A PRUDENT MAN

SHELBY KENT-STEWART

Wordsmiths, Ink LLC 

Published by Wordsmiths, Ink, Gilbert, AZ

ISBNs:
Paperback: 978-1-64184-261-7
eBook: 978-1-64184-262-4

I'll have her but I will not keep her long.
Richard III

TABLE OF CONTENTS

Part Two

Part Three

Part One

Debra

Friday, 16 June 2000

My husband. I say those words over and over in my head and yet I cannot believe it is true. How is it possible to feel such joy and still remember to breathe?

Tonight is the last that I will spend in this solitary bed, in this house that has known so much misery and death. It is such a large sad house but soon — in less than a year — it will be a school filled with the laughter of children, how wonderful! Charles has promised we will return one day so I may see it with my own eyes. I am grateful it will not be torn down as the lawyers were suggesting.

Tomorrow we leave for Paris where he will make another of my dreams come true. I will be a bride.

CHAPTER 1

ANNIE

Smoothly executing a sharp right turn without taking out a single pedestrian, Annie Heywood shot a grin at the figure beside her. "Told you I'd get the hang of it. From now on, we're driving and drinking domestic." She paused and scuffed her passenger's head. "Cheer up, pal, we've got this. New home, new life, new adventures."

Einstein, her five-year old Sheltie, sighed and closed his eyes.

She sat forward and gripped the steering wheel with both hands. Westport's Main Street was hard enough to negotiate for zippy little imports. For oversized vehicles, it posed a challenge she had no hope of meeting. And she could forget about parallel parking. Unless she was suddenly gifted with powers of levitation, it would be weeks before she attempted it.

For the second time in as many minutes, she felt a wave of anxiety. She was stalling, typical of the old Annie, the darling of denial, poster girl for procrastination. The new and improved model would have gone straight to the house, ripped down the sold sign and settled in. It was all she'd thought about, the only thing that saved her sanity through the difficult months. The house. Her house. Sightseeing could wait. She had years to explore. It wasn't Manhattan but at least it wasn't Greenwich with its restricted clubs and constricted minds. Whatever else it might become, Westport was her new home.

Two quick horn bursts from behind took her by surprise and she jumped. On the stress meter of life, she was deep in the red zone. Turning west at the stop sign, she started to relax. This was more like it, winding back roads beneath canopies of orange and gold, green lawns and well-maintained, unpretentious homes. This was the Connecticut she loved, the place that held her when reason told her to run.

The search started innocently, part lark, part curiosity. It was an excuse to leave the office early, to get in her car and drive. Things moved quickly after that, towns canvassed and eliminated for a variety of reasons, some practical, others personal. Before she knew it, she was looking in earnest, planning her future as her present fell apart.

They saved Westport for last, a quick lunch to scan the listings and, if time permitted, a few viewings. It was the bottom listing that caught her eye. The house was small, a modified saltbox of sorts, white with peeling blue trim on doors and shutters. Nestled among fat white birch trees on an acre all its own, it looked lonely and unloved. Her realtor was apoplectic but she was adamant. Two hours later, a signed contract made it hers.

That was in July. It was late September now and the landscape was different, tougher. In no time at all, the trees would slough their leaves and carpet the ground with color. Nature took care of such things. Even Einstein's coat was thickening. Contrary to the accepted wisdom, it was human beings who lost the cosmic crapshoot. In exchange for larger brains, they allowed themselves to be cloaked in arrogance and sent on their way. When the world turned cold, they were on their own.

After the initial viewing and offer, she deliberately stayed away. At first she'd been too busy, but somewhere along the line it became something else, a war of wills between her intellectual and emotional selves. The half she trusted saw it as a good investment while the other half kept her up nights, questioning her sanity and ridiculing her every decision. After a while, it was easier to fantasize from a distance. It became just another item on the list, another notation in her Day-Timer. And anyway, it was a little late for buyer's remorse. As of ten o'clock that morning, for better or worse the house was hers.

Spinnaker Lane was exactly as she remembered it, unpaved with overhanging limbs, sylvan and mysterious, perhaps a bit forbidding. She'd had it with manicured greenery and expensive Belgian block driveways. If it were up to her, every last one of them would be ripped out, crated up and shipped back to Brussels where they belonged.

On her right was the only other house on the lane, a grey clapboard Colonial with crisp white trim and pots of color on the front porch. From what she glimpsed of her neighbor during her first and only exploration, the house and its owner were a perfect match, neat and tidy.

The road tightened and forked to the left. Her property lay a few yards ahead behind a line of ancient pine trees. It was more or less what she remembered; more because of things she'd forgotten like the tiny stained glass attic window and the music of the brook as it snaked its way across the front of the house into the marsh. Less because of the one thing she'd chosen to ignore, the neglect that came with years of abandonment.

Reaching inside her tote bag, she felt around for her notebook then pulled back her hand. She hadn't been there two minutes and already she was obsessing. The list could wait. She needed to get the feel of the place, to come to know it. She needed to lighten up.

Einstein was on his feet, barking and pawing the seat. Annie followed his gaze to the wooded area on the far side of the property. At first she saw nothing, then a figure emerged, walking slowly, gesturing with one hand, holding something in the other. Annie squinted, then smiled. There was only one person in the world capable of making that entrance, only one who would be there for her at precisely the right moment.

Samantha Hogan stepped into the clearing and used the paperback to brush herself off. Einstein reached her first and she knelt down to receive his soft, wet kisses. Hanging back, Annie took her time, watching and appreciating.

Sam was a knockout, no doubt about it, but there was something else about her, a kind of divine presence. Once you got past the wild copper hair and drop-dead face, the trim body and grace of motion, you wanted to know more. The true beauty of her sister lay in the fact that you invariably got more. To those who knew her well, she was a person of extraordinary depth and compassion. To the millions of Brits familiar only with her small-screen persona, she was an addiction.

Having made his affection clear, Einstein bounded off to mark his territory and Annie moved in. "I can't believe you're here. They didn't kill you off, did they?"

After returning the hug, Samantha gave a theatrical flip of her hair. "Hell no, I'm still their token American bitch. They can't get rid of me. I make the rest of the cast look irritatingly saint-like. Right now I'm in the hospital undergoing a series of nasty tests. Pity really, poor Catherine's in for a rough road. I see a coma lasting, say, six weeks?" She brought the paperback from behind her back and waved it under Annie's nose. "Othello! Can you stand it?"

Annie grabbed the book from her and shrieked. "Make my day and tell me you're doing it on Broadway."

"Not a chance. Americans only tolerate Shakespeare when it's bizarre and edgy. I've wanted to play Desdemona all my life, and I'll be damned if I'm making my entrance on a Harley."

"You'll be fabulous. I'm so proud of you. How long can you stay?"

"Today's what, Friday? I have a wardrobe fitting Tuesday. I'll fly out Monday night."

Einstein had discovered the brook and was wading paw-deep in the clear rocky water. They watched him for a few minutes then looked back at one another. There was always so much to say, but this time Annie hardly knew where to begin. "I guess you got my letter."

"You mean the 'hi how are you sis how's the weather and oh by the way I'm not moving to Manhattan I've bought a home in Westport' letter? Frankly, I found it a little skimpy on the details.

When do I get those? And don't tell me I have to wait for the sequel. I hate sequels."

"Over dinner. When did you get here, how did you get here and how did you know I'd be here?"

"I flew in last night and crashed at a hotel near the airport. I tried your cell phone but of course it's on the bottom of your tote bag, more than likely in need of a charge. I took a chance and called the house in Greenwich. According to the aforementioned letter, Larry was in Tokyo for the month, so imagine my surprise. We had an awkward three-minute chat in which he grudgingly advised you were coming here after the escrow closing. I rented a car, a blue Toyota. Since there is only one Spinnaker Lane in all of Westport, I had no trouble finding it. Your neighbor Mrs. Allen invited me in for tea. Earl Grey. There now, those are details. See how easy that was?"

"You're pissed."

"I'm not pissed but exactly what is that you're driving?"

"It's a Ford F150…"

"It's a pickup truck, Annie, one of the many reasons I will never play Butte, Montana. Where's the Mercedes?"

"I traded it in. I needed a practical vehicle. Besides, it was too…"

"Gorgeous, classy, what?"

"Too Larry."

With a quick glance back toward the house, Samantha cocked an eyebrow. "He's worth millions, sweetie. Please tell me you didn't do something stupid."

"I asked for enough to buy this. That's it. No alimony, no mortgage payments. The Greenwich house was more his than mine anyway. I wanted a home and he wanted a shrine to his success. And before you ask, I let him have the house in Aspen too. I wanted to be free of all of it."

"Guess you showed him."

"I'm going to fix this place up, Sam, maybe resell it. I'm also thinking about writing a book about it. A lot of women are alone, trying to rebuild their lives. God knows, they don't need another self-help book. What they need is a practical guide for controlling their futures."

"Let's hope they have better lawyers than you or they won't be able to afford the book."

"Point taken. Any more questions?"

"Two. Who got custody of your hair?"

Laughing, Annie ran her fingers through her new boyish cut. "I donated it to *Locks of Love* but it's still me, blonde and perky."

"It suits you. I love it. Okay, last question. If we're not waiting for a moving van filled with expensive antiques, like a bed for example, then you've either got an inflatable mattress in the back of that thing or we'll have to go inside and wrestle Hansel and Gretel for their palettes. Which is it?"

"I've ordered a few things over the last couple of months. They're delivering a bed later this afternoon. I'm storing the rest until I figure out what I'm doing inside."

"The property is wonderful but what's the story with the house? It looks so sad."

"I suppose it is. It's been vacant for years." Fiddling with her keyring, Annie smiled despite her dread of the impending tour. "I guess I should warn you. The inside is a mess but it has loads of charm. What's so funny?"

"Your description. It fits half the leading men I know."

Throughout the walk-thru, Annie maintained a running commentary of her plans for the house, knowing full well her sister thought she'd lost her mind. From Sam's perspective, it was a derelict, cold and dark. Where Sam saw cramped spaces scarred by drooping wallpaper and chipped tiles, she imagined cozy rooms with endless possibilities. The tour ended in the kitchen where they stared at a spanking new stainless steel refrigerator, a large red bow taped across the door. Inside were a dozen bottles of good champagne and a gift card.

Samantha read the card and snorted. "I've been out of the country too long. What happened to fruit baskets and floral arrangements as housewarming gifts?"

"It's from Kay, my realtor. She went through a messy divorce about a year ago and we've sort of bonded."

"Too bad you didn't use her attorney."

"So what do you think of the house?"

"I think you'll make it wonderful, and I think you need to renegotiate your settlement." Samantha caught her look and put her hands up in surrender. "Okay, okay, I get it."

"It's not as bad as it looks, mostly cosmetic, nothing structural, except maybe the roof. I figure a year should do it."

"Then we'd better get started." After rolling up her sleeves, Samantha ran her finger across the top of the stove. "Knowing you, there are two things in the back of that practical vehicle out there. One is a coffeemaker and the other is a bucket of cleaning supplies. I suggest you toddle off and get them. We'll work for a few hours and then you'll treat me to an obscenely expensive dinner. On second thought, I'll treat you to dinner. Deal?"

"I have a better idea. Instead of coffee, let's crack open one of those bottles. If we can still walk by dinner time, we'll go out. If not, we'll order in a pizza."

"Hold it right there, Mavis. You want to have fun? What the hell's gotten into you?"

"You haven't called me that in years."

Samantha shrugged. "It's been awhile."

"What was so special about her?" The question had a more defensive edge than Annie intended and she softened it with a weak smile. "Go ahead. I can take it."

"Are you sure?"

"It was a long time ago, Sam. People grow up, make choices and spend their lives trying to come to terms with them. Fun gets pushed to the bottom of a very long list. If I remember correctly, Mavis wanted to do a lot of things including save the world. That didn't even make the list."

"The world's still there, more screwed up than ever. Besides, you'll need a project when you finish this one."

"Don't hold your breath. I'm not nineteen. I'm on the down-side of thirty, divorced, and my life has turned into a cliché. I'm not like you."

"Don't confuse bravery with bravado, Annie. I'm lousy with bravado, it's what I do best. I don't give a damn if you were Annie, Mavis or Helen of bloody Troy, you had more courage than anyone I've ever known."

"You're exaggerating."

"Like hell I am. I was there, remember? Kent State, my freshman year. You were a junior. It was May 4th, 2000, thirty years to the day when four students were shot and killed by the Ohio National Guard. An impromptu protest had broken out. A guardsman was burning in effigy with bits of his uniform dancing on the rising smoke. It was mayhem, and then I saw you crossing the Commons, pushing your way through the demonstrators. Your back was straight, that beautiful chin lifted in defiance. The fire was out before anyone could stop you. People were shouting at you, but you stood your ground. When the crowd was finally silent, you grabbed the microphone from the asshole agitating the crowd.

"You spoke for an hour without notes. You spoke with conviction, carefully enunciating the names of the dead. Allison Krause. Jeffrey Glen Miller. Sandra Lee Scheuer. William Knox Schroeder. You spoke passionately about who they were and who they might have become. You challenged all of us to channel our anger, to be the voices of the future, the ones who will never again allow dissent to be a rationale for carnage. It was a good speech because you knew your facts. It was a great speech because you knew your audience. I was so fucking proud to be your sister."

"That was a lifetime ago. I've changed."

"Wrong again. You're too thin and your hair is shorter, but you look exactly like you did in college. It's your spirit that's battered. Mavis is in there, Annie. We just have to reacquaint the two of you."

Debra

Tuesday, 4 July 2000

What an amazing country, my America! Tonight Charles took me to the beach and we watched as fireworks lit up the night sky. When we returned home, there was a wonderful film called '1776' on the television and I cried for the courage of those brave men. I cannot even begin to describe the pride and love I feel for my new husband, home and country. I know I have much to learn about the people and customs here but Charles is a patient teacher.

At this moment, my mind is filled with thoughts of Mama, how she would have loved it here, how unfair that she was called from this world without knowing Charles and the happiness he brings me. My grief is never more than a whisper away but my joy is constant. I hope she understands.

I have not written for several weeks and the words do not flow easily from my heart to the paper as they have in the past. Perhaps I should abandon this schoolgirl practice now that I have someone with whom to share my personal thoughts. And yet, there is something magical about imagining the life and love that will fill these pages.

CHAPTER 2

ANNIE

Groggy and disoriented, Annie opened her eyes and threw off the quilt. She was in hell. From the basement below, a timpani of clanks and thumps rose up through the floorboards and mattress to her throbbing temples. It was bad enough they'd polished off two bottles of champagne. At the very least, one of them could have remembered to turn off the furnace. She turned her head slowly to the side then down to the foot of the bed. Sam had always been a deep sleeper but, as a watchdog, Einstein needed work.

It was a little past four, the hour of dark thoughts, a bad time to be awake under the best of conditions but terrifying after a night of drinking. Careful not to awaken Sam, she scooted off the bed, adjusted the thermostat and opened a window. Tomorrow they'd take the bed upstairs and set it up in the master bedroom. Screw the floor refinishers. If and when they showed up, they could move it into the hall. She needed a semblance of order in her life, if only on the surface. Slumber parties were for preteens with good backs. The thought of Larry sleeping peacefully in their oversized, overpriced Biedermeier bed did nothing to improve her mood. Screw him too.

Grabbing a sweater, she eased out the side door onto a small concrete porch. From there, she could hear the brook and began to relax. Sam's visit, although welcome, had thrown her and the previous evening was not one of their best. There were the requisite number of laughs but the banter seemed forced, even cautious. Neither of them brought up her divorce.

It happened sometimes. One of them would step to the line and back off just short of crossing it. It had been that way since they were kids, emotionally tethered like twins, ultra-sensitive to one another's feelings.

Most of the time it worked for them. She'd known other siblings close in age, particularly those of the same sex, who were frequently rivals, fiercely competitive when it came to family, school and affairs of the heart. Not so the Sisters Hogan. They were enamored with one another from day one, as children openly affectionate, supportive and inseparable through their early teens and college years. The rough times, rare as they were, came when honesty was sacrificed in the interest of harmony, when words unspoken hurt more than truths told.

She took a deep breath of fresh cool air and smiled when the door opened behind her. "What took you so long?"

"I missed the anvil chorus. You might want to add a new heating system to that list I'm sure you have tucked away in your bag." Samantha eased down next to her on the step and put her fist in front of Annie's face. When she opened her hand, two fat joints lay side by side on her palm. "Happy weed?"

"No way. I haven't recovered from our last binge. How'd you get those through Customs?"

Producing a disposable lighter from her pocket, Sam lit one of the joints and inhaled deeply. "I didn't. There's a gas station about half a mile from this very spot. I stopped in to get directions. If the need ever arises, ask for Tony. He's packing more than a cute butt in those jeans."

Annie's mouth dropped open. "How many of those have you had?"

"I'm high on life. Know what would taste good right now?"

"After that last comment, I'm afraid to ask."

"Pistachio ice cream. Annie, remember that guy, Dwayne something from upstate New York? He was in one of your study groups. He'd smoke pot all night and eat pistachio ice cream. If he was high enough, he swore he could pinpoint the province in China where the pistachios were harvested. What a loser."

"Dwayne Beecham. He was just elected to the House from Texas or Tennessee, some red state. He was on CNN last week, ran on the family-values-high-five-for-Jesus platform. Oh, and he now has a southern accent and sounds like Jeff Foxworthy."

"Yee haw, what a country!"

Annie reached into Samantha's pocket and took the other joint. "You could come back, Sam. Mom mentioned you were offered a series."

"As usual, mom got it wrong. There wasn't an offer, just some discussions with my agent."

"If there were an offer?"

"I like working in the U.K. I'm relatively unknown here and I prefer it that way. Let's say I did a series or a film and it was moderately successful. How long do you think it would take before the tabloids got wind of my lifestyle? I'm an actor, not a martyr to the cause. I have no intention of becoming a rung on Dwayne Beecham's ladder to power and glory."

"He wouldn't dare. You know too much about his extra-curricular college activities."

"That's not my style. No one wins in a pissing contest. Anyway, I couldn't do that to Mom and Dad. I don't worry about you. In spite of your little speech yesterday, you're tough. It's different with them. All my life they've loved and accepted me for who I am. I won't be responsible for them spending their golden years dodging questions about my sex life."

And just like that, the reticence was gone, the barriers down. Annie took a final hit and let the ember die. "How are they taking my divorce?"

"Why are you asking me? Don't you talk to them?"

"Not really. Whenever I bring it up, they change the subject."

"Maybe they're afraid of saying the wrong thing. You're a private person and they know that. I don't think they ever saw it coming and, just between you and me, they never wanted to look. In their minds, you had it all, marriage to a handsome, successful stockbroker, a big house in a wealthy suburb, accolades for your AIDS work, everything parents could wish for their daughter. Bottom line, they thought they were finished having to worry about you."

"That's my fault. I didn't want to burden them."

"What did happen, Annie? He's been chipping away at you since you married him, even before that. Why him? From the time you were a little girl, all you ever wanted was your independence and a career in Archaeology. You could have had both. I was with you the day you received the letter from U.C. Berkeley. You were ecstatic over being accepted into their graduate program. A week later, you were married."

"You never liked him, did you?"

"I didn't trust him. You changed when you started seeing him in your junior year. You withdrew inside yourself, but after you broke up with him you came back to life. This amazing light seemed to emanate from somewhere inside you, but in your senior year when you let him back in, you lost it again."

"You were the one person I always counted on to be straight with me, Sam. Why am I hearing this now?"

"Oh no, you're not laying this on me. In the first place, you never asked my opinion, not once. In the second place, you were in love and wouldn't have listened to me and, furthermore, I don't blame you. I'm gay, remember? Read the manual. You still haven't answered my question. What happened?"

"Nothing. Everything. One day I thought we were happy and the next day it started coming apart. He wanted out of the law firm and I supported his decision, even though I never understood it. It wasn't as if he were doing pro bono work. The money was great but it was never enough for him. Wall Street changed him. He became crisp and flippant. He wanted me to reduce my hours at **Life House** so we could entertain more, so we could see and be seen by the right people. I thought he was joking when he said that. I think I even laughed. That was the beginning of the end, but the more I tried to pull away from him, the more possessive he became. The day he announced he wanted to install iron gates at the entrance to our property, I snapped. It felt like he was trying to imprison me. Four months ago, I woke up and couldn't breathe. That night, I moved into a spare bedroom at **Life House** and contacted a lawyer."

"What bothered you enough to leave, that he turned into Gordon Gekko or that you were with him for seventeen years and chose to ignore who he was? What about grad school, Annie? Wasn't that the agreement, you'd go back after he passed the Bar? Where was he the night you accepted the award for your AIDS work? I know where I was. I flew in from London and was seated next to you at the table. Mom and Dad flew in from Florida and were seated next to me. Where was Larry? That was five years ago, not four months ago. Why did you marry him? Were you ever in love with him?"

The barrage of discomforting questions made her insides clench. That they were asked out of concern and not morbid curiosity mitigated her sister's tough-love approach, but that didn't mean she was prepared to spill her guts. "Can we drop it for now? I'm hungover, sleep deprived and borderline high." Rising from the step, she flashed her sister a smile as pathetic as her excuses. "We need coffee. Stay here, enjoy the quiet and stop worrying about me. I'm fine."

Back inside, she took a deep breath and filled the water reservoir from the tap. Midway through measuring out the coffee, she dropped the scoop and leaned into the countertop, resting her forehead against the upper cabinet. She wasn't fine, far from it. Another opportunity had come and gone, another chance to tell the truth and she'd run. The same way she'd run from it twenty years ago. She was repeating a pattern, one she was determined to break. Secrets fed off the dark. The longer they stayed hidden, the more power they consumed.

Minutes later, she was back on the porch with two steaming mugs of coffee in hand. "I'm sorry, Sam. I guess it's a little too soon to talk about it. Forgive me?" The silence roared between them as the minutes ticked away. "Sam?"

"I had an interesting flight over, Annie. Lucas Markham's new book hit the stores yesterday. The woman in the seat next to me was reading it. Her husband's in publishing and the buzz is it's his best since his Pulitzer. They're predicting it will go to number one on the New York Times bestseller list before the week is out. It's been what, five years since his last one?"

"Something like that. I'm not particularly fond of his work so I don't keep track."

"But you were in one of his classes in your junior year, weren't you? God, he was good-looking, still is judging from the photograph on the back cover. Anyway, this woman kept going on and on about how remarkable it was, how only Markham could write something so titillating and still capture a mainstream audience. When I told her he was one of your professors at Kent State back in the day, she almost had a stroke. The more she talked about it, the more curious I became so I picked up a copy at the airport when we landed. I read it last night and she was right. It's a real page-turner, probably the most erotic thing I've ever read."

Nausea roiled up from the pit of her stomach but she managed to keep her tone light. "What's it about?"

"It's autobiographical. The first hundred pages or so deals with his parents, beautiful Sioux woman meets rich Texas oilman and they produce a son out of wedlock. She dies when he's five and his father takes him off the reservation and raises him. Blah blah blah Princeton, Rhodes Scholar, published his first novel at thirty, his second at thirty-three for which he earned a Pulitzer, tenured professor at Kent State by the age of thirty-six. He's surprisingly candid about his personal life, the fact that he'd never had a relationship with a woman that lasted longer than a night because he never found one who could challenge him on any level.

"And then in the spring of 2000, at the age of thirty-eight, he's making his way across campus and he sees a beautiful, spirited nineteen-year-old girl wearing overalls over a tank top, her blonde hair plaited into a French braid. He's noticed her before but on this particular day he sees her in an entirely different light. He's mesmerized by her untapped sexuality and intellect, her fearlessness. He thinks she's magnificent, like some wild, untamed animal. He wants her, it's as simple as that, and she becomes his obsession. And thus begins the most important chapter in his life, *Breaking Annabelle*, the title of the book. He seduces her, takes her away to a remote cabin in the woods of Minnesota and spends the next month teaching her everything there is to know about sex and submission. He adores her but his façade is that of a cold and demanding son of a bitch. She fights him on every level, emotionally, physically and intellectually but this only makes him want her more. My favorite passage is on page 317 where he compares fondling her perfect ass to winning the Pulitzer. Her ass wins hands down, no pun intended.

"Of course he doesn't break her. That's the irony of the title. She destroys him. On their last night together, he confesses his love for her and she rejects him. He's angry, so angry that he does the unthinkable, the thing he will regret for the rest of his life. He brands her. He ties her facedown on the bed and whips her with his belt until she passes out. When he realizes what he's done, he unties her and gets drunk. She's gone when he wakes up the next morning but there's a note. She forgives him but only if he stays away from her and she never has to see him again. He's so consumed with guilt and longing that he resigns his position at the university, boards a plane for Ireland and goes into seclusion for twenty years.

"So I'm lying in bed at the hotel reading this and thinking, wow, maybe I know this girl. Maybe she's the one he was watching the day of the demonstration, the one he couldn't take his eyes off as she held several hundred students in the palm of her hand. He was standing a few feet away from me and I remember thinking I'd never seen anyone stand so still. You always knew when he was around because every female student became a simpering pile of mush. He cut a dashing figure, I'll say that for him, tall, shoulders out to here with that perpetually tanned skin, those black eyes and hair. He knew it and played it up, always dressing in black and never without those damn cowboy boots and sunglasses. And that voice, deep and slow, with just a hint of a drawl.

"But then I thought, no, this couldn't be my sister because she was backpacking through Italy that summer with her Anthropology club, and she told me she got the scars on her butt from sliding down a rock face. But the most compelling reason it couldn't be her is that she would never keep something like that from me for twenty-years. You wouldn't, would you, Annabelle?"

The emotions racing through her were so numerous and convoluted, she didn't know which to deal with first. "I didn't know how to tell you, Sam. I know that's a lousy excuse but it's all I have at the moment. Did he use my last name?"

"Not in the body of the book. He saved that for the dedication: *For Annabelle Hogan Heywood, My Muse, My Love.* The pussy's out of the bag now, kiddo. You're screwed."

"I'll kill him."

"Too late. According to the book, you did that twenty years ago when you walked out on him. He never married."

"He reminds me of that in every letter."

"You're still in contact with him?"

"I've never been out of contact with him. We write letters but I won't see him or speak to him. Those are the rules. The book isn't about embarrassing me. He knows me better than that. He wants to stick it to Larry."

"Who will go ballistic when he hears about it."

"No, he won't. Lucas doesn't know him. Once he turns it to his advantage, he'll love every moment of the attention. He'll be the man who took me away from the brilliant and enigmatic Lucas Markham. As long as there's a star on the rise, Larry will find a way to bask in its glow. That's who he is."

"Did you love him?"

"I thought I did. He ruined both our lives the night he lost control. If he hadn't done that, who knows…"

"That's why you married Larry, isn't it? He was your plus-one, your insurance policy against changing your mind and running to Lucas."

"Something like that." Finally making eye contact, Annie saw a smile playing at the corner of Sam's lips. "You're enjoying this, aren't you?"

"A little. You'd better leave Mom and Dad to me. They were worried enough when they thought you were backpacking through Italy. I'll tell them Markham's a psycho and he made the whole thing up. They'll believe it because that's what they want to believe. And I accept your apology. You must have had your reasons for keeping it a secret all these years, but now that it's out there, I want details. How did it start?"

"It was a couple of days after the rally. I was short of the money I needed for Italy so I put the word out to some of my professors that I was interested in picking up some extra work, grading papers, typing, even some light housekeeping. I was leaving his class and he asked me to stay. He said he was working on a new manuscript and needed a typist, someone he could trust. He said he would pay me well but I had to work at his home for obvious reasons. I agreed to start that night."

"Were you attracted to him?"

"I never gave it a thought one way or the other. He was my professor. Besides, he had enough groupies. I'd broken up with Larry a month or two before because I didn't want any complications in my life. I was intent on getting into a good grad school and that's all I was thinking about. He met me at the door that night and was typical Markham, aloof and professional, the way he was in class. He called me Miss Hogan and showed me where I would be working. It was a large partner's desk in his living room. He sat on one side and I sat on the other. After about an hour, he told me to take a break, that there was coffee and tea in the kitchen and I could help myself. I asked him if I could get him anything and he said when and if he wanted something, I'd be the first to know.

"While I was in the kitchen, I noticed some dishes in the sink. I had to wait for the water to boil so I started tidying up. When I turned around, he was standing in the doorway glaring at me. That was a Wednesday night. I went there the next two nights and it was pretty much the same thing except Friday night after the break he said he didn't want me to work anymore, that I looked tired. He fixed two cups of tea and we sat at his kitchen table. Neither of us said a word for a few minutes and then he narrowed those dark eyes at me and asked me why I wanted to spend my life digging around in the dirt when only ugly, dried-up women did that. I laughed and said something to the effect that they probably didn't start out that way, that it was a consequence of working in arid climes. His expression never changed but something happened in his eyes. They got colder and darker and for the next half hour he tore into me. He criticized everything, the way I dressed, my work in his class, even the way I washed his dishes."

"He wrote that scene in the book, Annie. He said your laughter and the sound of your voice jarred something loose in him, an emotion so disturbing he almost took you on the kitchen floor."

"I left quickly after that but not before I told him exactly what I thought of him. I said there were at least a thousand girls on campus who would pay him to insult them but I wasn't one of them. I told him he was rude and arrogant, that I'd spend the weekend finishing his damn manuscript because I needed the money but, for the record, I hated his books. I found them to be self-serving diatribes, that he was no Norman Mailer and his latest stream-of-consciousness ravings made my teeth hurt."

"Ouch. That must have gone over well."

"I didn't wait to find out. I slammed the door behind me and threw up on his front lawn. When I arrived the next morning, he was gone but he left a note on the door telling me to start working on his ravings and to make myself at home. I worked for about six hours and left to finish an article for the school paper. It started raining around dinnertime, one of those spring thunderstorms that always put me on edge. The power was going on and off everywhere. I missed my bus and didn't get back to his place until around seven that night. I was drenched and in a pissy mood and we didn't speak for at least an hour. He finally got up from his side of the desk and sat across the room but he never took his eyes off me. I knew he was trying to make me nervous but I wouldn't give him the satisfaction, so I ignored him and kept typing. I was finishing up for the day when there was a loud clap of thunder and the power went out again. I was sitting there waiting for the lights to come back on when he pulled me from the chair and kissed me. I was so shocked I didn't feel his hand inside my jeans until it was too late."

"Holy shit. Did he say anything to you?"

"He told me if I moved he wouldn't be responsible for what happened next."

"And…"

"I moved."

"How did Larry get back in the picture?"

"When the fall term started, all I wanted to do was get my life back on track. I was fine for about three months until I got the first letter from Lucas. He begged me to forgive him and enclosed an open plane ticket to Ireland. He said he'd bought a home for us outside of Dublin. I was tempted but I knew I'd never be able to trust him. That letter brought it all back. I stopped eating and I couldn't sleep. It was right before the winter break and I was living in that little apartment off-campus. I'd seen Larry a couple of times after our break-up but always managed to keep him at arms-length. He came by one night and I was in bad shape. He insisted I eat and stayed until I fell asleep. I realize now it was wishful thinking, but he seemed different from the person I'd dated the previous year, not quite as sure of himself.

"By that time, Mom and Dad were living in Florida, you'd committed to doing that play in New York, and I couldn't face going home for the holidays. I decided to stay in Ohio and he stayed with me. It wasn't like being with Lucas but it was safe. I never told him about Lucas or that month in Minnesota. As far as he knew, I was in Italy and the scars were from sliding down that damn rock face. We were together constantly after the new semester began and then he was accepted into Columbia Law and I was accepted into Berkeley. He proposed the week before graduation and said he had everything figured out. Once he was finished with law school, I could reapply to Berkeley's graduate program and we'd move to California. I was grateful to him for sticking by me and knew if we were married I'd never use the plane ticket."

"You married a man you didn't love to keep from marrying a man you did love. Good plan. What about the BDSM stuff? Please don't tell me you and Larry were into that."

"Hardly. I suspect Luc exercised his right to artistic license when it came to the sex. Was he kinky? Yes, but for the most part, it was pretty vanilla, intense but vanilla."

"If you say so. What about grad school?"

"When Larry passed the Bar in New York, I brought it up to him and he said he wanted a wife, not a roommate and I should get my priorities straight. He said he had plans for our life and they didn't include me running off every six months to some godforsaken place. That was the last time I brought it up."

"Bastard. What happens now? I only hit the highlights of the book, Annie. It's raw, beautiful and praise-worthy, but raw nonetheless. Maybe you should move to London until things blow over."

"I can't hide from this, Sam. Victimization doesn't suit me any better than martyrdom suits you. Lucas didn't kidnap me. I went willingly and I don't regret it. I'm tired of secrets and exhausted from pretending to be something I'm not. Maybe that's why Luc chose this time to publish it. He wants me to remember who I was instead of regretting who I've become."

"You've always known who you are and now every red-blooded male in the world is going to know too. Before this thing goes away, you'll have to install a ticket booth." She pointed to a spot in the darkness. "I'm thinking right down there by the mailbox."

"Make it barbed wire and a gun emplacement and I might consider it. I've only been with two men and they both blew it. I'm swearing off."

"Two men in thirty-nine years? In this day and age, some people would say you're repressed."

"Get their names. We'll send them the book."

Debra

Wednesday, 5 July 2000

We drove around our beautiful Westport today. It is a lovely town with trees so high they seem to touch the clouds. And so many beautiful little shops filled with things I have only seen in magazines.

There is a theatre, the Westport Playhouse, where they put on plays with famous people from the cinema. Can this really be my life now?

We had dinner near a river called the Saugatuck and ate clams and drank champagne. Charles gave me a gift, a small gold heart with an emerald in the center to wear around my neck. I had almost forgotten it was my birthday. So much has happened in the past few months but now I have a husband to remind me of such things. He is kind in ways I cannot describe, intimate moments about which I will never write, not even here.

I hear him on the stairs now and must close…

CHAPTER 3

ANNIE

Successfully squeezing the pick-up between two 18-wheelers, Annie blew her breath out in a long whistle. She could have taken the back roads but on this particular day she needed to face her fears and knock them down one by one. Today her skills would be tested to the max, morning traffic on the Connecticut thruway.

In the sky above her, a passenger jet made its ascent out of JFK and over the Sound toward her sister's world. Twenty-four hours ago, Samantha boarded a plane following the same flight plan, giddy with excitement, ready to test and conquer her own doubts about the future.

The weekend had offered a reprieve from loneliness, but the barter was bittersweet. Together they had tiptoed through her life, peeling away the layers and exposing the truths, some stunning and hurtful, others funny and touching. The most shocking thing was how the years slipped by, seventeen years married, ten since she opened the hospice. It was the only thing in her life that made perfect sense, the one thing that could bring her to smiles and tears in the length of a heartbeat, **Life House.**

After exiting I-95, she drove five miles, made a few right turns and stopped at the end of a long driveway. The sign was simple, a flat piece of driftwood into which a line drawing had been wood-burned and sealed against the elements. It was a lighthouse situated on a bluff. The triangular beacon, instead of being directed out toward the sea, came from high above the water and bathed the solitary structure in light. It was primitive and childlike and it always made her smile.

She eased the truck around a blue paneled van and brought it to a stop, acknowledging the waves of a guest on the front porch and another who drew back a curtain in one of the lower floor rooms.

Releasing the tailgate, she pulled at a cardboard box full of books and broke a nail to the quick, the first of several irritating incidents waiting for her. She heard the two men before she saw them. They were rounding a corner from the far side of the house. One of them, the taller of the two, was pointing to the roof while the other made notes on a clipboard. Now what?

Sucking a drop of blood from her finger, she squared her shoulders before approaching them. "May I help you?"

The shorter man in paint-spattered overalls walked away while the other stood firmly in place. "No, ma'am, I think we've got it covered."

"Got what covered? There's nothing wrong with the roof."

"No, ma'am, the painting. You've got a mess here, the fascia's peeling and window frames are…"

Ma'am? "I'm Annie Heywood and you're…?"

"Carl Richards. Here's my card. When was the last time you had it painted?"

She glanced at the card before stuffing it in the pocket of her jeans. "About five years ago." To her own ears, it sounded more like a question than an answer and Carl Richards raised an eyebrow. "Okay, it's been ten years but we're on a very tight budget here. Have you spoken to the woman inside?"

"Mrs. Fredericks. She's a good woman."

"She's the best. You're here to give us an estimate?"

"No, ma'am, I'm here to figure out how much paint to buy. We're starting tomorrow. I'll bring you an invoice for the paint but the labor's at no charge. We'll get the porch done first so it's not out of commission for too long." He looked at the box on the tailgate. "That box is bigger than you are. Need some help?"

She waited for the 'little lady' tag line, then smiled and gave him a thumbs-up. "Got it covered, thanks."

The box was heavy but there was no way she was letting him carry it. Walking quickly to the ground floor kitchen entrance, she set the box on a counter and headed for the office.

"Ma'am? When did I become a ma'am?"

Cynthia Fredericks' large brown eyes peered over half-glasses. "And a happy Tuesday to you too, baby. I see you met our painter."

Annie let her tote bag drop to the floor in front of Cynthia's desk. "Yes, I met him but I thought we agreed we had to watch the budget. Furthermore, we can't let just anyone walk in off the street and start doing things. Contractors have to be licensed and bonded."

"How long you known me?" Cynthia produced a manila file from her in-box and waved it in front of Annie's face. "All right in here, certificate of insurance, copy of his license, everything but his marital status and I'll have that for you by the end of the day." She craned her neck so she could see through the plate glass window. "He sure is pretty for a white boy. Kinda got a Denzel thing going on there."

Annie knew where this was going and she had to shut it down pronto. "Don't even think about it. The ink isn't even dry on my divorce decree and if I were ever to date again, which I'm not, that patronizing putz wouldn't make the short list."

"Uh huh. You don't know who he is, do you?"

"Yes, Cyn, I know who he is. His name is Carl Richards. It says so right here on his business card." Richards. She knew that name and there was something familiar about him. "Oh, God."

Cynthia hefted her body off the chair and folded her arms over her ample breasts. "You white women need to get those rods removed from your skinny asses. Maybe it'll improve your eyesight. He looks just like his brother, bless his sweet soul."

"Oh, God."

"You said that but God's got nothin' to do with what killed that poor boy. Makes me mad as hell when one of those preachers says God don't love these people."

"You watched Fox News again last night, didn't you? Maybe Arthur needs to block it on your TV. It's bad for your blood pressure."

"You stop talkin' to that man about my health. He tried to slip me some frozen yogurt last night instead of my ice cream. And before you go, you make nice with that fella. His only brother died in here and he's tryin' to say thank you."

Annie knocked off a quick salute. "Yes, ma'am. Tomorrow I'll make nice and ask him to run by my place and give me an estimate on the interior. Happy?" She turned her head in time to see him driving away from the property. "I don't recall him here when Gary was dying or at his funeral for that matter."

"He was with Special Forces in Syria and they wouldn't let him come home. Don't you dare tell him I told you."

"I won't, but how do you know all this?"

"Because, Miss I Don't Need a Man, I looked into his eyes and saw a good heart. All you saw was that sorry-ass male you were married to."

"Good point. I need to work on that." Annie started to walk away but stopped when Cynthia held up an envelope. It was padded and large enough to hold a book. "What's that?"

"It came for you yesterday afternoon."

"Thanks, I'll open it in my office." She hesitated a moment before asking, "Did Sam stop here on the way to the airport?"

"Course she did. You think she'd come all the way from London and not see me? You're not the only friend I got in this world, Miss Annabelle Hogan Heywood."

"So you know."

"Know what, that some writer made up some sexy stuff about you and put it in a book? Samantha said it's all hooey. What else am I supposed to know?"

Annie felt the familiar twinge of guilt. They'd been through so much together, she hated lying to her. "And if it were true? Would it make a difference?"

"You have to ask, you don't know me very well. You got the kindest heart of anyone I've ever known. Wouldn't matter to me what you did. Just don't ask me to read the damn thing."

"Count on it. Was she here long?"

"Long enough to make the rounds and brighten everybody's day. That girl's gotta natural gift." Cynthia dove into her in-box again. "You know about this?"

It was a check written on a London bank made out to **Life House** signed by Samantha Hogan. Annie blinked back tears as she did a quick calculation from pounds to dollars. "This is almost twenty thousand dollars. We can buy a new van."

Cynthia snatched the check from her fingers. "We can get the old van fixed, buy a new washer and dryer and a dozen new mattresses. You folks are just plain pitiful when it comes to finance."

With a quick kiss on Cynthia's cheek, Annie turned on her heel in the direction of her office. "Don't let my sorry-ass ex hear you say that."

Behind closed doors, she slit the envelope open. The book slid out and landed in her lap, right side up. Resisting the temptation to turn it over and see his face, she opened the cover. Her eyes burned as she read the handwritten inscription:

I had to do it, baby. If I can't have the real thing, I'll take the memories. Yours, Luc.

You're biting your lower lip, aren't you? I do it better...

Cocky bastard.

Debra

Sunday, 9 July 2000

The church bells woke me this morning. What a lovely sound – just like home.

Charles was going to take me to Mass but he was sleeping so peacefully that I hadn't the heart to wake him. I must remember to get directions so I can go next Sunday.

The weather is pleasant, not yet too warm. I made tea and took it to the terrace with my sketchbook. The garden is beautiful but needs loving hands. I sketched for hours, thinking of mama, how unlike her I am. I believe Nature frightened her. She felt safe only when its beauty was framed by folds of liquid silk.

Tomorrow Charles will go into New York City and I will spend my first day alone in our new home. Perhaps I will call on our neighbor. She smiled and waved at me this morning. I would like to make a new friend here.

CHAPTER 4
ANNIE

RECOGNIZING MR. WRONG
When the Dream is an Illusion

Annie stared at the screen on her laptop and tried flipping the lines around to see if that worked better. When it didn't, she moved the cursor across the words and hit the delete key.

Whatever made her think this was a good idea? When did a 'practical guide for surviving divorce' morph into a *Lifetime* movie? Who was she to give advice? Mr. Wrong lived under her nose for seventeen years, nineteen if she included the years before the marriage.

The book wasn't happening, at least not yet, not until she put some distance between those warring voices in her head. She was a long way from sniffing out the Mr. Wrongs of this world and apparently she was equally challenged when it came to recognizing the good guys. If she needed further proof, she only had to look at Carl Richards.

She'd taken Cynthia's advice, made nice and given him the job of painting her own house, materials and labor included plus a little extra to soothe her guilt. As it turned out, he was just what he appeared to be, a kind, well-mannered guy raised on a Pennsylvania farm with his younger brother. He was very married and still making nice with his wife of eighteen years. Their fifth child was due in May.

Logging on to her e-mail, she dashed off a few quick lines to Samantha. After years of corresponding by snail-mail, their preferred method of keeping in touch, Sam insisted they start using the more timely method and she finally agreed albeit reluctantly. Letters were civilized and genteel, she had argued. There was something sad about reducing your life to a series of jumbled, badly-punctuated ramblings. No filters, no time to reflect. You thought it, you typed it, you hit the little 'send' box. The truth, Sam laughingly observed, was that Annie was loathe to sharing her life in real-time without benefit of self-censorship. Whatever.

The floor refinishers were back from lunch and she closed her laptop. They still had to sand the Master Bedroom and the noise was deafening, the vibration even worse. Earlier that day, she drove herself crazy checking every few minutes to make sure the plaster ceilings were intact. Despite the fans set up to blow the dust out the open windows, a thin layer coated everything in sight. What she needed was fresh air and a fresh perspective, and she knew precisely where to find both.

She'd take Einstein for a drive, head down to **Life House** and let him work his magic. He worshipped Cynthia and her home-baked dog biscuits and even tolerated her baby talk. But what he seemed to love most was walking through the rooms, slowly, almost reverently until a hand reached out from beneath a blanket and stroked his head. How he sensed their need for connection would forever be a mystery, but he would sit rock still until the hand withdrew or they fell back asleep.

Half an hour later she was almost there, the hospice in sight when she hit the brake and pulled the truck to the side of the road. The scene was magical, a downpour of red and gold leaves, twisting and turning on the breeze, laying a carpet of color all around her. She opened the window and inhaled the chilled October air and with it a flood of memories.

It was a day like this, a crisp and clear October day in 2009 when the idea was conceived. A friend of Larry's was recovering from surgery in Greenwich Hospital and she stopped by for a short visit. He was doing great and due to be released the next day. Relieved as she left his room, she walked toward the elevator. To this day, she would never know what made her stop and look into a room a few doors down from her friend's. It was so unlike her, stranger still that she lingered.

Alone in a room designed for two, a man lay swaddled in blankets, pale skin slick with perspiration, a cluster of dark red lesions on the side of his face. Somewhere in his thirties, he lay deathly still. Thinking he had passed away, she was about to run for help when a sharp intake of breath wracked his body and he opened his eyes. She couldn't remember if she returned his smile, but she did recall mumbling an apology and backing out of the room. But she would never forget the plump nurse with the coffee-colored skin who took her hand and helped her to a chair.

"What's the matter, baby, you know that sweet boy?"

"No. I thought…it's AIDS, isn't it?"

"Yes, it is."

"There's not a flower or a card in his room. Where's his family? He's dying and he's all alone."

"He's one of the lucky ones. His family's got money. That's why he's here. You don't want to know what happens to the others."

"Would it be okay if I sat with him for awhile?"

"Sure it would, honey, and when you're finished fillin' that boy's room with light and love, you come find me at the nurse's station. My name is Cynthia Fredericks. You might have some questions."

That was an understatement. For the next few months, she had nothing but questions. She talked to doctors, social workers, the CDC, HIV/AIDS patients, anyone and everyone who could provide her with the answers and guidance she needed.

'You have to get it right to do it right' became their unofficial Mission Statement late one night in Cynthia's kitchen when exhaustion and a Rocky Road-induced sugar hit gave them a case of the giggles.

She was concerned that Cynthia was killing herself, working all day at the hospital and long into the nights with her, poring over information and lists, then lists of lists. When Cynthia announced she was resigning her nursing position to devote herself full-time to the hospice, she was speechless. "Cyn, I know how much money you make. I can't ask you to give up your job. We don't even know if this thing will get off the ground or if we'll ever have enough money to pay you."

"You're not askin'. Arthur and the boys and I had a family meetin' and decided it's what I have to do. Besides, God cares about what's in your heart, not your wallet."

To their surprise, the birthing process was easier than the conception and infinitely more satisfying. The house was a gift donated by a colleague of Larry's in desperate need of a tax write-off. To the man who signed it over to them, the property was a white elephant money pit left to him by his mother, but it was so much more than that. A once-grand Victorian with a wrap-around porch and an elevator large enough to accommodate a wheelchair, it was everything. It was **Life House***.*

They needed an Advisory Board and they took on the arduous task of culling and cajoling from local area hospitals. Once a rotating staff of doctors and nurses was in place, it was left to Cynthia to line up a spiritual A-team, a task she undertook with a fervor that bordered on manic. How she got a Catholic priest, a Muslim cleric, a Presbyterian minister and a Jewish Rabbi to come together she would never say; but the afternoon they were observed playing pinochle in the **Life House** *kitchen, she finally attributed it to divine inspiration, whatever that meant.*

Four years later, when Cynthia and Arthur's oldest son succumbed to sickle cell anemia at twenty-one, all were present and each spoke eloquently of love and loss. Two years after that, those same divinely-inspired men delivered similar words for their younger son, dead at nineteen of a massive heart attack on a college football field.

Money was always an issue and they were relentless in their fund-raising activities. Medications and funerals were expensive and no one was off-limits when the coffers were depleting. A turning point came in 2012 when a country western singer wrote a song about **Life House**, *donating all profits from the sale of the album. It was dedicated to her brother, one of the first to die of AIDS in 1982, a little over a year after the first cases were reported in the United States.*

In one of her letters, the singer pleaded for answers: why it took the death of a Hollywood icon in 1985 for mainstream America to put a public face to a private hell; why, until then, no one seemed to care that close to fifty-thousand of their sons and daughters, brothers and sisters had already died of the disease; why so many had to die alone, abandoned by their families out of fear and ignorance; or why it had taken almost a decade for the government to utter the words and begin educating the public. The questions were rhetorical but made the grief no less real.

The blessing was that, for a variety of reasons, AIDS-related deaths had been declining in the U.S. since the mid-90s and with it the **Life House** *waiting list. Nonetheless, it was still an on-going battle in a war for those with no voice or hope, a war they were prepared to win. If she couldn't save the world, she was prepared to fight for her small corner.*

Snapping out of her reverie, her mind touched on something, backed away, then grabbed at it again. The sensation was new to her and she sat for a few more minutes, not knowing what to make of it.

It was later that night, right before nodding off, when she was able to put a word to the emotion she felt at that moment in that place. Free. She was free for the first time in more years than she could remember.

Debra

Monday, 10 July 2000

Mrs. Allen is so charming! She asked that I call her Helen and we talked for hours. She made tea and invited me to accompany her to Mass next Sunday. Her husband passed away last year after a long illness and I told her about mama, how she had lingered and how I cared for her. We have so many things in common and I know we will be good friends.

For the first time, I went out on my own and took a walk to the Post Road. It isn't far but I felt as if I were finally a part of this town I love. I even purchased a few things from the pharmacy and market. Charles was so proud that I found my way around. He has left again to pick up Chinese food for our supper. I think I will surprise him by setting the table on the terrace.

Tomorrow I think I will be less ambitious as I am quite tired from all the excitement. It has been a wonderful day!

CHAPTER 5
RYAN

Peter Ignatius Ryan is a man who seeks comfort in continuity. Seven days a week he will rise early, shower and shave, down his first black coffee of the day and proceed to dress: black pants, shoes and raincoat, rain or shine, white shirt buttoned at the neck, no tie. He will leave his tidy Mission district apartment, walk approximately five blocks, purchase his second black coffee of the day and continue the final block to his tidy Mission district office.

The exception to this routine presents itself on this very day, the 20th of October, every year for the past 10 years. Today he will walk to his refrigerator and withdraw flowers purchased the night before, retrieve his aging Toyota from the parking garage and head south on U.S. 101 where, for the next four hours, he will focus on the road in front of him, looking neither left to the rolling hills nor right to the Los Padres National Forest.

Only once did he made the mistake of taking Route 1 along the ocean, past iconic landmarks like Monterey and Big Sur, through the picaresque hot spots of Big Creek Bridge and Ragged Point. The beauty depressed him. He felt alienated by the waves rushing against the cliffs, the endless miles of deserted beaches, even the sea lions at rest against the giant rocks.

This was the place where his sister finally found the happiness she deserved, a lifetime removed from their childhood. Here, from a distance, she would write of it, sullen hard-edged verses of concrete and grime, deprivation and crime. Here she found literary success, purchased her home overlooking the sea and met the love of her life.

For the final few miles, he will turn on the radio, flipping the dial until he finds music suitable to the occasion. The visits are always difficult. Birthdays were never enjoyed in the Ryan family, merely endured. This one promised to be more painful than most. His sister would be turning forty.

Reaching the hamlet of Cambria, he slows his car for the final few turns and parks. The rest of the journey is on foot. Here the ocean is upstaged by the sound of the wind in the trees and an occasional tinkling of wind chimes. Had he bothered to ask about the variety of trees, he would have learned they were the largest stand of Monterey Pines in the state of California, that there were over twelve hundred trees on the grounds including Monterey Pines, coastal live oaks, Toyon and California Pepper trees. It never occurred to him to ask.

When he arrives at his destination, he removes the cellophane and rubber band, wads them into a ball and tucks them in the pocket of his raincoat. The flowers he puts in a tall glass vase and adds water from a plastic bottle. He places the vase on the headstone and closes his eyes. When he opens them, he looks briefly at the words chiseled in the granite:

Theresa Ann Ryan
October 20, 1980 – July 8, 2010

Turning to leave, he makes a quick sign of the cross. He is there no more than five minutes.

Had someone been observing him, they would see a tall man a few inches over six feet, well-built, though it would be hard to tell because of the raincoat. They would see a thick crop of black hair atop a face routinely described as ruggedly handsome, a description he would consistently dismiss with a disdainful wave of his hand. They would see a good man, a pious man, possibly a priest. They would be wrong.

Peter Ignatius Ryan is a murderer, a cold-blooded taker of life. He has envisioned the scene a thousand times, finding the ghost who destroyed the only beauty in his life, torturing him as he had tortured her, watching him die as he had watched her. Only then would he and his sister find peace.

CHAPTER 6

ANNIE

"How are rehearsals going?"

Samantha made a gagging sound. "Let's just say I wish I really were in a coma. Wait, I am in a coma. I'm only dreaming I'm going to set British theatre back to the Stone Age."

Annie rolled her eyes. "You'll be brilliant and you know it."

"Tell that to the Bard. Rumor has it they can hear him shrieking all the way to Liverpool. Where are you? It sounds like you're speaking from inside a cave."

Crouching down, Annie ran her hand over the smooth wood floor. "I'm in my bedroom finally. No furniture yet but I have a beautiful new floor and it only took six weeks to get them out here. They finished sealing it yesterday."

"Don't knock progress. Listen, sweetie, are you going to make it across to see your sister murdered or not? We open November 27th which will be a royal pain for you with Thanksgiving weekend and all, a horrible time to fly, but maybe you could come over a week early and bring me tea and sympathy and valium, lots and lots of valium. Annie? Annie, did I lose you?"

Annie used the sleeve of her sweatshirt to wipe a layer of dust from the cover of a book. She peered behind the radiator before putting the phone back to her ear. "I found something. It must have been lodged behind the radiator and the floor guys found it."

"What kind of something?"

"It's a diary or journal of some sort. There aren't many entries and it's not a child's. The handwriting is beautiful, almost calligraphic. There's a date, July of 2000, and a name inside the front cover. Debra Hastings."

"Well, unless there's something juicy and prurient in it, I have to dash. Call me over the weekend or e-mail me and let me know when you're coming. I love you."

"I love you too."

Annie read the first entry and snapped the book closed. She felt uncomfortable invading someone's personal thoughts and she felt something else, something that seemed a bit too close to envy. Had she ever experienced the kind of joy that took her breath away?

That was enough of that. Tucking the book under her arm, she headed for the stairs. On her way to the kitchen, she stopped to build a fire in the living room fireplace. She fed Einstein, grabbed her pre-made salad and a bottle of water from the fridge and pulled a rented DVD from her tote bag.

Thirty minutes into the film, she ejected it. She'd done it again, been seduced by a great ensemble cast in a film about depressed rich people. Evidently scripts about depressed poor people weren't attracting A or B list stars, nor were scripts about happy rich people. Come to think of it, she didn't know too many happy rich people. She knew wealthy people who played at being happy, the way kids play at being superheroes, but she could not think of one person of wealth who didn't appear miserable most of the time. Or maybe they were happy and were pretending to be unhappy as some sort of bizarre penance. Or perhaps she missed the memo that declared 'those of wealth and privilege will refrain from exhibiting enthusiasm or joy for thou art the chosen ones and no one wants to be around a giddy person with four homes, three yachts and a private jet.'

Einstein nuzzled her hand and she let him out. When she returned to the living room, she added a log to the fire and avoided glancing at the diary on the mantle. She should throw it on the flames and be done with it. It was none of her business and, besides, Mrs. I'm So Joyful I Can't Breathe was probably divorced by now, a single mom raising three snotty teenagers with tattoos and nipple rings.

She started channel-surfing. A slasher film held her interest for five minutes, a walking tour of Pompeii and Herculaneum occupied another ten and, for almost half an hour, she sat mesmerized by a show featuring the nastiest coven of brides this side of Transylvania. She watched it to the end, hoping at the last minute a member of one of the wedding parties would run down the aisle yelling at the groom to save himself, that she would eat their young. It was the type of reality programming that made her cringe and want to trade in her vagina. On the other hand, these banshee babes might be on to something. Start the marriage off as a Harpy instead of being driven there by some selfish, egocentric…

What the heck was wrong with her? PMS? Larry. She hadn't thought of him in days and here he was rummaging through her subconscious, pissing her off in absentia. Was she still so vulnerable that she couldn't watch a movie or TV show without making some sort of connection to their so-called life?

It was a little early for bed but she was suddenly exhausted. Before she could talk herself out of it, she grabbed the diary from the mantle.

She spent a fitful night running through the streets of Pompeii. Several yards behind her, a man ran screaming, his upraised hand holding a nine-inch carving knife. He was wearing a wedding dress, a Vera Wang.

CHAPTER 7
RYAN

Ryan shrugged off his raincoat and threw it across a chair, thought better of it and hung it on a hook behind the door. He had to keep the chair free for a new client, another SFPD referral. At least this time it wasn't a frantic wife on the trail of a philandering husband which, of late, there seemed to be an inexhaustible supply. They never saw it coming, or so they said. His record was four minutes in determining why the poor bastard had fled the jurisdiction of home and hearth.

He checked his phone for messages and made some notes. His emails offered little more than the usual barrage of spam, all of which were handily dispatched. He had twenty minutes, enough time to make his usual round of calls and present a demeanor that would suggest he gave a shit about his next client's drama.

His initial impression of Marcia Banning was positive. She looked him in the eye and offered him a firm hand across his immaculate desk. He liked her look, neat and simple, white blouse, dark skirt and black pumps. Her make-up was minimal, hair shiny, a little shorter than shoulder-length and natural, dark brown with a few errant grays here and there. He placed her age as early fifties and found her far less objectionable than most, probably because she was a female version of himself.

She didn't fidget, sat perfectly erect in the chair, legs crossed at the ankles, hands folded loosely in her lap. When she spoke, her voice was soft but not so low that he had to ask her to repeat herself. She also used her words economically which he found most agreeable. He felt it would not be necessary to tell her to get to the point, that he would have to dig for background which was how he preferred it. Information extraction was like an archaeological excavation. All the good stuff was buried.

Sitting forward, Ryan laced his fingers together atop the desk. "When did you last speak to your sister?"

"Last January. We met for dinner in Sausalito. I believe it was the 17th."

"Ten months ago. Is it unusual to go that long without some sort of communication?"

"Not particularly. We lead very different lives, Mr. Ryan."

"Meaning?"

"Our parents were both classical musicians and we were raised in an atmosphere of refinement, even gentility one could say. Susan relished the lifestyle, the elegance of it. My brother and I hated every moment of it. He and I left home in our teens to study abroad. Susan stayed with our parents until their deaths in 2017. They died in a car accident in Oakland."

"Your sister is the oldest?"

"No, the youngest by several years. She turned thirty-eight on June 7th."

"That's odd. The first born is usually the more compliant and obedient. The youngest child is typically more rebellious."

"Very little about our family was typical, Mr. Ryan. Our parents were always on the road with one symphony or another. My brother and I were left to our own devices much of the time. Susan came along when their careers were winding down. I think they realized they missed a lot with Franklin and me and tried to compensate with their youngest child. At least that's the way it appeared." Her voice trailed off and she frowned. "I don't think I've ever thought of it in those terms before. That sounded rather harsh, but I loved my parents and I love my sister. You have to find her."

"You said the two of you lead very different lives. Can you elaborate?"

"I teach music at a small private school. My husband passed away earlier this year, but I have a wonderful circle of friends and I'm still close with my brother. I'm very active in my church and I volunteer at two local hospitals several times a week. Susan never made friends easily. She was always aloof and guarded, even as a small child. I can't ever remember her dating, but I wasn't living at home during those years so I really have no way of knowing. She writes music but I think it's more a hobby than a vocation. I doubt she's ever actually sold anything or I'm quite sure I would have heard about it. She leads a very solitary life, especially since the death of our parents."

"Why are the police not taking her disappearance seriously, Mrs. Banning?"

"When our parents were killed, Susan took it very hard. She became even more reclusive and difficult. She refused to leave the house and she stopped taking care of herself. Even the most basic hygiene seemed too much for her. I thought perhaps she was clinically depressed and suggested she consult someone, a psychiatrist or therapist, but she refused. My brother and I even discussed court action to see that she got help but we never went through with it. Around that time my husband was diagnosed with cancer and Raymond was touring with a road company of some show. He's also a musician. We let her down, Mr. Ryan. We abandoned our sister."

"You're not answering my question, Mrs. Banning. Why are the police not pursuing her disappearance? Please understand that I can make a phone call and get this information from the detective who referred you to me."

"I lied to you on the phone yesterday. I wasn't referred by the police. We haven't reported her missing."

"You gave me a name, Detective Robbins."

"I called the precinct last week and asked for the Missing Persons Division. A Detective Robbins answered the phone. I wrote down the name and hung up. I thought you'd be more inclined to see me if it were a referral. I'm sorry I lied to you but we want to keep this low-key. We don't wish to involve the authorities yet."

"Why not?"

Her composure slipped and Ryan sensed she was either debating her options or trying to remember the script.

"Our parents were very well-known in the classical music world. It would be embarrassing if it became public knowledge that Susan flipped out and was living on the streets."

"Embarrassing to whom?"

"You don't understand. She could be anywhere, doing anything with anyone. We don't want that kind of publicity. Will you help me or not?"

"Frankly, I'm not at all sure that I will. Firstly, I don't like being lied to and, secondly, I consider sins of omission even worse than lies and not nearly as creative."

Marcia Banning looked down at her hands, folded demurely in her lap. When she eventually made eye contact, her expression had hardened. "If you must know, our parents left everything to her and now it's gone. We want to know where the money is and if she's alive or dead. To be honest, I don't care either way."

"I suspected as much. You've done your homework, Mrs. Banning. I assume that is your real name. The clothes are a nice touch, by the way, as is your reference to the Church. Which church is it in which you're active, Our Lady of Perpetual Greed?"

"Don't you dare judge me. Everything I've told you is the truth. I presented myself in such a way that you'd be more inclined to take my case. I know about your sister, Mr. Ryan. I also know you gave up your career with the police department to track down the man who murdered her. Our motives may be different but I think you'll find there are stunning similarities to what happened to your sister and what I suspect happened to mine."

Rising to his feet, Ryan put his fists on the desk and leaned forward. "We're done here. I suggest you call Detective Robbins."

His height and build would usually intimidate even the most resolute criminal but Marcia Banning sat quietly, neither shaken nor stirred. "What's troubling you, that I lied to you, that my motives aren't as pure as yours or that your sister's killer might have been operating under your nose for the past ten years? That you might have passed him on the street or been in line next to him," she paused and nodded toward the paper cup on the desk, "getting your morning coffee."

"You seem to know a lot about me for someone whose life is so full of good friends and philanthropic pursuits. I wonder where you find the time. How do I know you're not working with him to determine how much information I have, how close I am to finding him?"

She laughed, a deep throaty sound that made him pull back. "They were wrong about you, Ryan. You're not smart. I doubt you could find your dick with a flashlight."

Ryan dropped his head and took a deep breath. If there were even a remote chance this woman had information, he needed to hear it. "You have five minutes and you can start by telling me who you've spoken to about this case."

"A week ago, I contacted another private investigator, George Adams. He agreed to take the case but then he mentioned your name and said the circumstances sounded familiar. I sensed the two of you were not exactly buddies. He said you were a bit peculiar, that you'd been on the fast-track to becoming Captain but left the force because you didn't like the way your sister's case was being handled. He also said you had a reputation for being a pompous prig. The police have a nickname for you, did you know? They call you Brother Ryan."

He did know and he didn't have a problem with it. He also knew George Adams, a former cop with a reputation for never meeting a suspect he didn't want to shoot first, Mirandize later. "Go on."

"I remembered your sister's case but I knew nothing of you until I met with Adams. When he went to the men's room, I left his office. I assumed you and I could help one another."

Ryan sat back in his chair. "Why the pretense? When you spoke to me yesterday and made the appointment, why didn't you just lay it out about your sister?"

"Because he led me to believe you had strict criteria for taking on new cases, that you were a religious zealot and wouldn't approve of my reasons for wanting to find my sister, all of which is apparently true."

"None of it is true but that's beside the point. My issue with you is you lied which does not portend a healthy working relationship."

"I'm not quite the monster you think I am, Mr. Ryan. You don't know Susan. She was a selfish, horrible child who grew into an even more despicable adult. Raymond and I didn't elect to go to Europe to study. I was fifteen and he was sixteen when we were shipped off because Susan told our parents she saw us having sex. I was sent to Switzerland and he was sent to the U.K. All we ever had was each other, but not in that way, never in that way. The accusation almost killed my brother. Our parents didn't even know us. Prior to that, we saw them three months out of every year, but Susan was the baby and she traveled with them everywhere while we were left in the company of whatever nanny answered their ad first.

"Our mother's family was wealthy. We are talking about a considerable amount of money, almost fifty million in cash, real estate and stocks. If Susan is alive and well and living the good life that's one thing. I'll admit I'm not happy about it but I'll accept it since I have no choice. Raymond won't join me in any kind of lawsuit even though I've been told we have grounds. I don't agree with him but I respect his decision. He's been through quite enough with our family for one lifetime. On the other hand, if someone has profited from her death and is living off the money, I want it…him found."

"And if I find them living the good life together? Have you considered that possibility?"

This time her laughter was shrill and bordered on the hysterical. "No, I can truthfully say I have not. But if it's true and someone has married her with the idea of finding peace and comfort, he's going to earn every penny."

CHAPTER 8
ANNIE

Annie pushed her hands deeper in the pockets of her jacket and closed her eyes as the truck backed up, taking with it another limb from the tree overhanging the driveway. If she didn't get it trimmed soon, there'd be nothing left of it.

Back inside the house, she put the kettle on for tea and walked into the living room. With each delivery, her vision for the house became a reality; today the rugs, tomorrow the upholstered pieces, after that the accessories she'd been hording in the garage. Before long, she could start thinking of it as a home instead of another project.

The weather had turned bitter and she adjusted the thermostat. She was chilled to the bone and squiffy from lack of sleep. She rarely remembered her dreams but last night's was scary, payback for reading the damn diary. She was ten the first time she went against her instincts. All her friends rode their bikes across Mr. Howard's property but only Annie Hogan ended up in the emergency room with a broken arm. Crime may not pay but it was the little indiscretions, the small moments when personal ethics were compromised, that hurt like hell. Why was that? And what was the big deal about reading the discarded meanderings of someone who apparently thought so little of them that she stuffed them behind a radiator and went on with her life. It wasn't as if she had desecrated the Dead Sea Scrolls.

What she needed was sleep, a nice warm fetal-position power nap and she'd be fine. When she woke up, she'd go on-line and see about flights to London. Or maybe not. It wasn't fair to leave Cynthia alone at **Life House** over the Thanksgiving weekend and she wasn't at all sure she wanted to. Holidays were important for the guests. What no one ever mentioned was the one thing never far from her mind: that for some it would be their last.

She was on her way back to the kitchen when Einstein started throwing a fit, pawing and barking at the door. Looking up, she saw her neighbor approaching the back steps. Sighing, she put on a smile.

"Mrs. Allen, what a nice surprise."

"Hello, dear, and hello to my friend Einstein," she said, reaching into her pocket for a dog treat.

"I was just going to have some tea. Will you join me?"

"I'd love to. It's rather brisk today, isn't it?"

"Yes, it is. I'm glad you're here. I was going to stop by your place tomorrow after my morning run. I wanted to apologize for all the trucks going in and out of the lane. I've been doing a lot of work on the house and I'm sure it's a bit intrusive."

"Not at all. I like the activity. I believe this house has been waiting for you. You're an interior decorator, are you not? I think your sister must have mentioned it. How is she?"

"Sam's great. She's opening in Othello next month in London. I'm very proud of her. I haven't been in the design business for a while. It was something I dabbled in during the early years of my marriage." She bit her tongue instead of adding it was her whack-job former husband's idea to keep her busy and off his back about grad school. Her only consolation was it cost him a small fortune to get her accelerated certificate through the New York School of Interior Design.

"I don't think I'd enjoy that, going into someone's home and trying to please them. You do something else though. You work with AIDS patients, if I remember correctly."

This time her smile was genuine. How often did people make the mistake of thinking the elderly were addled, their faculties blurred? This woman was sharp as a tack. "Yes I do. A friend and I run a hospice in Riverside."

"That's lovely, dear. Perhaps you'll let me visit some time. My eyesight isn't as good as it was, but they have books with large print and maybe I could read to them."

"That would be wonderful. We have a nice library and I'm sure we have books you could read, even borrow if you'd like."

Preparing the tea, she noticed the diary on the counter and felt the familiar nudge of a guilty conscience. As inconspicuously as possible, she slid it into a drawer.

"Mrs. Allen, did you know the people who lived here before me?"

"Oh my, that was a long time ago. Twenty years." She kept petting Einstein's head but was looking out the window toward the trees. Her expression was mournful, so much so that Annie wished she'd kept her mouth shut. "I only met him that once, the night she died. I don't think I've ever seen a man more sorrowful or miserable. He was almost crazy with grief."

Convinced she'd misheard the older woman's words, Annie gripped the edge of the countertop. "I'm sorry, I'm not…what did you say?"

"She was so beautiful. Debra. She had an old-fashioned reserve about her but she wanted desperately to fit in here. The poor child never had the chance. I was angry at God for a long time about taking her. I'm ashamed to admit that but it's true. Anyway, dear, we've forgiven one another so it's all right now."

"Mrs. Allen, are you saying the woman who lived here, Debra, passed away in this house?"

"No, I don't believe so. It was on the way to the hospital. Yes, I'm certain of that."

"That's terrible. How long did they live here?"

"Less than a week. It was right after Independence Day, around the 7th or 8th of July when she became ill and died. I remember because she visited me earlier that day and mentioned watching the fireworks with her new husband."

Annie's hand was shaking as she returned the cup and saucer to the table. "I'm sorry, but I'm really confused. You're saying this couple, Debra and her husband, moved in here in July of 2000 and she died several days later?"

"That's right. What is it, dear? You don't believe in ghosts, do you?"

"That's not what…it's just that…what happened to her, how did she die?"

"You know, I never found out exactly how she died. I was sure there would be a notice in the newspaper or an announcement about a funeral but there never was. I always intended to call the newspaper and inquire but I kept putting it off. Sometimes these things get away from me."

"But you said you met her husband that night. Didn't he tell you what happened?"

"You have to understand how upset he was and it was the middle of the night. He could hardly speak when he came back to get his things. I suppose he couldn't bear to spend a night here alone without her."

"And you never saw him again?"

"No, I never did." She sat quietly for a few minutes and added, "I seem to recall the owners tried to find him, but I have no idea if they were successful."

"The owners? I thought Debra and her husband owned it and sold it to the Stanley family trust."

"No, dear. This property has been owned by the Stanley family since long before I moved here in 1974. It used to be several hundred acres but they've sold most of it off through the years. The last people to live here for any length of time were two men." She lowered her voice to a whisper before adding, "I think they were gay. Such nice men. I was sorry to see them go. They moved out in the mid-80s to somewhere in Florida."

"They were probably renting then, Debra and her husband. That makes sense."

"Oh my, you know I haven't thought of this in so long. No, I don't think they were renting. Someone came to my home several weeks after she passed away and was upset that people had been living here without permission. I believe I was rather rude to him, suggesting that lovely girl and her husband had broken in. What a fuss he made."

Broken in? To quote Sam, what the bloody freaking hell? "Who was he, do you remember?"

"I'm sorry, dear, is it important? Perhaps I still have his card. I rarely throw anything away. Please don't assume I'm one of those doddering ratpacks who keeps thirty-year-old newspapers on top of the television. Everything is neatly filed away."

"Mrs. Allen, there's nothing doddering about you and I'm sure you're neat as a pin. It's not important. I hope you don't think I'm being nosy. I'm curious about the history of the house."

"Key West, that's where those nice men moved. I'm sorry, did you say something?"

Evidently, they both needed a nap. Annie formed a question but let it go. She was feeling uneasy. The diary ended on the date of Debra's mysterious death and the woman sitting across from her was one of the last to see her alive, to serve her tea. She felt as if she had just wandered into a sequel of *Arsenic and Old Lace.* The words came out before she had time to think about them.

"Why don't you come to dinner tomorrow night? We can eat in the living room in front of the fire. I should have some real furniture by then."

"That would be lovely. May I bring something?"

"No, please don't. I mean, it's okay, I'll take care of everything. Around six?"

"That's perfect but I'll have to be home by eight. I can't miss my show."

"That's fine. I usually try to get to bed early during the week. What show do you watch?"

"CSI reruns. I'm addicted to it. I'm fascinated by the fact that they take decomposing corpses and find evidence to put the villains away, aren't you?"

Annie wasn't sure how to respond so she nodded. Decomposing corpses? There went that night's sleep. "Don't you ever have nightmares from watching that kind of show, Mrs. Allen?"

"Oh my, no, but I have stopped watching CNN when they have those dreadful Senate hearings. They keep me up all night." She rose to leave and reached over to pat Annie's hand. "And please, dear, call me Helen."

CHAPTER 9
RYAN

Morning in the Mission district was his favorite time of day. He liked the bustle, the sounds and smells, even the verbal skirmishes when diversity met the reality of commercial discourse. He thought of it less as a melting pot and more as a molting creature that periodically shed its skin, reinventing itself every decade or so to adapt to new cultures. If its soul was Latino, it was the bloodlines of countless immigrants that fed its heart. It was also one of the few topics to which Ryan took proprietary umbrage when someone criticized it. The creature's Irish blood ran in his veins too. It was where he had lived his entire life and where he planned to die.

Reluctantly, he closed the window and dropped the blinds, shutting out all activity on the streets below. He wanted to hear the tape again, to close his eyes and concentrate on Marcia Banning's tone and the quality of her facts, and to satisfy himself that he had not missed a word, a syllable that might change the direction of his investigation.

Less than twenty-four hours earlier, right after her hysterical outburst, he excused himself, leaving her alone in the office. Moments before, he had touched two buttons beneath his desk, one to activate the hidden camera on the bookcase and the other to start a recording device inside his desk, a dated piece of equipment dubbed the Tricky Dictaphone by his former partner. He rarely did this before committing to a case but this time he was looking for specifics, a rifling of his desk or a cell phone call to an accomplice. For over ten minutes, he watched and listened via remote receivers hidden behind the paper towel dispenser in the men's room.

Something wasn't quite right with the Widow Banning but he couldn't put his finger on it. Granted, he'd confirmed several elements of her story, including her parents' deaths and their reputation as superb, albeit temperamental, classical musicians. A phone call to the American Federation of Musicians led him to the whereabouts of the brother, Raymond Pierce, currently playing trumpet in a dinner theatre production of **Chicago** outside Branson, Missouri.

So what was bothering him? Yes, she had lied and he'd called her on it. Or maybe it was the simple fact that for over ten minutes she did nothing more suspicious than open her handbag and check her make-up. Usually after the first five minutes, his solitary visitor would become restless and stand up and stretch, walk to the window or glance at the books and photographs lining the back wall of his office. No one was that patient or disinterested, unless of course they suspected they were being observed. Ryan shook his head. What was that expression? *Just because you were paranoid didn't mean someone wasn't after you?* Or something to that effect. Nevertheless, he had a different take on it: *Better safe than sorry.*

He hit the 'play' button, rewound to the moment he re-entered the office.

R: *I'll take your case, Mrs. Banning, but if at any time I find you are not forthcoming or distort the truth, we are done. Is that clear?*

B: *Yes, very clear. Where do we start?*

R: *Your parents. Do you have a copy of the police report on their accident?*

B: *Why is that important?*

R: It's important because I want to see if there are any unusual circumstances surrounding their accident.

B: What kind of circumstances? You don't think one of us…

R: Do you have a copy of the police report or not?

B: I'm not sure if I kept it, but I'll look for it.

It sounded like an equivocation or the response of someone who didn't give a damn, probably the latter. He stopped the tape and reread the report emailed to him earlier that morning. Their Mercedes had run a stop sign, clipped an SUV and overcompensated by spinning into a brick wall. Neither of the Pierces were wearing seatbelts and both died on impact. The owner of the other vehicle walked away with a broken arm and enough cash to purchase a fleet of Hummers. According to the autopsy report, Mr. and Mrs. Pierce had blood-alcohol levels of .1 and .09 respectively. Temperamental and gassed to the gills, the Pierces were a fun couple.

R: Who initiated the dinner between you and your sister on January 17th?

B: Susan called me earlier that day at school. Frankly, I was shocked. We hadn't spoken in two years, not since our parents' funeral, and here she was calling out of the blue. I was surprised she even knew where I worked. She sounded different, not at all like the sister I knew. She even asked how I was doing, how Raymond was getting on. It was a very odd conversation. She said she had news, something exciting to tell me and suggested we get together that evening for dinner. My first instinct was to say no, that I was busy but I agreed to meet her, more out of curiosity than anything else.

R: What was the name of the restaurant in Sausalito?

B: The Blue Pearl.

R: Who chose the restaurant?

B: Susan, which was also peculiar. Here I was practically convinced she was agoraphobic and she wants to have dinner in Sausalito of all places.

R: Do you know if she'd dined there before?

B: I don't believe so, although I can't be certain. You have to understand how shocked I was by her appearance.

R: How so?

There was a rustling sound on the tape as his client pulled a small manila envelope from her handbag.

B: This is a photo of Susan four years ago. My parents pulled some strings with the Arts editor of the Chronicle to do a feature article about her musical compositions. You know, daughter of classical musicians continues their legacy etcetera. You may keep that if you wish.

Stopping the tape, Ryan held the black and white photograph beneath the light of a desk lamp.

Susan Pierce looked older than her thirty-eight years. Her pale skin was puffy, her thin lips held together as if the whole experience were distasteful and somehow beneath her. In an obvious attempt to make her face appear thinner, her dark hair was pulled severely off her face which gave her a vaguely masculine quality. Even the white turtleneck, designed to camouflage the thickness of her neck, looked frayed, as if it had been pulled from the laundry hamper. Her lack of make-up and jewelry only added to the austere persona of one uncomfortable in her skin. If the intent was to make Susan Pierce appear erudite and capable of producing classical compositions, it failed miserably. Had the photograph been in sepia tones instead of black and white, she could have easily taken her place in a gallery of long-forgotten spinster aunts.

Before resuming the tape, Ryan scanned the clipping again and made a note of the by-line. He didn't recognize the name but over the years several articles had been written about his sister's work and at least two appeared in the Chronicle.

B: And this is the woman who met me for dinner last January.

The second photograph was a five by seven color shot of two women seated side by side in a banquette. On the left, a handsome woman with long auburn hair smiled seductively for the camera. The table blocked most of her body from the waist down but, even so, Ryan could see that Susan Pierce had shed at least fifty pounds. Her make-up appeared flawless and skillfully, if not professionally, applied. Her white shirt was crisp and clean, collar pulled jauntily up behind her elegant neck, around which hung a double-strand of turquoise nuggets. Another woman was seated beside her but the image had been carefully outlined and filled in with a red marker pen. The two red horns protruding from the top of her head were a telling addition.

R: Who took this photograph?

B: You mean his name? I have no idea. We had just been seated when Susan pulled a digital camera from her bag and asked a waiter to take it for us. That photo arrived in the mail three days later.

R: I take it the evening did not go well.

B: Obviously, but then I never expected it to. You have to understand that when Susan extends an olive branch, you must be prepared for thorns. Do you know what she did the day she told our parents the lie about Raymond and me? That morning she went into the garden and picked flowers for our rooms. Two days later we were put on separate planes to Europe. Trust me, this is about more than losing weight and a trip to the cosmetics counter. You can't see the rest of her clothes but they're high-end all the way. Her boots cost more than my car.

R: *She's a very wealthy woman, Mrs. Banning. She can afford the best of everything, cosmetic surgery, a personal trainer, a stylist. It's a remarkable transformation and four years is a long time.*

B: *She said she had met her soul-mate, the man of her dreams. She said he understood her, that he knew why she isolated herself and her talent needed only to be nurtured before the world could appreciate it. He told her he wanted to take her away from everything and everyone who had hurt her. Does any of this sound the least bit familiar to you?*

R: *Mrs. Banning, I have agreed to look into the disappearance of your sister. I have no intention of sharing the details of my sister's life or death.*

There were, how had she put it, stunning similarities in Susan Pierce's life and his sister's but there were also minor differences. In spite of her difficult childhood, Theresa had emerged a caring, loving person who channeled her anger into her work. She was a critically-acclaimed author of several books by the time she met the 'love of her life', the madman who would take that life. There was also the difference in their ages, which he tended to dismiss. All in all, he had to admit the things they shared, reclusive lifestyle, interest in the arts and financial independence were compelling common denominators.

B: *You must have loved her very much. I'm sorry for your loss, Mr. Ryan. I should have said that to you earlier.*

R: *I beg your pardon.*

B: *I see the pain on your face. Susan and I were never close and Raymond and I have never been able to regain the kind of bond we had before she ripped us apart, but I lost my best friend when my husband passed away and I know how it stays with you every moment of every day.*

R: *How did she meet this man, her soul-mate?*

B: *I asked her that but she seemed reticent about sharing any details. It was so obvious that, for several minutes, I thought she was making it all up, that she was trying to make me feel bad that I had lost my husband and she had someone. I know that sounds horrible but our history had been so poor and it seemed so out of character for her to share this with me. The only thing that led me to believe there was a man was the way she looked, the way she carried herself. Although at one point, it almost felt as if…*

R: *As if what?*

B: *As if she'd been coached. There were several times when she would start to say something then stop herself or change the subject. When I asked what he did for a living, she smiled but then excused herself and went to the ladies' room. When she returned, she went into this long spiel about a piece of music she'd written and how there was some interest by the San Francisco Symphony in performing it later this year.*

R: *What precipitated her sending you this photograph?*

B: *She wanted me to sign away my rights to the estate and relinquish all future claims. I refused and she left.*

R: *What do you mean she left? She left the restaurant?*

B: *Yes, we were having coffee and she picked up her bag and left.*

R: *Did you follow her? Did she have a car? Was she picked up?*

B: *I have no idea and at that moment I couldn't have cared less. The waiter came with the bill and I paid it. Typical Susan.*

R: *How did she suggest you relinquish your rights? I assume she wanted something more than a verbal agreement.*

B: *She had a document with her. She said I could take it with me and we should meet the following day and execute it with her attorney.*

R: *Do you have the document?*

B: *Absolutely not, I wanted nothing to do with it.*

R: *I assume it was an official document. Did you see the name of the law firm?*

B: *I wouldn't touch it but she told me who it was, Emerson and Nagel. They've handled my family's affairs for years. Thomas Nagel was a friend of my father's.*

R: *How did she present it to you? What reason did she give for wanting you to relinquish your rights after all this time?*

B: *She said she'd been thinking about it for some time and wanted to get on with her life and not have a lawsuit hanging over her head.*

R: *What kind of settlement did she offer you in exchange for signing the document?*

B: *She offered us a million dollars each. I laughed at her.*

R: *Has anyone discussed this with your brother? Perhaps he wouldn't find it amusing to be giving up a million dollars.*

B: *I've told you. He wants nothing from her except to be left alone.*

R: *Did she indicate how she planned to get on with her life? What changes she intended to make?*

B: *No and I didn't ask. I was angry and hurt if you can believe it. I suppose I inferred from the way she'd been talking that she was going to start a new life with this man, whoever he was.*

R: And neither your sister nor anyone from the law firm has contacted you since January 17th?

B: No.

R: Have you tried to contact her?

B: Two weeks ago, I drove to her home. It was the first time in almost thirty years that I'd been near it. My husband and I used to joke about it. He called it the House of Usher and we would drive miles out of our way to avoid it. But this particular day, I woke up depressed and decided to confront her. I'd been thinking about it for months, that perhaps I made a mistake in refusing the settlement. I was prepared to accept it on the condition that she tell me why she ruined our lives, but when I got there, it was as if I were paralyzed. I parked in front for an hour or so, studying every detail of the house, the wrought iron gates, the Palladian window on the second floor that was my room. I tried to imagine myself inside, to think of one day when I felt I was part of a family, one hour when my brother and I were as important to our parents as their next European tour. The longer I sat there, the angrier I became. I felt foolish and pathetic. Finally, I went up and rang the bell by the gate.

R: Mrs. Banning, do you need a few minutes?

B: No, I'm fine, thank you. An elderly man answered the intercom. He told me he had no idea who Susan Pierce was, that his daughter and son-in-law purchased the home in September. He told me if I wanted any more information, I should come back when they were home.

R: Did you contact them?

B: No, I couldn't. I have a friend who's a realtor and she looked into the details of the sale. The home was sold for seven and a half million dollars on September 27th, almost a month ago. I have a copy of her notes. The name on the escrow papers is Susan Pierce.

R: What about the contents of the home?

B: I have no idea.

R: I assume there were some valuable pieces, antiques, perhaps some important art?

B: I know I must sound naïve but I never even gave it a thought. I was a teenager when I left that house. Everything looked old and dark and disgusting, but I'm sure there were some valuable pieces.

R: Then that's our starting point. It's entirely possible we can track the contents right to their door. Mrs. Banning, are you all right?

B: The day before I contacted George Mason, I got a phone call at my home. It was around eleven o'clock at night. Normally I don't answer the phone that late unless I recognize the number but this was a strange area code so I picked it up. It was a woman. She said my sister was in trouble, that someone was trying to kill her. She wouldn't give me her name, saying she didn't want to get involved but that Susan begged her to call me. I laughed, Mr. Ryan. I told her I would be the last person on earth my sister would call. I told her never to call me again and to tell Susan to go to hell.

R: I assume you made a note of the number?

B: Yes, and I called it the very next morning. It's a gas station in Sedona, Arizona, a pay phone. One of the attendants happened to walk by and pick it up. No one had any idea who could have made the call. I couldn't believe I'd been so heartless. If I thought she was really in danger, of course I would want to help her. I'm so confused by all of this. One minute I hate her and the next I think she may have been as much a victim as Raymond and I. But the timing of the phone call seemed strange. It was only a week before that I had gone to the house.

R: Do you have the number of the payphone?

B: It's on the notes about the house sale. It's circled there.

R: Did you contact the police in Sedona?

B: And tell them what? That a strange woman called me in the middle of the night from a pay phone in the middle of the Arizona desert to enlist my help for a sister I…I hate?"

Ryan hit the 'stop' button. There it was, the thing that was bothering him. He missed it yesterday because he was concentrating on her facial expressions and body language. Today it jumped off the tape. Guilt. Marcia Banning's odd behavior, her frequent forays into multiple personalities, were not a result of duplicity but shame, the remorse she felt for ignoring her sister's call for help; and her pride, her fear and distaste of having her family's dysfunction played out in a public forum.

He rose and walked around the room, opening the blinds and windows. He wanted to air out the space, to cleanse it of the rancor and hostility that hid in every corner of his personal and professional life. It was not his place to judge Marcia Banning, any more than he could fault the women who sought love and found betrayal.

He made a few more notes and a list of the calls he'd make before contacting the airlines. But first, he'd listen to the last few minutes of the tape.

R: Mrs. Banning, this is important. Did your sister mention anything about this man that might help us find him? Did she describe him in any way, his age, physical appearance, anything? Did she mention any friends of his whom she might have met, any hobbies or the kind of car he drove?

B: I'm sorry, I've gone over it a thousand times in my head. Once she dropped the bomb that she had someone in her life, she steered clear of it and any reference to him. That's why it seemed a fabrication. When I first met my husband, I couldn't stop talking about him, how handsome he was, how accomplished and kind. I wanted to shout his name from the rooftops.

R: You've thought of something. What is it?

B: You know there was a moment toward the end when we were arguing about the release. She was very frustrated and mumbling to herself, but I'll swear she mentioned a name. How odd that I just remembered that.

R: Mrs. Banning, please.

B: Charles. It was Charles, I'm sure of it.

CHAPTER 10

ANNIE

Annie took a sip of wine and stared into the fire. She should have cancelled. Early this morning, they lost another guest at **Life House**, a long-time resident and friend to all. Although his decline was mercifully swift, neither she nor Cynthia found consolation. No matter how one tried to dress it up, death meant loss. They spent the entire day handling the details, notifying relatives, making funeral arrangements, setting the date for the memorial, a bittersweet tradition. The Final Good-bye.

She glanced across at her dinner companion who had spoken very little and eaten almost nothing of her meal. Either Helen had picked up on her mood or she was lost in some deep funk of her own. Maybe it was the fish. She knew she should have prepared a chicken dish. Who didn't like chicken? Or maybe she was ill. She did seem frailer than the day before and a bit distant.

"Helen, are you feeling okay? We could do this another time if you'd like me to walk you home?"

"I'm sorry, dear, I didn't sleep well last night."

"That's my fault. I shouldn't have opened old memories yesterday."

"Death is a part of life. The dead need to be remembered."

Annie could have kicked herself. The one subject she wanted to avoid was any discussion of the home's previous occupants, at least for this evening. "Would you like some tea? I picked up a chocolate cake."

"Debra was an artist. Did I tell you that? The first time I saw her, she was sketching by the creek. We waved to one another. I have something to show you. Where did I leave my pocketbook?"

Before Annie could respond, Helen was on her feet, headed for the kitchen. When she returned, she held out a small pen and ink drawing in a plain black frame. It was a beautifully rendered study of herself, many years younger, an incredible likeness.

"This is amazing. Did Debra do this?"

"Yes, the day she came for tea. She said she always carried a sketchbook with her and she asked if I would mind. It took her almost no time and she gave it to me right before she left. I had it framed."

"The frame is perfect. She was very talented but then she had a wonderful subject."

"You're very sweet, Annie, just like her."

"What was she like?"

Helen folded her napkin precisely as she had found it and laid it on the table. "We had a daughter, our only child. She was nine when she passed away with leukemia. When I first saw Debra, I thought 'why there she is, that's the way my Linda would have looked.' She had black wavy hair and beautiful brown eyes. I've always regretted I didn't tell Debra that, but I was afraid it would make her uncomfortable."

"I'm sure she would have been flattered."

Annie sensed the older woman was struggling with something and rose to clear the table to give her some space. In the kitchen, she filled the kettle and leaned back against the countertop. The way things were going, it was just a matter of time before they both broke down in tears. She had to get through the next couple of hours. After that, she could cry her eyes out. Back in the living room, she laid out the cups and saucers and sat back down.

"Annie, are you a religious person?"

Ah, boy. She had very definite ideas about God and organized religion but now was not the time to share them. Sticking as close to the truth as possible, she chose her words carefully. "I believe in a higher purpose, but I wouldn't say I'm religious. I hope that doesn't offend you."

"Oh my, no. I'm only asking because my religion frowns on certain things and I'm a bit confused about something."

"Confused?"

"I dreamed of Debra last night."

"Considering we discussed her yesterday, that's not surprising."

"This was different. I've heard that sometimes people who have passed away come back in dreams to visit. Do you believe in that?"

"Yes, I do. I like to think the dreams I've had of my grand-mother were visits. We were very close."

"But that would mean there's an afterlife."

"Is that what's troubling you, that the Catholic Church doesn't condone that sort of thing?" Crap, she'd been careful to avoid quoting anything from Debra's diary and here she was babbling on and spilling the metaphorical beans. The good news was Helen appeared to be lost in her own thoughts. "I'll get the tea."

This was ridiculous. She hated lying and was terrible at it. She debated showing Helen the diary to let her see how fond Debra was of her but shot down the idea. Perhaps some other time. At the moment, she needed to serve the dessert and keep things upbeat. "I'm afraid this cake is very rich. If you'd prefer, I have some fat-free cookies. You know, I read a funny article the other day about…"

"She was angry with me."

"Angry? Why would she be angry with you?"

"I've thought about it all day and I think she was angry because I didn't try to find out about her funeral. That I kept putting it off."

"Many people believe those who pass on don't take negative emotions with them."

"I didn't know that."

"We have quite a few books on the subject at **Life House,** and I'd be happy to bring you a couple. I'll think you'll find them comforting."

"Yes please, dear. I'd like that."

Helen finished off her cake and Annie stole a glance at her watch. It was only 7:30. By eight, she could be soaking in her tub with another glass of wine.

"I'll take a spot more tea, Annie. I'm so enjoying this."

Or not. Annie reached for the tea pot and Helen moved from her chair to the sofa.

"Does it upset you to talk about her, Annie? I'm only asking because you seemed rather anxious when we were speaking of her yesterday."

Annie started to reply but thought better of it. Maybe it did upset her. No one liked to think of a vibrant young woman dying tragically before her time, a woman who viewed the world through the eyes of a child, who had loved her husband and adopted country with such passion. Maybe it was guilt, not so much over reading her private words, but of the brief moments of envy that Debra found true love and Annie Hogan Heywood had not come close. If there were such a thing as angry spirits, maybe Debra visited the wrong house.

Picking up the wine bottle and her glass, she took the chair opposite the sofa. "Tell me about her."

"Are you sure?"

"You said it yourself, Helen. The dead need to be remembered. Maybe we could consider this a memorial to her. Where was she from?"

"She was Canadian but she didn't refer to herself that way. She used another word, a French term."

"Quebecois? Was she from Quebec?"

"Yes, that's it. She was from Quebec. She had a beautiful accent."

"Did she tell you anything about her family?"

"Oh, yes. She came from a very old family. I remember now. She said one of her ancestors had been the first French baby born on Canadian soil. She even told me the name but I can't recall it."

"That's an impressive lineage."

"Her father had something to do with the Government, but he passed away right after she was born. She was raised by her mother. She was an only child and I got the impression she had a rather sheltered childhood. I gather they were very well off, although she would never say that. She was much too refined to talk about such things. She did speak about their home, that it was very large and how it was going to be turned into a school. I believe she said her husband arranged that. My, she was so in love with him."

"How old was she?"

"I'm not sure, dear, but she couldn't have been more than twenty-five or twenty-six. Wait, she did tell me. Her birthday was a day or two before we spoke. She was twenty-six."

"That's awfully young to die so unexpectedly. Did she mention being ill?"

"No, I'm quite sure I would have remembered that. She seemed the picture of health."

"I know you only saw her husband that one time but do you remember what he looked like?" Not for lack of trying, Annie couldn't picture him. One day, she envisioned him as dark and dashing and the next as blond and preppy.

"I said I only met him once. I caught a glimpse of him driving down the lane one day and the next day I saw him in the hardware store. He was very good-looking, a bit taller than average with sandy blond hair. He reminded me of one of those young men in the movies, you know the ones who ride those board things in the ocean."

"A surfer?"

"That's it, a surfer."

"Can you guess his age?"

"I'm terrible with age. Everyone looks young to me. I would say he was approximately the same age as Debra, perhaps a year or two older."

"You're amazing, Helen, the details you remember."

"You know what they say about the elderly, dear. We can remember what we were wearing on our seventh birthday, but we can't recall what we had for breakfast on any given morning."

Annie laughed. She liked this woman immensely, the way she lived her life and got around. In their brief relationship, she had detected not a hint of self-pity or fear over facing her future alone. "I seriously doubt that applies to you, Helen."

"Sometimes it does, but then I think it's God's way of filling our minds with happier times. In the end, does it really matter what we did two days ago or what we had for breakfast?"

She had to think about that. Two of her grandparents died from complications of Alzheimer's, their battle to preserve their dignity and hold on to the simplest daily detail heartbreaking, much more so than the physical deterioration.

"What happened that night, the night she died?"

"The last time I saw her they were dining on the terrace. It wasn't quite sunset but they had a candle on the table. I thought that was so romantic. I was walking to the mailbox before it got too dark, and I heard them laughing. That's what made me look in this direction. It must have been around midnight when I heard their car driving out of the lane toward Compo Road. It woke me and I got up and looked over here. It was summer so I had the window open. Normally noise from the outside doesn't wake me. I'm not sure why it woke me that night. I looked over and the house was completely dark. I thought that was strange."

To say the least. "Now I'm confused about something, Helen. You said someone questioned you and implied that Debra and Charles had broken in and were living here illegally. Assuming that was true, how did they manage without furniture or electricity or even running water?"

"Well, let me think a moment. It seems to me that dreadful man said something about the house being furnished and the utilities were kept on because the Stanleys sometimes used it as a guest house. Yes, I'm sure that's what he said."

"That makes sense, especially with the sump pump in the basement. It runs constantly. I'm sorry, you were saying?"

"What was I saying, dear?"

"About that night. Their car woke you around midnight."

"Oh yes, I had a devil of a time getting back to sleep. It happens sometimes. I had gotten out of bed to walk over and turn the television off. I didn't have a remote control back then. That's when I heard the car again, only this time it was going very slowly and the headlights were off. I know because I peeked out my bedroom window."

"Did you happen to note the time when you saw the car return?"

"No, but I do recall I watched a movie after I was awakened the first time. It was just starting and I watched it until the end. That's when I got up to turn off the television."

So roughly two hours unaccounted for. "You said you spoke to him that night. Did he stop by your home?"

"No, I sensed something was wrong and I thought, Helen, they don't know too many people here and you should be a good neighbor, so I put on my bathrobe and got a flashlight and started toward the house, toward here. The car was empty when I reached the driveway but the trunk was open. I remember that because there was a light inside it. I assumed they were in the house but there weren't any lamps lit that I could see. I walked to the front door and it was open. That's when I heard someone running on the stairs. I called out her name and then his but he must not have heard me because he almost ran me down. I stepped aside just in time. He was so upset, poor thing."

"How do you know he was upset?"

"Who wouldn't be? His sweet wife of only a few weeks had just died."

"When you finally spoke to him, what did he say?"

"He was already back at the car when I called his name again. That's when he turned and saw me. He was very cross at first. Here's this strange woman in a housecoat, skulking about his house in the middle of the night with a flashlight. I was a bit taken aback but then I introduced myself and he apologized and told me Debra had collapsed and he was rushing her to the hospital when she died in the car. I couldn't believe it. I started crying and telling him how sorry I was and…"

"And…"

"He stood there."

"But you said yesterday that he was crazy with grief, that you'd never seen anyone so miserable. Was he crying?"

"No, he wasn't crying but I'm sure he was grief-stricken."

Okay, this was weird. Either Helen was projecting her emotions on to him or the guy was in shock. Or he could have been pumped full of adrenaline and feeling as if he had to do something, that he needed to take control of the situation.

"I'm sorry, Helen, what were you saying?"

"I was asking if you've ever lost someone close to you."

"Only my grandparents, but I lose people I care about all the time, much too often, and I cry every time."

"When our daughter died, my husband never cried. He would get very quiet and sit in her room for hours, but he never shed a tear. I'm sure he felt he had to be strong for me. Men don't like to show their emotions."

Maybe it was a Canadian thing or a French thing. She knew the British could be annoyingly stoic, stiff upper lip and all that. Only the Irish cried at the drop of a hat. "What part of Canada was he from, do you recall?"

"He wasn't Canadian, dear. He was American, from somewhere in California, San Francisco I think. Yes, because she mentioned the Golden Gate Bridge and how he promised to take her there."

Then again, maybe it was a California surfer thing. Maybe he had paddled his board into the surf and dropped flowers, crying like a baby. Annie was feeling the effects of the wine and getting punchy. She also felt the beginnings of a wicked headache, the kind that started right above her left eye and lingered for hours. It was time to wrap things up.

"What happened after that? He was standing there and then he…"

"He got in his car and left."

"Just like that? Did he say good-bye or offer to walk you back to your house?"

"No, but he was in a hurry. I assumed he was going back to the hospital."

There was always so much paperwork involved with a death, a fact with which Annie was all too familiar. Maybe he had to get back and sign some papers or he'd returned to the house to pick up Debra's clothing for the mortuary.

"Did he happen to mention which hospital he took her to?"

"I don't believe so. Do you think I should have asked him that?"

"Under the circumstances, I probably wouldn't have thought to ask him either. I'm sure whatever you said was perfect and he appreciated your concern."

"Have we started the memorial yet, dear? My show starts in half an hour. I've had such a good time, Annie, and I've so enjoyed this game."

"Game?"

"The courtroom game. How did I do?"

"Do?"

"With my testimony. I feel like a witness in an episode of *Law and Order*."

Way to go. She'd managed to turn a perfectly harmless dinner into an interrogation. "You were great. I'll tell you what, I'll try to find out where Debra is interred and if it's around here, we'll visit her grave. Would you like that?"

"I would, dear, but you didn't even know her. Are you sure you want to go to all that trouble?"

"It's no trouble. Debra would only be a few years older than me had she lived. Who knows? We might have become friends."

"I think that's very possible. You both have a sweetness about you, your sister too. You said she's in a play next month, didn't you?"

"Othello. She's playing Desdemona."

Helen's expression turned wistful and she closed her eyes. "O thou foul thief, where hast thou stowed my daughter?"

Feeling a chill, Annie pulled the collar of her sweater up around her neck. "Nicely done. Samantha would be impressed."

"My husband taught Literature at the University of New Haven. He loved to read Shakespeare to me. That was before television."

If that was a hint, Annie was on-board. Twenty minutes later, walking back to her house from seeing Helen safely into hers, another line popped into her head:

> *Nay, lay thee down and roar;*
> *For thou hast kill'd the sweetest*
> *innocent*
> *That e'er did lift up eye.*

Damn.

CHAPTER 11

RYAN

Deputy Police Chief James Januski added his dollar bill to the one on the table and grinned up at the pretty waitress. "I'm feeling lucky today, Maria. It's gotta be 80 degrees, maybe warmer."

She craned her neck around a passing busboy, smiled and scooped the two bills off the table. "You feel lucky every week, Jimmy. Thanks to you, my son will be going to college."

"Your son's what, three?"

"Three and a half. We're shooting for Harvard. The usual?"

"Hold the bacon. I'm off bacon so even if I beg you, no more bacon."

"Okay, so wassup?"

"Nothing's up. I'm eating healthier, that's all."

"And I am Penelope Cruz." She snapped her fingers. "You watched **Charlotte's Web** with your nephew again."

"Don't be ridiculous."

"Yes, you did. You told me the same thing when you saw that other movie. What was it called?"

"It was called **Babe**. Now go away. And no bacon…ever."

Directly behind him where he'd caught the tail-end of the conversation, Ryan shed his raincoat before taking his usual seat at the table.

Jimmy leaned in. "Next week, no raincoat, okay?"

Ryan added a sugar packet to his waiting latte. "Quit complaining. You're losing a buck a week. I'm risking heat stroke. She wants her kid to go to Harvard."

"So I've heard. You look like shit."

"Whatever you do, avoid the mussels at the Blue Pearl in Sausalito."

"Did they recognize her?"

"A waste of time. The place is mostly a tourist trap. She's not a regular. You get any hits?"

"Yeah, I got hits. I got about twelve hundred hits on scumbags with the name Charles and that's just in the last year. A couple of domestic violence cases look interesting. We're following up."

"This guy doesn't beat them up, Jimmy. He can't risk getting nailed for a black eye or a split lip. He's smooth, even charming, until he gets what he wants from them."

"Them? It sounds like you're already convinced there's a connection between Theresa and this Pierce woman."

Maria placed their lunch plates in front of them. Before Ryan could protest, she rested a hand on his shoulder. "No cheeseburger for you today, Ryan. You look like hell. Your face is paler than my ass. Soup and bread for you and go easy on the lattes. You will thank me later."

"You just blew your tip."

They ate in silence until Jimmy pushed his plate away. "This Banning woman sounds like a flake, Pete. Could be a crime junkie or a lonely woman looking for attention."

"Not a chance. Too many of her facts check out. I found the furnishings from the Pierce house, a storage facility on Turk Street. The house closed escrow on September 27th. On the 20th, they rented three eleven by eighteen bays to a Susan Pierce. All the paperwork was done by email. Two days later, they got a check for over six thousand dollars to cover the first six months. Two days after that, a moving van shows up and fills the three bays. The guy couldn't remember the name of the moving company but I've got calls into all the big ones."

"Jesus. You don't think…"

"We'll see. I gave him the date. The guy's new, only been there six months. They're computerized, but it could take awhile. I'm going over there later with a few bucks to ease his burden. It's a longshot."

"It's a hell of a lot more than we've come up with."

Ryan let the comment slide. He knew Theresa's case was a sore spot with his ex-partner, but there was more than enough guilt to go around. He'd worked the case himself for a solid year before he cleaned out his desk, dropped his shield and gun on Jimmy's desk and never looked back. No finger pointing, no drama, no farewells. The only things he left behind were letters to the Chief of Police, the Mayor and anyone else he could think of, laying out the reasons that his friend and partner, James Januski, should top the shortlist for Chief of Police.

If he was going to find her murderer, he would do it without the constraints and politics of the SFPD. Within a month, he had his P.I. license, an office and Jimmy's assurance he'd do everything in his power to help.

Together they had brainstormed the facts surrounding her murder countless times, looking at it from every angle. None of it made sense. The fact that her body was discovered in a vacant lot not a mile from where he was sitting and two hundred miles from her home in Cambria turned out to be red herring. Believing it to be a revenge kill, together they had pored over all his collars trying to establish a link and came up with nothing. Now serial killer was added to the mix.

Jimmy was right about one thing. The Turk Storage lead was a good one. When Theresa's home was burned to the ground, no furniture or personal effects were found in the rubble. Where did it go? He knew enough not to get his hopes up but, damn, all he needed was a name.

When he came back to Planet Earth, Jimmy had just finished a call on his cellphone and was shaking his head. "Another dead end. No activity on Susan Pierce's credit cards since September 30th, almost a month ago. She bought a set of luggage at Louis Vuitton. We're still working on the airlines but she didn't use her credit card for the tickets to Arizona."

"They didn't fly. He couldn't risk being identified by airline personnel and he couldn't ask for separate seats or Susan Pierce would get suspicious. My guess is they drove."

"You really think this guy's that smart?"

"I know he's smart. I talked to the owners of almost every home on Susan Pierce's street yesterday, even the hired help. No one, and I mean no one, saw a guy entering or leaving the house in the last year."

"That sound right to you? Even rich people need a repairman now and then."

"You've seen those houses, Jimmy. They're mansions with gates and intercom systems. Most of them are set back off the street behind high walls. You're in a car with tinted windows and a remote to the gate, you can come and go as you please. I'm telling you, this guy is like vapor."

"What about the Pierce woman? She must have had some kind of household staff."

"I spoke to the housekeeper next door who claims she used several different services to come in and clean. She said she'd think about it and call me if she remembered any names."

Jimmy's cellphone rang again. This time he got up and walked a few feet away. When he returned, he was smiling. "When you get to Sedona, you'll have the full cooperation of the police chief there. His name is Roland Cody."

"Thanks, Jimmy. How'd that happen?"

"The Chief made the call. She likes you. You have a lot of friends, Pete. You need to remember that."

Ryan reached for the check. No response was called for and he wouldn't have known what to say anyway. Jimmy was his friend, his only friend when it came right down to it, a world apart from everyone else. He knew guys had pals or buddies and 'best friend' sounded childish, like something a kid would say on a playground. Nonetheless, it was true. He was also the only one still living who called him Pete. The truth was he didn't know he had a lot of friends and wasn't sure he wanted them. Maybe it was a holdover from Iraq. He'd gone over with two friends from the neighborhood and came back alone.

He pulled out cash to pay the check and added a twenty dollar tip for Maria. He was still hungry but at least he didn't feel like running to the head.

Polishing off his iced tea, Jimmy sat back in his chair. "Wish I were going with you to Sedona. It's beautiful. Mary Jo and I spent a week there a few years ago. They have those jeep tours that go up into the canyons. Pink Jeep Tours, that's what they're called. You should do it."

Rising from the table, Ryan grabbed his raincoat off the chair. "I'll do that. Maybe I can fit it in between my aura cleansing and regression therapy."

CHAPTER 12

ANNIE

The room was still in darkness when Annie opened an eye and groaned. It was way too early to be awake and there was no way she'd get back to sleep. As she pulled the blankets up around her chin, a question bobbed to the surface and stayed there. What really happened to Debra Hastings?

She was losing it. Samantha was the Drama Queen and sensible Annie was the level-headed one. Maybe she needed to see someone and talk it out. She hadn't had a good night's sleep in weeks. Could it be a delayed reaction to the divorce? Was there some mandated grieving period she was supposed to know about? Her tried and true method of dealing with life was failing miserably. In the past, staying busy and focused while channeling her inner-Scarlett had seen her through the worst of days, so what happened?

Stress happened. For starters, she was in a new home in a new town. Sam was pushing her about a decision on London, she had a funeral tomorrow, a meeting with the accountant next week and, as of yesterday afternoon, her garage was flooded. Definitely stress.

Before throwing back the covers, she reached over and stroked Einstein's head. He acknowledged her hand with a gentle lick and fell back to sleep. The little shit.

She briefly closed her eyes against the glare of the bathroom light, grabbed the edge of the countertop and stared into the mirror. All things considered, it could be worse. It was nothing a good night's sleep, a facial and a round of boisterous sex wouldn't cure. Startled, she jerked upright. "Whoa, where did that come from?"

Where indeed. She'd done enough research to know it was a perfectly normal response, the need for touch and intimacy, a way to feel alive. It was Death, the dark aphrodisiac. The Grim Reaper shows up and the first thing you want to do is jump somebody's bones. On the plus side, she was glad it was out there, floating around the universe among other unlikely concepts like world peace, campaign finance reform and Martin Scorsese's overdue Oscar, any of which had a better chance of success than sex anytime in her future.

Downstairs, she opened a bottle of aspirin, popped two in her mouth and washed them down with a slug of day-old black coffee. It was her father's sure-fire cure for a morning headache, something to do with shrinking or enlarging the capillaries, one or the other. Making a face, she pitched the rest of the coffee into the sink before starting a fresh pot. While it was brewing, she logged on to her computer. Like it or not, she had to try and find out where Debra was buried. A promise was a promise. With any luck, she could make a few calls and be on to the garage by noon. Big whup.

Problem. Her files and rolodex were at **Life House**, all their contacts with local funeral home directors and administrators. This was just as easy. She'd bring up the list for Fairfield County and have all the phone numbers at her disposal.

Blinking at the screen, she fell back in her chair. There were nine pages of funeral homes and cremation facilities. She counted almost seventy then stopped and started from the beginning, noting only those within a reasonable radius of Westport. There were still way too many of them and, even if she were able to talk any of them into searching their files, the records were twenty years old. It could take weeks. More than likely, he shipped her body back to Canada where she could be laid to rest with her parents.

A better plan was to search the local newspapers, but a quick run-through of their sites proved to be another non-starter. Only a few displayed death notices on-line and none back to 2000, which meant doing things the old-fashioned way and schlepping to the library.

Einstein made his presence known so she let him out, poured herself a large mug of coffee and logged on to her e-mail. She had thirty-two new messages, thirty of which were junk. Of the remaining two, one was from Samantha urging her to firm up her flight plans. The second was from Cynthia written the previous evening. It was a reminder they would be welcoming a new guest later in the day, a transfer from Norwalk Hospital, and not to worry about a thing. She would pick him up, take him home and make him comfortable.

Annie smiled at the wording. Cyn won that argument many years ago, a real doozy. For many reasons including insurance issues, Annie wanted local guests brought to **Life House** via ambulance. It was safer, faster and they would have help moving them in. The debate lasted almost an hour when Cynthia squared her shoulders, fixed her with *the look* and asked, "You bring friends to your home in an ambulance?" That was that, and she was right. By the time their guest arrived at his new home, he knew he had at least one person in his world who cared more about his dreams than his disease, at least one person who was in his corner, willing him, empowering him to fight the most important battle of his life.

She perked up and reread the e-mail. Cynthia was going to Norwalk Hospital, and unless he was too upset to be thinking clearly, Charles would have driven Debra there. In the middle of the night with little traffic on the thruway, it would take him less than ten minutes. The only other possibility was Bridgeport Hospital but it was twice the distance. No, he would have taken her to Norwalk, she was sure of it. It was close to I-95 and well-marked. He couldn't miss it.

Cynthia started her nursing career at Norwalk before transferring to Greenwich and she still knew people there. How tough would it be for her to cajole them into looking through their files? Hospitals kept impeccable records, they had to.

She died on the way to the hospital.

So she was still alive, or at least Charles thought she was still alive, when he put her in the car, which meant there would be some record of receiving her body. An autopsy was a given. A twenty-six-year-old woman doesn't die without raising a red flag. She knew a couple of people in the County Coroner's office but they were always overworked so she'd save them as a last resort. Starting with Norwalk Hospital wasn't a perfect plan and it might not produce the information she wanted; or they could get lucky and everything, including the final disposition of Debra's body, would be there for them in black and white. Either way, the ball would be in play.

She typed a CliffsNotes version of what she knew about Debra Hastings and checked her date of death against the last entry in the diary. When she was done, she reread it, buying time. She shouldn't be doing this, adding another thing to her best friend's already full plate. Thanks to an early flu season, they were understaffed as it was, and here she was, responsible Annie, taking the day off to clean out her garage. Or she could make it up to her by foregoing London and being there during the Thanksgiving holiday. Even better, she would insist that Cyn and Arthur take that entire weekend for themselves, a B and B getaway in Vermont, all expenses paid.

"Sounds good to me," she said aloud and hit the send key.

CHAPTER 13

RYAN

Ryan accepted a watery orange juice and thanked the flight attendant, easily matching his tone to her level of enthusiasm. Odds were, she didn't want to be there any more than he did. He hated flying, always had. In the first place, he wasn't built for it; and in the second place, he knew way too much about airline security, an oxymoron if he ever heard one.

From his aisle seat, he twisted around and looked toward the rear of the cabin. Several seats back, a male passenger in a *Planet Hollywood* jacket made eye contact before looking away. Air Marshal. Poor bastard. One day he's doing his job, watching and observing, putting his life on the line to keep the friendly skies friendly. The next day he's filing a Surveillance Detection Report on a father of four from Dubuque who wants an aerial photo of the Golden Gate Bridge for his kids. Our guy has gotten the word, a memo outlining a new quota system. File one SDR a month and you get a raise, a bonus, and maybe a special assignment. But hey, what's the big deal? There's something in it for everyone. Washington, with its *seek and ye shall fabricate* system, gets its paperwork, our guy gets to hone his skills in creative writing, and Daddy from Dubuque gets his name on a terrorist watch list.

Meanwhile, the winners were the assholes who knew enough not to use their smartphones to snap photos out the window of an aircraft, the ones who got a pass because the system was clogged with crap. The losers were a few whistle-blowing sky guys who think the quota system stinks and the American people who couldn't care less. Since the story broke a few years back, it was business as usual: tuck the kids in, slug back the Kool-Aid and switch the channel to *Dancing with the Stars.*

Ryan checked his watch. They were still an hour out of Phoenix. Once he landed, he had a two-hour drive to Sedona. After that, it was anyone's guess when he would sleep again. He would have preferred driving the entire way, retracing the route taken by Susan Pierce and her companion, stopping along the way to see if anyone recognized them, but as of this morning a twelve hour drive was out of the question. Things were moving fast.

Rousing him from a sound sleep, the call came a little after 4 a.m. and he wasn't happy, even less so when he heard the information imparted. An hour earlier, an Ultralight pilot had called the Sedona police department to report an odd sighting. At dusk the previous evening, he was flying low a few miles east of the 17, somewhere between Sedona and Mormon Lake. He was chasing a pack of coyotes when they stopped abruptly, much more interested in what was on the ground than above them in the air. Curious, he maneuvered the craft around and did a fly-over. It looked like a pile of clothes and some hair, reddish or brown, he couldn't be sure. He thought it might be a mannequin. Damnedest thing, he'd never seen anything like it. His wife nagged him all night and insisted he report it. You never know.

Cody made the call, a courtesy from one cop to another. It was stretching the point but Ryan was grateful. The tip-off was the hair, sounded familiar, and then he remembered the call from San Francisco. Could be something, could be nothing but they had to start the search right away. There was a lot of land to cover and they'd be doing most of it on ATVs, maybe a chopper, depending on how many damn hikers were lost in the canyons. Fully awake, Ryan jotted down his cellphone number and thanked him. He'd be on the next flight out.

He'd been on the Pierce case only a few days, but he knew in his gut it was connected to his sister's death. Two financially-comfortable women, single and living alone, creative and reclusive, finally meet the man who will appreciate and nurture their talents, their soulmate. New Age bullshit.

The big break would come if he could connect Theresa's property to the storage facility but yesterday afternoon was a bust. The genius on the desk forgot to look through his files and whined for ten minutes about how busy he was. Ryan took the hint and waved a hundred dollar bill under his nose. Find out if someone rented a bay in late June, early July 2010, come up with a name and it's his. Call him day or night if anyone showed up to remove items from the Pierce bays and there would be five more bills just like it. Find a rental agreement, no matter how old, signed by someone with the first name Charles. If the lead panned out, he'd buy him a car. Spread the word.

What was this monster's game? He didn't get Theresa's money, at least none that he knew of. She never changed her will which meant she hadn't secretly married the sonofabitch. When her estate was settled, it all went to her only living relative, to him, everything but the insurance on the house. Since arson was suspected, the insurance company denied the claim. It took months to research the fact that no one had taken out a policy on her life. The house was stripped clean before the fire, but you don't murder someone over a couple of loveseats and a dining room set. Artwork? Her taste ran to black and white photography, not fine art. Jewelry? None that he knew of. The only thing she owned of any value was a pair of diamond stud earrings, his gift to her on her thirtieth birthday. She never took them off, not even in death.

His attempt at finding the moving company that picked up the contents of the Pierce house was also a colossal waste of time. He'd put calls into all of them, even the small independent ones that boasted a labor force of starving students and meatheads. The same with Theresa's stuff. Ten years ago, he'd been all over them, likewise rental car companies offering oversized paneled vans. Hell, he'd even searched the want ads for guys with pick-up trucks, the ones who would haul away your grandmother for a six-pack. Nothing.

He was getting ahead of the facts. For all he knew, Susan Pierce and her soulmate were sipping margaritas at a pricey resort. The pilot said he was flying at dusk, more than likely a trick of the light.

The plane banked. Ryan felt it start to descend and closed his eyes. Within seconds, he was asleep.

CHAPTER 14

ANNIE

Surveying the damage, Annie made a mental note to call her realtor and advise her against recommending Stevie Wonder as a home inspector. Even she could see the driveway was pitched in the wrong direction, that whenever there was a storm like yesterday's the rain would take the path of least resistance directly into the garage.

It could have been worse. Instead of slogging through packing paper and empty boxes, she might have been trying to salvage their contents. Only a few days before, she unpacked the last of them, putting them in place around the house or storing them in the attic.

She glanced at the pile behind her, a growing mountain of soggy cardboard and debris. No way was she going to get it all in the back of her truck, not tonight anyway. She was chilled to the bone and exhausted. She thought about calling it a day, taking a nice hot shower and crawling into bed with a good book. It must be late, at least five o'clock, but she was too close to being done to quit. Another hour and she could work her way to the back wall. The garage would be empty, even the junk left by the former tenants. It didn't look too bad, a few pieces of avocado laminate, a pile of old floor tiles and some large black garbage bags, probably leaves from a fall clean-up. She leaned the broom against the grill of the truck and rubbed her lower back. At least tonight she'd sleep.

It took less time than she thought. She was right about the bags. Surprisingly light, they were filled with leaves, mostly compost. The musty sweet smell reminded her of home and her father's garden. He'd throw a fit if he saw her property in its current condition. Come spring, the first thing on her agenda was tackling the landscaping.

She threw the last of the tile on top of the mound and rubbed her gloved hands together. Almost there. The laminate pieces, backed by three-quarter inch plywood, were heavier than she anticipated and she had to drag the first one to the pile. She had the second one halfway there when she stopped and turned around. Something behind it caught her eye, something white. It would have been easy to miss, buried as it was beneath a layer of leaves against the rear wall. Dropping the piece of laminate, she looked around for a light switch. It was getting dark and, gloves or no gloves, she wasn't reaching into a pile of dead stuff without some light.

Careful to make sure she wasn't standing in water, she flipped the switch. The light bulb crackled and went dark. In less than a minute, she was back with a flashlight.

It was a plastic bag, not thin like the ones from a supermarket, a heavier gauge and larger. Finding a dry spot on the floor, she knelt down, removed the gloves and started working on the knot. Freed at last, she upended the bag and spilled the contents on the floor but there was nothing there but some used paper towels, wadded into balls and dumped in a bag for discard, something she'd done a thousand times. She laid the bag beside them and smoothed it out, the words **Panda Palace** printed in green.

He's bringing home Chinese food.

"We gotta problem."

Annie yelped and fell back on her butt, the flashlight flying from her hand. When she could catch her breath, she scrambled to her feet.

"Damn, Cyn, you scared the living crap out of me!"

"You about done here? We need to talk."

"Why is it so dark and why didn't I hear you drive in? What's wrong with your headlights?"

Cynthia picked up the flashlight and directed the beam into Annie's face. "It's after seven o'clock and I had to park down the road, almost killed myself walkin' in here. There's a limb the size of a Buick blocking your driveway."

Annie took the flashlight from her and aimed it in that direction. "It must have come down in the storm last night. I haven't been out today so I didn't see it. I know, I know, I should have called you but time got away from me. How'd everything go? Wait, what's wrong? I know something's wrong. You're always home at this time making dinner. What happened? Please tell me you didn't have an accident."

"You finished?"

"Sorry, must be the adrenaline."

"Uh-huh."

Inside the house, with the lights turned on and Einstein sated by Cynthia's cooing, Annie set a pot of decaf tea between them. She didn't know whether to start asking questions again or wait for her friend to open up. Cynthia hated driving after dark so whatever was up was probably bad. Or she was pissed. It was that damned email. She knew she shouldn't have sent it. The least she could have done was follow it up with the phone call.

Annie reached across the table and patted her hand. "What's up? Whatever it is, we'll handle it together like we always do."

"You ever wonder why I went into nursing?"

It was bad, maybe not *Game of Thrones Red Wedding* bad but bad. "I've never met anyone more loving or compassionate than you, so I guess I assumed it was a calling."

"My mama was a nurse."

This was uncharted territory and Annie held her breath. In the eleven years they'd known one another, Cynthia never discussed her childhood or any details of her life before Arthur and the boys. Whenever she reminisced about her own family, Cynthia would nod and smile in the right places but she never offered anything about her own.

"She worked at Norwalk Hospital, Intensive Care. We were living in Stamford then too, a little house, just me and mama and my grandmother. She had me when she was seventeen, even married the man but he left after I was born. I was so proud of her. She'd put on that uniform and she looked like some African princess, tall and thin.

"One night around dinnertime, she gets a call. One of the ICU nurses is having car trouble and she has to cover for her on the nightshift. I was only eight and didn't understand. I start crying, saying it wasn't fair and it was our time together. She was runnin' late but she sat me down and told me what a privilege and blessing it was to look after the sick. She told me before I go to sleep I should pray for all those in her care. She said she was lucky to have such a wonderful daughter and she hoped one day I'd be a nurse so I could carry on that blessing."

She stopped speaking and took a sip of tea. Annie had no idea where the story was going or what precipitated it, but she knew grief when she saw it. She'd been there with her and helped her bury two sons.

"She sounds like an amazing woman. Why haven't you ever told me about her or your childhood?"

"I didn't have a childhood, Annie, not after that night. She never came home, never even made it to the hospital. My grandma was sick with worry and knew something wasn't right when the hospital called. She called the police that very night. They came the next afternoon, stayed maybe half an hour, looked around and saw a woman of color, single with a child. Probably just took off was what they said. It was the staff at the hospital that raised a fuss. They put up posters, offered a reward for information, even organized searches. One of the doctors had a brother who was a reporter. He did a story about her, about how the police didn't seem to care much. That got everyone's attention but by then it was too late. They found her car a month later in upstate New York, abandoned in some woods. Took me years to get my hands on the police report. There was blood all over the backseat. They never found her."

"How could you keep something like this from me?"

"Because it hurts my heart. Someone took that precious woman and murdered her. Because when I think about it or talk about it I have to remember what it must have been like for her, how frightened and alone she was."

"Then how…"

"How do I keep my faith? I knew you'd ask me that. Truth is, I didn't. I was mad at God for a long time until I met Arthur. He reintroduced us you might say, God and me. When I held our first child, I knew I'd never question him again."

Mad at God. The words sounded familiar. Helen. Was this about Debra?

"Cynthia, sweetheart, listen to me. I never should have asked you to look into the Debra thing. I had no idea about your mother. I was tired when I sent you the email. Besides, it's not the same thing. Debra wasn't murdered."

Cynthia pulled a sheaf of papers from her handbag. "She never showed up at Norwalk Hospital, Bridgeport neither, nor Greenwich. The county medical examiner never performed an autopsy on her. She wasn't buried or cremated in the state of Connecticut or New York and there's no record of her body being flown to Canada for interment. No death certificate, no obituary, no nothing."

Stunned, Annie stared at the papers littering the table. "When did you do all this? I sent you that email just this morning. How… why…okay, let's take a breath. I gave it some thought while I was cleaning the garage. Maybe Helen confused the whole incident with an episode of CSI or a movie. Maybe it never happened. Maybe Charles and Debra had a fight and he took her to the airport and sent her home. He's upset, he comes back to get his stuff and he's embarrassed to tell Helen the truth, that she's left him. When she described his mood, it sounded more like anger than grief to me. He'll never see this woman again, so he concocts a story. Maybe in his mind she is dead."

"You've spent some time with this woman. You think she's confusing reality with some TV show?"

"No, she's pretty with it. She also remembered a lot of details, but I still think the second scenario is possible. For all I know, Larry's telling everyone I'm dead. Wait, what about San Francisco? Helen thinks Charles was from there. Maybe he had her flown back to his home town and she's buried in a family plot or…"

"No one gets flown anywhere without a death certificate. You should know that."

She did know that but clutching at straws seemed the lesser of two evils. A death involved a mountain of paperwork and sometimes shit happened, computers crashed, files disappeared and human mistakes were made. "Then that leaves us with the second theory. He takes her to the airport and she goes back to Canada where she's been living a wonderful life for the last twenty years. She came from a wealthy family, which means she didn't spend the day cleaning out her garage."

"This is serious, Annie. You have any idea how many women in this country are killed each year by their partners? I looked it up. About fifteen hundred, a little over four a day, and that's not counting the ones that go missing, their bodies never found like my mama."

"Sorry, that was pretty callous. You dropped a couple of bombshells on me and I'm trying to process them. I don't know where to go from here."

"You go to the police is what you do, get them involved."

"You're joking. It's been twenty years. This isn't a cold case, it's a non-case."

"Do I look like I'm joking? It took them longer than that to prosecute the boy who killed that pretty little girl in Greenwich. Moxley, Martha Moxley.

"There was a body." The moment she said it, Annie wished she could pluck it from the air before it reached her friend's ears. "I didn't mean that the way it sounded, you know that."

"I know this. I know there's not a day goes by when I don't pray they'll find my mama's remains. I know she deserved better than being dumped somewhere, cold and alone, or thrown into some icy water for eternity. I know if someone had seen her as a human being, something more than a profile or a statistic, they might have found her alive."

"God, Cynthia, I don't know what to say to you or how you've managed to keep it together. Let's wait a few days before we get the police involved. I don't want them frightening Helen or making her feel any guiltier than she already does. As it is, she thinks Debra is visiting her in her dreams because she's angry at her for not following up on her disappearance."

Annie searched for an excuse, something, anything to steer Cynthia away from steamrolling her on this. If she was going to the police, she was taking more than harebrained theories. "There was an incident not long after Debra and Charles left. Some guy went to Helen's house and implied they had broken in and were living here illegally. He asked a lot of questions. I didn't think too much of it at the time. I had him pegged for some over-zealous property manager trying to cover his ass for a broken window or something. She said she might still have his card. Maybe he can shine some light on all of this. If that doesn't work, I'll contact the family that owned this place, the Stanleys."

Cynthia reached across the table and squeezed her hand. "You're a good friend, Annie, and I love you. I laid a lot on you tonight, wish I'd done it a long time ago. We'll do it your way, but you have to promise me something. Tonight, before you go to sleep, you pray that man isn't out there hurting other women."

CHAPTER 15

RYAN

It was either a good day or a bad day for hikers. Three choppers were circling in the distance. No sooner had he pulled the car to the side of the road than two white police cruisers crested a hill behind him and sped past, sirens shrieking.

Before alighting from the car, he reached inside his duffel bag. The binoculars were a last-minute addition and he was glad he remembered to pack them. He panned the area to the east and grabbed the map. He was at the junction of I-17 and Hwy. 179, the road into Sedona. The cruisers continued north on the 17 and he was tempted to follow them and blow off his meeting with Cody. All the activity was in the general direction of the sighting reported by the pilot.

Changing the game plan was a bad idea and Ryan nixed it. Even if whatever was out there turned out to be a false alarm, he needed Cody. The town of Sedona was his territory and that's where Ryan wanted to be. Cody had been more than cooperative, staying in touch by cellphone, keeping him in the loop with the progress of the search, even filling him in on the jurisdictional issues.

He turned his attention to the map. He was still in Yavapai County and would be for another ten miles. Four to five miles south of Sedona, he'd cross the county line into Coconino. At that point, the line made a ninety-degree angle north for another ten miles or so and then veered left, toward the west. He could see why there might be problems with jurisdiction. Even though Sedona was technically in Coconino County, it was practically sitting on the line that divided the two counties east and west. Theoretically, it was possible for a Sedona landowner with enough property to be a resident of both counties. His investigation could easily turn into a territorial tug-of-war. As much as he liked operating alone, he needed an ally, someone to help him circumvent the proprietary morass.

As he put the binoculars to his eyes for a final look, two of the choppers split off, one heading north, the other heading southwest while the third was hovering. Reluctantly, he pulled back on the road and floored the accelerator.

Roland Cody. It sounded like a name manufactured by old Hollywood, the kind used in B westerns. He sounded okay, efficient but not overly officious. His voice was low with an accent Ryan couldn't place. He pictured him somewhere between fifty and sixty, white hair, like that lawyer who was all over the television a few years ago, the big guy who wore the fringed buckskin jackets. Jerry Spence.

Maybe Cody was a little too efficient, a little too eager to be in on the action. Maybe he was angling for a better job in a bigger city or he liked seeing his name in the papers. At some point, he'd have to remind him he was no longer on the force and had no influence over SFPD hiring practices. The other possibility was the Chief had played Cody to ensure his cooperation and confided in him about his sister's murder, how poor old Ryan was wasting his life chasing ghosts. He hoped not. Theresa's story was off-limits. The last thing he wanted was someone looking over his shoulder, watching him, waiting for a sign that revenge was clouding his judgment.

Then again, who could blame the guy for wanting out of this Godforsaken place? He never understood why people flocked to the desert. For most of the two hour drive, he'd seen nothing but bare hills and brown earth dotted with patches of scrub.

The last few miles were a little more interesting and the road was no longer straight and flat. He lowered his speed, not sure how the rental car would take the curves. The scenery was changing, closing in on him. There was now less brown and more green, every conceivable shade of it, from the tight low shrubs that crept along the desert floor to the spiky bushes and trees with leaves that looked like feathers. In contrast were the rock formations, rugged jutting masses the color of sunburned flesh. Beautiful was the way everyone described the Red Rocks, even Jimmy, who mentioned that some of them had names like Cathedral Rock or Coffee Pot Rock. Ryan didn't care. It wasn't their names that interested him, it was their secrets.

He found the motel with minutes to spare. It was low-slung in the typical territorial style, adobe colored with vigas poking through a foot or so below the flat roof. Cody suggested this place because it was clean, close to his office and shared a parking lot with a decent diner.

Ryan parked the car in front of the motel, got out and stretched. There were only two cars in front of the diner and one was a black and white at the far end. A tall woman wearing a dark blue uniform had her back to him, her elbows resting atop the cruiser. She was on her cellphone, obviously a heated discussion judging by the way her long black ponytail danced with the movement of her head. Either he was early or Cody was waiting for him inside the diner. Maybe the woman was his partner. She looked muscular, like she could take care of herself. No backup needed there.

The diner was empty except for a man and woman seated at the counter. The attending waitress smiled and made a sweeping gesture with her arm. Ryan took a seat in the booth farthest from the couple and reached for a menu. When he heard the door open, he looked up and glanced back outside at the patrol car, his faith in his powers of observation dwindling by the second.

Cody grinned and accepted a hug from the waitress before approaching the booth and extending his hand. "You must be Ryan. Roland Cody. Welcome to Sedona."

"You're Navajo."

"You're Irish. Let's order, I'm starved."

The waitress took their orders and Cody leaned back. "They still haven't found anything. I'm beginning to think that pilot was inhaling more than engine fumes."

"You know the guy?"

"Nah, he's from Cottonwood, south of here. He's a wreck, by the way. Now he's convinced it was a woman lying out there."

"I saw a lot of activity driving in, three choppers and two cruisers that almost ran me off the road."

"That's nothing. Last count, there were fifty uniforms on the ground from both counties. There's a lot of territory to cover. The choppers go in first and sweep the area for anything that looks suspicious. If they find something, they radio it in. Depending on where it is, the county boys go in on foot to preserve any evidence."

"Does it happen often, bodies dumped in the desert?"

"It's happened a time or two but mostly we deal with idiots. Once or twice a month some damn fool mistakes his Range Rover for a dune buggy and then we get a call or, like I told you, hikers go up in the canyons and can't find their way out."

The diner was filling up and Ryan noticed that every person made their way to the booth to chat with Cody. Equally impressive, Cody knew them all by name. "You're a popular guy."

"Goes with the job. You bring that photograph of Susan Pierce? I've got a deputy stopping by in a few minutes to pick it up."

Ryan pulled a photograph from his shirt pocket and handed it off across the table. "This was taken last January at the Blue Pearl in Sausalito. Susan Pierce is on the left. The devil on the right is my client, Marcia Banning, her sister."

Cody chuckled. "I take it this isn't your handiwork."

Carefully omitting any reference to Theresa or how Marcia Banning had come to hire him, Ryan took him through a more detailed account of Susan Pierce's life, filling in the bits and pieces absent from their brief telephone exchanges. His narration ended with the phone call from Sedona two weeks earlier, the one claiming her life was in danger. A lot of it Cody already knew so he mostly listened. The few questions he asked were solid, and Ryan was beginning to think he'd misjudged him. There was more to Roland Cody than window dressing with his central casting good looks and the hair thing.

The deputy came and Cody introduced them. He gave instructions that the photograph be cropped, enlarged and circulated to everyone on the force. If the woman was spotted, she was not to be approached and he was to be contacted immediately. Furthermore, whoever called it in better keep her in sight, like a Jumping Cholla on a coyote's ass.

The waitress brought their food and they dug in. Ryan relaxed for the first time since the early-morning phone call. He was always keyed up after a plane trip and the drive hadn't helped. The fact that Cody appeared to know nothing of Theresa eased his mind even further.

A few more people drifted into the diner and Ryan searched their faces. He was deep in his own thoughts when Cody threw another question at him.

"Sorry, I missed that."

"The woman who called your client from the gas station, did she have an accent?"

"She didn't mention an accent, but I should have asked. I'll give her a call."

"Might be a good idea. We have a lot of undocumented immigrants working here as cooks, housekeepers, nannies. The hotels are pretty good about checking their paperwork, but we have a population of over twenty-one thousand which adds up to a lot of private homes and a relatively small labor force. If she was undocumented and working for the Pierce woman, that would explain why she wouldn't leave her name or contact us directly."

"I don't suppose Susan Pierce made it easy for us and purchased a home here in the last year?"

"Not under her real name. We've checked the escrow closings going back three years. I'll have them go through the records again. Maybe we'll get lucky with the name Charles."

"You won't. He doesn't leave a paper trail. What about rentals?"

Cody waited for the waitress to take their plates and move beyond earshot. "That makes more sense. We have a lot of them here, second homes. The owner takes some flattering photos and puts them on the internet. In season, he can make a bundle. Even off-season they do well, enough to pay the mortgage, taxes, and still come out ahead. We have a few agents who specialize in short and long term rentals. We'll check them out tomorrow, but my guess is it was a private deal to save the commission, also no way to track it."

Excusing himself, Ryan headed for the men's room. That he hadn't asked about the woman's accent rankled him. He tried calling Marcia Banning, and when she didn't answer, he left a message on her home phone.

Cody was back outside on his cell when Ryan returned to his seat. Before he could signal for the check, the waitress approached and placed two plates of apple pie on the table. "It's on the house. I'll get you more coffee."

"I appreciate that. It's Laurie, right? I'm new around here. Chief Cody a good guy?"

"He's not just good, he's awesome. I think it's the first time everyone in this town has agreed on something since I've lived here. My mom needed by-pass surgery a few months ago and the bills were over the moon. Chief Cody and his wife found out about it and held a big barbeque, a fund-raiser I guess you'd call it. They raised almost twenty thousand dollars. Yeah, he's a good guy, smart, kind of a hunk too, don't you think? Gosh, don't tell him I said that."

"Count on it."

She was still blushing when she fled from the table as Cody approached, his expression grim. "They found something, a woman's skirt and a lot of blood. They don't have much more daylight so they're taping off the area and heading in. They'll be out again at first light. Nothing much we can do until tomorrow morning."

"I take it we're not invited."

"Trust me, that's the last place you want to be. The piece of clothing was found less than a half mile from the county line. There's an expression your people use when there are too many chiefs and everyone's running around trying to cover their asses and no one knows what the other one's doing."

"A clusterfuck."

"That's it. I'll have to tell my wife that."

"It's also called a circle jerk. Sounds better."

Cody smiled but it never touched his eyes. Ryan knew the look. At one time or another, he'd seen it on the face of every cop he ever worked with. It was the shock of realizing the horror one human being was capable of inflicting on another. As the silence dragged on, Ryan watched him rubbing his thumb against a large turquoise cross suspended around his neck by a thick silver chain.

"What kind of a name is Cody?"

"Old Indian tradition. When we killed a white man, we would eat his heart and take his name. My grandfather liked the name Cody better than William."

Ryan raised an eyebrow.

"Old Indian joke. Buffalo Bill died at 71 of kidney failure. Far as I know, he still had his heart. It's just a name."

"How'd you end up here?"

"I was a cop north of here near Monument Valley. Kayenta. I wanted out."

"Kayenta. Why does that sound familiar?" Recognition dawned and with it Ryan's respect and embarrassment for not doing his homework. "You're that Cody, the cop who broke that case a couple of years ago, the wealthy couple who were murdered."

"I got lucky."

Ryan remembered the case and luck had nothing to do with it. A middle-aged couple from Phoenix won some money playing the lottery, a lot of money as he recalled, enough to get them out of their mobile home and into a custom-built dream home in a better neighborhood. They also purchased a luxury RV and were going to spend a few months traveling around the country. After a couple of days and they hadn't checked in with their daughter, she called the police. Within hours, every cop in the state was mobilized. The next day their RV was found abandoned, stripped clean. Their bodies were discovered a few days later on Navajo land near the Four Corners. Kayenta. Their throats were slit and they were buried Navajo-style. It was the lead story on every major news outlet for weeks.

"I remember the case. You were on the FBI's shit list as I recall."

"Probably still am."

"They thought they had it all tied up with a couple of your local boys."

"The feds were all over us. My people were scared to death. Truth is, I was scared too.   You remember the Leonard Peltier case?"

Everyone in law enforcement knew the case and everyone had a different opinion on Peltier's guilt or innocence. It was viewed as a cautionary tale when dealing with the Feds. "Back in the seventies, somewhere in the Dakotas."

"1975, the Pine Ridge Indian Reservation in South Dakota. A lot of people remember the outcome and the trial. Two federal agents are gunned down and Leonard Peltier gets two consecutive life sentences in a trial so full of holes you could drive a fleet of trucks through it. You happen to remember why the Feds were there in the first place? A couple of local ranch hands reported that a Pine Ridge man, Jimmy Eagle, beat them up and stole a pair of cowboy boots. Cowboy boots, for God's sake, and we've got two dead white people on our land, rich white people."

"What led them to your boys?"

"Stupidity mostly. Don't get me wrong, those guys were bad news. I was always busting them for something. They drank too much and pissed off way too many people for their own good. I never did find out who talked to the Feds, but the next thing I knew, they're being hauled away. Someone said they saw them drag racing out near where the bodies were discovered, drunk out of their minds, crashing into each other, raising holy hell."

"But you had another theory."

"Not right away. I'm not proud of it but all I felt at the time was relief. The FBI had their suspects which meant they'd be gone soon. My people could breathe again. I slept that night for the first time in a week."

"What turned it around?"

Cody added cream to his coffee. "You married?"

"I'm waiting for hell to freeze over."

"Then you don't know how damn irritating it is to live with someone who knows you better than you know yourself. My wife Lita, that woman knew, and what's worse, she knew I knew those boys didn't kill those people. She never said a word but I'd catch her looking at me, waiting for me to do something. You sure you want to hear all this?"

"I enjoy any story where the Feds get pissed off."

"First off, it was the burial. There were no footprints leading to the graves or away from them. Before the dirt was thrown on, the bodies were covered in blankets, a Navajo design. I asked my eight-year-old to go on the computer and see if she could find anything about Navajo burial customs. I wanted to know what was out there. Took her less than two minutes. It was all there, no footprints left behind for the dead to follow, the absence of tools, the blankets, everything. So we're supposed to believe these two drunken lowlifes sobered up enough to pull off a ritual and then celebrated by whooping and hollering around the grave."

"What about the blankets? They're expensive, couldn't they trace them?"

"Not these, they were made in China. I found a stack of them in a shop in Wickenburg. Truth is, something bothered me about the son-in-law from the beginning. The day after the bodies were found, he showed up wailing with grief, demanding justice for quote the kindest people I've ever known unquote. Seemed a little excessive for one whose wife was inheriting over a hundred million dollars, but the Feds bought it and I kept my trap shut. I had some vacation time coming so I decided to take a few days and nose around. I drove down to Phoenix and went by the decedents' home. Never seen anything like it. They must have had a hundred thousand dollars in electronic surveillance equipment around that place, cameras, infrared devices, you name it. These were not trusting people and I had a hunch they didn't leave their paranoia behind.

"Then there were the neighbors. A couple of them were out in their yards or walking their dogs. They had no obligation to talk to me but as it turned out they were more than happy to share their thoughts about the Flemings. Whoever said you shouldn't speak evil of the dead didn't live on that street. I don't know if they threw a party when the news hit about the murders, but I guarantee they thought about it. The husband would start drinking around noon everyday and by nightfall he was out threatening the dog walkers with a gun. One of the neighbors finally called the cops on him. They show up and he's stumbling drunk, screaming in the middle of the street, repeating over and over, 'You know who I am?' at the top of his lungs. By this time, the whole neighborhood is standing out in the street begging the cops to take him."

"Let me guess."

"You're in Arizona, my friend. Everyone carries a gun, no law against it. No law against being a loud-mouth drunk either, especially if you're rich."

"The son-in-law had a decent alibi, if I remember."

"Not that decent. He was dabbling in real estate and claimed he was with out of town clients the entire weekend. The guy and his wife, a couple from Minnesota, vouched for him. That was good enough for the Feds. It took me two days to find an old yearbook from ASU with a photo of Minnesota dude and the son-in-law mugging for the camera in their tennis whites. Things fell apart after that. The trial's set for next month. The daughter's already divorced him and won't give him a nickel for his defense. Last I heard, he's using a public defender."

"That was good police work."

"Come on, Ryan, my twelve-year-old could have solved that case."

"So what happened? You think the FBI was looking for payback for Pine Ridge?"

"Nah, if I believed that, I'd call it quits. Most of those boys who showed up in their dark suits and wraparound sunglasses weren't even born when Pine Ridge went down. You were a cop, a good one I hear, so you know how it is. You get focused on a suspect and you stay there. Those young bucks made it easy for them. They were surly and uncooperative. Three months later, I got a call about this job and I grabbed it."

Along with his powers of observation, Ryan concluded he needed to work on his assumptions too. He was dead wrong to think Cody might want the spotlight. It was the FBI that held the news conference and took credit for the arrests. Cody's name was a footnote in an article that came later and he subsequently refused all requests for media interviews. It was only due to an intrepid journalist that the truth finally came out that it was Cody and not the Feds who broke the case. So what made this guy tick?

"I know why I'm here, Roland, but you've got a town to run. You've gone above and beyond the call and I'm grateful, but I'd like to know why."

Cody reached into his hip pocked and pulled out his wallet. Tucked inside was a plastic accordion photo holder that he spread out in front of Ryan. Eight faces smiled up at him, all female. The youngest looked to be about five, the oldest somewhere in her early twenties. They all bore a resemblance to one another. With long black hair, some braided, some straight and parted in the middle, they had the same dark eyes and were strikingly beautiful.

"I've got eight good reasons. Men who prey on women deserve their own special place in hell."

"Amen to that. You're a lucky man, Roland."

Cody scooped up the photos and put them back in his wallet. "And you, Ryan, I sense a deep sadness here." He made a fist and brought it to the front of his shirt, just below his breastbone. "The problem with locking people out is that our spirit gets locked in. In time, it withers and dies."

"Old Indian saying?"

"Old Indian wife, but don't tell her I said that."

Ryan reached into his other shirt pocket and withdrew another photo, placing it in front of Cody.

Cody picked it up. "This isn't Susan Pierce. This woman looks like an angel."

"She is. Her name's Theresa. She was my sister."

CHAPTER 16

ANNIE

Opening the driver's side door, Annie looked over her shoulder, hiked her skirt up around her waist and felt around for the ground with her left foot. If someone knew a ladylike way to enter and exit a truck with a skirt and heels, she'd like to hear it.

The men were still working to clear the limb from the road, moving it enough to get through the lane. She had a couple of hours before the funeral, sufficient time to stop at Helen's and remind her to look for the property manager's card, then it was off to **Life House**. If she could stay on-point and keep Helen's chatter to a minimum, she'd have an hour or so to get acquainted with their new guest and make the rounds. After the funeral, if she were still on her feet, she'd spend a few more hours getting things together for her meeting with the accountant. It was still a week away but she liked to be prepared.

The one thing she would not do is dwell on the fact that she wasn't sleeping. A couple of hours last night, three or four the night before were now the norm. Who wanted to waste their life sleeping anyway? How many people could boast they'd seen every infomercial ever made and knew the dialogue from nine seasons of *Seinfeld*?

She rang the bell, then knocked and called out Helen's name. This was odd. Helen was an early riser. Annie cupped her hands around her face and put her nose to the glass. She could see just enough through the curtains on the other side of the door to determine the house was dark. Her breath was fogging up the glass and she wiped it with her sleeve.

Stepping off the porch, she turned and faced the front of the house. The garage was attached on the left so there were no windows into the main part of the structure. On the right side of the house, two windows were positioned approximately four feet off the ground, her best hope of sneaking a peek inside the living room through to the kitchen. With the grass still soggy from the recent rain, she took off her heels. By the time she reached the windows, her stockings were soaked and she realized she'd misjudged the height. Right beneath the windows, the ground sloped about a foot, the bottom of the frames touching the center of her forehead. No way was she going to jump up and down in her stockings, even if she had the energy, which she didn't.

Treading as lightly as she could, she made her way back to the front porch and pounded on the door. One of the men started up a chainsaw and now she had that irritating noise to contend with. Annie yelled out her name again but it was lost beneath the din behind her. Ready to give up, go back to her truck and use her cell to call Helen's phone, one of her feet slipped off the edge of the step and she landed ass-first on the graveled path.

The chainsaws stopped and she turned to see the men gawking at her, their expressions a predictable mix of humor and concern. Attempting to be as modest as the situation would allow in a tight, knee-length skirt, she got to her feet and waved.

"Good morning, dear. Are you here to see me?"

For the second time in twenty-four hours, she'd fallen on her backside and come close to a heart attack. "Helen, there you are. What are you wearing?"

The older woman smiled, put her arms straight out from her sides and turned in place, showing off a pair of loose-fitting pants rolled at the ankle and an oversized blouse, all in white.

Annie took a closer look. The buttons on the blouse were the symbols for Yin and Yang. "I give up."

"It's my Tai Chi outfit. I ordered it from a catalog."

"You do Tai Chi?"

"I certainly do. I took a class at the Y last year. I can't do all the positions, Kick Tiger with Right Foot for example, but I can do most of the other ones. I usually do them inside but the weather is lovely today and the air smells so fresh after the rain, I thought I'd do them on the back patio."

"You do Tai Chi?"

"You look lovely today, dear. I don't think I've ever seen you all dressed up. I'll bet you have a luncheon with your girlfriends."

"I wish. Unfortunately, I'm going to a funeral."

"Oh, I'm sorry. Is it someone you know?"

Annie took a breath. "Yes, it's someone I knew very well, one of our friends at **Life House**. Oh gosh, look at the time. Helen, remember the other night you mentioned a man who came by shortly after Debra passed away? You know, the man who made the fuss and accused them of breaking in? Remember? Helen?"

"I do remember and I found his card just yesterday."

"That's great."

"Well, good-bye, dear. It's always nice to see you."

"Wait. Do you suppose I could borrow the card? I'd like to follow up with him on something to do with the house."

"I'll get it and I'll bring a towel for your feet. They look wet."

In the cab of her truck, Annie cranked up the heat and put the envelope on the seat beside her. She was pulling into the driveway at **Life House** when it occurred to her the envelope was large for just a business card. If Helen grabbed the wrong thing and she had to go through the whole rigmarole again, she'd shoot herself.

The card was clipped to the front of another envelope. It was addressed to Mrs. Charles Hastings, 7 Spinnaker Lane, Westport, CT 06830, the letters USA written in red ink across the bottom and postmarked July 7, 2000. The return address was smudged but she could just make it out, everything but the six-digit postal code: Jacqueline Gauthier, Box 760, Shawnigan Lake, B.C. The letter was unopened.

After giving Cynthia a quick peck on the cheek, Annie pulled back. "Why aren't you dressed? We have to leave in twenty-five minutes."

"I don't know where you're going, but I'm staying right here. I got work to do."

"The funeral, remember?"

"You might consider turning on that expensive cell phone of yours. I left you two messages this morning, one an hour ago and another thirty minutes after that."

Annie dropped in a chair beside her desk. "What's going on?"

"His family called me first thing this morning. Said they'd reconsidered and wanted his body flown back to Wyoming for burial. I already notified the mortuary. By tomorrow afternoon, that poor baby will be back with his family."

Normally, upon their death, the procedure for disposition of a guest was straightforward and devoid of the storm and fury raging around the life of their most recent loss. In almost all instances, the family of the deceased was notified immediately and arrangements were made to return the loved one to his family for the final interment or cremation. It was rare that a family refused receipt of the body since **Life House** assumed all costs, even rarer that time, distance and compassion had not tempered their discomfort or denial with the cause of death. In this case, however, their three attempts to notify the parents of their son's passing were met with stony silence followed by a string of Biblical quotations that lasted until one of the parties finally broke the connection.

"You called them again, didn't you? I thought we agreed we weren't going to guilt them into anything. What did you say to them?"

Uh oh, not only was she getting *the look* but this time it would be accompanied by *the voice*, the one that dropped an octave and was perfectly-modulated, each syllable enunciated with razor-sharp precision.

"Firstly, I didn't agree to anything. Secondly, I used several Biblical quotations of my own which I have no intention of sharing. Thirdly, guilt is a noun, not a verb. And as a postscript, they're paying to have the body flown back."

"You used *the voice* on them, didn't you?"

"I did."

"Well, knock it off, it scares me."

"Precisely."

Annie couldn't help but smile. The voice was Cynthia's secret weapon, the one known only to family, a close circle of friends and those unlucky enough to get on her bad side. Larry hated *the voice*, insisting it made her sound pretentious. Her mother, on the other hand, couldn't understand why she'd ever use the other one, 'the one that sounded so Black'. The irony of *the voice* was that it was as much a part of Cynthia as her DNA. It was who she was, well-educated with an I.Q. in the 140s and an innate sense of purpose. Using the African American dialect was how she chose to facilitate that purpose and live her everyday life. It was, for lack of a better explanation, the other side of her unique personality, the woman who could soothe a fevered brow and render hope with just a few whispered words. She was also acutely aware that the outside world's perception of her was based on what came from her lips, not from her heart. She simply didn't care. Prejudice was their cross to bear. She had more important things to do.

"You're good, I'll give you that."

Cynthia returned her smile and winked. "Good's got nothin' to do with it. Sometimes you have to fight fire and brimstone with more fire and brimstone."

"Where is everyone?"

"Doctor Roberts just left, said to tell you hello, Tracy and Paige are upstairs changing the bed linens and…"

Annie jumped to her feet. "Is that a piano? We don't have a piano."

Putting her finger to her lips, Cynthia guided her from her office across the foyer through the arched entrance to the living room. At the far end, a man in a flannel shirt and faded jeans was seated at a baby grand. The frailty of his frame belied the power and passion with which he embraced the music of Rachmaninoff, *Rhapsody on a Theme by Paganini*, one of Annie's favorites. Even on a good day, it could reduce her to tears.

Every chair was filled, every empty space occupied by a wheelchair. Even the housekeeping staff had abandoned their chores and were watching from the back stairwell.

At the end of the piece, his body language changed and he sat up straighter, moving his head in quick rhythmic jerks to the tune of *Linus & Lucy*.

Annie joined the girls on the steps and listened for another fifteen minutes until fatigue got the better of him. As he rose from the bench, she went over to him, introduced herself and kissed him on the cheek. On her way out of the room, she took a long moment with each man there, catching up, letting the warmth of their smiles breathe life into her tired body.

Cynthia was hanging up the phone when Annie rounded the corner to her office. "The piano stays. I don't care how much you paid for it. If I have to, I'll sell one of my kidneys. He's amazing. Nice touch, by the way, having him play the Rachmaninoff."

"You think I don't have anything better to do than keep track of your musical tastes? Besides, they want healthy kidneys. If your insides don't look any better than your outside, you got nothin' to worry about."

"What's wrong with my outside?"

"Nothin' a good night's sleep won't fix. Here, I got you a few pills from Doc Roberts. He thinks you need to get your sleep cycle adjusted."

Annie took the plastic vial and dropped it into her bag. "I hate taking pills. Out of curiosity, where did you get the piano and how much did it cost? I have to put it on the books for the accountant."

"You ain't gonna like it."

"Try me."

Cynthia held up an envelope and Annie grabbed it. When she was finished reading the card inside, she put it back in the envelope and ripped it up.

"What'd it say?"

"It said here's this year's baby grand gesture. Happy Birthday, Love Larry. Oh, and as a postscript, he suggested we have dinner one night."

"Bein' away from you must have improved his sense of humor. What'd he mean about a grand gesture?"

"We weren't speaking last year on my birthday. He showed up that night with a diamond Rolex. I wasn't very gracious and accused him of doing what he does best, making grand gestures."

"What happened to the watch?"

"I'm driving it. Wait a minute, we get a new guest who happens to be a world-class pianist and a piano is delivered as a birthday gift, a week early I might add, from my ex-husband. Tell me you didn't have something to do with this."

"You want another watch? Here, you can have mine."

"Cynthia?"

"He called me over the weekend. He said he wanted to get you something for your birthday and asked if I had any ideas, something you might have mentioned. You've been talkin' about getting' a piano in here for years so I suggested it. He wasn't jumpin' up and down at first until I reminded him he could claim it as a donation. You sure know how to pick 'em."

"Don't I just. Thanks, sweetie, I love the piano."

"I hate to bring this up, Annie, but I heard back from the M.E.'s office in Westchester County. They never performed an autopsy on a Debra Hastings nor anyone matching her age and description around that date. You give any more thought to what we talked about last night, about calling the police?"

"We may not have to. I stopped by Helen's this morning to remind her to look for that card, you know, the man I assumed was the Property Manager. She found it yesterday. It was clipped to this."

Cynthia took the letter and scanned the front. "British Columbia. That's clear across the country from Quebec. We need to open this letter."

"I know, I almost did it earlier but Helen's held on to it for twenty years and never opened it. How do I explain the fact that it's open when I return it to her?"

"I'll be right back. You get on the computer and try to find out where Shawnigan Lake is."

When Cynthia came back, she held two pieces of pink stationery in one hand and the envelope in the other, its flap wavy from a recent steaming. She made photocopies of the front of the envelope and the letter, slid it back inside the envelope, glued the flap and smoothed it out.

Annie started to read aloud, quoting snippets of information displayed on the computer screen. "Shawnigan Lake is a village on Vancouver Island about forty miles north of Victoria. There are only about four thousand residents. Not a lot there except some restaurants and a couple of private boarding schools. It's beautiful. Look at these pictures."

Cynthia closed the door to her office and began reading. *'Dearest Debra, my little cousin married. I can hardly believe it, and an American. How exciting and how wonderful that you have such a good man in your life. When your mother passed away, I worried you would be alone. I only wish I could have been beside you at your wedding but an elopement is so much more romantic. And in Paris of all places. I was sorry to hear your wedding photographs were lost. How on earth did that happen? I was also happy to hear that your family home is being turned into a school. I have such fond memories of the summers I spent there with you, going to concerts and museums. Victoria is beautiful, as you know, but Montreal is so alive. As for me, I am enjoying my summer hiatus, doing a little tutoring and helping around the store. The tourists arrived last month en masse and it seems our little village becomes more popular every year. Won't you please consider planning a trip here with Charles? There is a lovely new Bed and Breakfast right on the lake. Please do try and come. I'll make all the arrangements. I wasn't going to burden you with any unhappy thoughts, especially now when you're starting your new life, but we've always shared everything and I feel you should know. Tom and I have broken off our engagement or, to be more accurate, Tom has broken off our engagement. It happened over a month ago and left me very sad but today the sun is shining and your letter has filled me with renewed hope. I wanted to speak with you instead of communicating by mail but your phone must be unlisted as the operator could find no number for you in Westport, Connecticut. When you get this letter, please call me at 250-555-7676 and please continue to keep me in your thoughts and your life. I will always keep you in mine. Your loving cousin, Jacque.'*

"That's convenient, no wedding pictures. Sounds like they were close. Are you calling or am I?"

"I'll do it. What's the number again?" Annie punched in the numbers and waited. After what seemed like an eternity, she ended the call. "No answer and no machine. This number's twenty years old. Maybe she moved or Tom the rat bought her a piano and she forgave the jerk and married him."

"Try information."

Not holding out much hope, Annie gave the information operator a name and the town in British Columbia. Within seconds, she had the number. "It's the same, I'm surprised. I guess she never married. I'll try it later from home. While I'm at it, let me try Bert what's-his-name. Maybe he'll remember something."

CHAPTER 17

RYAN

Ryan tapped lightly on the open door to Cody's office. "It's not that I don't love your company, but I thought we agreed we'd meet up later."

Studying a map that took up most of one wall, Cody had his back to him. When he turned around, Ryan stopped in mid-sentence. The man looked beat, like he'd pulled an all-nighter. His skin was ashen, his uniform and hair filthy.

"Sorry about the early-morning wake-up call, but I figured you'd want to be in on this."

"You figured right. Your deputy didn't say much. I take it they found her."

"They found someone but they're not sure who it is. Right now, there are a lot of tired county boys out there engaged in a territorial shouting match. So much for your people civilizing this country."

"It's only been daylight for thirty minutes. You said they weren't working through the night."

Cody poured two mugs of coffee and handed one to Ryan. "Right around the time they were shutting it down, they found some remains, a hand and a foot. That got everyone's blood up so they brought in some portable lights and kept looking. They're flying the evidence to Prescott and Flagstaff as fast as they pick it up."

Ryan joined him at the map. "I may be retired from the force but I know procedure. Why are they splitting up the evidence?"

"You see that dotted line that runs east and west about four miles south of here?"

"Yeah, I see it. It separates Coconino and Yavapai counties."

"The foot was found here." He pointed to a spot just above the dotted line then moved it an eighth of an inch below the line. "And this is where they found the hand."

"You've been out there all night?"

"Nah, I've been up here." He indicated a spot north of the town.

The layout of the streets resembled a diagram of the human intestinal system. While a few streets ran north and south, east to west, most of them wound around and came to abrupt stops. The spot where Cody had his finger was just east of one of the dead-ends, miles from the county line and the found remains. Working from the legend, Ryan tried to calculate the distance a coyote or mountain lion would have to travel dragging pieces of a human being.

Cody flopped back in his chair. "A week ago we had a fire up there, big home, expensive, not even a year old. Went up like a pile of dry kindling, right down to the foundation, everything but one wall made of quartz, the fireplace. The owners were out of the country. The husband's a lobbyist. Their primary residence is in Georgetown. They planned to spend six months here, six months in D.C. The house sits pretty much alone out there on a good size piece of property. When the owners built it, they paid to have the road extended by half a mile. It's not even on the map. Everyone figured the fire was caused by some kind of electrical problem since the contractor lost his license a few weeks after he worked on their place. The insurance company sent an investigator and he found some frayed wiring in what was once the laundry area. He signed off on it. Electrical failure. I should also mention the owner's wife sits on the board of the insurance company."

"How nice for them."

"Last night, I couldn't sleep. I kept thinking about your sister, what you told me about her house being destroyed by a fire so I called a friend of mine, a former arson investigator in Seattle. I met him at a conference five years ago and we hit it off. When he retired last year, he moved here. We met up at the house. Even working in the dark, it took him less than half an hour to find traces of accelerant. We spent the next few hours picking through the rubble, looking for anything that might give up a fingerprint."

"The furnishings were destroyed with the house?"

"Far as we can tell. This morning I called the owners. They're back in the country at their Georgetown home. They knew Susan Pierce's folks and stayed in touch with Susan after they were killed. Sometime around the middle of September, she called them and asked if she could rent the house for a couple of months."

"Sonofabitch."

"She told them she was getting married, that they were going to Paris and have the wedding there but they wanted a place to unwind while they cleaned up a few legal matters. They were happy for her, told her to stay as long as she wanted, that they wouldn't need the house until after the first of the year."

"Why didn't she contact them if she thought her life was in danger?"

"Beats me, unless she knew they were out of the country."

"Someone must have seen this guy, Roland. You can't live somewhere for weeks without someone noticing you. He had to leave the house at some point, go to a restaurant, get a haircut, buy a newspaper, something."

"You have any idea how many tourists we get through here in a month, how many faces come and go? Even if we had a photograph of him, I doubt anyone would recognize him. He doesn't want to be caught so he stays low, sends her out for everything they need. What's she going to do, rock the boat? Not likely with a Paris wedding in her future. He was in and out of the Pierce home for months before they left the San Francisco area and how much luck did you have finding one person who could describe him? Cambria's a small town, I looked it up. How many people there even knew your sister had a man in her life? You said it yourself, the guy's smart."

"Domestic help. Susan Pierce wasn't the kind of woman to clean her own toilet."

"I asked the owners about that. They used a service when they were in town, Helping Hands. She said she told Susan about them but has no idea if she called them. It's privately-owned, not a big company and not a franchise. They employ between forty and fifty women at any one time, rotate them around so they don't get too familiar with any one client and get hired away. They still have a big turnover, it's the nature of the business."

"You talked to the owner?"

"My wife did. Lita teaches school, special needs kids. One of the owner's kids is in her class. She's going through her records to see if she ever sent someone out there, said the name Pierce sounded familiar. She's also putting together a list of employees, everyone who worked for her over the last six months. She said she'd try to have everything pulled together by noon."

"What about a landscaping service or bottled water deliveries?"

"I asked about the landscaping but what they have out there doesn't need much maintenance, mostly desert plantings with a drip system. They didn't have anything delivered or picked up on a regular basis. What about the Banning woman? Did she call back?"

Not for the first time since meeting Cody, Ryan felt like a rookie. In all his years on the force, he'd never met a more dedicated cop, nor a smarter one. He anticipated everything and acted on it. On the case less than twenty-four hours, Cody had more information than ten years of spinning his wheels produced for him. "She said the woman who called had an accent, a thick accent, definitely Spanish. She insisted she told me but, trust me, she didn't. I have it all on tape. Nonetheless, I should have asked. Maybe I am too close to this."

The phone rang and Cody answered it, his demeanor changing as he listened. The haggard look was gone and its place cold determination. "Sit on her. We'll be there in half an hour." He hung up and looked at Ryan. "A boutique owner at Tlaquepaque recognized Susan Pierce's photograph."

"It's not even eight o'clock. People start work early around here."

"Johnny, the deputy you met yesterday, was walking through the plaza and saw a woman changing out her window display. He thought what the hell and gave it a shot."

"Sounds like I got here just in time."

Turning, Ryan recognized her instantly from the photo. She had long blue-black hair, enormous brown eyes and was stunning. In her hand, she held a hanger with a freshly-laundered uniform covered in plastic.

"You must be Pete. I'm Lita. Is it raining?"

Cody kissed her on the lips and took the uniform. "I'll grab a shower and change. Go easy on him, honey. Give it a couple of days before you start in on him."

Ryan grinned. "He said you were a handful."

"He should know. How long will you be staying in Sedona?"

"Until I find Susan Pierce or get a lead on the guy I'm looking for. You have seven daughters?"

"Sure do. The youngest is five and the oldest starts college next year at ASU. She's going for a degree in Criminal Justice. Just what we need in the family, another cop."

"She's got big shoes to fill. Roland's one of the best. He's always one step ahead of me. By the way, what's a talakee…?"

"Tlaquepaque. It's beautiful, not kitschy like many of the structures in the Southwest. It was built in the '70s, started out as an Arts & Crafts village. Over the years it's changed and become a little more high-tone. There are some nice restaurants and high-end clothing stores, a few good galleries. You'll like it."

"How far is it?"

Lita headed for the map. "We're here and Tlaquepaque is here, ten minutes tops. Sorry, I've got to run. Come to dinner tomorrow night. You can meet our girls. I'd invite you tonight but I'm hoping Cody will get home at a decent hour and catch up on his sleep. I'll make meatloaf."

"I'm not sure I'll still be here but I appreciate the invitation."

When Cody reappeared, all the telltale signs of a night spent digging through a burned out house were history. He looked refreshed and resolute. "That wasn't an invitation. Save yourself some grief and accept. I'll drive you over and bring you back to the motel. The house isn't easy to find." He kissed his wife good-bye and watched her walk away, waiting until she was out of earshot before adding, "You got any gall bladder or stomach problems, I'd skip the meatloaf."

Buckled into the patrol car, Cody cleared the parking lot and glanced over at Ryan. "That comment you made earlier about being too close to this. Sounds like someone's said that to you a time or two."

"Who hasn't."

"Anyone say it that you cared about?"

"The last time I heard this speech I was seven, something to do with sticks and stones if I remember right. There's a reason surgeons don't operate on family members. You really believe an investigation can't be compromised when a cop is too close to it?"

"Depends on the cop. I doubt there are too many of us who haven't kicked ourselves for not asking a question that turns out to be important later on. I know one thing. If something happened to Lita or one of my daughters or my sister, I'd be on the case and I'd stay there until I found the bastard."

"How'd the two of you meet?"

"Her mother moved Lita and her two sisters to Kayenta when Lita was fourteen. I was in my last year of high school and she was in her first year. I knew she was the one the minute I saw her. Don't think I spoke more than a dozen words to her the entire year, but the day I left for U of A, I went to her house and told her to wait for me. She didn't say a thing, just looked at me and nodded. I came back after I graduated and she was gone. She's smart as a whip, skipped a year of high school. She was at ASU on a full scholarship. I caught up with her there, begged her to come back, told her we'd get married right away. Nope. She waited for me and now it was her turn. If I loved her, I'd wait. So I did."

"That's quite a story."

"She's quite a woman, works her tail off teaching all day, great mother, runs a local charity and still finds time to host an on-line support group."

"What kind of support group?"

"I'll let her tell you about that. We're here."

Tlaquepaque was just as Lita had described it and Ryan was impressed. Someone did a beautiful job of replicating a traditional Mexican village right down to the architectural details, ironwork and tiled fountains. Everywhere he looked, his senses were fed by the sights, smells and sounds of another time and place.

The boutique was located on the ground floor of what looked to be an artery of the main building. Just outside was a small courtyard with several stone benches. The deputy was sitting on the one closest to the door and he jumped up when he saw the two men approaching.

"Chief Cody, Mr. Ryan, she's inside. Her name's Carol O'Toole."

Before entering the shop, Cody walked the deputy a few steps away from the door. "Your shift doesn't start for another hour. You bucking for a promotion?"

"No, sir. Everyone knows what's going on out there, what they're finding. I thought maybe I'd get here before the shops opened and got busy. People might be more cooperative if they don't have customers to deal with. I'll go grab some breakfast and come back when my shift starts."

"Like hell you will. I think maybe you should listen in, hear the kind of questions we need answered. If you're going to have my job one day, I want you prepared."

Carol O'Toole was a woman in her mid to late forties, attractive and well-tended with a cultured British accent. She seemed cool and composed as the three men entered her shop and the deputy handled the introductions.

"Chief Cody, I met you at that fund-raiser a couple of months ago. How can I help?"

"My deputy tells me you recognize the photograph of Susan Pierce. Was she a customer of yours?"

"Yes, I looked it up while we were waiting for you. She purchased some items on October 8th."

"How did she pay for the merchandise?"

"She paid in cash which I found surprising considering the amount, a little over fifteen thousand dollars."

Cody looked around the shop and then back at her. "I'm sorry. Did you say fifteen thousand dollars?"

"I know what you're thinking, that it doesn't look like I have fifteen thousand dollars worth of merchandise in the entire store. We don't keep stock in the traditional sense. Seventy-five percent of our merchandise is ready-to-wear but very high-end. I'll bring in a dress, for example, but only one in that particular style and in only one size, usually a six or an eight. The other twenty-five percent of our inventory is strictly couture from Paris or Milan."

"But you keep records of what people purchase."

"We do better than that. We take a digital photograph of every piece of clothing or accessory that's brought into the store. When a client makes a purchase, we open a file on them and put a copy of the photograph in it. That way we know what they've purchased, their size and the type of garment or jewelry that interests them. I go through the files periodically, and if there's something new of a similar style, I'll contact them and send it out on approval. Or they may ask for a particular thing I'm not currently carrying in the store. If I happen to come across it at market, I'll bring it in and either hold it for them or send it to them, again on approval."

"Did that ever happen with Susan Pierce, that you sent something out to her on approval?"

"No, I'm sorry. Here, I made a copy of her file for you. There's a photograph of everything she purchased. Chief Cody, what is this about? Is she in some kind of trouble with the police?"

"Her family in San Francisco is worried about her. Pete and I are trying to find out where she is and if she's okay. Was anyone with her, another woman, a man?"

"She was alone."

"What was her mood, happy, sad, in a hurry?"

"I'm not sure how to answer that."

"Carol, we appreciate the fact you have to be discreet about your clientele, but this is important. I can assure you it won't go any further than this room."

"Well, frankly, she was a bitch. She found fault with everything, the lighting in the shop, the way the jewelry was displayed, literally everything."

"But she still spent fifteen thousand dollars."

"People shop for any number of reasons, Chief. If they're bored, it gives them something to do. If they're sad, it makes them happy. If they're happy, it makes them happier. Studies show there's an adrenaline rush, like gambling. Of course, it's only temporary until the next time they require a fix."

"What about need?" asked Ryan. "Don't people buy things because they need them?"

"Not in my shop. No one needs a twenty-five hundred dollar skirt unless they're dressing for a Red Carpet event. My point is, Susan Pierce was none of those things. She was a spite-shopper, a rarity but we get our share." She paused and smiled. "I can tell by your expressions you have no idea what I'm talking about. Think of it like this. Imagine you're a woman married to a wealthy man. The two of you have a fight over something or you can't stand the sight of him. What is the one thing that matters to him above everything else? Money. So you put on your lipstick, grab the black American Express card and you go spend his money. He can't divorce you. You'll take half of everything he owns and for the few hours that you're indulging yourself, you're also getting back at him."

"But you don't get many of those."

"No, thank God, and I've never had one in my store quite as verbal. I almost asked her to leave. Two other shoppers ran out. I think they thought she was crazy. She'd point to something and say Charles will hate this, I'll take it, or Charles despises red, wrap it up."

Ryan and Cody exchanged a look.

"You're sure the name was Charles."

"You don't forget a name that's thrown out there a dozen times in less than an hour."

"Did she say anything else about this Charles, give any reason why she was angry with him?"

"No, but then women like her don't confide in women like me. The trappings may be upscale but I'm still here to serve them. The only exception to that rule is occasionally their hairstylist or manicurist, but Susan Pierce didn't put me in mind of the type of woman that would confide in them either. She was a very strange woman. I don't know any other way to describe her."

"She didn't mention the fact that she was going to Paris to get married, nothing like that?"

"Definitely not. I assumed she was married or in a long-term relationship. Perhaps I misread her."

"Just a couple more questions. Was she carrying any shopping bags or parcels from another shop here?"

"No, none. She was carrying a Louis Vuitton handbag though, the real thing, not a copy."

"Did you notice which direction she went when she left here?"

"I'm sorry, I didn't notice. As she was leaving, another customer came in and started asking questions about an item in the window. I didn't see which way she went."

The deputy cleared his throat. "Excuse me, ma'am, but did she ask any questions about where to go for lunch or maybe where to get her hair done, anything like that?"

"No, I don't think…wait, she did mention she felt tense and thought she might need a massage. I remember thinking to myself, sweetheart you need more than a massage. Before she left, I gave her the card of a very good masseuse. She didn't acknowledge it but she did put it in her handbag. I must have put it out of my mind because I felt guilty inflicting her on someone I know. I have another one of her cards in the back. I'll get it."

Cody turned to the deputy. "When she gets back with the card, call the woman and find out if Susan Pierce went to her for a massage. If she did, pay her a visit. You know the questions. If she didn't, grab some breakfast and then talk to as many of the shop owners here as you can. If you need help, let me know and I'll send someone over, but if anyone else recognizes her, you do the interviews, got it? And check in with me every hour, sooner if you get something."

"Yes, sir."

When Carol O'Toole came out of her office, she was carrying two large shopping bags, one filled with clothing and the other with what appeared to be cosmetics. She dropped them at Cody's feet, handed him the card and asked, "Would you mind very much taking these to Lita? I was going to drop them off after work but I have a dental appointment." She started laughing. "Chief Cody, you should see your face. These aren't for her. She's much too smart to shop here. I don't buy the merchandise and I own the shop." She lowered her voice and added, "They're for the women's shelter."

CHAPTER 18

ANNIE

Annie pulled to a stop and rested her arms on the steering wheel. Impressed was putting it mildly. This morning the driveway was a disaster area. What the men accomplished in a few hours was nothing short of a miracle. Not only was the wood from the limb split and stacked neatly against the house, but the pile of debris from the garage was gone. Things were finally shaping up. For the first time since moving in, she could use the garage for its intended purpose instead of a repository for other people's junk.

She made a wide turn, put the truck in neutral and executed another unladylike exit from the vehicle. The white plastic take-out bag and its contents were strewn across the garage floor where she left them the night before. Now the only question was what to do with it. If it were proven Debra met with foul play, this could be evidence. Bending down, she folded the bag carefully, using only the edges while trying to leave as few fingerprints as possible.

The wadded up paper towels looked different in the light, smoother, with some scraggly edges that might have been pulled off a notebook. Or a sketchbook. Picking one at random, she was careful to remove the wrinkles without tearing it. When she was finished, she rocked back on her heels. It was an eight by ten drawing of her home, so perfectly detailed it took her breath away.

There were a total of five, each drawn from a different perspective around the property. One was of the front door with

143

the two fat birch trees standing as sentinels in the foreground. Another was of the brook as it tumbled its way into the marsh. She must have been sitting on the front porch when she drew the fourth one. It was the line of pine trees that formed the boundary to the property to the west, trees so old and tall they blocked the sun. Did she know their history when she drew them? Before there was a lighthouse off Fairfield Beach, sailors used them to navigate their way through Long Island Sound.

The fifth one confused her. It looked like a sketch of the side patio, the one off the living room. She recognized the two low brick columns that held the carriage lamps but there was something between them in the background she couldn't quite make out. It looked like a baby crawling across a large boulder protruding from the earth. Was it creative visualization, a baby to share her new home and life? The thought depressed her. Whatever the drawings were, they weren't trash. Debra had signed each of them in her beautiful script.

By the time the truck was in the garage and she entered the house, the depression turned to anger. Einstein sensed her mood and approached slowly, licking her hand as the anger dissolved into tears. Kneeling down, she took his face in her hands and whispered, "He killed her. I know he did."

She sat with him for a few more minutes before getting to her feet. Maybe later she'd take one of the damn sleeping pills but it was still early, not quite three. The hours spent at **Life House** were productive. She'd still be there if Cynthia hadn't shooed her out, telling her to go home and get some sleep, that she was frightening the guests.

Before going upstairs to change, she put on a pot of decaf coffee and turned to the pile of drawings on the kitchen table. She pulled out the one with the baby on the rock and walked through the kitchen into the living room. Einstein followed as she opened the French Doors and stepped onto the patio. There was nothing beyond the columns, nothing but high grass neglected for what appeared to be decades.

Einstein left the patio to relieve himself by the brook but was back in record time. He was always sensitive to her moods but today he was more attentive than usual. Instead of running off to bark at the birds, he stayed close, always keeping her in sight. The sun was behind the house and she felt a chill. "Come on, boy, we have phone calls to make."

They were half-way through the door when she turned and walked back across the patio into the high grass. She took only a few steps when her toe hit something. Parting the overgrown mess, she saw it, a stone baby a little larger than life-size crawling across a massive boulder six feet long and a foot high. She felt another wave of anger, this one almost knocking her off her feet. When it receded, she made a silent vow to a woman she would never know. *We'll get the bastard, Debra. Charles will pay for what he did to you.*

Fifteen minutes later, dressed in jeans and a turtleneck, she picked up the phone and dialed the number in British Columbia. If she calculated right, it was only twelve-thirty in the afternoon, give or take an hour. The voice on the other end startled her.

"Hello?"

"Is this Jacqueline Gauthier?"

"This is her daughter. She's gone into the village. Who's calling please?"

"You don't know me but my name is Annie Heywood. I'm calling from Connecticut."

Silence.

"I'm trying to locate your mother's cousin, Debra Hastings."

"I'm sorry, who are you?"

"My name is Annie Heywood. Six weeks ago, I purchased a home in Westport, Connecticut. I believe Debra lived here for a short time after she was married in 2000. I was cleaning out the garage yesterday and found some drawings of hers and I thought she might like to have them. Do you have any idea where she is? They're beautiful and I'd like to send them to her."

"Debra died many years ago, Miss Heywood."

"I'm sorry to hear that. Please, my name's Annie and you are…"

"Lisa."

"Hi, Lisa. I hate to bother you with all this but do you know any details surrounding her death?"

"Not really. She married an American and moved to the States. I don't think she lived there very long before she passed away."

"Do you know if she was ill?"

"I really don't know anything. I didn't even know about her until two years ago when I came across a letter she'd written to my mother. She doesn't like to talk about Debra. It makes her sad."

"I'm sure it does. Can you answer just a couple more questions, please?"

Silence.

"Do you have any idea where she's interred, if she was buried in Canada?"

"No, I don't."

"She was from Quebec, I believe. She made a friend of one of my neighbors and told her she was Quebecoise."

"Yes, she was raised in Montreal."

"I also recall she told my neighbor her childhood home was being turned into a school. You wouldn't know the name of the school, would you?"

"That was in Debra's letter, the one I found, but it's not a school."

"How do you know?"

"We went there last year when I graduated from high school. It was my graduation gift from my mother. We had a wonderful time. While we were there, mother suggested we drive by Debra's house. She spent some summers there with her and said it was a wonderful old house."

"It's still a private residence?"

"It's an office building, a horrible ugly thing."

"You wouldn't know the address or the street, would you?"

"Mother may know but…Miss Heywood, Annie, I really have to go. I'll be late for my shift."

"Your shift?"

"I work at a coffee kiosk in Mill Bay. I'm also studying art at university."

"You're an artist, how wonderful. Debra was a very talented artist."

"I guess it runs in our family."

"Lisa, I wouldn't ask if it weren't important, but do you think your mother would speak to me if I called back at a more convenient time?"

"I'm not sure. Your number is here on our I.D. and I'll tell her you called. If she wants to speak with you, she'll call you back. Is that all right?"

"Of course. Thank you, Lisa. One last thing, are you still living in Shawnigan Lake? Perhaps your mother would like to have Debra's drawings. I could send them to her."

"I'm sure my mother would love to have them. Good-bye, Annie."

Annie stared at the phone as the connection was broken. She learned nothing from the conversation but what she already knew, that Debra was dead and no record of her death existed. Cynthia was right. She had to take what she had to the police, lay it out for them and let them do their thing. They had resources and manpower and she had neither. Bert Kennedy was another waste of time. The phone number on his business card now belonged to a Day Spa.

Pacing, she mentally put the facts in some semblance of order that would sound credible. She knew enough to keep her voice level and free of emotion, otherwise they'd take her for a crackpot or worse. Where was Samantha when she needed her? She'd know exactly how to bait the hook and reel them in. With just a look, she could get them to reopen Lincoln's assassination.

"Okay, here goes."

Einstein lay stretched out on the floor, his head between his extended front paws, watching her every move. When she finished her soliloquy, she threw up her hands. Einstein was sound asleep. Not that she blamed him. With what she had, she'd be lucky if all the police did was fall asleep.

To begin with, she forgot to ask Lisa about Debra's maiden name. The cops would need that to verify she'd existed at all. Furthermore, most of what she knew about the night Debra died came from an eighty-something woman whose memory of the events didn't exactly jibe with the facts. As far as physical evidence, she had next to nothing, a twenty-year-old journal, a discarded Chinese take-out bag and some drawings. And finally, there was the property manager, Bert Kennedy, who was MIA. Without him or some record of the so-called break-in, she had squat.

What she needed was a phone book, another relic of the pre-computer age. Cynthia was so insistent that she go home, she left her laptop in her office. She vaguely remembered bringing in a phone book a few days after she moved in. It was covered in plastic and left at the base of the mailbox. She found it on the top shelf of the coat closet tucked beneath the staircase, one of the few places yet to be scrubbed down and painted. She lived alone in a three bedroom home with more closet space than she knew what to do with and she had no future plans to do any serious entertaining. For the time being, it would remain a catch-all.

She pulled the top one down and with it came the one beneath it. It was dated 2002-2003 and looked pristine, as if it hadn't been used. Several others were stacked similarly and she pulled them all down. The oldest was dated 1983-1984. While she was at it, she decided to get rid of them so she piled them up and carried them out to the recycling bin. On her way through the kitchen, she slid the two most recent ones onto the table. She wanted to check Bert Kennedy's phone number, the one on his card, with the 2002-2003 book, perhaps even find a home phone number for him.

Grabbing a bottle of water from the refrigerator, she sat back down and ripped the plastic off the newest book. There were a number of listings for Kennedy but none with the first name Bert, no Albert either. She flipped over to the yellow pages and searched until she found a heading for Property Management. There were three listings but none for Westport Properties Ltd. The third listing caught her eye and she circled it, Stanley Properties, Inc.

It had to be the same Stanley that owned properties scattered around the county and it made sense they had taken up the slack from Kennedy's defunct business. It was a Greenwich exchange and address. She knew exactly where the office was. Her gynecologist was in the same building.

The phone was answered by a cheerful young woman evidently hired for her sparkling personality rather than her knowledge of property management. No, she did not recognize the name Bert Kennedy; no, she did not know if Stanley Properties, Inc. had taken over the properties formerly managed by Westport Properties Ltd.; and no, Mr. Bryce Stanley was not in the office today. When Annie finally asked a question that elicited an affirmative answer, she grabbed it and made an appointment for the following morning at 10 a.m.

Turning her attention to the phone book dated 2000-2001, she found the listing for Westport Properties under Property Management and checked the number against the one on the card. They were the same which confirmed that Bert Kennedy's business was no longer in existence. Her last hope was he had retired, was still living locally but now preferred the anonymity of an unlisted number. If that were the case, she could call him, ask the questions and cancel the meeting with Bryce Stanley which she wasn't quite sure why she made in the first place.

She rifled the white pages until she came to the Ks. The page listing his home address and phone number were marked with a bright orange card about three inches long by one inch wide. It was stuck in the crease a third of the way down the page. She pulled it out and put it aside. She tried the number, but just like his office number, it was reassigned to another party.

Annie checked her watch and stretched the kinks out of her upper body. It was still way too early to try and sleep. Einstein would need to go out at eight for his last duty call of the day which meant she had three hours to kill. A walk? Why not, they could both use the exercise. When they got back, she'd order a veggie pizza and settle in on the sofa. With any luck, she'd fall asleep there and forego the sleeping pill.

After depositing the two phone books back in the closet, she scooped up the plastic wrapper and orange tag from the table. There was something printed on the back of it, something she hadn't noticed when she took it out of the book:

**Turk Street Storage, San Francisco, CA 94102
(415)555-7418.**

Einstein was awake, waiting patiently by the door. It was freaky how he sometimes read her mind or had she been talking to herself again? She threw the plastic and the card in the trash, grabbed the leash and they were off.

Half an hour later they were back and Annie was pawing through the trash. When she found what she was looking for, she dialed the number and waited.

"Turk Street Storage."

"Hi, is this a storage facility?"

"Yeah, what can I do for you?"

"I'm not sure. What kind of a storage facility?"

"The kind where you store stuff."

"Right. Do you know if a man named Charles Hastings has a, what do you call it, a…"

"A bay?"

"That's it, a bay. Is there any way for you to check and see if a Charles Hastings rents a bay there?"

Silence.

"Hello, are you there?"

"Yeah, I'm here but we don't give out that kind of information."

"I understand that, but I'm his sister and I can't remember the name of the facility where he stored our parents' furniture. He's living in Europe now and I need to know if this is the right place."

"Listen, lady, I'm kind of busy. Give me your name and a phone number and I'll call you back."

"Sure. My name is Annie Heywood, H-E-Y-W-O-O-D, and my phone number in Connecticut is 203-555-4323. Any idea when you might be calling me back? Hello?"

Damn, she should have gotten his name before he broke the connection. He was in a hurry, that was obvious, but she hoped he had taken down her information before hanging up. More than likely, it was another wild-goose chase, but if he didn't call her back by tomorrow afternoon, she'd give it another try. She had no idea what the ramifications were of Charles Hastings having a storage bay in San Francisco or if, indeed, he had one but it seemed an odd coincidence.

The walk relaxed her and she yawned. Pizza was a bad idea, too heavy, so she opted for cereal. When she was finished, she put the bowl in the dishwasher and reached for the plastic vial in her tote bag. Einstein had peed against every rock, tree and shrub in the neighborhood and would be fine until morning.

She turned off the light in the kitchen, checked the locks and climbed the stairs.

CHAPTER 19

RYAN

"I could be wrong but I sensed some chemistry back there."

Ryan shucked his raincoat and threw it in the back of the patrol car before settling in. "Not my type."

Cody's cell phone rang and he answered it. Within seconds, Ryan's cell was buzzing and he stepped out of the car to give them both some privacy. By the time he finished the call and rejoined Cody, he'd concluded his call too.

"That was the owner of Helping Hands. Two weeks ago, she got a call from Susan Pierce, needed a one-time cleaning. She sent out a woman named Maria Hernandez. She hasn't heard from her since, never even came by to pick up her check. I've got an address. She might be more inclined to open up if she doesn't see a uniform. How's your Spanish?"

"Passable."

"Let me know if you run into trouble. You okay, Pete?"

"Yeah, that was Jimmy, my former partner. He ran Susan Pierce's credit cards again and there's still no activity which means she didn't use them for tickets to Paris."

"You and I both know she never made it to Paris."

"I hope you're wrong. What's the latest on the search?"

"Haven't heard a thing. I'll check in again when I get back to the office but I wouldn't get my hopes up. A body out there wouldn't last more than a couple of days."

"The timing's off. You said the house burned down a week ago. The pilot reported the sighting a little over twenty-four hours ago. Where was she for six days?"

"The will to live is powerful, my friend."

"Christ, you're not suggesting she was alive when he took her out there. How much do you have to hate a person to leave them in the middle of the fucking desert, knowing what will happen to them?"

Even as he said the words, Ryan's thoughts went to Theresa. She was savagely beaten and left to die in the middle of a vacant lot. Months later, when he could bring himself to read the autopsy report, he learned there were signs of rodent activity around her face and hands.

"You're assuming he hates them."

"If that's a theory, I'm all ears."

"Something's been bothering me ever since you told me about your sister. He meets these women, spends a lot of time convincing them he's their savior and then he murders them. Why? What's he getting out of it? It's not money, at least it wasn't in Theresa's case. She left everything to you. Susan Pierce? I doubt we'll find any record of a wedding. He's not going to put his real name on a marriage certificate, and without that, he's not getting a dime."

"Unless she changed her will or put all her assets in both their names."

"That make sense to you, that he'd go to all the trouble to stay under the radar then have his name show up on some bank records?"

"So, what, he's some kind of sadistic patron of the arts with a God-Messiah complex?"

"Makes about as much sense as anything else. You've been involved in this longer than me, Pete. What do you think?"

"I think I'd like to know if there are any other victims who fit the profile."

Cody pulled the car into his parking space ad turned off the ignition. "We've got one, probably two women, well-off, never married, both involved in the arts, who meet a mystery man and end up dead. Throw in the fact they're unsolved and you may narrow it down to a few hundred. Could take months to get any feedback through official channels. There's a reason cold cases are cold."

"I know the drill. You have any better ideas?"

"Maybe."

***

Using the rental car's GPS, Ryan slowed his approach to Maria Hernandez' home and parked across the street. The neighborhood was mostly small older homes, working class, judging from the number of pick-up trucks, some better maintained than others. The Hernandez home was one of the good ones with its fresh coat of white paint and pots of flowers on the front porch. Off to one side was a make-shift shrine to the Virgin Mary, her blue and white gown faded by years in the sun.

He pulled down the visor and loosened the top button of his shirt, his attempt at casual missing the mark. He could be wearing cutoffs and a t-shirt and would still look exactly like what he was, an uptight ex-cop.

After knocking on the door, he waited. Somewhere deep inside the house a radio blared rock music. He tapped louder and the music stopped. He thought about knocking again, calling out her name, but he stopped himself. If he were to gain her confidence, it would have to be because of trust, not fear.

As he was walking back to his car, a voice behind him stopped him mid-stride. "You want something, mister?" An attractive young woman in low-slung jeans and a halter top leaned against the frame of the door, her arms crossed just below her breasts. It was the body language of one accustomed to attention and the ability to dispatch it with prejudice.

Ryan kept his distance, stopping just short of the steps leading up to the porch. "My name's Pete Ryan. I'm not a cop, and I don't give a damn if you're from the planet Krypton and were dropped here illegally from the mothership. I need to speak with Maria Hernandez. I need her help."

The woman stepped aside and waved him in. When they were both inside, she motioned him to a chair. "Are you a priest?"

"I'm not a priest. Why do you assume that?"

"You made the sign of the cross when you saw the Madonna."

"I'm Catholic. Old habits die hard."

"What is it you want with my mother, Mr. Ryan?"

Deliberately slowing his movements, he took Susan Pierce's photo from his pocket and held it up to her. "Your mother worked for this woman approximately two weeks ago. Her name is Susan Pierce and she's missing. Right after she worked for her, I believe your mother made a phone call to this woman's sister, telling her she was in trouble, that someone was trying to kill her. The gas station where the phone call was made is less than a mile from this house."

"You have the wrong person. My mother doesn't do housekeeping."

"Look, miss, I meant what I said out there. Your mother's not in any trouble. I'm afraid the same can't be said of Susan Pierce. If what we suspect is true, they're picking up pieces of her out there in the desert."

The woman's eyes widened then narrowed. "You have identification?"

Ryan produced his P.I. license and business card. She examined them closely and returned them to him. "How do I know you're not him, the man in that house?"

"I have Chief Cody's card. Call him, he knows me."

"Chief Cody is a good man. Then you must also know his wife. What is her name?"

Knowing she was testing him, Ryan finally smiled. "Her name is Lita and she's a lot like you, a real ball buster."

"Si, it's part of our charm. I made the call, Mr. Ryan. I'm Maria Hernandez."

"My client, Marcia Banning, said the woman who called had a thick Spanish accent."

"I suppose it depends on who's listening."

"Tell me about them. You may be the only person in this town who was in that house while they lived there. It burned down a week ago."

She nodded. "I heard. I was there all day, almost seven hours. She was very difficult and unpleasant. Look around you. I know how to clean a home but nothing pleased her. I never saw the man, not once. She let me know that I shouldn't bother him, that he was in his office and I was to stay out of that room.

"She was very different with him. She would go in and out of that room every hour or so, quietly like a little mouse, trying to do things that would please him, taking him coffee or his lunch on a tray. I would hear her trying to talk to him, something about a piece of music she was working on, and he would say terrible things to her."

"What kind of things?"

"That she should get her hair done, that it smelled bad, or she was putting on weight again. He told her to go back to her piano and leave him alone."

Ryan's stomach lurched at the thought of Theresa being subjected to that kind of cruelty. "And this went on in front of you? They didn't care that you heard all this?"

"Have you ever been in service to a wealthy person, Mr. Ryan? They want you efficient, humble and invisible. Pretending not to understand or speak English makes me a non-entity to them. They can go on with their lives, be as unpleasant to one another as they choose and the ignorant Mexican girl will never tell their secrets."

"What was his voice like, young, old? Did he have an accent?"

"You all sound alike to me. I'm sorry."

"Tell me about the phone call to Marcia Banning. What did Susan Pierce say to you to get you to make that call?"

"She didn't say anything to me but I know something about domestic violence. It starts out as verbal abuse. One day you are being humiliated, just like her, and the next day your head is shoved into a wall."

"I'm confused. Are you saying she didn't ask you to make the call?"

"No, she never asked me to make the call and I never said anything about him trying to kill her. What I said was I thought she was in trouble and she needed help."

"How did you know who to call?"

It was the first time she averted her eyes and looked uncomfortable. "There were some papers on the counter in the kitchen. They looked like some kind of application, for a passport I think. On the form, it asked for the name of a relative and she listed Marcia Banning as her sister. There was an address and phone number. That was what gave me the idea to call."

"How did her sister react when you told her she was in trouble?"

"Your client is not a nice woman, Mr. Ryan. She told me to tell Susan to go to hell. Is she really dead?"

"We're not sure. They're still searching the area where some remains were found."

Maria made the sign of the cross.

"You never went back to Helping Hands to pick up your check. What's that about?"

"Susan Pierce came into the kitchen as I was writing down the phone number and she screamed at me, told me she wasn't paying me to snoop around, that I should finish and leave. I was sure she would report me and I would be fired anyway."

He knew she was telling the truth but something didn't gel with her story. "You're saying Susan Pierce was horrible to you, demanding and unreasonable and practically kicked you out of the house and you still called her sister to get her some help."

"Yes, that's what happened."

"I don't get it. Why would you do that?"

"When you are in an abusive relationship, you don't understand what is happening. You are not yourself. You become whoever or whatever the man says you are. You think when you do what he wants he will change and become the person you loved. But mostly you are alone. You do not tell your family because you are embarrassed, and until the day he hurts you, you never think it will happen. That is why I called her sister."

"I'll see that your check is sent to you. What about your job, do you want it back?"

"No, but thank you. I've been here almost six months, time to move on. I only rent this place anyway. I like it, though. I've been happy here."

"Why are you leaving?"

Maria looked down and again crossed her arms, but this time the language of her body screamed protection, not defiance.

"He's still out there looking for you, isn't he?"

Maria nodded, her eyes filling with tears.

"Where will you go?"

"I think a big city this time. It's easier to get lost."

Ryan took another of his business cards, turned it over and wrote out two names and their contact information. "The woman is a friend of mine in San Francisco. She waits tables at a nice café in the Mission District. Tell her Ryan sent you, that you need a job and a place to live. She'll help you and she won't ask questions. Jimmy is my old partner, a cop and a good one. Call him if you ever need him. His home phone number's on here too."

She took the card and brightened. "Her name is also Maria."

"You'll like her. Sit tight, I'll be right back."

When he returned, he handed her a check.

"I can't take this, Mr. Ryan. I'll never be able to pay you back ten thousand dollars."

"It's not a loan. Hell, it's not even my money, I inherited it. Consider it a gift from my sister, a down payment on your new life. Maybe if someone like you had given a damn, she'd still be alive."

Back in his car, Ryan waited for his anger to subside. When he glanced across at the house, Maria Hernandez was standing in the door, her right hand over her heart.

He started the engine and drove until the house was out of sight then pulled the car to a stop and reached for his cell phone. He left it in the car while he was in the house so he wouldn't be interrupted. Now it was beeping, alerting him to voicemail messages. There was only one and he listened, jotting down the phone number. Letting the car idle, he dialed the number and identified himself. When he was finished taking down the information, he thanked the kid on the other end, reminding him to call if he heard from the woman again and he'd make it worth his while.

Ryan sat for a few more minutes, planning his next move. His inclination was to call the woman, find out if there was more to her story than coincidence. His cop instincts told him to wait and think it through. If he called her back instead of the guy from Turk Storage, she might get spooked and try to protect her brother. At the very least, he had a last name, Hastings. Charles Hastings.

His first call was to Jimmy who assured him that he'd run the name right away and get back to him. His second call was another to Turk Storage. Under no circumstances was anyone to call the woman back. If she called again, they had to put her off by saying they were still trying to find the information. More importantly, they had twenty-four hours to complete the review of their files to determine if someone named Charles had rented bays there in the last ten years. After that, it would be done with a court order and out of his hands along with the promised cash. It was completely up to them. He had no idea if the bluff would work, but he could swear he heard files opening and keys clicking before he hung up.

On his way back to Cody's office, Ryan picked up sandwiches and two large coffees. Over lunch, he filled him in on his meeting with Maria Hernandez, everything but the last five minutes of their conversation.

"I also got a call from the kid at the storage company. A woman phoned him about an hour ago asking if a Charles Hastings had a bay there. He put her off, told her he'd look it up."

Cody made a note of the name. "I'll run it though the Arizona DMV, see if anything comes up. You get the woman's name?"

"Annie Heywood. It's a Connecticut number. She told him Charles Hastings was her brother and she was trying to track down the storage facility where he stored some of their parents' stuff."

"Sounds reasonable enough. You gonna follow up with her?"

"As soon as I figure out the best way to handle it. If there's a chance this Charles is connected to the case, I don't want her shutting down and protecting him."

"Could be just a coincidence, unless…"

"Unless she's working with him and doing a little investigating on her own," added Ryan. "You got a computer I can use?"

"Use mine. I'll get them started running the name Charles Hastings."

Ryan took Cody's chair and logged on to the internet. The name Charles Hastings brought up nothing. When he typed in the name Annie Heywood, he got luckier. There were two sites, the first of which referenced a column in the *Stamford Advocate* devoted to Interior Design. He clicked on it and several columns were displayed, the most recent dating back a year, nothing since. The second site was the homepage of **Life House**, an AIDS Hospice located in Riverside, Connecticut. Established in 2010, it was run by two women, Cynthia Fredericks and Annie Heywood.

Working his way through the site, Ryan was impressed. The place looked more like an upscale retreat than a healthcare facility. Obviously, that was the point since their Mission Statement focused on the dignity of living with the disease and not its deadly ramifications. To their credit, they had also put together an august Advisory Board including healthcare professionals, spiritual advisors and local benefactors.

Cody came up behind him. "You get something?"

"Yeah, take a look and then go back to the homepage and give me the phone number. I have an idea."

"Chief Cody, Mr. Ryan, do you have a minute?"

Looking less composed than a few short hours ago, Carol O'Toole stood in the doorway.

Ryan stood up and Cody went around his desk to greet her. "Carol, come on in. Is everything all right?"

"Everything's fine but may I see the photograph again, the one of Susan Pierce?"

Ryan pulled a copy from his pocket and handed it to her. She took it and compared it to a photograph pulled from her handbag. "Is there any way to enlarge it? It's the necklace. I was concentrating on her face when the deputy first showed me the photograph but then, after your visit this morning, I started thinking about the turquoise necklace she was wearing. I went through my files and found this."

Cody took her photo and put it against the one of Susan Pierce. "Looks like a couple of strands of turquoise to me. You can buy these almost anywhere."

"I know jewelry, Chief Cody, and she didn't pick this up in a t-shirt shop. Please, can you enlarge your photo or give me a magnifying glass?"

Cody took the photograph and left the office. When he came back, he had a blow-up of the necklace around Susan Pierce's neck.

Carol O'Toole laid the two photographs side by side on the desk. "It's the same necklace. See how the chunks of turquoise are individually knotted, not separated by silver beads. That way, if the cording breaks you don't lose any of the nuggets. The knotting takes time and makes the piece more expensive. Look at the center stone, the way the matrix stops halfway down and blossoms out at the bottom. The two stones on either side are almost perfectly matched, more oval than round. It's the same necklace."

Ryan weighed in. "The photograph of her wearing that necklace was taken on January 17th of this year in Sausalito. Maybe she bought it from you on a previous trip here."

"You forget, I keep records, very good records. This necklace was sold on December 22nd of last year to a Charles Tyrrell."

"I don't suppose you've got an address and phone number for him?" asked Cody.

"Sorry, just his name. I'm not sure if we even asked him for additional information. It was three days before Christmas. You can't imagine how busy we were."

"Who helped him with his purchase?" asked Ryan.

"According to the sales slip, I did but I don't remember him. There was a man who came in during the Christmas rush and all the girls were giggling about him, saying he was probably a movie star but I'm not sure if it's the same man who bought the necklace."

"What made them think he was a celebrity?"

"He was expensively-dressed and he wore a cowboy hat pulled forward on his head and large sunglasses that hid most of his face. He looked as if he were trying to conceal his identity."

"Anyone hazard a guess as to who it might have been? Was he a certain type, Clint Eastwood or Mel Gibson? Help me out here, I haven't been to the movies in ten years."

"It's no use, Chief. I called the two girls who were working with me during the holidays last year and neither of them remembers a thing. I know he paid cash. I went back and checked the receipts for that day."

Cody took the card from her and copied down the name. "I'll get them started running this name too."

When they were alone in the office, Ryan approached her cautiously. She looked ready to burst into tears and consoling two weeping women within an hour was beyond his skill set. "Who's minding the shop?"

"No one. I closed it up to come here. She's dead, isn't she?"

When he didn't respond, she walked to the window. "It's a small town, Mr. Ryan. That's the reason a lot of us came here in the first place, for a sense of community and the beauty. There's a legend that Geronimo made frequent pilgrimages here to renew his spirit. I don't know if it's true but there is something magical about the place. I wonder how much longer it will be that way. Apparently it's changing." She turned away from the window and looked him in the eye. "I said some terrible things about her this morning. I wish I could take them back."

"You answered our questions and sometimes the answers aren't pretty. The information you gave us was valuable and we appreciate it, especially taking the time away from your shop to come over here. If it helps, the identity of the body hasn't been confirmed."

"I've got to get back. Tell the Chief I said good-bye."

"Carol, not all change is bad. It might even be good for your business."

She offered him a half-smile. "It's not my business I'm worried about. It's my spirit."

CHAPTER 20

ANNIE

Grabbing her mug of coffee, Annie walked around the front of the house toward the flagstone terrace. The weather was into its second day of unseasonable warmth and she wanted to enjoy it while it lasted. All too soon the northeast would be under a blanket of snow and ice.

She gave a sidelong glance at the spot between the two columns then shifted her eyes toward the brook. She felt sad and relieved at the same time. The rock and baby were gone, reclaimed in the night by the high grass.

Maybe it was a sign. Earlier that morning, after a good night's sleep, she made a decision. "Balance." The word came out while she was brushing her teeth. She had no idea what it meant and even less idea how to achieve it, but she was fairly sure she didn't have it.

She knew only two things for certain: she did not want to end up a pathetic pill-popping divorcee and sleuthing was not her forte. In the first place, she was bad at it, and in the second place, she didn't need the drama. Intrigue was Larry's thing. He could sit for hours, advancing theory upon theory about how to twist a situation to his advantage or extract information when none was forthcoming.

After her meeting with Bryce Stanley, she was done. She'd take whatever he knew, add it to the list and drop it in the hands of the police, everything but Debra's drawings. Those she would send off to Jacqueline and Lisa Gauthier.

She made another decision too. When she got to the office, she was booking her flight to London. It was a selfish thing to do but she had to get away and concentrate on something other than death. She needed her sister, to tap into her incredible energy and zest for living. She also needed to know if the contentment she'd felt for a few short weeks was real or if she were one of those people who required turmoil to give their life meaning. Most of the changes she'd made were external, things she could feel and touch. What she was desperate for was a reconnection to who she was and what would make her happy long-term.

Before she even made it though the front door, Annie heard the piano. Today it was a medley from the musical **Annie**. She was laughing as she rounded the corner and blew a kiss to the pianist.

On the way to her office, she stopped by Cynthia's desk. "Thanks for the pills, sweetie, I feel almost human. I fell asleep on the sofa and slept for twelve hours."

"You're lookin' better. You ever get hold of that woman in Canada?"

"Yep, yesterday afternoon, not her but her daughter. She was very sweet but she didn't know much beyond the fact that Debra died shortly after marrying and moving here. I had no luck with Bert Kennedy. Apparently he's left the area. I couldn't find a recent listing for him, so I have an appointment with Bryce Stanley of Stanley Properties. My guess is he took over the management of the properties from Kennedy and may have some files lying around. It's worth a shot."

Annie considered telling her about the drawings and her call to the storage company but decided against opening another can of worms. "What's going on around here?"

"Nothing much, pretty quiet. Samantha called a few minutes ago looking for you. She didn't sound happy."

"She's not. Listen, Cyn, I know I've been going back and forth on this London thing, but I need to know how you really feel about me being away during Thanksgiving."

"You need to go, that's how I feel about it. You'll kick yourself from here to Sunday if you miss her opening."

"Tell you what, I'll make it up to you. How about I treat you and Arthur to a romantic weekend in Vermont?"

"How about you creatin' a little romance in your own life instead of worrying about ours. We're doin' just fine in that department, thank you very much."

Inside her office, Annie opened her laptop and logged on. She had just enough time to book the flight and call Samantha with the good news.

Cynthia appeared in the doorway. "You got a brother stashed away somewhere I don't know about?"

Annie was checking her calendar against the dates scrolling down the screen. "Yeah, I keep him in the attic and bring him out for special occasions. Wait, why are you asking me that?"

"I took a call late yesterday afternoon, right before I was leaving. A man said he'd come across our website, that he was looking for a hospice for his brother. I started asking him the usual questions, when he was diagnosed, his T-cell count, what medications he's on, you know the kind of questions we ask."

"And?"

"And he answered them all, didn't stumble once. It was like he was reading them off a script."

"Maybe he was. Maybe he was looking at his brother's medical records and was prepared for the kind of questions he knew you'd ask."

"I've been doin' this for ten years and only once has someone been that prepared. He sure didn't sound like he had a brother who was dying. People who call here for the first time are in bad shape. They're feeling guilty and helpless that they're having to turn the care over to someone else. I spend the first ten minutes calming them down."

"Okay, so he's an exception. Maybe his brother was sitting there and he needed to keep it together for his sake."

"You got a short memory."

It took her a moment to connect the dots and Annie shook her head. "Oh, hell." Less than a day after their website was up and running, a man claiming to have a brother stricken with HIV called and kept Cynthia on the phone for over an hour, asking and answering her questions, probing her about the principals involved, their personal mission and even their finances. The next thing they knew they were being targeted by several fundamentalist Christian groups and **Life House** was viciously attacked in at least one publication under the title ***The Devil's Work***. Ten years later, they were still receiving hate mail. "Give me his number, I'll deal with him."

"That's the other thing, he wouldn't leave a number and he blocked it on his phone, came up as a private number."

"He was asking personal questions too? Is that how it came up about me having a brother?"

"He said he'd heard of you, maybe through your brother, thought maybe he'd met him somewhere."

"Did he happen to mention if my brother had a name?"

"Yes, he did. He said he couldn't remember his last name, but he thought his first name was Charles."

"What did you tell him?"

"Tell him? I didn't tell him anything. I hung up the phone. I also put a note by the phone warning everyone not to pick it up if the number is blocked. Should have done that a long time ago. If someone needs to reach us, they can darn well let us see where they're calling from. Otherwise, they can talk to the voicemail. Annie, you all right?"

"I'm good, although it's strange the name Charles popped up, don't you think?"

"I never even thought of that, never made the connection. It's a pretty common name, Annie. Our UPS man is named Charles."

"You're right, this whole thing is creeping me out. I'm going to the police sometime today."

The phone rang and Cynthia turned on her heel to answer it in her own office. As usual, she had the last word. "It's about damn time."

***

She was ten minutes early, but she needed the extra time to collect her thoughts. The timing of the phone call was weird but she'd convinced herself it was a coincidence. She even toyed with the idea of calling the storage place again, asking them if they called **Life House**, but decided to let it go. Anyway, she was sure she never gave them her office number. Cynthia was also right about the name Charles. It wasn't all that uncommon. Her uncle on her father's side was named Charles.

Inside the building, she found the directory next to the elevator and had to look twice before she found what she was looking for: Bryce Stanley, Attorney at Law. According to the smaller print below his name, his specialty was Estate Planning. In even smaller print below that, she finally saw what she was looking for: Stanley Properties, Inc. The suite number was the same, 202-203 on the second floor.

As she was being escorted into his private office, Annie was told he was finishing up a meeting in the conference room and would be with her shortly. A half hour later her patience was wearing thin. Ten minutes after that she was ready to leave when the door opened and Bryce Stanley walked through it.

She was prepared to rip him apart. What she wasn't prepared for was his striking good looks or the warmth of his smile as he reached for her hand.

"I'm Bryce Stanley. Sorry about the wait. What can I do for you, Mrs. Heywood?"

"It's Ms., Annabelle, Annie."

"Okay, Ms. Annabelle Annie, what can I do for you?" He paused. "Annabelle Heywood, why do I know that name?"

Crap. Since Luc's book, she rarely used her full name. Thankfully, the blowback from his tell-all had been relatively mild. A few raised eyebrows, a comment here and there, and the occasional reporter who promised her the sun, the moon and the stars in exchange for an interview, all of whom she shut down with three words. Wrong Annie Heywood. "You may have seen it on some escrow papers. I bought the home on Spinnaker Lane. I believe it was part of your family trust."

"There has to be a story behind why your parents named you Annabelle, other than the fact it fits you perfectly."

The flush she felt extended from her hairline down to her toes. Was he flirting with her? "I was named after my maternal grandmother. She passed away a week before I was born."

"You look familiar. Have we met, at a party perhaps?"

The question threw her. "I doubt that. I've hosted some charity events that you and your wife might have attended but…" Now he was laughing at her. "Did I say something funny?"

"The idea that my ex-wife would attend anything that didn't involve a red carpet and a gift bag is amusing."

"She must have done something right. Are those your boys?" She nodded at a silver-framed photograph on the credenza behind him.

"Twins. They're at Oxford. Your hair was different, longer. Were you ever a redhead?"

"That sounds like my sister Samantha."

He snapped his fingers. "That's it, Samantha Hogan. She's on that show in the U.K., what's it called?"

"Victoria Street."

"She plays the vixen, the American crime reporter."

Annie laughed. "Vixen, I haven't heard that expression in a while. She prefers to think of herself as the bitch who makes everyone else seem irritatingly saint-like."

"She does a good job of it. I was in London for a few months last year and got hooked on that damn show. Come to think of it, I heard a nasty rumor about her. I hope it's not true."

Nasty rumor? Her good mood vanished. If he brought up her sister's sexual orientation, he'd be wearing whatever was in the mug on his desk. "What rumor would that be, Mr. Stanley?"

"That she's leaving the show and concentrating on the theatre."

"Oh that. Not really. They have her character in a coma while she's doing a limited run as Desdemona. In Othello." No, she was playing Desdemona in the *Vagina Monologues*, you idiot. He was quite the Anglophile, his bookshelves filled with beautiful collections, everyone from Chaucer to Shakespeare.

"When does the run begin? If I'm over there, maybe I'll try to catch it. Are you going over for it?"

"I'm planning on it. It opens November 28th and ends in mid-January."

"You're prettier than she is. I suppose you've heard that before."

She'd heard it all her life but she didn't believe it then and she most certainly didn't believe it now. "No, I can't say I have. Look, I appreciate you seeing me and I'll try to make this brief. Twenty years ago, your family had a property manager named Bert Kennedy of Westport Properties. I tried the number on an old business card but it now belongs to a salon or day spa. Do you have any idea how I can reach him?"

"Bert Kennedy. I remember him. He was a funny little man, nervous, took his job very seriously as I recall. He passed away. Are you a relative of his?"

"No, I'm not a relative. You don't happen to know what happened to his business, do you?"

"He was the business, a one-man band. After he died, my brother took over management of the family properties for a few years, until he got bored, and then I stepped in. Most of the properties have been sold off anyway so there's really no need for a management company per se. What's this about?"

If she had to go through the story again, she'd throw up. Besides, the whole thing would sound ridiculous, like she had nothing better to do with her life. Not that it mattered what he thought. "I'm doing research for a book on Westport. I thought he might be a good source for information on the area. You wouldn't have any idea how he died, would you?"

"Heart attack, I think. If you'd like, I can make some phone calls and get back to you."

She'd forgotten to eat again and was feeling slightly off-balance. It didn't help that he was staring at her. She lowered her head, hoping the weakness would pass.

"Annie, are you all right?"

"I'm fine. I tend to be a little hypoglycemic."

"Do you have glucose pills with you?"

"Are you a doctor too?"

"One of my sons is hypoglycemic. Sit there, I'll be right back."

When he returned, he popped the top on a soda can and knelt down by her chair. "Here, sip this." Her hand was shaking when she tried to hold the can and he took it from her and put it to her lips, holding the back of her neck with his free hand. The intimacy of his touch sent a shockwave through her body and she took a quick intake of breath.

By the time he got to his feet and was behind his desk again, she was feeling better. "Thank you. I'll go have a seat in the waiting room for a few minutes so you can get back to work."

"You'll do no such thing. You'll sit there until I'm sure you won't fall down."

His tone was sharp and she felt the heat creeping up to her face and kept her head down.

"How do you like the house? Did you have to do much to it?"

"You've never seen the house, have you?"

"You have me there. I'm embarrassed to say I've never seen it but I'm probably the only man in Fairfield County who hasn't."

"What does that mean?"

"It's not important. Are there any problems with it?"

"None that I didn't know about before I purchased it, except maybe the driveway. It's pitched in the wrong direction and the run-off goes straight into the garage. It's something that should have been caught in the inspection. Anyway, it's not your problem."

"I've been known to take on a lot of issues that aren't technically my problem."

The silky smoothness of his voice combined with a look she could only describe as dangerous triggered something and she looked away. He was a player, the type that made a game of conquests. They bred like rabbits among the wealthy. No one was that good-looking or charming except when they wanted something. It was time to leave. "Of course you do, you're an attorney but I'm happy to say I don't have any issues."

"You have issues you're not even aware of but you're still adorable."

Getting to her feet, she grabbed her tote bag and made it to the door, relieved she didn't wobble. "Babies are adorable, puppies and kittens are adorable. I know your type, Mr. Stanley, and I've had my vaccination. I'm immune. Thanks for your time."

Back in her truck, she exhaled and dropped her forehead against the steering wheel. Puppies and kittens? It was now official; she'd lost the ability to be civil to any member of the opposite sex. Fuck you, Larry.

CHAPTER 21

RYAN

Ryan looked at the clock beside his bed then back at the ceiling. 6:13. For the better part of an hour, he'd been staring at the ceiling, thinking.

More often than not, this was the most productive part of his day, the time between waking up and a hot shower. It was as close as he would ever come to meditating, of letting go and allowing his thoughts to wander and explore, to peek into places he would not normally venture. He was too pragmatic to put much credence in remote viewing, even though it was rapidly gaining credibility with law enforcement. In the seminars, they referred to it as intuition. On a good day, Ryan called it instinct. Today he called it bullshit.

Maybe Sedona was the problem. The place wasn't laid back, it was comatose. Cody was the exception. He was as sharp as they come. Even with no sleep, his brain was working the angles, anticipating and moving forward. Ryan figured he'd last about a month before he ended up running through the scrub, drinking cactus juice and cooking rodents on a wooden spit.

He'd been there less than forty-eight hours and already he was losing his edge. He blew the call to the hospice and the woman hung up on him. The cardinal sin was his, over-preparation. His answers were rehearsed and slick, as if they were nothing more than a prelude to the question about Annie Heywood's brother. He should have delved deeper before making the call and done his homework on the women. It was no wonder she was guarded and skittish. Several sites beneath the **Life House** homepage, he found a link to an article that turned his stomach. It was in a fundamentalist Christian publication. He made it only halfway through the article before clicking off in disgust.

He'd give it another day or so and then try again, but this time he'd speak to the Heywood woman herself, find out what her story was. In the meantime, he was stuck there, at least until the remains were identified or they came up with another lead. The names Charles Hastings and Charles Tyrrell were run in California and Arizona with surprisingly few results, all of which were eliminated for one reason or another.

The masseuse was another dead-end. Susan Pierce never called her nor had she visited any of the other shops or restaurants at Tlaquepaque, at least as far as the shopkeepers could remember. Today the deputies were expanding their inquiries to the tourist traps, t-shirt and trinket shops, as well as local beauty salons. He wasn't holding his breath. If Susan Pierce had reverted to her reclusive ways, it was out of desperation, depression or maybe both.

Marcia Banning called him twice during the preceding twenty-four hours and during the second call he prepared her for the worst, even going so far as to ask if she could get obtain her sister's dental records. She was subdued at first then almost manic in her replies. By the end of the conversation, he was sure he could hear the dollar signs popping in her head.

Today he was on his own, at least until noon when he and Cody would hook up and try to refine their game plan. It was fine with him. He wanted to do some nosing around, maybe hit a few of the better hotels and resorts. If Charles Tyrrell was in Sedona the week before Christmas, there was a better than fifty-fifty chance he stayed at a hotel and rented a car.

That was another curious thing about the two cases, one he hadn't really considered in any depth. Neither Theresa nor Susan Pierce owned a car. His sister preferred a Vespa to more traditional modes of transportation, renting a car only when she needed to travel beyond her safety zone, and Susan Pierce was never issued a California driver's license. It was strange but there was very little about the two cases that wasn't. Susan Pierce could easily afford to hire a car and driver when she needed to get around and Theresa simply didn't give a damn about owning one. She liked the wind on her face and the freedom. If the weather was bad, she stayed in or she walked.

It was another item on the victim profile that may or may not be important. At this point, it was anybody's guess. If Cody had a plan to find out if there were any other victims, he was playing it close to the vest, uncharacteristically so. When he brought it up again, Cody put him off, assuring him he was working on it, whatever that meant.

He sat up and swung his legs over the side of the bed, rubbing his arms to get the circulation back. If his mood didn't improve, he'd find a way to beg off from the dinner invitation, and if that didn't work, he'd have to pick up a bottle of wine. Maybe someone would know what went with meat loaf. He sure as hell didn't.

CHAPTER 22

ANNIE

She hesitated only a second before nosing the truck to the left, the opposite direction from the Post Road and I-95, either of which would take her back to the office. Instead, she steered the vehicle through the familiar back roads to confront her past, a necessary step to putting it behind her.

Larry's acknowledgement of her birthday was unexpected but not nearly as unappreciated as she made it seem. It was a childish thing to do, tearing up the card and dismissing the gift, as if she were the injured party. It was she who wanted the divorce, not the other way around. So why was she still so angry?

She opened the window. How many times had she driven this same road, preparing herself for whomever would walk through the door? Sometimes it was Larry, the man she married, the one who could make her laugh with his pratfalls and horrible jokes; but for most of the marriage, it was the other one, the stranger who loosened his tie with one hand and mixed his martini with the other, the one she didn't recognize.

The farther she drove away from the center of town the larger the properties and homes. Architecturally, they were beautiful, oversized and obsessively maintained, but there was something cold about them, as if no one actually lived in them. She knew better. Behind the grand façades, there were children and dogs, spilled milk and dirty paw prints on the pricey limestone floors. She rarely saw children at play outdoors or kids shooting hoops.

This was back country Greenwich. Everything a child needed was in computer rooms and media rooms and bedrooms fit for royalty, their work and play monitored like specimens in a laboratory. In many ways they were royalty, little princes and princesses who would eventually ascend to their privileged places in the world.

She'd been inside many of the homes, several professionally, but more often than not for social occasions when Larry worked the room like a politician. Immensely popular, he was always the first asked to play golf or crew for a weekend of sailing. He was, after all, the Golden Boy, a self-made multi-millionaire by the age of thirty-five, the one who walked away from a lucrative law practice to pursue the **real** money. Of course, no one ever said that. To even allude to it was considered tasteless and tacky. One just assumed by the way one lived they had made it big.

It still amused her they took such pains to avoid the subject of money, all the while competing to see who could flaunt it the fastest and spend the most doing it. For many years it was home gyms, then wine cellars. The current rage was cigar rooms where the men retired with their port or brandy. Smoking was yesterday but cigars were in, Larry had quipped, and she needed to get on-board.

A Greenwich patrol car eased around her and she half-expected to be stopped and questioned. There were few pick-up trucks in this part of Fairfield County, except those belonging to the hired help. When he was well past her, she breathed a sigh of relief.

The house lay just ahead and she slowed. The monogrammed iron gates were a new addition, one they argued about before she left. As it turned out, she was right. They were ridiculous and pretentious. The library and billiard room were bad enough, but the gates were the deal breaker. At that point, he was out of control and she wanted off the bus before they crashed and burned.

A glimpse of black behind the gates caught her eye and she pulled off onto the shoulder. The gates weren't the only things he'd added since she left. A shiny new Ferrari was parked just outside the front door on the circular Belgian block driveway. She pulled up far enough to see the license plate: CARPE D M.

Well, good for him. He seized the day and lost his mind. Who said men couldn't multi-task?

She gave it another few minutes then smiled and whipped the steering wheel around, executing a near-perfect U-turn in the middle of the narrow road. It was the best twenty minutes she ever wasted. She felt vindicated, released from the guilt she'd carried for over two months. She hadn't left the marriage after all. He had chosen narcissism over love and had the toys to prove it. His daddy would be proud.

Samantha's words rang in her ears. *You need to lighten up on yourself, kiddo. You never had a prayer.*

***

"You been smilin' ever since you walked in here. Somethin' new you're not telling me about?"

"Well, let's see. Among other things, I learned I've lost the ability to have an intelligent conversation with the opposite sex and I'm okay with it."

"What's that supposed to mean?"

"It means bring it on. Did that guy call back, the one from yesterday?"

"No, but I'm ready for him if he does."

"Do me a favor, Cyn. Just this once, if he calls back and I'm not here, give him my home and cell phone numbers. I want to talk to him. We're not going to be blind-sided again."

"If you say so."

"I need to do a couple of things and then I'm headed back to Westport. I'll call you after I've talked to the police. Wish me luck."

"You don't need luck from me. You'll do just fine."

She booked her flight to London and wrote a quick e-mail to Samantha. Before logging off, she typed in a name and waited. There wasn't much there, a brief bio on Robert Gibson Stanley, the Stanley family patriarch until his death in 1998. It was his grandfather who amassed their fortune in the late 1800s, taking up tobacco growing in the Connecticut Valley near Windsor, a particularly good tobacco used for cigar wrappers still being grown. The profile mentioned two sons but gave names for neither. There was very little about the properties they owned and nothing of a personal nature. Evidently old money was more discreet than new money.

The website for Bryce G. Stanley, Attorney at Law, was even less informative, a photo and a brief description of his legal services, a textbook example of the less is more approach to marketing. With offices in Greenwich, Palo Alto and Santa Fe, all pricey locales, he was obviously doing well. She took a closer look at the photograph, surprised to see it wasn't retouched. Even the scar near his left eyebrow was visible. Piercing blue eyes looked right through her, much the same as they did when she was in his office. His features were in exactly the right proportion, lips full but not too full. The crowning glory was his hair, gunmetal grey brushed back off his face, a little longer in the back where it met his collar. What the photograph could not convey was the way he looked in his clothes, well-built and irritatingly masculine. He was the whole package, and he had the moves to go with it, touchy-feely stuff that would send most women swooning. So why was he practicing on her? Then again, why not her? His type rarely missed an opportunity to hone their skills on the local talent, even if she were a commoner.

She was still smiling when she closed her laptop. "Get over yourself, pal. You're not laying a paw on my issues."

Her meeting with Detective Saunders went well, much better than she anticipated. Besides being a hottie, he was interested and polite, nodding in all the right places. That he asked very questions she attributed to the fact that her narration was polished and precise, much more so than the day before. As planned, she left everything with him but the drawings, which she never mentioned. Walking her to the front door of the brick building, he thanked her and told her he'd keep in touch. Whether he did or not remained to be seen. At least he didn't fall asleep.

CHAPTER 23

RYAN

It was close to 5:00 when Ryan answered the knock on his door. Inside the dimly lit motel room, the television was tuned to a local station out of Flagstaff. At the bottom of the screen, the words **Breaking News** streamed across in red and yellow. The volume was down.

Cody collapsed in one of the two chairs. "I can't handle any more caffeine. You got anything stronger in here?"

Ryan handed off a pint of Jack Daniels he'd been nursing for the better part of an hour. After taking a long pull, Cody screwed the cap back on and set it on a side table. "Let's go easy on this stuff. Lita will skin both our asses if we show up for dinner hammered."

"So that's it. Susan Pierce walked out into the desert of her own free will and committed suicide by being eaten alive by the local wildlife. Why didn't we think of that? I could have been enjoying the sights for the two last days, maybe taken one of those jeep tours or hunted for little green men in the canyons. How'd they make the identification anyway? They haven't said a thing about that."

"They stopped the search around noon. Whatever was out there is scattered to the four winds. They got some prints off the hand, but she was never fingerprinted so that didn't do them any good. They'll send some skin samples for a DNA comparison with her brother and sister but that'll take time. It was the skirt, the one they found with the blood on it. I knew it the minute I saw it, same color suede with those little dangly things along the bottom. I had Carol O'Toole's photographs with me and there it was, big as life."

"And she's sure the skirt was one of a kind, not some mass-produced thing."

"Carol called the woman who made it, lives right here in Oak Creek. She only made one in that color. She'll swear to it."

"They're serious about not pursuing it as a homicide? They seriously believe she just wandered off?"

"Her sister and brother make a good case for it. I heard they were flying in."

"You just missed it, the interview with the grieving siblings. They could barely talk they were so broken up. Their sister was a saint but deeply unhappy. They blamed themselves. They knew she was troubled, talked about suicide all the time. They cut the interview short, claiming they needed some private time to grieve. Five minutes later, the lovely Mrs. Banning called and fired me."

Cody grinned. "Bet you never saw that coming. Did you tell her you had her on tape?"

"I was tempted, but I knew she'd claim the mystery man was a ruse to get me to take the case. She's a piece of work. We know she lied about what Maria Hernandez said to her on the phone. I half hoped Maria would crash the news conference and tell them what she knew."

"Maria Hernandez left town last night or early this morning. Her rental place is clean as a pin but she's gone. She say anything to you about leaving?"

"Does it matter? They've made their decision. Case closed."

"Look at it from their standpoint, Pete. They didn't find enough of her to determine a cause of death; no one saw a man or knew anything about one living with her here. Her own brother and sister claim she was unhinged and threatened suicide, and the only thing that might have given us any forensic evidence was burned down and officially written off as an electrical fire.

To top it off, it's an election year. The county prosecutor isn't about to open a case he can't close. Am I forgetting anything?"

"What about the couple in D.C., the ones who rented her the place here? She told them she was getting married."

"I'm betting her brother and sister will shoot that down quick, saying she was always making up stories, something like that. The last thing they want is a prolonged investigation. The sooner this thing is put to rest, the sooner they get their hands on her money."

They sat in silence, staring at the TV screen until, as if on cue, a replay of the interview with Marcia Banning and Raymond Pierce filled the screen. Ryan turned the volume up. Three minutes later, he hit the power button and the screen went to black.

Cody slapped his thighs. "Time to hit the trail. Look on the bright side, Pete. It's meatloaf night."

It took them almost twenty minutes on back roads, mostly dirt, but it was worth the trip. His first view of the property was an adobe wall that seemed to spring from the earth and wrap around it, melding seamlessly with the environs. Ryan recognized a few trees that surrounded the wall, Junipers and Cottonwoods mostly. Others, like the Crucifixion thorn and Hackberry, Cody pointed out on the ride over.

Inside a pair of high wooden gates, the house was even more impressive, low and sleek, nestled snugly against the base of a large rock formation.

Ryan gave a low whistle. "How the hell did you find this place?"

"Couldn't find it, that's why we built it, took us almost eighteen months. Got the land at auction. Some fool developer bought the land, thought it'd be a nice setting for some condos, even ran the power and water in. He went bust after six months. Now you know why we wanted to bring you out and take you back. We'd be sending out the choppers for you by tomorrow morning."

"You built this?"

"Not really all that tough when you've got eight women living in a mobile home. That can be pretty motivating."

The interior of the home was as beautiful as its exterior; but where the outside blended with the colors of the earth, the inside danced with color. Jewel tones of green, blue and burgundy leapt off the artwork and rugs, baskets and pottery, all handsomely displayed against whitewashed walls and polished wood floors. In the middle of the open plan, between the kitchen and great room, a fireplace took center stage. Made entirely of river rock and open to both rooms, it rose from the floor and pushed its way through the log ceiling.

The rooms adjoining the large open space were filled with activity. In one, a girl of about seven practiced her scales on an antique upright. In another, one of the sisters huddled in front of a computer while her sister did homework on the far side of a partner's desk. Others were busy in the kitchen or dining room. The house hummed with humor and purpose and Ryan felt his energy spike. With seven girls in the house, he expected a scene from *Little Women*, demure little things, all ruffles and lace, bent over embroidery hoops or books of poetry. Instead, he saw a well-oiled female machine, each young woman perfectly at ease with who she was, where she was going and the most efficient way to get there.

Lita greeted them warmly and took Ryan's raincoat. A television was on in a corner of the great room and the three of them turned toward it. They were airing the interview again, the one with Marcia Banning and Raymond Pierce. Pulling a remote from her pocket, Lita switched it off, turned back to them and deadpanned, "So how was your day?"

The dinner was delicious but Ryan was even more surprised by the level of conversation around the table. It was spirited and intelligent. No subject was off-limits, every question posed by one of the girls answered in a forthright manner by one or both of her parents. This was new to Ryan, the concept of a family in harmony, but he was enjoying it. When the subject eventually turned to Susan Pierce, he was ready.

The question came from the oldest, the future cop. "Mom said you were surprised they aren't investigating her death as a murder, Mr. Ryan. Do you think it's because she's a woman?"

At least he thought he was ready. "I'm not sure how to answer that. Under the circumstances, it wouldn't make any difference if it were a man or a woman. They don't believe they have the evidence."

"Don't you think they were a little quick in making that decision? Do you really believe if it were a man out there, they wouldn't have kept looking for him? Mom, what do you think?"

Lita smiled, reached over to her daughter and smoothed her hair behind her ear. "You know what I think, sweetheart, but I also think we need dessert."

The two older girls started clearing the table and another excused herself and left the room. When Ryan looked over a few minutes later, she was back in front of the computer.

When they were all seated again, one of the younger girls asked, "Daddy, what's a pandamenic?"

"I'm not sure I know that word, honey. Can you use it in a sentence?"

The girl frowned, concentrating on forming the words. "Hurting women is a pandamenic."

Cody turned to his wife. "I think you better take this one."

"The word is pandemic, honey, and it means widespread or all over the world, like a disease. What you heard me say was that violence toward women is a pandemic."

She accepted the explanation then asked, "But why?"

"I know." A new voice was added to the mix, one who was silent for most of the meal, watching and observing. Ryan couldn't remember her name but he knew she was nine years old.

"I think it started with the cavemen. One day they went out to kill something for food but they couldn't find anything and got mad. When they got back to the cave, one of the men wanted to use his club on something, so he beat up his wife. When she didn't pick up a rock and hit him back, he decided it was easier than sneaking up on a wild animal."

One of her younger girls started giggling. "That's silly. What did he do for food then?"

"He let the other men hunt."

Ryan put his head down so they wouldn't see him smiling. Her explanation made as much sense as anything else.

"Kara is our budding sociologist, Pete," interjected Lita.

"Anthropologist, mommy. I want to be an anthropologist."

"And you will be, sweetie, but let's not forget that for every bad man who hurts women, there are many more good men like your daddy and Mr. Ryan. You just have to learn to tell the difference."

Ryan nodded his thanks. He was glad he came and didn't make some last-minute excuse. Even his initial discomfort over the topic of violence was gone. Perhaps if Theresa had been part of this discussion in her formative years, she might still be alive. If, indeed, knowledge was power, there were seven young women who would not make the same mistakes she did.

"Do you like music, Mr. Ryan?" asked one of the girls.

"I love music."

"Do you play an instrument?"

Seeing only a piano, Ryan figured he was safe. "I play the violin, the fiddle actually."

Before he could protest, several pairs of hands were dragging him into the great room, pushing him into a chair in front of the fire. One of the girls produced a violin and handed it to him as if it were a precious gift. It seemed to be in perfect tune and he lifted it to his chin.

He was tentative at first, but after a few seconds, he closed his eyes and let the strings convey the emotions he kept submerged. It was an Irish ballad, as old as heartbreak itself. He played it for Theresa and Susan Pierce, for Maria Hernandez and the eight women seated around him. He played it for the women who had loved him, the ones he'd pushed away. But mostly he played for himself. It was the one time when his soul was completely at peace, when he could channel his anger into passion.

The next tune was more upbeat. Halfway through the second piece, he sensed a change in the room and opened his eyes.

One of the girls was standing in the doorway of the room with the computer. She looked flushed. "Mom, Dad, Mr. Ryan, I think you'd better come and take a look at this."

Reaching the computer first, Lita gently moved her daughter aside and took the chair. Ryan and Cody moved in to stand behind her.

Ryan bent down and peered over Lita's shoulder. "What am I looking at?"

Cody motioned him to a corner of the room. "Kim set up a link to Lita's chatroom for abused women, the one I mentioned yesterday. It was Lita's idea. You said you wanted to know if there were any other victims that fit the profile. I'm not sure how the damn thing works but they set up a link to an email address in your name so victims or their families could contact you directly. It's posted on the website."

"We just talked about this yesterday. Your daughter did this? She's what, sixteen or seventeen?"

"She's sixteen and she's been using a computer since she was four. She's also been designing websites and fixing computers for folks around here for the last two years."

Ryan looked at Lita and Kim, then back at Cody. "I don't know what to say. Help me out here."

Cody clapped him on the shoulder. "Don't thank us yet, Pete. You're still a long way from tracking the monster down, but you will. And after you do, you might want to come back, take some vacation time and look for those little green men, maybe play the fiddle again."

"Pete, let me show you what Kim's done," Lita said from across the room. She turned to her daughter. "You did good, sweetheart. You're my girl."

The homepage of the website was no-frills, simple and easy to navigate. With a header that read ***Are You a Potential Victim?***, it laid out a simple point-by-point profile of the type of woman likely to be targeted by their predator. Beneath the bulleted points, the two known cases involving Theresa Ryan and Susan Pierce were summarized, their identities and locations concealed by fictitious names. At the very bottom of the page was an email address.

After familiarizing him with the site, Lita rose from the chair. "As of five minutes ago, you had seventy-three emails, and the site's only been up and running three hours. Don't get your hopes up. Over half of them will be hoaxes or worse. We get them all the time. Others will be family members of women who've gone missing. The women they're writing you about won't fit your profile but they're so hungry for answers they'll clutch at anything, say anything in the hope that someone will listen and help them. Most people don't realize that at any given time close to twenty thousand women in this country are missing. I don't know any other way to do this and limit the number of responses you'll get. Looks like you have your work cut out for you. Let me know how we can help." She handed him a printed copy of the web page. "I wrote our email address on there for you too."

Rarely at a loss for words or a quip, Ryan was speechless. He simply couldn't find the words. "I don't know what to say."

Lita's smile was warm but her eyes held a sadness he hadn't seen before. "Say you'll find the bastard."

"That's a given. With a support group like this, failure's not an option."

Cody joined them. "Where do you go from here?"

"I'm headed back tomorrow morning. I was going to drive but now I think I'll fly." He held up the printed copy. "I've got my work cut out for me. All I need is one good lead."

Turning to Cody, Lita kissed him on the cheek. "You look beat. Why don't you tuck the girls in and go to bed. I'll drive Pete back to his hotel. I won't be long."

Cody shook Ryan's hand. "Stay in touch, my friend, and stay safe."

They drove most of the way in silence until Lita asked, "Where'd you learn to play the violin? You're very good."

"My mother's brother. He came over from Ireland once a year and brought his fiddle."

"You're full of surprises."

"That's me."

"I had a visit this morning from Maria Hernandez. She left Sedona. She's moving to San Francisco. You wouldn't have anything to do with that, would you?"

"I hardly know the woman."

"Then I guess you wouldn't know anything about the thousand dollars she gave me for the women's shelter."

"Nope."

"I know all about the money, Pete. Don't worry, your secret's safe with me. You know, when this whole thing is finally over, you might want to consider joining a police force in, oh I don't know, a picturesque town in the middle of nowhere? I'm pretty close with the Chief of Police and I could put in a good word for you."

"This place is growing on me, but I don't think I could ever leave the Bay area."

"Because of your sister?"

"Something like that."

She pulled up in front of the hotel and turned off the ignition. "They're both gone, Pete. Your father can't hurt her anymore."

Ryan looked out the side window into the darkness. "How do you know about that?"

"I hear him and I lock my soul in a shiny silver box. My heart beats and I will it to be still. He is the mist that hides the moon and haunts the sun. I am lost."

"I don't know what that means."

"It's from her first book, *Hummingbird*. With those thirty-eight words, your sister described the horror of child molestation. Have you read any of her books, even the ones about her childhood?"

"Why should I? I lived it."

"Did you?"

"Look, Lita, I'm grateful for everything you've done, more than you'll know, but can we talk about this some other time?"

"How old was she, eight or nine when it started? I was ten."

"I don't get this. How can you even think about it, let alone discuss it with a stranger?"

"You ate my meat loaf and didn't bat an eye. Only a friend would do that. Come on, Pete, what should I do, be like you and cloak myself in a black shroud and hope it will conceal the pain? Wounds don't heal if they're wrapped too tightly. What happened to us was dark and foul. Theresa brought it into the light and aired it out."

"My sister trusted three men in her life and they all betrayed her."

"I know about your father and the man who murdered her. I assume you think you're the third."

"She was seven when I turned eighteen and joined the army. Our mother died a year later. I knew our old man was a mean drunk but I had no idea what he'd do to her. She was eleven when I got back. It'd been going on for two years. She was nine years old. I didn't find out about it until several years after that. By that time, the old man was dead. I should have known about it. Why didn't she tell me?"

"Keeping secrets is what we do, Pete. We're ashamed and frightened and we think it's our fault. Child molesters are vile but they're also smart. They can smell the fear and humiliation and they use it, manipulate it. I slept in a room with two of my sisters and he still found a way to get me alone and tell me I was his precious girl, that no one could ever find out that he loved me more, that it would break my mother's heart and tear the family apart."

"Lita, for God's sake…"

"Did you think this kind of thing only happened in big cities or when there was a drunk in the house? My father never touched a drop of alcohol. He was the pastor of the Baptist church in our village."

"How the hell have you managed to have a normal life? Most people would kill to have your marriage and seven well-adjusted kids."

"That was the easy part. I found the person with the key."
"What key?"
"The key to the shiny silver box."

PART TWO

CHAPTER 24
ANNIE

Annie slammed the door and rammed the key in the ignition. In the building behind her, another man lay bleeding in the dust. They were dropping like flies.

He came to her nine years ago, the ink still wet on his Accounting degree, begging for a chance to prove himself. He knew about their work at **Life House** and wanted to be a part of it, gratis if he had to. The experience would be great, and if she was satisfied with his work, she could refer him to a few of her friends. She hired him on the spot but insisted he be paid the going rate. She'd do her part by sending him monthly reports, bank statements and staying on top of expenses. Her brief to him was short and sweet: keep an eye on their cash flow, keep them on track and out of jail. Today, he had a staff of thirty, a luxurious suite of offices in Darien and a *Who's Who* client list, many of whom were her referrals.

Typically, they would speak by phone once a month, analyzing disbursements and making corrections that didn't involve the health or emotional security of their guests. If a shortfall loomed, it was easier to raise funds a little at a time than making a pitch for the "big money". They hadn't spoken in months and her attempts to reach him by phone were annoying but not necessarily a predictor of doom. At the very least, he would email her or call to set up their quarterly meeting. Not this time. It was she who insisted on the meeting.

The tip-off came when she arrived for the meeting and found herself in a windowless office opposite a stranger, a fresh-faced minion who was unprepared, unprofessional and unapologetic. Without so much as an introduction, he rushed into the room, pulled her file from a stack on his desk and announced that **Life House** was in trouble. Her last four monthly reports had been misplaced until that very morning, a euphemism for *look around you, lady, this is a big fancy pond and you're nothing but a little fish, a non-profit fish at that.*

Once again she had chosen the bliss of ignorance and once again it was coming back to bite her in the ass, only this time it involved the lives of others. For the past four months, they were flying blind. That they were being sucked into the engines of a 747 was the last thing she expected. The bottom line was bad. Without an infusion of cash, **Life House** would be forced to close its doors in six months.

Taking it in, Annie sat stock-still. She wasn't completely naïve when it came to their financial exposure. For the past two years, the cost of everything had risen, fuel for the van, medications, but especially the property taxes, almost double what they were the previous year. What might have prevented the disaster was if someone had been monitoring things, the someone who now occupied a corner office and was too busy to return her phone calls. After a few minutes, the only sound she heard was the beating of her heart.

She had two choices. She could thank him for his time and leave with her dignity intact or she could make a scene, something she might regret. Whichever way it went, the nasty little man in front of her was just the messenger, and a lousy one at that.

Gathering up her things, she left his office without a word. On her way through the reception area, instead of walking straight through the double glass doors and into the parking lot, she veered right. Marty's office was the last one on the left and she burst through the door, stopping just inside. She expected him to be perturbed, maybe a little embarrassed. What she was not prepared for was his look of shock or the contempt on the faces of the couple seated across from him.

She recognized the couple immediately, the Prescotts, her former neighbors, the ones Larry courted like a dog in heat, the ones she avoided like a virus. They were the dregs of the ruling class, the kind who spent their considerable time and money keeping the country clubs restricted and the neighborhoods white. The husband, a former Enron board member who had the bad taste to boast of it, helped put the *con* in conservative and his wife was worse, narrow-minded and brittle.

Annie smiled and feigned surprise, briefly touching her hand to her lips. "Oops, sorry, but I have a message for Marty," she said to the couple before turning her gaze to her former friend and accountant. "I ran into Seema at the DNC fund-raiser the other night and she wanted me to thank you for the generous donation. Oh, and Derrick wanted me to remind you he's holding your spot at the NAACP convention next July if you're still up for giving a speech." As a final parting gift, she blew him a kiss and closed the door.

Back in her truck, she took several deep breaths. By evening, Greenwich would be abuzz and Larry would be vindicated for his failed marriage. His ex-wife was not only a bleeding heart do-gooder, she was something worse, a Democrat.

Her dark mood continued until she pulled into Spinnaker Lane where it darkened appreciably. A truck was blocking her entrance to the driveway, a big freaking truck, its backend pointed toward her house. She put the truck in neutral and set the parking brake before getting out. The noise from a jackhammer was deafening. Squeezing her way between the truck and the shrubbery, she advanced as far as she could and came to an abrupt stop. Her driveway was gone, reduced to a pile of black chunky rubble in the bed of the truck. The noise stopped but she remained rooted to the spot.

One of the men saw her and approached. "You Miss Heywood?"

She opened her mouth to speak but nothing came out.

He handed her a sealed envelope and turned away to give her a moment of privacy. She opened it and pulled out an ivory card with a single initial engraved in black. *Hope you're remembering to eat. Dinner one night? You're still adorable.* It was handwritten and signed *Bryce*.

Annie replaced the card in the envelope. "Please put it back."

The man stepped closer, thinking he'd misunderstood. "Ma'am?"

"The driveway, I want it back."

"I can't do that, Miss Heywood. We've already broken it out. You can't put down broken asphalt. Anyway, Mr. Stanley's one of my best customers. We do all his commercial work. As it is, I'm about a week late. He called me last week and said to get over here, that it was urgent because your garage was flooding when it rained. He was right. Your driveway was pitched in the wrong direction. Ma'am?"

She was staring in the direction of two neatly-stacked piles partially covered by a tarp. "What's that?"

Visibly puffing himself up, the man smiled, obviously pleased with himself. "Belgian block, the best they make. I handpicked it myself."

She put her fingers to her temples, closed her eyes and hoped when she opened them she'd still be in bed and the entire day was one long nightmare. No such luck. "I'm sorry, I didn't catch your name."

"It's Harold, Harold Sawyer. I own the company."

Stepping up beside him, she looped her arm through his, gently maneuvering him so he had an unobstructed view of the house. "What do you see, Harold?"

"A house?"

"What kind of house?"

"A farmhouse?"

Close enough. "That's right, a farmhouse, not some gaudy neo-classical nightmare or faux Mediterranean monstrosity with a cigar room and a billiard room and stupid iron gates with my initials on them."

His mouth opened as if to say something then clamped it shut.

"Never mind. Here's what you're going to do. You're going to load up all that Belgian block and take it to your house or Mr. Stanley's house or back to the yard where you bought it, and tomorrow you're going to replace the asphalt on my driveway, pitch it in the right direction, and then you're going to give me an invoice for which I'll write you a check. Okay, Harold?"

"Sorry, I can't do that."

"Can't do what?"

"Can't do any of it. Mr. Stanley will have my ass."

"Now listen carefully. I've had a bad day, a really bad day, and the only thing I wanted was to come home, play with my dog and lock myself in the house so I wouldn't be tempted to go out and shoot someone. But guess what? I can't get to my home because what was my driveway is now rubble in that big fucking truck in the middle of the road. So here's your choice. You either agree to everything I've laid out or I go inside and call the police. I own this house and you're trespassing, no, make that vandalizing my property. And if you're worried about Bryce Stanley coming here and getting upset that you haven't done what he asked, get over it. He's never going to know because he's never coming here."

Something resembling sympathy touched his face and he nodded. "I get it. You two had a fight and he's trying to do something nice, you know, like get back in your good graces."

"A fight? You have to be together to have a fight. We're not together. We've never been together. I've met the man once."

He looked around for a place to run but she held him fast. When he realized he couldn't get away from her, he exhaled. "I may only be an employee of his but I've known him almost thirty years. My dad owned this company before me and worked for Mr. Stanley's old man. We go way back. I've never known him to pull me off a job to do something personal and believe me, lady, this is personal."

She didn't want to hear any more. If she had to process another revelation, she'd lose it. Even worse, she was taking out her anger on the wrong person. "Okay, Harold, you win. We'll do it your way, everything but the block. I promise I'll make sure Mr. Stanley knows you tried to carry out his wishes. Deal?"

He seemed satisfied with the compromise but evidently felt compelled to give it one more shot. "You sure you don't want it?"

With a sidelong glance toward the covered stacks, she nodded. "I'm sure."

Einstein was waiting for her just inside the door, clearly upset at the noise and the fact he was missing all the action. It was his domain after all and he didn't appreciate being left out of the loop. Annie soothed him and together they walked back outside with three bottles of water for the men. After adding his own voice to the melee and receiving the appropriate number of pats and rubs, he seemed content to follow her back inside the house.

Her phone chimed, alerting her to voicemails. Word traveled fast. There were three, one each from Cynthia, Marty and Larry, presumably all calling for different reasons but the same assumption, that she was in meltdown. A lot they knew. Somewhere between her missing driveway and the side door, she came out of disaster mode, her survival instincts on high-alert, her mind racing with ways to solve the financial crunch.

The house was the solution. It was fully paid for and she could refinance it, take the proceeds less the down payment and Keep **Life House** solvent for several years; or she could sell it outright and find a smaller place. Either way, the money problems would go away, at least temporarily. She'd have a mortgage payment to deal with but she had that covered. Interior Design was her fallback. She left the business on a high note and referrals were still coming in. Only this time she'd be smart about it. She didn't need to write a hefty rent check for a storefront when she had two empty rooms upstairs.

Her days of being the *socialite designer* were behind her, a whispered moniker she fought from day one. Done right, interior design was a lot of work and not a hobby, but she understood why some thought otherwise. She would target her marketing elsewhere, Westport and Weston where she was relatively unknown. After today, Greenwich was off-limits.

Good, that was settled. Inertia was a killer, a devourer of the spirit. She'd learned the hard way that action, almost any action, was preferable to complacency. But this decision felt right, so right in fact that she picked up the phone and played back her messages.

Evidently Cynthia didn't get the news. She was chipper and upbeat, just checking in and letting her know everything was fine. The other two calls from Larry and Marty were strange and she played them both again. The accountant apologized for not meeting with her himself, made no allusion to her earlier performance, and suggested she approach Larry for the money to put **Life House** back in the black. Given that he knew almost nothing about their relationship since the divorce, it was an odd thing to propose. Even stranger was Larry's phone call offering her the money. In and of itself, the offer wasn't out of character but the terms he tacked on right before hanging up made her wince. Knowing her, she would want to keep it professional so she could always use the **Life House** property as collateral.

So that was it. The boys had buddied up and, if her suspicions were correct, there was someone else in the playpen with them. She pulled a business card from her notebook. Owen Chandler, Chandler Development. For months, he'd been buying up homes adjacent to **Life House**, beautiful older properties either handed down to a generation that didn't appreciate them or maintained by the elderly who struggled to afford them. She was privy to some of the details and didn't trust him, telling him as much when he showed up one day sniffing around the property, a vulture with a Hermes briefcase. If she had to hock every last thing she owned, she would hold on to **Life House** and its precious two acres. Owen Chandler could take his plans for a condominium development and executive retreat and go straight to hell, along with his two new pals.

She wasn't sure which was worse, that Larry was capable of selling her out or he thought she was stupid. In the end, it was probably a draw. In their years together, she'd done very little to disabuse him of his belief that he could get away with almost anything. He was who he was, the guy who never missed an opportunity. As for Marty, he did his job, keeping her in the dark until her options were limited.

The truck was heading out for the day and she watched it go, happy for the silence. Long after it was out of view, she kept her eyes on the narrow road, lost in thought. She should have been angry or hurt but she felt neither. Determined, yes, but angry? Not so much. After awhile, she picked up her phone. In spite of the fact that her past kept tugging at her, she had to keep moving forward. Baby steps were for toddlers. She had to sprint.

Her first call was to Cynthia and she filled her in on the meeting, their money issues and how she intended to fix them. Knowing her friend would blow a gasket over Larry's part in their financial mess, she left that part out, simply stating that she was replacing their accountant. If Cynthia inferred anything from their conversation, she kept it to herself.

She looked at her watch, surprised at how the afternoon had flown. It was after five, closing time for most businesses, but at least she could get the ball rolling by contacting her realtor. Kay would have a handle on which lending institutions to approach, the ones best suited to her needs. When her phone went to voice-mail, Annie left a message.

Detective Saunders was next on her hit list. It was a week since they met, long enough to review the information and make some inquiries. Despite her best efforts to let the whole thing go, Debra was on the periphery of everything she did, making her presence known when she least expected it. After dialing Saunders' number, she looked over her shoulder to the refrigerator where the drawings were held in place by tiny magnets. She felt guilty for not sending them off to Debra's cousin but every day it became more difficult to part with them.

He was working on it, the detective assured her, and thanked her for her interest before hanging up. Her interest? She wasn't reporting a jaywalker. It was a murder investigation. For the second time that day, she felt the sting of a brush-off. That this time it was done with polite indifference and not arrogance made it no less irritating.

Her last phone call was to Bryce Stanley, and even as she punched in his number, she had no idea what to say to him. She should probably apologize for her behavior in his office but she'd play that part by ear. As far as the driveway was concerned, she was torn. Half of her saw his gift as pushy and presumptuous, but then there was the other half, the squishy half that appreciated the gesture.

After several rings, a female voice answered the phone, identifying herself as Bryce Stanley's assistant. Annie gave her name, and judging by the woman's over-the-top response, was sure she'd been prepared for the call. Several minutes of chit-chat later, she was advised that Bryce was on his way to London. It was a last-minute thing, a soccer injury sustained by one of his sons. She could call him at his flat or on his cell phone if she would like those numbers. Annie demurred on both, offered the requisite wishes for his son's speedy recovery and thanked the woman for her kindness. She felt immensely relieved.

Behind her, Einstein let loose with several sharp barks followed by a low growl. Annie turned, expecting to see someone at the side door. What she saw was a flash of blue and someone running away from the house toward the road. She managed only a glimpse before he disappeared behind the dense trees but she could tell he wasn't very tall, about her height, and young judging by the way he moved.

Taking her time, she walked through the other ground floor rooms and looked out the windows. There were reports of minor vandalism around town and she wasn't taking any chances that he'd left some companions behind. Other than deliveries or unscheduled workmen, there was no reason for anyone to venture down the lane and run away as if his life depended on it.

On her way back to the kitchen, she peered through one of the windows toward the side porch. There was a box, long and white, tied with a large red bow that wasn't there a half hour ago. Retrieving it, she set the box in the middle of the kitchen table and stared at it. Either someone was trying to make amends or Stanley got wind of her rebuff and decided to pursue a more traditional courting ritual. Whichever it was, she wasn't in the mood.

It was only after removing the ribbon that she noticed the name of the florist was nowhere on the box, no label, no engraving, nothing. Puzzled, she eased the top off and folded back the tissue. Inside were a dozen white lilies, the petals dry and withered, the stems limp. Along the inside edge of the box, she found a small white card, the message and signature printed as if done on a computer.

She watched it slip from her fingers and flutter to the floor. Time slowed down even as her heart raced. She kept her eyes averted, looking anywhere and everywhere but at the card. Somewhere far away, she registered the ringing of a phone but was powerless to move, held fast by the words etched deep inside her head.

CHAPTER 25
RYAN

Ryan let the phone ring until it went to voicemail and hung up. Either Annie Heywood was dodging his calls or he missed her. According to the Fredericks woman with whom she'd spoken a few minutes prior, she was home.

He should have tried harder to ingratiate himself with Cynthia Fredericks, maybe come clean about his investigation, but there was an edge to her voice that stopped him cold. She was obviously following some agreed upon scenario, giving him her partner's cell and home numbers, but he sensed she was none too happy about it.

Ever since his return from Arizona a week ago, he'd put off calling the hospice again, hoping to put a little time and distance between his first attempt, an unqualified disaster. He even considered unblocking his number this time around but he wasn't prepared to do that yet. It was too easy to trace an address from a phone number. If and when he came face-to-face with his quarry, it would be on his terms.

The more he thought about it, the more the incident smelled like a red herring. The fact that Heywood never followed up with the storage company made a strong case for it. Maybe she was just what she appeared to be, a woman with a brother named Charles who'd gone off to Europe and left her holding the bag, dealing with their family's property. By now she might have reached him and had the name of the right facility or…or what?

He turned a sour glance to the yellow lined tablet before him and noted Annie Heywood's name, phone number and the time. Frustrated, he ripped the page off the pad and added it to the pile on the right side of his desk, the one designated for follow-up. It was the closest thing he had to any real system and it sucked.

As much as he hated to admit it, he needed help. A mere twenty-four hours after arriving back in San Francisco, the number of responses to the website had tripled, increasing exponentially with each successive day. At last count, there were well over a thousand. After almost a week of plowing through them, he hadn't made a dent. Still, the idea appalled him, having to share his space with someone. Other than Jimmy and his brief liaison with Cody, he preferred working alone. It was another inside joke among his former fellow officers: *Didn't Play Well with Others* would be chiseled into his grave stone.

Getting to his feet, he stretched and walked to the window. His ass hurt and his eyes stung, a condition he attributed to the poor quality of his computer. Purchased over a decade ago, it was large, slow and temperamental, just like him.

He tensed and looked toward the door. He could have sworn he heard something in the hall. It was a small sound but one that didn't belong there. He was alone on the floor, at least he should have been. Easing back around the desk, he slid open the bottom drawer and retrieved his service weapon, a SIG Sauer P226, his eyes fixed on the slice of light beneath the door. A commotion on the street below diverted his attention and he looked back toward the window. The entire episode lasted only seconds but when he glanced back down an envelope lay half in, half out of the office. He covered the distance in two long strides and opened the door. The hallway was empty but he distinctly heard footsteps in the stairwell.

For a minor fender-bender, the ensuing dust-up between the drivers was drawing a crowd and Ryan spotted her standing apart from the group, taking it in. Careful not to frighten her, he touched her lightly on the shoulder. "Welcome to the big city. I see you made it."

Maria Hernandez turned and smiled. "I would have knocked but I didn't hear anything so I assumed you were out or busy."

"I was practicing my impression of Dirty Harry."

She seemed to find that funny and Ryan waited until her laughter stopped. "Mark Hopkins, pretty fancy. I was hoping they'd give you a job at the café."

"They did offer me a job but I wasn't comfortable there. The people are very nice and I love Maria, but it's too public. I'm not sure I'm ready for that yet."

"I should have thought of that."

"I don't mind housekeeping. Thanks to you, I had a good letter of recommendation from Helping Hands and the Mark Hopkins hired me right away."

Ryan held up the envelope and check. "I thought we agreed this wasn't a loan."

"You're a generous man, Mr. Ryan, but I can't take your money. I plan to pay the other five thousand back when I can."

"Four thousand and you don't owe me a penny. I know about the check you gave Lita for the shelter. I like her but she can't keep a secret worth a damn." When he tried to give her back the check, she shook her head and he stuffed it in his pocket. "You on your way to work?"

"I'm finished for the day. I work the six to two shift."

An uncomfortable silence floated between them and Ryan inclined his head toward the building. "I have to get back upstairs. I'm expecting some phone calls and I need to find someone to fix my damn computer." He was about to end the conversation when he remembered seeing a computer in her Sedona rental, a pretty sophisticated set-up. As quickly as the idea occurred to him, asking her to take a look at his antiquated system, he nixed it. She already felt obligated to him and he didn't want to take advantage of that.

"What's wrong with it?"

"What's wrong with what?"

"Your computer. You said you were getting someone in to fix it."

"It's a pain in the ass. I hate the damn things."

"So you have no idea what's wrong with it."

"Not a clue."

Upstairs in his office, Maria removed her coat and folded it over the back of one of the chairs. He waited for her to make a comment about the age and size of his monitor but, to her credit, she did neither, nor did she seem to notice the mess on his desk that passed for a filing system. When she was comfortably settled in, she hit a few keys and turned to him. "It's frozen up. I'm going to reboot."

"If that's computer talk for kicking it across the room, be my guest."

Between small talk, Ryan answered her questions about his specific needs and watched, fascinated, as she brought the machine back to life. Her actions were precise and not the least bit tentative. "So when you're not cleaning houses and hotel rooms, you're what, a cyber-superwoman?"

She took her eyes off the screen long enough to smile at him. "No offense, Mr. Ryan, but a gifted ten-year-old could have fixed this."

"Speaking of gifted kids, have you talked to Lita since you got here? I'm sure she'd like to know you're okay."

"I spoke with her a couple of days after I arrived. I needed her advice."

Ryan waited. She seemed on the verge of explaining herself but he didn't want to push her. Finally, after a few minutes, she dropped her head. "I don't understand. How could everyone dismiss Susan Pierce's death as a suicide?"

"Not everyone did, just the people in charge."

"That day in Sedona, when you came to my house, you said I may be the only person who knew she wasn't alone in the house. You think I should have come forward, don't you?"

"I'm not sure it would have made a difference. Evidently there were other things at play, like greed and politics." He was tempted to let it go at that. Now that he'd let her off the hook, she could finish up and leave. "Did Lita tell you about the website?"

"Yes, but only in connection with my concern over Susan Pierce's murder and whether or not I should go to the police with what I knew." She stopped speaking and waved her hand over the unruly stacks of paper in front of her. "Is that what this is all about?"

"I'm afraid so."

"Maybe I could give you some help, file some of it away or make some phone calls."

"If you want a job, just ask. If you want absolution, go see a Priest."

"I have a job but thank you for the offer."

"I apologize. That was out of line. You were the only one who cared enough to try and help her."

She looked back at the computer screen, made a few more moves with the mouse and pushed away from the desk. "I've done about as much as I can on this but it's still very slow. You might consider getting a new one. I can come back and transfer your files, get it up and running. The newer ones have much thinner monitors which will give you more room on your desk." She hesitated a moment before asking, "Are these all responses to the website?"

"Most of them. I print everything out and separate them based on how legit they sound. Ninety-five percent don't fit the profile. Some are bored crime-junkies and a few of them are looking for advice on dating. One of them said Charles sounded cool. With the other five percent, I try to get their phone numbers so I can follow up, engage them, get them talking."

The phone rang and he motioned for her to stay seated. The call turned out to be a woman who supplied her number and for whom he left a message earlier that day. The call lasted only a few minutes before the woman ended it abruptly.

Ryan put the phone back on the desk and did a double-take at Maria's horrified expression. "What?"

"Is that your idea of engaging them? These women are reaching out, Mr. Ryan. You're asking them to trust you and then you're speaking to them like they're suspects, not victims. If I were on the other end of the phone, I'd have hung up on you too."

"In case you've forgotten, this is a murder investigation, not a hot-line for the romantically-challenged. I don't have time to be warm and fuzzy. This guy could be out there right now, working on his next victim."

Maria was on her feet. She leaned in to face him across the desk, her eyes ablaze. "Then get someone in here who does have the time. Regardless of whether or not they fit the profile, they're in pain." She grabbed the pile of papers off his desk and waved them in front of his face. "And while you're at it, get someone to set up a filing system for you."

"And you learned all this where, at the Days Inn School of Interrogation and Procedures?"

She lowered her eyes to slits and lashed him with an endless harangue in Spanish. By the time she finished, she had her coat on and was reaching for the door knob.

"Ouch."

She whipped around. "You speak Spanish?"

"I caught the suggestion of a place to shove my computer when I get a new one."

"I apologize for that."

"I've heard worse."

Glaring at him, she leaned back heavily against the door.

Ryan suspected she knew he'd been goading her, but he also knew she was buying time, trying to determine how much of her tirade he understood. Keeping his face expressionless, he pulled a set of keys from a desk drawer walked and toward the door. When Maria stepped aside, he opened it and headed across the hall, using one of the keys to access the office across from his. Inside, he went directly to the window and opened it, allowing the cool afternoon air to circulate and cleanse the room of stale cigar smoke.

"The guy who had this office died a month ago. His kids came in and cleaned it out, everything but the desk and chair. I have an account at the office supply store around the corner. Charge whatever you need but make sure you get a good computer and printer and don't even think about bringing in your personal one. You'll need it after hours.

"The job pays a thousand a week and I'll cover your health insurance." He took her check from his pocket and ripped it up. "We'll consider this a signing bonus but don't thank me yet. Other than Cody, I haven't worked with anyone for five years and there's a good reason. I like it that way. Any questions?" He dangled the office keys in front of her. "Time to step up or shut up, Maria. You think you can do a better job with the website, here's your chance to prove it."

When she didn't take the set of keys, he laid them on the edge of the old oak desk. "Use my office until you get the phones hooked up in here. Everything you need to know, including my password, is on a piece of paper in the center drawer. Lock up when you leave. The blue key is for my office. The cleaning service locks the downstairs door when they're finished around eight."

She took the keys from the desk and held them tightly in her hand. When she turned around toward his office, he was putting on his coat. "Where are you going?"

"Somewhere quiet where I can think, where I can get a cup of coffee in something other than 60% post-consumer recycled fiber and something to eat that doesn't have to be scraped off a piece of plastic. And then I'm going to follow up on everything I should have been following up on for the past week. Let me know when you get the phones hooked up in the other office."

"But that could take days, maybe even weeks." She walked back into his office and stood in front of his desk. "Exactly what am I supposed to do with all of this?" When he threw her a look, she put her hand up. "I'll figure it out."

"Good answer, and before I forget, there's a gun in the bottom drawer. Try not to shoot yourself."

Before he even made it to the stairwell, he heard the door slam behind him. Ryan allowed himself a grin. That went well.

On the street, he walked briskly at first and then slowed. Maybe it went a little too well. Something was nagging at him, not so much anything she said but rather a look in her eyes. If he didn't know better, he would swear it was she who set him up. And if he really thought about it, he could swear he saw Lita's fine hand in things. *Give him a week to realize he's in over his head and then drop by. But whatever you do, let him think it's his idea.*

Sonofabitch, he wasn't just off his game, he wasn't even in the right league. On the other hand, what difference did it make whose idea it was? He needed to spend time out of the office and he needed help with the website. As for Lita, the damn woman should have come with a warning label. Thank God she was Roland's problem.

He changed his mind about the coffee and food. What he needed was a drink, preferably in a Sports Bar, somewhere testosterone had a fighting chance against estrogen.

CHAPTER 26

ANNIE

"It's a threat. Read the card. It's there inside the baggie. I thought you could check it for fingerprints or DNA or whatever. I touched it when I first opened the box and dropped it on the floor, but I was very careful about handling it when I picked it up."

Mike Saunders reached inside the open floral box on his desk and pulled out a plastic bag. He flicked his eyes briefly toward another man whom Annie didn't recognize and back at the card. "Debra is at peace. Let her go. Charles."

His delivery sounded deliberately benign, like he was reading a recipe for Chicken Piccata. "Okay, maybe it's more of a warning than a threat but look at the flowers. They're lilies, dead lilies."

"When did you say this was delivered?"

Annie kept her hands folded in her lap, her initial anxiety fast becoming frustration. "About twenty minutes ago."

Saunders flipped open a file on his desk. "You called me at 5:13. The call lasted approximately three minutes. You're telling me this was delivered right after we spoke."

"That's right."

"And you have no idea who delivered them."

"What I said was I have no idea who arranged to have them delivered. The person who put them on my steps was a young guy in jeans and a baseball cap and sweatshirt. There might have been a hood on the sweatshirt but I can't be sure. I only caught a glimpse of him as he was running away."

"How do you know he was young if you only saw his back?"

"I guess I assumed he was young by the way he moved. He was running very fast and he jumped a split rail fence and a stack of Belgian block in the driveway."

"Uh-huh."

"Detective, I'm a little freaked out here. What about the fact that the florist's name isn't on the box?"

"You're a writer. I don't remember you mentioning that when you first contacted me."

Annie wasn't sure where he was going with the question but she needed to calm down and stay alert. "I wouldn't call myself a writer. I wrote a column for a few years for a local paper."

"You had an interior design business in Greenwich from 2007 to 2012 and you run an AIDS hospice in Riverside, is that right?"

"Are you kidding me with this? You're investigating me?"

"It's just a background check, nothing to get upset about."

"Really? Well, oddly enough, I am upset. I came to you because I believe a murder was committed. I brought you her journal and the letter from her cousin and…"

"And a take-out bag from a Chinese restaurant, not exactly a smoking gun."

She didn't find a gun but she wished she had one with her now. And to think, she had a naughty dream about this…this cranky pants, not once but twice. "Look, Detective Saunders, is there someone else I can speak to, someone…"

"This is a police station, not the customer service desk at Neiman-Marcus. You're stuck with me. Maybe someone's playing a joke. They know about your research and they're trying to pull your chain."

"That's ridiculous. There are only two people who know about my research as you call it, and one of them is my sister and the other is my best friend."

"What are their names?"

"Samantha Hogan is my sister. She lives in London. Cynthia Fredericks is my partner at **Life House**. We've known one another for eleven years. She's the one who talked me into coming here in the first place. She's also the last person in the world who would want to frighten me."

"What about your ex-husband or your neighbor, Helen Allen?"

"My ex-husband doesn't know anything about it and Helen is in her eighties. She's pretty with it for her age but she's not exactly what you'd call a prankster. Anyway, it can't be her. She doesn't know I believe Debra was murdered. I thought it might upset her."

"But in your initial statement, you suggested we talk to her, that she'd seen them together and might be able to identify the man, or at least give us a description of him."

"Yes, but I also told you she was elderly and asked that you not alarm her, you know, show a little discretion in your questioning. I'm sure I also mentioned she might not remember things exactly the way they happened."

"But she was there and you weren't, isn't that right?"

If he were trying to rattle her, he was doing a bang-up job of it. Nevertheless, she was determined to keep her cool. "That's true, but I think she may have misread his actions that night as grief instead of guilt or fear he'd been caught in the act."

"The act of murdering his wife."

"Exactly. Detective, I have no idea where you're going with all this but I came in here a week ago to try and do the right thing. Regardless of how you dance around it, a woman has disappeared. One minute she's eating Chinese food with her husband and the next minute she's gone. I don't know what happened to her but I know what didn't happen to her. She wasn't taken to a hospital, she wasn't autopsied and she wasn't flown back to Canada for interment. Furthermore, her family hasn't heard from her since 2000, something you might have confirmed had you bothered to make a phone call."

"What makes you think we haven't?"

"Well, have you?"

"Sorry, Miz Heywood, but you said it yourself. We're investigating a possible homicide and we're not obligated to keep you informed of our progress."

"But…"

He looked at his watch again and grabbed his coat off the back of the chair. "Sorry, I've got to run. We'll send a patrol car by your house every couple of hours for the next few days. If you'd feel better staying with a friend, keep us informed where we can get in touch with you. Anything else you need, ask Detective Robinson. See you tomorrow, Lou."

Once he'd bolted from the room, Annie turned to the only other person in the room, a stocky dark-skinned man leaning back in his chair, his hands locked behind his head. He looked more like a prizefighter than a detective. She knew he'd been watching them and now he was grinning. "This isn't funny. Where is he going?"

"To pick up his kid from soccer practice."

Annie stood up, uncertain of what to do next. "Is he always like this or is it me? Do I remind him of his ex-wife or something?"

Detective Robinson leaned forward. "I don't see any horns, turn around. Nope, no pointed tale."

"Why is he so rude?"

"He can't figure you out. Most women find him irresistible, fall all over themselves when they're sitting in that chair. Some women even make up stories to get him to pay attention to them. Must be that winning personality of his. You act like you couldn't care less."

"Believe me, it's no act. He's attractive enough but so far I haven't seen a personality. We haven't met, I'm Annie."

"Lou Robinson, happy to meet you. He thinks you're hot."

"Excuse me?"

"You heard me but you didn't hear me, if you get my meaning. That's what he told me after you came in here last week. She's hot."

"Be sure to remind him of that when you find my decomposing body."

The detective's voice took a more serious tone. "If someone really wanted to threaten you, he'd find a more sinister way to do it. The flowers seem a little theatrical, a little too cute."

"Cute? Look, I don't want you to break any departmental rules or anything, but is anyone taking Debra's disappearance seriously?"

"Mike's taking it seriously but he's being cautious. He got burned a couple of years ago. A guy came in here saying he witnessed a woman being abducted by a guy in a van. He gave a full description of the woman right down to the kind of shoes she was wearing. Mike caught the case, ran his ass off for weeks."

"I remember that. The man who reported it was from out of town. He was staying at the Westport Inn and saw the whole thing outside his room late one night."

"Except it didn't happen. The guy was getting background for a screenplay. By the time Mike figured it out, the department wasted thousands of dollars chasing down leads."

"I don't remember reading that in the paper."

"Some favors were called in with the media to play it down. They figured after a few months the public would forget about it, chalk it up to another case gone cold."

"They were right. I was one of those people." She walked toward a bulletin board where half a dozen photographs and newspaper clippings were tacked up, many yellowed with age. "Is that what these are, cold cases?"

"Yeah. Those particular cases are ones that Mike's dad worked when he was a detective in Stamford. He's long-retired now but he still stops by from time to time and they talk about them. Some of them go way back."

Annie reached up and touched one. It was a color headshot of a little boy who couldn't have been more than five or six. He had red hair and a sprinkling of freckles across his nose. His smile was wide and toothy. "I thought this was some kind of urban legend, cops obsessing over unsolved cases into their retirement years. I'm glad to know it's not."

"Depends on the cop and the case. That little boy's mama locked him out of the house when he wouldn't eat his dinner. Someone picked him up, sexually assaulted him and cut his throat, dumped his body about a mile from his house. Nice neighborhood too, just up the road from the Merritt Parkway off Long Ridge Road."

"I don't know how you guys do this."

"Same way you do with that hospice of yours. That can't be easy."

"It's different. When the moment comes for them to pass over, they know they're loved, not like…" Annie's breath caught. Partially hidden behind a wrinkled news clipping, the flyer almost escaped her attention. The photograph was of a smiling, beautiful woman, her uniform and teeth a brilliant white against her black skin. Her face was thin with high cheekbones and incredible eyes, familiar eyes. "Just like an African princess," she whispered. "What do you know about this case?"

"Between you and me, that's the one that keeps Mike's dad up nights. He's even talked to me about it a time or two. I know he wishes he'd done things differently. She was a nurse at Norwalk Hospital. Got in her car to go to work one night and that's the last anyone saw of her."

"Did he tell you it took them an entire day to follow up on her disappearance or that they implied she'd run off with someone and left her only child behind? Did he tell you that because they dragged their feet, the only thing they ever found of her was her bloody car? Did he tell you any of that?"

"Yeah, he did. He told me all of it. Now you tell me how you happen to know so much about the case."

Annie took the offered tissue and wiped her eyes. Where his manner had been loose and friendly, he now seemed guarded. Even his voice sounded different, cold and professional. She was confused. "What?"

"No one could know those details unless…"

"Unless what, I'm doing research? Her daughter is my best friend, Detective, and she's been grieving for forty years, not knowing where her mother's body is or what happened to her. I'm sorry your friend's father is losing sleep, but my friend lost a hell of a lot more than that."

"It was the eighties, a different time."

"Is that the official explanation?"

"It's all I got. Your friend look anything like her mother?"

"Not really, except for the eyes. She followed in her footsteps, though. She's a nurse too."

"That the reason this other case is so important to you?"

"I hadn't really thought about it, but I guess it is. I hate the idea that someone can disappear and no one's looking for them."

"You think it would do any good if I stopped by and talked to your friend, tried to explain things, maybe apologized?"

"I don't know, let me think about it. I appreciate the offer." She picked up her tote bag and swung it onto her shoulder. "And thanks for talking me off the ledge."

He extended his hand and Annie took it gratefully. "You and Saunders have the whole good cop bad cop thing down pat. Do you ever switch roles and get to play the bad cop?"

He gave her hand a squeeze and winked. "Nah, it'd never work. I'm much too pretty."

***

Annie closed her eyes and let her body slip deeper into the water, felt its warmth on her face, let it cradle her, womb-like, until the need for air forced her up to take a breath. She had no idea how long she'd been there but the water was cooling, the bubbles reduced to floating islands. When they caught the light of the candle, they shone iridescent, like clusters of tiny pearls.

On the floor beside her, Einstein gave a low growl. The patrol car again. If she moved her head to the right, she could see into her darkened bedroom, watch its headlights spray the walls, disappear and then bathe the room in red as it drove away from the house, back into the night.

She didn't want to dwell on the frequency of the patrols or the possibility that Detective Good Cop played down the incident to pacify her. In fact, she didn't want to think about the day at all. She'd had them before, days so poisonous that the only way to purge the emotional toxins was with a hot bath and a good cry, but even that wasn't going as planned. So far, she hadn't mustered a single tear.

Reaching up to turn on the hot water, she jerked her hand back as Einstein barked, followed by another growl, this time more menacing. She saw another flash of white light. What the heck? It wasn't even five minutes since the last one. It was a good thing there weren't more homes on the lane or they'd think she was into something nefarious, like a meth lab or call-girl service. She hoped Helen was asleep. Tomorrow she had to bring her up to speed and explain as gently as possible what her suspicions were about Debra, everything but the dead flowers and the note.

She waited for the familiar red glow of the taillights. When it didn't come, she stood up and grabbed her bathrobe off the hook. Something was up. She was sure she heard a car door close. Einstein heard it too and was on the move, barking and growling at the top of the stairs.

It was probably nothing, one of the officers coming to check on her. She should have thought of that and had a pot of coffee ready. It was a Hogan thing. No matter how weird things got, her dad always thought a pot of coffee would fix them, the stronger the better.

She flipped on the bathroom light and did a quick once-over in the mirror. She'd be lucky if she didn't scare him to death. With her face flushed and her hair slicked down and wet, she looked like a lab rat.

Before heading down, she took Einstein by the collar and led him back into her bedroom, closing the door behind her. Under normal circumstances, he was all bark and no bite but this was far from a normal day and she didn't want to risk it, especially with someone carrying a gun.

She started down the stairs, stopping a few steps short of the bottom. The front door was directly in front of her, across a small vestibule. From this point, with the porch lights on, she should have been able to see the top of his head through the fan window in the door but there was no one there.

The other possibility was he had gone to the door off the kitchen, the one she referred to as the side door. It was the first one you came to from the driveway and it faced the front lawn. People who didn't know the house usually made that mistake and went there first. It was an odd set-up but not uncommon in older homes. She walked to the left, through the dining room, and looked through the window toward the porch, the same porch where she'd found the box of flowers. Nothing.

That left the French doors in the living room but that made no sense at all. That room was on the far side of the house. Why would anyone go there, unless his orders were to periodically walk the property and make sure everything was buttoned down? In that case, he would need a flashlight to navigate the overgrowth and she would have seen a beam or something.

There was one more possibility and she went with it. She'd simply missed the taillights and the sound came from the ancient oil heater in the basement. The only thing that couldn't be explained was Einstein's incessant barking and growling. Clearly, he didn't have her knack for threat assessment and rationalization.

Before going back upstairs, she wanted one final look so she doused the outside lights. With no overhead streetlamps, it was impossible to see more than a few feet beyond the house and definitely not as far as the driveway. The only other light that might have helped was a single carriage lamp on a post near the mailboxes a few feet down the lane, but it burned out weeks before and she never replaced the bulb.

This was getting silly. If someone were there, they would have rung the bell or knocked. She was safe inside her home in the middle of a fairly good-sized town with homes all around her — and she was being protected.

So why was she walking into the kitchen to get a flashlight? It was the stuff of bad horror flicks, the heroine about to venture outside alone, a silly woman who always prompted her to scream at the TV: *Jeez, lady, are you nuts? There's a guy out there with a machete!*

She braced herself and opened the French Doors, panning the patio with the flashlight. When she was satisfied no one was lurking about, she stepped off the flagstones and turned toward the front of the house.

"I love what you've done with the driveway, Annie. I could have killed myself, not that you'd give a shit."

Annie gasped. It was the last thing she expected to see draped across her front steps. His clothes looked as if he'd slept in them and the yellow exterior lights gave his face an inhuman pallor. She didn't dare speak. If she opened her mouth, she wouldn't be responsible for what came out. Instead, she pointed the flashlight toward the entrance to her property. No wonder she couldn't see a car. It blended with the night.

"You lying whore. How could you do this to me?" Larry Heywood used his free hand to pull himself up by the wrought iron handrail. In his other hand, he was waving a copy of Markham's book.

He lost his balance and Annie ran forward to catch him. "You're drunk, Larry."

He pushed her away. "Yeah, I've had a few. You wanna know why? Because for the last three hours, I've had to listen to everyone at the Club laughing behind my back because I couldn't keep my hot little wife satisfied. Did you think I wasn't going to find out about this?"

"You were supposed to be in Tokyo until next week. I planned to tell you about it when you got back."

"And this afternoon when you barged into Marty's office and laid some shit on him in front of the Prescotts? What the hell was that about? They're pissed, by the way."

"I don't give a damn what the Prescotts say about me and you shouldn't either. I'm calling a cab to take you home. You can pick up your car in the morning." She turned away from him and took a step toward the back patio.

"I need to use the head."

"Go around to the other door. There's a powder room behind the kitchen." Satisfied he'd regained his footing and was heading in the right direction, she backtracked through the French doors. By the time she turned up the thermostat and finished preparing the coffee, he was standing in the entrance to the kitchen. It was obvious from his appearance he used the time to do more than relieve himself. His hair was neatly combed and his face was ruddy, evidence of a cold-water splash.

"Why'd you do it, Annie? Why'd you have to embarrass me?"

"Which betrayal are we discussing first, yours or mine?"

"I don't know what the hell you're talking about, and why didn't you return my phone call today?"

She looked down at her hands. They were no longer trembling. She kept staring at them, not wanting to look at him, refusing to acknowledge he was in her space, challenging her. "It was my way of not dealing with your narcissism and selfishness, of not confronting the fact that you'd sell me out and take away the only thing in my life I'm really proud of. Did you really believe that because I lived with you for seventeen years and looked the other way while you ruined our marriage that I couldn't see you for what you are, that I'm so pathetic I couldn't connect the dots?"

"What dots?"

"Your latest scheme, Larry. The one that involves Marty setting me up, you coming to my rescue and then calling in the loan on **Life House**. Those dots."

He took a clumsy step forward. "I was pissed at you for leaving me."

"I didn't leave you. I left a house. You hadn't been there for a long time."

"I'm here now, baby."

Annie recognized the tone. She'd almost forgotten how he would change his demeanor to manipulate her, how he could lapse in and out of sobriety at will. Toward the end of the marriage, there were times when she believed the slurred words were a stunt, an attempt to mitigate his bad behavior. But this was no act. The only other time she'd seen him this drunk was the night before she left, not one she cared to repeat.

"Not for long. Here drink this. I'm calling a cab."

Before she could react, he moved toward her, knocking the mug from her hand. Shocked, she watched the hot liquid arc and splash to the floor and heard the mug shatter on the tiled floor. She tried to twist away but he pinned her against the counter. She felt his hands inside her robe, groping, felt his breath on her face as his mouth tried to find hers. The more intense her rage, the less she struggled.

Sensing her starting to yield, he relaxed against her and Annie struck, bringing her hands to his chest and pushing as hard as she could. He stumbled back, found his footing then lost it, finally coming to rest against the refrigerator.

She backed away from him. "Get the hell out of my house!"

He was breathing hard but keeping his distance, trying to get his balance. When he could finally stand, the words came out in short, breathy bursts. "I almost forgot. You can only get off if someone's beating the shit out of you." He started removing his belt. "No problem, baby. If that's what you want, I'm happy to oblige."

Einstein was barking again, pawing at her bedroom door, and someone was banging, someone at the side door, a man in uniform. He looked angry. Behind him, in the distance, she saw the flashing lights of a patrol car.

Adjusting her robe, she covered the distance to the door and opened it.

The officer stepped inside. Taking a few seconds to assess the situation, he focused first on the belt in Larry's hand. "Everything all right in here, Miss Heywood?"

Annie took a step back, surprised he knew her name. "It's okay, officer, my ex-husband was just leaving."

He directed his attention behind her. "Is that your car, sir?"

Before Larry could answer, Annie nodded. "Yes, it's his car but he's not going to be driving it tonight. I'm calling a cab to take him back to Greenwich."

To her further surprise, the officer took her by the elbow and walked her back through the side door and out onto the small porch. He looked uncomfortable, unsure how to broach the subject. "I've been here a few minutes, Miss Heywood. I know you think you can take care of yourself but I've seen this kind of thing before. You sure you don't want to file a report? I can take him in, let him sleep it off."

She felt the tears building but managed to keep them at bay. "It's tempting, believe me, but I can handle him."

"No offense, ma'am, but the hospitals are full of women who thought they could handle the situation."

She glanced over her shoulder through the window in the door but she couldn't see Larry. When she turned back, she shook her head. "I'm fine, really. I have a feeling he's already starting to sober up. Listen, I just made a pot of coffee and I could scrounge another mug if you'd like to take it with you."

"I'll call the cab company. They'll get here faster. I'll take the coffee and move the cruiser down the lane a bit. When I see the cab pick him up, I'll bring back the mug and be on my way."

"Thank you, officer, for everything."

The first thing she noticed when she went back inside was the floor. It was spotless. Larry was seated at the table, staring into a mug of coffee held between his hands.

She filled another mug and took it outside to the waiting cop. When she returned to the kitchen, it was five minutes before either of them spoke. Annie stood by the door, her eyes on the lane, watching for the cab that would take him away.

"He knew your name, Annie. What's going on?"

"Nothing's going on."

"You're shaking."

"I was in the bathtub when I heard your car."

"Ah, the old bath and a cry ritual."

The remark stung like a slap in the face. He knew her so well and yet his words and actions were those of a stranger. Waves of fatigue and emotion swept through her and she fought to keep it together.

"How do I make this right, Annie?"

"Ask me again when you're sober."

"This is your dad's coffee. Give me another minute."

There it was again, the inside joke, another reference to better days. It was vintage Larry, using charm to worm his way out of trouble.

"For what it's worth, I'm sorry."

She took her eyes off the road long enough to study his face. "Sorry for what, for calling me a whore, for attacking me in my own home or for trying to sell me out? You've had a busy day, Larry, it's hard to keep up."

"I'm sorry for all of it. I'll give you the money, no strings attached. We both know you let me off easy on the settlement. It's no big deal."

"Thanks, I've got it covered."

"It's there if you change your mind. And just so you know, I'm still pissed about the Prescotts, having to listen to them mouth off at the Club."

"You must be having a bad day. Any other time you would have spun it to your advantage. 'See guys, that's why I dumped the whacko.' And since when do you mind being the center of attention?"

"It's complicated."

"You didn't. Please don't tell me you're involved in some shady business deal with those people."

"I'm seeing their daughter."

"You're seeing Miranda Prescott? Does her husband the Count know about it?"

"They're getting a divorce. She's been back in the states for a few months. It's getting serious."

"Wow, that is news. Congratulations. You do realize the title doesn't transfer. It's not like a car."

"That's funny. I'll have to remember that. You've still got it, Annie, the gift for badinage."

She looked back toward the lane, wearying of the game. "Now it's badinage. When we were married, you called it smart-mouth. Do me a favor, save the pretentious bullshit for your new in-laws. They'll eat it up with a cuiller."

"A what?"

"Look it up."

He got up and refilled his coffee, but instead of sitting back down, he rested his hip against the countertop. "Did you love him?"

"I can't do this tonight, Larry. You deserve an explanation and I'm sorry I didn't tell you about him sooner but I just…"

"Small and yielding, naked and lovely, she crawls into my lap and rests her head on my shoulder, her hand on my heart; and in those exquisite moments, I know the ecstasy of Heaven and the torment of hell. With each breath, each murmured word of love, she holds my soul within her grasp. Do you have any idea what I would have given to have you do that to me, crawled up in my lap and told me you loved me?"

"I never denied you anything except when you were drunk."

"That's true. All I ever had to do was reach for you and you were always compliant. How did you do that? How could you separate yourself, love me so much in the bedroom and despise me in every other room of the house?"

"You were different there. It was the one place I didn't have to compete with your ambition and obsessive need for acceptance by those shallow, vapid people you call your friends. Be honest, Larry. In spite of what you said earlier about being laughed at, has Luc's book hurt your reputation in the slightest?"

"I've taken a little ribbing but there wasn't a man there tonight who didn't envy me."

"God, you're so predictable. Your cab's here."

She moved aside to let him pass but he stopped in front of her and put his hand on her cheek. "I still love you, you know. Just say the word and I'll send the crazy Countess packing."

She put her hand on top of his and gently moved it away. "It's too late, Larry. Just try to get it right this time."

He was almost through the door when he stopped and turned toward her. "Don't judge me, kiddo. It's not that easy living in the shadow of a saint, the one who always does the right thing. I know the cop wanted to take me in and I know you saved my ass. Even in college, you were the first one into the fray, railing against injustice, civil rights, world hunger, all of it, like some freaking latter day Joan of Arc."

"As usual, you're exaggerating, but what I don't understand is if you held me in such disdain, why would you want to marry me, spend your life with me?"

"Maybe I thought some of that fire and passion would rub off on me. I was like Icarus, except I didn't get burned up, I got frozen out. Making money is the only thing I'm good at and you hate me for it."

"That's not true, I don't hate you. I hate what the money did to you, and it isn't the only thing you're good at. You were a brilliant attorney. The firm loved you. You would have made partner within the year."

"That was your dream, not mine."

"My dream? I must have missed that when I was working two jobs to put you through Law School."

"I guess you did because I hated every minute of it. I didn't want to be a partner. I wanted to run the place. Hell, I wanted to own the building. I wanted it all."

"Now you have it all so why the anger?"

"You really don't know?"

"No, I don't understand any of this."

"You lost your spark, Annie. You gave up on me and then you gave up on yourself. You became the long-suffering wife, but here's the punch line: you got it back. I knew it the minute I heard about your performance in Marty's office, and then when I saw you tonight, I went kind of crazy because the old Annie's back and I'm out. Tell me something. Did you feel anything when I told you about Miranda?"

"I can't do this, Larry, not tonight."

"That's what I thought. You're a liar, Annie. You never loved me. You've always belonged to Markham. I just leased you for seventeen years."

She watched him walk toward the cab and thought of a hundred things she could have said, things she should have said, but her reserves were depleted. Perhaps tomorrow she would wake up and feel all the emotions she should have felt at that moment, anger, guilt, even jealousy; but for now, she felt blessedly numb.

After the officer returned the mug, she walked through the house and extinguished the lights. Upstairs, she sloughed the damp robe and crawled beneath the sheets, pulled her dog close and kissed the spot between his ears. In a day filled with drama and chaos, she found she only had one regret, that she ignored her own voice, the one warning her not to go outside.

As it turned out, there was a man with a weapon and he knew how to use it. His words found their mark and drew blood, especially those with a ring of truth. All things considered, she would have preferred the machete.

CHAPTER 27

CHARLES

Richmond. Charles Richmond. He liked the sound of it. It didn't have the elegance of Hastings but it would do. Hastings was his favorite, perhaps because it was his first. Unfortunately, the same could not be said for Debra. Looking back, only two things set her apart from the others, her innocence and enthusiasm, both irritating in the extreme.

She was beautiful but then they all were, except the last one. Beauty was part of the criteria, an important part, and with Susan he compromised his standards in the interest of the game. He wouldn't do it again, play Pygmalion. It took too much time and provided too few guarantees. On their last night together, she was as crude and obnoxious as the day he met her. Equally disappointing was her talent for music composition, mediocre at best, derivative and soulless. She left him no choice. By making him angry, she orchestrated one final piece, perhaps her best, her grisly finale. He would have loved to see her face when she gained consciousness, alone and bleeding, surrounded by predators miles from anyone who would hear her screams. He wondered what she looked like after several days of exposure, if they were still hacking and sawing her remains, probing them for evidence.

It felt strange to be breaking his pattern, hunting again for the second time in a year. What was it the behaviorists called it? Escalating. His activities were escalating. He begged to differ. Susan didn't count. It was ludicrous to imagine he could be labeled with some crime show psycho-shit. He was no serial killer. They were all wild-eyed unkempt losers driven by sado-sexual fantasies and perversions. He was a gentleman, rarely giving into fits of frenzy and cruelty and only when provoked. He was also patient. The years between the kills were proof of that, a spiritual rationing of sorts. *Bet you can't kill just one.* But he could. Five women in twenty years, six if he were lucky, was hardly a crime spree. It was another part of the game, the anticipation. He enjoyed it almost as much as he relished the execution. Months became years, the years turned into months and the cycle began anew. In the meantime, he continued with his life.

He had to get it right this time. It could well be his last. He wanted another Theresa, the archetype, independent and willful, her looks exceeded only by her intelligence. He remembered moments, infrequent though they were, when he forgot about the game. They were good together, especially in bed. She took his absences in stride and never questioned him. When she couldn't have him with her, she preferred solitude, having time to write. It was that part he found so agreeable, that she kept her own counsel and relied on no one. It was crucial to the game. Friends and family were poison.

Her brother proved the point. He was the only family she had and she wanted them to meet, was becoming insistent on it. His excuses were wearing thin and, with them, her trust. Was it because he was a cop? He laughed when she asked the question. In the next moment, his hands were around her throat. That was the money-shot, the one Susan stole from him, the eyes turning from disbelief to terror. Cut and print.

He poured a half cup of coffee from the thermos and looked at his watch. He liked to be there early, around sunrise. Late-night lovers making early-morning exits would put a crimp in things but this morning, like the previous six, she was alone.

It was 6:15. If her schedule held, in fifteen minutes she'd be waking up. Almost instantly, a light would go on and she'd appear at the door to let her dog out. Shortly thereafter, she would open the door, walk half the length of her driveway to pick up the paper, call her dog and lead her back inside the house. For the next hour all would be quiet as she read her paper, showered, dressed and attended to a few housekeeping chores. It was during that hour when he would leave, just long enough to grab breakfast at a local diner, refill his coffee and use the facilities.

He pulled a notebook from his briefcase and rested it against the steering wheel. So far, she had varied her routine only once. Wednesday mornings she attended a yoga class in town. Other than that, her life was regimented and solitary, devoted mostly to her work, no interruptions, no one coming to call. It was the way he liked it, the way he insisted on it. Once he was in their lives, it was easy to isolate them, to make himself the center of their universe.

She appeared at the door and he liked what he saw, everything but her hair. It was blond, a departure for him. All the others had dark hair, long and flowing. She went against type but rules were made to be broken, some rules anyway. Everything else was a perfect fit. She had a beautiful face and lovely hands, his mother's hands.

It was her hands that first attracted him, a little over ten months ago, a few days before Christmas. He was in Sedona, a quick trip in and out, just long enough to get the lay of the land. On his way out of town, he stopped somewhere for a gift for Susan and a quick lunch. Wandering through the plaza, he saw her in a gallery, working the clay on a stand in front of her, oblivious to the growing knot of onlookers. He stood back, impressed by her concentration and poise as she answered questions, endless inane questions about the casting process, her vision for the piece in progress, on and on.

Only once did she look up and meet his stare, but the Stetson and sunglasses all but covered his face. When she looked back down, he moved beyond her line of sight and walked the gallery. Her talent was exceptional, especially the wildlife. One piece in particular, a life-sized eagle in flight, was breathtaking in its conception, each bronze feather sculpted in exquisite detail. When he sensed he was attracting the attention of a sales clerk, he picked up a brochure and walked casually out of the gallery.

For months she never crossed his mind, and then one night, lying in bed with Susan while enduring her clumsy attempts to arouse him, he thought of her, the way she used her hands to bring the clay to life, a perfect melding of passion and purpose. From that moment on, he thought of little else.

The brochure long discarded, he remembered her name, Morgan Evans. The rest was easy. His computer and a few well-placed phone calls gave him everything he needed to know. She was thirty-nine, divorced, no kids. While she maintained a small apartment in Sedona, her primary residence was an hour and a half away, Tonto Hills, ten miles northeast of Scottsdale. Rough and remote, it bordered Tonto National Forest and was absent the usual amenities including paved roads and vegetation beyond the ubiquitous scrub. Local color was provided by the residents, an eccentric mix of artists, anti-social wing nuts and cowboy wannabes.

Her home was modest, more casita than house, her studio a converted two-car garage, but what it lacked in size it made up for in views. Floor to ceiling windows provided a magnificent panorama of the Superstition Mountains and wildlife that wandered in from the surrounding hills. It was a good place to be inspired, an even better place to observe without being harassed. Apparently no one cared, least of all him. His cover story was flawless.

Charles Richmond was a location scout for an independent film company out of Vancouver. That explained the odd hours and repetitive visits, the need to study the lighting and survey the terrain. Location shoots were costly, everyone knew that. Some hastily-printed business cards and a backseat full of thrift shop photographic equipment were a cheap investment. Human beings were gullible and predictable. Throw in a few props, some showbiz bullshit and they'd be pissing themselves.

Today was the day. It felt right. When he got back, he would approach her, feel her out about using her home, at least for the exteriors. He couldn't risk another day. His window was narrowing. In less than three days she was due back in Sedona for another one-woman show. He'd have to make his move here, give her something to think about while she was away. Sedona was out of the question, too soon.

He started the car and gave a final glance toward her house. Game on.

CHAPTER 28

ANNIE

It was the noise that woke her, a dissonant opus of thumps, clanks and whistles. Amid the sounds, she swore she heard violins. Spike Jones meets PDQ Bach.

Annie bolted to a sitting position and grabbed the alarm clock. It was 6:01 in the morning. The oil heater again? Not unless it shimmied its way up the basement stairs and out the side door. Whatever was going on was coming from the front of the house, not beneath her. Where was Einstein? He should have been throwing a fit.

The racket persisted and she stumbled out of bed, grabbing her robe off the floor. When she reached the window, she opened the blinds. Larry's car was gone but the big truck was back and, behind it, another car she didn't recognize. The driveway was buzzing with activity, men everywhere. She took a moment to wipe the sleep from her eyes and get her bearings. Was it really this light at 6:00 in the morning?

She called out for her dog and stepped into the bathroom. Minutes later, she was headed downstairs. Passing through the dining room, she saw a man sitting on the steps, his back to her and Einstein's head buried in his lap. She rounded the corner toward the side door. It was open, only an inch or two, but open nonetheless.

Mike Saunders gave the dog a final rub and got to his feet. "I found him wandering down the lane. You should keep a better eye on him. Someone might pick him up. Mrs. Heywood, did you hear me?"

"Of course I heard you, Detective. I'm not deaf, at least not yet. How did you get my door open? I'm sure I locked it before I went to bed." But she wasn't sure. The last thing she remembered was Larry's voice and the look on his face before he walked through the door.

"It was open when I got here fifteen minutes ago. How can you sleep this late with all the commotion?"

"Late? It's 6:00 in the morning."

"It's after nine. Rough night?"

"Very funny. My clock must have stopped." She examined the door around the lock, checking for scrapes on the fresh paint.

"I see your husband picked up his car. Maybe he used his key and opened the door."

Annie felt her face flush, more from embarrassment than anger. "He's my ex-husband and he doesn't have a key. Why are you here, Detective? Slow day around the water cooler?"

"Flynn was doing his job. His orders were to patrol and report. Did he hurt you?"

"Only my pride. Officer Flynn was wonderful. Please thank him again for me."

"I'm confused about something. Yesterday you said the kid who delivered the flowers jumped the fence and a pile of block. I don't see any block."

She switched gears. There was a moment when he almost sounded human and just as quickly morphed back into RoboCop. "The contractor must have taken it away. I didn't want it."

"Come again?"

"It was there last night, on the other side of the fence near the truck. If you don't believe me, ask one of the guys."

"I'll do that. Look, Mrs. Heywood, we have to talk."

"I know where this is going. First, they blow you off with a sporting event and then they break up with you." Was that a smile? Whatever it was, it was gone. "That was a joke, Detective."

"I need permission to walk your property, maybe nose around inside the house if that's okay."

"Help yourself. I'm going to make a pot of coffee and grab a quick shower. Can we talk after that?"

"Whatever you say."

She leaned around him. "What are they listening to out there?"

"Vivaldi's Four seasons, Spring."

Well, what do you know?

Mascara or no mascara? Screw it. Sergeant Friday wouldn't know the difference. She applied some lip gloss and stepped back from the full-length mirror. The jeans and sweatshirt were anything but hot. On the other hand, she looked rested and refreshed, remarkably so considering the events of the previous evening. The capper to a less than perfect day was the dream, another one in which Mike Saunders took center stage. What was it about snarky men that made her blood rush to all the inconvenient spots? She didn't doubt for a moment he had women swooning over him. He had that Daniel Craig vibe going on, not so much in looks but in temperament, all business on the outside, a raging volcano in the sack. "Don't go there," she said to her reflection and turned off the light.

Back downstairs, she saw him talking to Harold Sawyer. When they were finished, the detective nodded and they shook hands. Trying to appear disinterested, she busied herself at the kitchen sink until she heard his knock at the door. When she waved him in, he stepped inside, Einstein at his heels.

Annie poured a mug of coffee and held it out to him. "Looks like you've made a friend."

"I called Jacqueline Gauthier's home this morning. She's in Europe but I spoke to her daughter who confirmed the fact that no one's heard from Debra since the summer of 2000. I also had an interesting chat with your neighbor. She confirmed what you told me but has a slightly different take on things."

His voice was business-like and brusque, even more so than before, and it set her on edge. "I'm sure she does, and I suppose Harold explained about the Belgian block?"

"You know what they say, nothing says romance like a pile of over-priced building products. He took it back to the yard this morning."

"Well, look at you, a music buff and a comedian. Do you take anything in your coffee, cream, sugar?" *Battery acid?*

"No, thanks. You didn't mention Bryce Stanley. Any chance he sent the flowers? Maybe you were spending too much time on this other thing and not enough time on him."

That did it. "Not that it's any of your business, but Mr. Stanley and I are not involved romantically. I met him once over a week ago in his office. His family owned this property before me and I guess he felt responsible for the problems with the driveway. As far as this *other thing* is concerned, I never mentioned Debra Hastings. Why would I? It was hard enough coming to you, which I'm now seriously regretting."

"I'm sorry you feel that way but at this point everything is my business. You did come to me and now we're looking for a missing person."

"Wrong again. She's not missing, she's dead."

"Did you do those? They're beautiful." He was staring at Debra's drawings on the refrigerator.

"Debra did them. I found them in the garage. I was going to send them to her cousin."

"They're evidence. I'll have to take them with me."

She felt cornered. It was getting to be a habit, the urge to run, to get in her truck and drive away, the farther the better. She was tired of fighting, of being on the defensive.

"I'll be careful with them and get them back to you as soon as possible, fair enough?"

"Do me a favor, Detective. Don't start being nice to me. The only thing holding me together right now is anger."

"At me in particular or the world in general?"

"Take your pick. Maybe it's a delayed reaction from last night."

"Bad divorce?"

"Do you know of any good divorces?"

"Mine. With one exception, it's been the highlight of my month."

"Oh." For whatever reason, their eyes rarely connected but this time they did and she had to look away before she said something stupid.

"Mind if we sit? I have a few questions."

Some of the tension was gone but his new-found geniality unnerved her. "I hate to open old wounds but why the change of heart? I thought you pegged me as a crackpot."

"Cops don't expect people to do the right thing. Cynicism and suspicion come with the badge, an occupational hazard."

She thought of Cynthia's mother, the way she looked in the flyer above his desk. Perhaps callousness came with the territory or maybe it was genetic, handed down from father to son, like heart disease or male pattern baldness.

"Is something wrong? If you're not up to this now, I can come back later or you can stop by the station."

She waved it off. "I'm okay. What is it you want to know?"

He removed a notepad from his breast pocket. "I haven't run the property records yet but you said you purchased this home from the Stanley family."

"It was part of their family trust. From what I understand, they owned a lot of land around here but it's been sold off over the years."

"And when you went to Bryce Stanley's office it was to complain about the driveway?"

"No, I went there to see if he knew how to get in touch with the former property manager. I was going to start with him, to see if he remembered any details about the break-in."

He flipped a few pages of the pad until he found what he was looking for. "Bert Kennedy. What did Stanley tell you?"

"He told me Kennedy had passed away, that his brother took over management of the properties for awhile until he got bored or something to that effect. I also asked him if he knew how Kennedy died and he said he thought it was a heart attack."

"Bert Kennedy's brother took over his business?"

"No, Bryce Stanley's brother. He didn't mention his name. The meeting was a waste of time."

"Not necessarily. You got a new driveway out of it."

"Let it go, Detective."

"And you never mentioned Debra or Charles or any of your suspicions? Wasn't he curious why you wanted to contact this guy Kennedy?"

"I told him I was writing a book about Westport and I thought Bert Kennedy might be a good resource for background on the area. It was the only thing I could come up with."

"That's it? You walked into his office, asked about Bert Kennedy and mentioned your driveway. A week later he sends a crew out here, rips out your old blacktop and spends thousands of dollars on Belgian block."

"I have no idea why he did that unless he thought I was going to sue him or lodge a complaint against the estate or something. He doesn't know me. Anyway, the whole encounter lasted less than ten minutes."

"Have you been in contact with him since that meeting?"

"I tried calling him yesterday, to thank him, but his secretary said he's in London. One of his sons was injured in a soccer match. Come to think of it, the two of you have a lot in common."

"I doubt it."

"You don't even know him."

"I know his type. I have to deal with them everyday. They think they can buy their way out of trouble. I would have thought you'd had enough of that."

"Now just a minute," she said, rising from her chair. "What's that?"

He'd reached into his pocket again and was holding something between the tips of his fingers. "One of the workmen found this on the ground. He thinks it blew off your windshield."

Annie took the check and unfolded it. It was drawn on one of Larry's accounts and payable to **Life House**. The amount shocked her and she sat back down.

"You set me up. Tell me something. Does this passive-aggressive thing work on most people?"

"I don't know. I'm trying it out for the first time. How am I doing?"

"You suck at it. Are we done here?"

"Almost, just a few more questions. Did anyone call you back from Turk Storage?"

"No, but there was a strange phone call not long after I called them, within an hour or so. A man called **Life House** and spoke to Cynthia, made up a story about his brother having AIDS. He said he knew my brother. He mentioned the name Charles."

"Why didn't you tell me about this before?"

"I forgot about it."

"Did he leave a callback number?"

"No, and his number was blocked."

"You said you found the Turk Storage card in an old phone book. Do you still have it?"

"I threw away some older ones but I kept that one. I'll get it."

When she came back, he was standing at the sink, refilling his coffee. "You wouldn't happen to have any more of those evidence bags would you, the giant economy size?"

"I have no idea what you did for amusement before I came along but the answer is no. Will a shopping bag do?"

"That's fine. Two more things and then I'm out of your hair. You'll have to come by the office and get fingerprinted. We'll need to separate your prints from whatever we find on the other items."

"I'm in the system. I was fingerprinted when I opened **Life House**. What else?"

"You're not going to like it."

"Compared to what, all the fun we're having so far?"

"I want to bring in a cadaver dog to sniff your property."

It was another of those moments when Annie feared her heart would stop.

"It's probably nothing but there are a couple of spots where the ground looks uneven, like it's been disturbed. Someone may have had a vegetable garden out there. It could be anything."

The door to the basement was in the kitchen and Annie nodded toward it. "Have them check the basement while they're here. There's a raised spot next to the sump pump. It's about four feet off the ground and extends back eight or nine feet toward the north wall. I think it's filled with dirt but it's definitely creepy. Einstein won't go near it."

"I'm impressed. I thought by this time I'd be picking you up off the floor."

"Death doesn't frighten me. I've seen too much of it. Besides, I don't think you'll find anything. According to Helen, Charles left for a couple of hours, between midnight and two a.m."

"If she's remembering correctly, and even if she is, what was he doing between the time they had dinner and the midnight drive?"

"I'd rather not think about that. I said death doesn't frighten me. Murder terrifies me. You read Debra's diary. She was sweet and trusting and…"

"Vulnerable. Sometimes that's enough. The locksmith's here."

"I didn't call a locksmith."

"I did."

"But I had the locks changed when I moved in."

"Your door was open when I got here. This isn't a request, Annie."

Annie? That was new as was the intensity in his eyes when he said it. At some point, she'd have to think about why she liked the sound of her name coming from his lips. "What happens now?"

"You go on with your life. I'll try to get the dog out here this afternoon, tomorrow morning at the latest but I'll let you know." Downing the last of his coffee, he walked to the sink and rinsed the mug. On his way out the door, he threw a final comment over his shoulder. "Good call on the block. It doesn't suit your house."

Annie closed the door behind him and collapsed against it. He exhausted her. One minute she wanted to slap the crap out of him and the next she wanted to jump his bones. Dealing with one of his personalities was bad enough but evidently he had several, all equally taxing. And now thanks to him, she was more confused than ever. All she wanted was someone to take her seriously, to find out once and for all what happened to Debra; but now that things were moving forward, she dreaded it. The idea she might be buried in her yard made her sick. There was comfort in the theoretical. When things turned practical, she was thrown.

She picked up the check. He was right of course. It had payoff written all over it. She couldn't believe she was even considering it. Yesterday she had a plan, a good one. But today? Today she saw things differently. It was a lot of money, enough to keep them going for a couple of years. It wasn't about her principles. It wasn't about her at all. It was about **Life House**. Perhaps she could think of it as a loan and pay it back over time. And while she was at it, she could go upstairs and cut her wrists.

She ripped the check into pieces.

You go on with your life.

Easy for him to say.

CHAPTER 29

RYAN

He had to go with his instinct. He'd been a cop too long to ignore the niggling, persistent tug at the back of his brain. If he was wrong, she'd never know. No harm no foul, but if he were right?

The unruly piles were gone, replaced by manila files. He flipped the cover on one and thumbed through the pages. The emails were alphabetized with notations, some in red, others in blue. Still others were highlighted in neon yellow. If nothing else, she was organized.

He pulled a pair of disposable gloves from his pocket and put them on. Freed from its clamshell packaging, the new mouse was in the other pocket. He compared the new one with the old one. Satisfied that it was a close enough match, he made the switch. He noticed she'd been messing with his computer again. Instead of a plain blue screen, tropical fish were swimming back and forth through bubbling water.

"You know that's not a real aquarium." Maria hefted a cardboard box to the top of his desk and smiled. "I'm glad you're here. I was going to call you."

He kept his hands in his pockets. He was still wearing the gloves, another rookie mistake. "I needed some phone numbers from my desk. It's not even seven. What are you doing here?"

"It's my first full day of work. I wanted to get an early start. It's nine o'clock on the east coast. People are much more pleasant in the morning, don't you think?"

"I hadn't noticed. What's in the box?"

"Some supplies and a coffee maker. The new computer is coming today and the phone lines will go in between 12 and 5 this afternoon."

"There's a coffee shop around the corner."

"And now you will only have to step across the hall, unless you want me to set it up in here."

"I like their coffee."

"Suit yourself. Your messages are under the lamp."

"As long as you brought it in, you may as well set it up."

Maria rolled her eyes. "I'll be right back. There's a file in that stack marked Ryan. You might want to look through it."

The gloves removed, he was going through the file when she returned. "How late did you stay here last night, Maria?"

"I'm not sure. I lost track of time but it must have been ten or eleven."

"That's too late to be roaming the streets. This isn't Sedona."

"I don't roam, I walk purposefully, and I can take care of myself. I'm a big girl."

"I don't care if you're Captain Marvel. From now on, you're out of here by eight. I need my beauty sleep and don't want to be roused in the middle of the night because you've been mugged." He motioned to the file. "What am I looking at here?"

"It's the email on top, the one highlighted in yellow. It came in last night around nine o'clock."

"It's a little cryptic but it could be something."

"It is something. I've already spoken to her. Her name is Barbara Kruger. Her daughter Ellie disappeared in 2015 from her home in Templeton, a few miles north of San Luis Obispo and half an hour from Cambria. She was thirty-two, an artist and a promising one. She'd been seeing a man for a few months, but as far as her mother knows, no one close to her ever met him. His name was Charles Vaughn."

"How does she know his name?"

"Mr. and Mrs. Kruger were living in Dallas. A week before she disappeared, Ellie called them and was going on about this new man in her life. She wanted them to come out for a visit and meet him. She mentioned his name and her mother wrote it down. She doesn't know why she did that."

Ryan reached for the phone. "I have to get to Dallas."

"They relocated in 2016. They live in Atascadero, the next town over from Templeton. I have their address and I've pulled directions off the internet. I thought perhaps you'd want to drive but I'll make airline reservations for you if you prefer. You can fly into San Luis Obispo and rent a car there. It's half an hour from the airport."

"I'll drive. I might have missed this email completely. She sounds angry, even a little nuts."

"She is angry. For five years, she's tried to get the police to take her daughter's disappearance seriously. That's why they moved from Dallas, so they could stay on top of it, but they're still running into a brick wall. She's almost given up. The only reason she responded to the site was because a friend saw it and badgered her into it."

"Maybe there's a reason the police aren't investigating."

"And maybe there isn't. Maybe it's just another woman who's fallen through the cracks. How can you of all people sit there and defend them?"

"I'm not defending them, Maria, but I was on the other side of the fence for a lot of years, remember?"

"It's something I'm trying to forget. Are you going or not? I told her I'd call this morning and let her know."

"I've got a stop to make first but tell her I'll be there early afternoon. Is that it?"

She pulled another file from the stack and handed it to him. "Here, take this. The Kruger's phone number, address and directions to their home are in there."

"This is good work, Maria. Anything else I should know?"

"Yes, Ellie was their only child. Try to be compassionate. They're still in a great deal of pain."

"Aren't we all."

***

Atascadero was similar to other towns that dotted California's central coast, a study in contrasts, an incongruous tangle of surf shops and day spas, thrift stores and fancy grills. It was vintage California, a contradiction in terms, a town struggling against the interests of those hell- bent on erasing its identity.

The back roads were much the same, a confluence of styles, older farms situated comfortably next to sprawling new estates. The common denominator was land, two to five acre properties, most bound by fencing to keep things in, not out. Here animals ruled. They were everywhere, horses, goats, even donkeys, one enormous petting zoo. To his surprise, Ryan liked it. For a city boy, it felt like country living at its bucolic best, all winding roads, rolling hills and trees, every specie of tree as far as the eye could see.

He made the final turn and slowed the car. On the opposite shoulder, a deer eyed him suspiciously, took a tentative step and leapt across the road. A flock of wild turkeys came next, squawking their disapproval and displaying their annoyance.

The home of Howard and Barbara Kruger sat alone on the side of a hill. Even in an area of architectural diversity, this one stood apart, a contemporary dwelling with jutting rooflines and walls of glass. It was surrounded by trees, pines and venerable California oaks. In the pasture below, two horses grazed contentedly, completing the pastoral picture. Without even stepping inside the home, Ryan knew the views of the valley would be spectacular.

Alighting from his car, he watched a man round a corner and walk quickly toward the garage. Within about a minute, a late model Mercedes was backing out. The driver, somewhere in his sixties, looked none too happy as he revved the engine and sped past Ryan's car.

Barbara Kruger was a woman who wore the mask of one in perpetual grief, a look he recognized. He introduced himself and followed her into the expansive living room. As he suspected, the view dominated the space.

When they were seated, he pulled a small tape recorder from his briefcase. "Do you mind if I record our conversation? It's less distracting than taking notes."

She sat erect, her elbows resting on the arms of the chair. "Whatever."

"Was that your husband pulling out?"

"He won't be joining us. Howard has chosen to deal with Ellie's disappearance in his own way. I don't agree with him but I respect his feelings."

"How is he dealing with it, Mrs. Kruger?"

"He isn't. He believes one day she'll walk through the door, give us a kiss and tell us about her latest adventure."

"I see."

She smoothed an imaginary wrinkle from her pants, unwilling to meet his eyes. "I'm sure you don't but that's all right too."

"Has he felt this way from the beginning, from the time Ellie disappeared?"

"No, he was the one who suspected something was wrong from the beginning."

"I don't understand."

"When you're going through something like this, it's like you're in deep water. One minute you're sinking to the bottom and the next minute you're bobbing to the surface and trying to stay afloat. And then someone throws you a line and you reach for it. That's what the police did with us. They threw us a line and my husband grabbed it. I didn't want it. What I wanted was the truth."

"The police don't believe she met with foul play."

"She's a missing person. Apparently that's police jargon for 'we'll keep the file open but not pursue it.'"

"Can you tell me about her?"

"Our girl was a handful, Mr. Ryan. She was never into narcotics or anything like that. Her drug of choice was saving lives. Even when she was little and there was something on the news about a disaster somewhere, she'd cry and beg us to go there so we could help. When she was in fifth grade, she heard about a fire at a school in Pennsylvania. The next thing we knew, the police were at our door. They picked her up outside a pawn shop, trying to sell her bicycle for bus fare to Philadelphia. We were beside ourselves. We tried everything, reason, discipline. We even stopped watching the news but nothing worked. She ran away twice in high school. I can't even remember the incidents now but each time we brought her back, her response was always the same. But I wanted to help.

"She seemed to calm down in college. Her first two years at Middlebury were wonderful for all of us. She found her voice through her art. In September 2003, just days after the new fall term started, she disappeared again. We were frantic and contacted the police. A week later, she called us from Santo Domingo. She saw the devastation caused by the earthquake in the Dominican Republic and wanted to help."

"She sounds like an extraordinary young woman."

"That painting, the one behind you. She did that when she got back. She was only twenty."

Ryan turned around in his seat. It was a large canvas, powerful and disturbing.

"I think it's my favorite of all her work because it defines who she was and how touched she was by tragedy."

"And your husband really believes she's off somewhere doing good deeds?"

"Three years ago when Hurricane Maria devastated Puerto Rico, he never moved from that spot for a week. He watched every minute of the coverage convinced he'd see her there, serving food or God only knows what. That was two years after she disappeared. Nothing has changed."

"Were you forthcoming with the police about all the times she disappeared?"

"At the time, it never occurred to us to be anything but forthcoming."

"What about private investigators? Did you ever consider hiring someone who could work outside the parameters of law enforcement?"

Her body stiffened. "Yes, we considered it. We considered it to the tune of over twenty-thousand dollars. We've hired two. You'll be our third. How much is it going to cost us this time?"

"Did you read the website, Mrs. Kruger?"

"Yes, I read it. I thought it was a come-on, a marketing ploy to drum up business. Know someone who's gone missing? I'm your man."

The longer they talked, the more agitated she became. He knew the reasons. Once again, she was being asked to rummage through her daughter's life, to describe the indescribable and relive the nightmare. He had a choice. He could take his time and gain her trust or he could shock her, go against his instincts and discuss the brutal realities of the other two murders. The website laid out only their profiles, carefully worded to avoid the gruesome details. He waited another long moment before resuming. "I assume the other two investigators gave you written reports. I'd like to see them."

"I'm sure you would but I'm not paying you to rehash their failures."

"I'm not here to take your money, Mrs. Kruger. I'm here because of your daughter. I know you're angry. I understand that. You're either going to help me find out what really happened to Ellie or you're not, but one way or another, I'm in your life."

"Forgive me for saying this, but no one is that altruistic."

"Altruism has nothing to do with it. I have my reasons for wanting to find this man, but for the time being, they're my reasons and don't concern you. It would be helpful if you trusted me, but I'll accept it if you can't make that leap. I'm not the most trusting person in the world myself. All I ask is your help but if you can't give me that, then I'm afraid we have nothing further to talk about."

"We don't have the reports. I threw them away."

"Why?"

"Because they reached the same conclusion as the police, that she'd taken off with this man, this Charles. I didn't want my husband to read the reports. I thought they would only validate his psychosis, his total detachment from reality."

"Fair enough. Do you mind if we backtrack a bit? How did Ellie end up in Templeton? Maria said you and your husband were living in Dallas."

"I was born and raised in Templeton. I met my husband in college and we moved to Texas after we were married. Ellie was raised there but she spent the summers here with my parents from about the age of seven. When my mother passed away, she left the house to Ellie. After she disappeared, we kept it vacant until 2018, and then we rented it to a young couple. They still live there. We put the proceeds from the rental income into an account in Ellie's name."

"The house wasn't destroyed by fire?"

"Why would you assume that?"

"It's not important. Did the police send out a forensics team to gather evidence at her home, fingerprints, DNA?"

"No. The most they did was look around for evidence of violence but nothing was disturbed. There was no blood, no signs of a struggle, nothing. It looked to them as if she had packed a few things and simply driven away. Her purse was gone and her toiletries. There were some empty hangers in the closet and a drawer or two were cleaned out. Everything else appeared normal."

"Ellie owned a car?"

"If you can call it that. It was a VW bus, an old one. It worked for her because she could take her paintings around to art shows and galleries. It was a wreck but she loved it. It had rust spots all over the body but she painted over them with flowers and birds. That was Ellie."

"Would you happen to have any information on it, a title or some insurance papers, something with the VIN number?"

"No, she kept everything like that in a metal box. It was gone as well."

"Did anyone try to track down the vehicle?"

"Mr. Ryan, perhaps I'm not making myself clear. Once the police heard about her history, there was no crime, and since my husband was willing to go along with their conclusions, there was very little I could do."

"What about money? Did Ellie have an inheritance from your parents or your husband's parents?"

"She was your typical starving artist. We offered to subsidize her but she loved her independence. She took odd jobs here and there when she needed something special but nothing that lasted any length of time."

"I assume she wasn't making any real money selling her art."

"She was just beginning to make a name for herself on the Central Coast. Earlier that year, a magazine did a very complimentary article on her and several galleries were showing her work but making a living as an artist can take years."

"What about credit cards? Were the police monitoring the activity?"

"She didn't believe in credit cards. She felt the system was skewed toward those who extended the credit, not those who received it."

"Smart girl. Tell me about Charles Vaughn. Try to remember everything she told you."

"We spoke every Sunday around one o'clock. We both looked forward to it. During one of the calls, she sounded different, like she did when she was a little girl, giggly and excited. I thought perhaps she had sold a painting or a gallery was interested in her work, something like that. When she told me she had met someone, I was floored."

"Why was that?"

"A couple of years before, she'd been seeing someone quite seriously but he was killed in a motorcycle accident. She was desolate and swore she'd never let herself love that way again. That was the first time I'd heard her express interest in anyone since then. She said his name was Charles Vaughn, that he was a photographer. That's how they met. She was working on some sketches at Morro Bay and he was there setting up shots. I believe he told her he was working with a writer on a book about California's beaches or some such thing. They started talking and then went to dinner. After that, they saw one another whenever he was back in town.”

“He didn’t live around here. You’re sure of that?”

“I’m not sure of anything, only what she related to me. She said he traveled a lot, all over the country doing freelance work, that he tried to spend a few days with her every couple of weeks. She also said he was very attentive and possessive. That worried me but apparently she found it captivating.”

“This is very important, Mrs. Kruger. Did she give you any physical description of him, his age, height, color of his eyes, anything?”

“Only that he was handsome and very intelligent. I did get the impression he was a few years older than she.”

“Why was that?”

“She said he loved classical music. I guess I assumed a man close to her age would prefer something more contemporary. You have to understand, we only had the one discussion about him and we talked mostly about her feelings and how they were together. Frankly, I don’t think she wanted to go into much detail until we actually met him. Perhaps she thought we’d be disappointed if she built him up too much. I don’t know.”

“How soon after that phone call did you lose contact with your daughter?”

“That was the last time we spoke. The following Sunday we were supposed to firm up plans to travel here. Charles was coming back and she wanted her father and me to visit and spend some time with both of them. When she didn’t answer the phone, we thought it was a little strange but we certainly weren’t panicked. I tried at various times to reach her during the following week but I never caught up with her. When the following Sunday came and went without talking to her, we were very worried so the next day we flew here from Dallas.”

“Did you contact the police right away?”

“When we arrived on Monday night. Tuesday we spent the day at her home and then we talked to her friends and her employer at the time. She was picking up extra money by waiting tables in a small restaurant on El Camino Real. It's no longer there."

"What did her employer tell you?"

"That she hadn't shown up for work one night. They tried calling her but, again, she never answered the phone."

"What about her girlfriends?"

"I didn't realize that one of her friends had relocated to Europe. When we were finally able to contact her, she knew nothing of Ellie's new relationship. Her only other good friend here was Connie Wright. She's married now with two children. We run into one another from time to time at the supermarket but it's uncomfortable for both of us."

"Why uncomfortable?"

"For a couple of reasons. Mainly, I think she feels that when I see her with her children, I'm reminded that Ellie may never have that opportunity."

"I assume Connie never met Charles."

"She tried dropping in one day when she knew he was there, but Ellie told her he was napping. Connie said she seemed nervous about her being there so she left rather quickly."

"Did Ellie confide in her anything that could be useful?"

"No, nothing. The police did speak with her and one of the investigators I believe, but she wasn't any help. In fact, she may have contributed to the theory that Ellie had picked up and left."

"How so?"

"Not too long before she disappeared, they ran into one another at a local hair salon. At first Connie said it was old Ellie, bright and upbeat, but when she brought up Charles' name, Ellie shut down. She was surprised. She thought everything was going well in that department. They chatted for awhile about this and that and then Ellie blurted out she might be going away, that it was a secret and Charles would kill her if he knew she was ruining the surprise."

"But you said they were good friends. I thought women confided in one another."

"You shouldn't believe everything you see on television, Mr. Ryan. Contrary to what most of the writers conjure up, mostly male writers by the way, not all young women spill their guts over martinis and a salad. I spent many hours with Ellie and her girlfriends over the years, enough to make me want to pull my hair out. Young women today have sent our sex back to the Dark Ages. Where we wanted to be independent, they want to be taken care of. Even worse, they buy into the belief that when a man is possessive and jealous it means he loves them. When they get older, they may or may not see it for what it is, but by then it's usually too late. At the same time, these young women are bombarded with a cultural message: if you're alone, there must be something wrong with you. When a man comes into their life, instead of being vigilant, they become deaf, dumb and blind. Many of them withdraw from their friends. They stop going to the movies or meeting for coffee, whatever. Perhaps it's a proprietary thing or maybe they just don't want to run the risk that a girlfriend will point something out they don't want to hear. Personally, I suspect the latter."

"Did Connie tell the police what Ellie said about going away?"

"Yes, but I'm sure she had no idea at the time it would have the ramifications that it did. I know she blames herself for derailing the investigation, even though I've told her she did the right thing."

"What about neighbors? Did anyone see a man arriving or leaving?"

"No. Her home is even more remote than this one. My parents owned a small horse farm on about four acres. It's very private."

"Can you give me directions to her home? I'd like to drive by there."

"Of course. Mr. Ryan, will you answer a few questions for me now?"

"I'll try."

"The other two women, the ones on the website. They're real, aren't they?"

"They're real."

"And my Ellie? I assume you think she's a victim too or you wouldn't be here."

"I've just started looking into your daughter's disappearance, Mrs. Kruger. It's way too early to make that kind of assumption."

"But you suspect a serial killer, don't you?"

"I never said that."

"You didn't have to. How long have you been working on these cases?"

Ryan chose his words carefully. "The first case came to my attention in 2010, the second one a few weeks ago."

"2010? You've been working on this for ten years?"

"Yes. Do you have a photograph of Ellie, something taken around the time of her disappearance?"

"They took a photo of her for the magazine piece. I'll get it."

When she got back, she handed him a large white envelope. Ryan pulled the photo out, glanced at it and slipped it back inside the envelope. "She's lovely. I have to ask. What do you think happened to your daughter?"

"She's dead. I've known it from the moment we got here on that terrible Monday. Call it a psychic connection, a mother's love, whatever you want but I know Ellie is gone. There's no way she would have done this to her father and me, run off without a word in five years. I don't care how much in love she was or how hard he tried to control her. She would have found a way to let us know she was all right."

"It's possible the years got away from her. At the time, she may have been caught up in the moment, a romantic escapade, but at some point she woke up and realized what she'd done. Now she's afraid to face the consequences. It wouldn't be the first time."

"The consequences or me? I know what you're thinking. I've seen it on the face of every person who's sat in that chair, including the police. You look at me and see an angry, judgmental woman. You may not believe this, but at one time this shattered, dysfunctional couple was considered light-hearted and fun. I don't think Ellie ever understood us either. She thought we were angry when she ran off. We weren't. We were frightened out of our minds. The truth is we were proud of her. Who wouldn't be? When most of our friends' children were whining about not getting a new car or trips abroad, our daughter was reaching out to make the world a better place. But we couldn't encourage her to just take off when she felt like it. We made mistakes. We know that now. Perhaps if we had embraced her goodness and independence, she might have…"

"I wasn't thinking that, Mrs. Kruger."

"Then you're the first. One of the investigators even verbalized it. I don't blame your daughter for running off. If I were your child, I'd run off too."

"He was an asshole."

She smiled for the first time and looked down at her watch. "I'm sorry to cut this short but my husband will be coming home any minute. Are you staying in town or going back to San Francisco?"

"I'm going to drive by Ellie's house and nose around town a bit but I'm headed back tonight. I'll be in touch in a few days after I've had a chance to check a few things out. If you think of anything else, please give me a call day or night." He handed her his business card. "My cell phone number is on there."

"Why is he doing this, killing these women?"

"I wish I knew. What I do know is that Ellie is another part of the puzzle, an important part, and if she's alive I'll do everything I can to find her and bring her home. But I'm not going to lie to you, this could take time."

Barbara Kruger got to her feet. "Then I'm going to have to ask a favor of you, a big one I'm afraid. Unless you find Ellie's body, don't let my husband know what you suspect. I'd rather he live with the lie than have to face the loss of both of us."

"You're leaving?"

"I'm dying. I've been diagnosed with a brain tumor, inoperable. I have less than six months."

"Aren't there treatments?"

"I've chosen to forego them. Let's chalk it up to the fact that I'm a coward and let it go at that."

"I have no idea what your reasons are but you're no coward, Mrs. Kruger. As far as your husband finding out, I can't guarantee what will happen if we find this guy and learn the worst about Ellie. It may be out of my hands."

"Then I want you to tell him before he sees it on television or some stranger knocks on our door." She reached out and put her hand on his sleeve. "I know I have no right to ask but please, Mr. Ryan, promise me."

"Why me? You hardly know me."

"I'm not sure except I sense you've known your share of loss as well."

Ryan took her hand and held it between both of his. "You think she's waiting for you, don't you?"

She nodded.

"And if she isn't? If you're gone and she's alive?"

"Then I'll be waiting for both of them, won't I?"

CHAPTER 30

ANNIE

Despite the rocky start, Annie thought the day went well. She'd made appointments with two prospective accounting firms, finished three loads of laundry and taken a nap. While they were not the most productive eight hours of her life, she believed tearing up Larry's check made them, hands down, the most expensive.

The phone call from Bryce Stanley, coming as it did on the heels of Detective Giggles' departure, was a nice surprise. At the very least, it took her mind off Debra's resting place and the impending visit from the cadaver dog. Even more surprising was the tone of their conversation, chatty and comfortable, quite different from what she imagined. His son was back in his flat, the injury painful but not life-threatening. He'd sustained fractures in the first and second metatarsal bones of his right foot and would probably sit out the rest of soccer season.

Annie clucked sympathetically, asked about the London weather and thanked him for the driveway. When she could put it off no longer, she told him about refusing the Belgian block. To her immense relief, he laughed. Although he would have liked to take the credit, the block wasn't his idea. His instructions to the contractor were to fix the problem and make it look nice. If he had to guess, it was probably left over from another job. The last few minutes of their conversation were broken up by a weak signal. When they finally said good-bye, she was more confused than ever.

Tonight was a different story. It was Friday night and she was bound and determined to have fun. It was Arthur Fredericks' fiftieth birthday and birthdays were important around the Fredericks home, even more so since the deaths of two of their sons. Birthdays celebrated life, another year well-lived, another year in service to their faith. While there were always private moments of reminiscence and reflection, their parties were never maudlin. On the contrary. Arthur and Cynthia were gracious hosts who entertained at the drop of a hat, raucous, joy-filled events with music, laughter and a spirited collection of friends and colleagues who, once they arrived, were reluctant to leave.

Annie stole a glance over her shoulder. The cake was riding smoothly, a yummy confection of chocolate and strawberries, Arthur's favorites. On the floor, sheathed securely in bubble wrap, were eight bottles of champagne, a good chunk of her housewarming gift.

Pulling up in front of their house, she looked at her watch. By now, the cul-de-sac should have been filled with cars. Something was wrong, she could feel it. She hit the pavement running.

Cynthia stepped out of her front door and put her hands up. "I knew you were going to panic when you drove up here. Everyone's fine. We had a change of plans is all."

Annie stopped short and bent forward, rested her hands on her knees and exhaled. "Thank God." When she straightened up, she studied the face of her friend, trying to read her expression. "What kind of change of plans?"

"We decided to keep it small, just the three of us."

"You don't do small. You do big and noisy and fun."

Cynthia looked past her toward the truck. "You got cake in there?"

"Yes, I have cake, enough cake to feed half of Stamford. And booze, eight bottles of champagne, enough to get the other half blotto."

Arthur Fredericks walked up behind his wife and put his hands on her shoulders. "Sounds like a party to me. How you doin' Annie? You look good, sweetheart."

At fifty, Arthur appeared a good ten years younger. In spite of the tragedy that marked his life, his face was smooth and unlined, like beige porcelain. He was a shade or so lighter than his wife with dark brown eyes, the exact color of the freckles across his cheeks and cleanly-shaven head. He was a fine-looking man but his greatest asset was his kindness. Annie adored him.

"Happy birthday, sweetie." She went forward to give him a kiss. "I suppose you still want your present, right?"

Dinner was delicious, a vegetable lasagna prepared in Annie's honor and served in the kitchen, one of her favorite places in the world. If love had a smell, it would be just like the Fredericks' kitchen, lemony, with just a hint of soap and cocoa butter. It was where they hatched their dream and brought it to fruition, where they cheered their successes and mourned their losses. It was like home, only better.

Over cake and coffee, Arthur opened her gift and leapt out of his seat. In no time at all, the bluesy voice of Bessie Smith came through clear and strong. When he rejoined them, he looked sad.

Annie reached over and touched his arm. "So I did good?"

"Better than good. I didn't know that collection existed. Thank you, Annie."

Clearing the table, Annie sensed a change in the atmosphere. The air felt different, as if the oxygen were leaking out through some invisible rent. Grief could do that, descend like an unwanted guest. From the corner of her eye, she caught a glance between her friends, a reaching out of hands, silent offerings of love and support.

She kept her back to them and took her time loading the dishwasher. When she was finished, she took her seat at the table. "God, I've missed this. So what's new? We need to catch up." When they both seemed reluctant to speak, Annie laced her hands on top of the table. "Okay, me first. Larry showed up last night and almost got thrown in jail, they're sending a cadaver dog to the house in the morning to see if Debra's in my back yard, I tore up a check for half a million dollars, Bert Kennedy didn't die of a heart attack, he was killed by a hit and run driver in Norwalk and Wednesday night I have a date."

Arthur was the first to speak. "Who's Bert Kennedy?"

Cynthia shushed him. "You have a date?"

"I'm going to dinner with Bryce Stanley. He's the one who told me about Bert Kennedy. He was curious so he did some digging."

"Who's Bert Kennedy?"

Cynthia took the question, patiently explaining about the property manager and how he figured into Debra's disappearance. When she was done, she turned her attention back to Annie. "Okay, now you want to replay the part about Larry and the half a million dollars?"

"He came to the house last night. He'd been drinking. Things got a little out of hand but it all worked out. This morning he came to pick up his car and left a check on my windshield. I tore it up."

"That's the Reader's Digest version. You gonna fill in the details or not?"

"Not tonight. Anyway, it's your turn. What's new?"

Now she knew she wasn't imagining things. She'd shared too many dinners over too many years not to know something was wrong. "Come on, guys, I know something's up." Annie felt a chill. If one of them was seriously ill, she'd have to hold it together no matter what.

Cynthia reached for her hand. "Arthur got a promotion, baby. They want him to head up the I.T. Division."

"But that's incredible!" She looked from Cynthia to Arthur. "Congratulations!"

Arthur managed a half-smile and nodded.

"He'd been offered it twice before but never told me," added Cynthia. "Only this time I found out before he could turn them down."

"I don't get it. Why would you do that, Art?"

He shifted in his chair. "The job's in Atlanta, Annie."

Once again, Annie's world trembled on its axis but she got to her feet, went directly to the refrigerator and withdrew a bottle of champagne. "I don't know about the two of you, but I need a drink, and if this doesn't call for champagne, nothing does." It was the last thing she wanted but she had to get up and move around. It was either that or throw up.

Following her lead, Cynthia pulled three flutes from the sideboard and took the bottle from Annie's hands. "You better sit down before you fall down. We need to talk this out."

Annie did as she was told. "There's nothing to talk out. It's a wonderful opportunity for both of you and I couldn't be happier. You have to do this. It'll be a fresh start in a new place, something I should have done. Besides, I can visit. I love Atlanta and I love…" She lifted her glass. "To your new job, your new life and to old friends."

The champagne was cold and delicious and they may as well have been drinking lighter fluid. After several minutes of miserable silence, Annie tried again. "Come on, you two, this is silly. Tell me everything. When is all this happening?"

Cynthia got up and left the room. Arthur watched her, barely keeping it together. "Everything she loves is here, you, **Life House**, even our boys. I can't do this to her, Annie."

"You're not doing it to her, Art, you're doing it with her. Believe me, there's a difference. Besides, you deserve this. You've worked your ass off for that company, late nights, weekends, all the travel. She'll be fine. It's just a lot to take in. As far as the boys' graves, does it matter where they're buried? They live in your heart, remember?"

When Cynthia returned, she put a piece of paper on the table in front of Annie. "Here's a list of people you might want to start calling to replace me. If you want, I can call them over the weekend and get them in next week."

Annie stared at it. Her mind was racing and it was all she could do to keep up. Before she could stop herself, the words tumbled out. "What do you know about **The Acres**?"

"I know they spent about five million building it. It's on seven acres with a pond and a couple of indoor pools. I also know a couple people from the hospital who work there. What's goin' through that head of yours?"

"I heard a rumor they've opened a separate wing for AIDS patients." That was a lie. In a moment of panic over their cash flow, she called them to see if the **Life House** guests could be accommodated if they were forced to close the doors. Even worse, she took a tour without telling Cynthia. As a hospice facility, the place was unequalled. By their own admission, the owners had followed the **Life House** model and designed the facility for the living, not the dying. It had a movie theatre, fully-equipped salons for men and women and an ice cream parlor.

"Annie?"

"Sorry, my mind went blank for a moment." Another lie. "When do you have to be in Atlanta?"

"The first week in January, right after New Year's."

Six weeks? It was a pitifully short time to expect people to uproot themselves and leave everything familiar, but it was the corporate way or the highway, the quickest route to career suicide.

"Annie?"

"Cyn, in the first place, you can't be replaced. You're the heart and soul of **Life House**. And in the second place, I've known about this less than ten minutes. Please don't ask me to make any decisions tonight." She looked around the room and over her shoulder to the living and dining rooms. Two years ago for their anniversary, while Cynthia and Arthur were lying on a beach in Aruba, Annie had seized the moment, redecorating those two rooms from floor to ceiling. The planning had taken months but the reveal was well worth the effort. Cynthia shrieked then cried her eyes out, big fat tears of joy. "I love this house. I doubt you'll have any problem selling it."

"We have an offer already, one of the guys at work."

Annie wasn't surprised but the finality of it struck her like a blow. "Are you going to accept it?"

They both nodded.

Now the energy in the room seemed charged, as if the slightest ripple would create a spark and send them hurling through space. Annie didn't move, afraid of being the catalyst. While part of her wanted to stay, to say all the right things and make them laugh and feel good about their excellent adventure, another part of her wanted to run.

In the end, she took the coward's way out, kissed them both good-night and walked quickly to her truck. Circling the cul-de-sac, she saw them in the open door, arms wrapped around each other's waists, heads leaning into one another, a single silhouette. It was a touching tableau, the perfect image of who they were. It was also the one she would summon when they were gone.

Pulling onto I-95 for the short drive home, a knot began to form in her stomach and a memory surfaced, both sweet and terrifying. It was a childhood game that Samantha relished and Annie tolerated with big-sisterly patience. They were only about five and six but the recollection survived along with the sensation, the unreasonable dread.

As children, they shared a room and sometime after good-night kisses and lights out, they would pull all their dolls and stuffed animals onto the full-size bed. For the next hour, the bed was a raft in the middle of the ocean. Even then, Samantha showed a remarkable talent for drama, setting the scene with high waves and circling sharks. Annie knew it was make-believe but that made it no less frightening, the pink shag carpeting no less deep and threatening. Almost immediately, she would feel her stomach knot.

She smiled at the symbolism. Annie Hogan Heywood, adrift at sea. How poetic, how pathetic, how true.

CHAPTER 31

RYAN

Jimmy Januski sipped his coffee and waited while Ryan settled in across from him before launching the opening salvo. "I almost forgot how handsome you look in the morning light. You're a goddamn Adonis, you know that?"

"What light? It's six o'clock in the morning. Remind me again why we're meeting at this ungodly hour on a Saturday."

"Because in an hour I'm running a sensitivity seminar and I'm going to be tied up all day, that's why."

Ryan chuckled. "Gosh, that's a shame. What is it this time? Can't be Gay Pride. That was months ago."

Jimmy lifted the mug in a mock toast. "Tis the season, my friend, that wonderful time of year when everyone takes exception to something or someone. This year it's Holiday Harmony. Who knew all that singing and dancing and diversity means the end of civilization as we know it. Maybe I'm getting old, but I remember a time when the fruitcakes were under the tree, not threatening to blow it up."

"Since when did sensitivity become an issue when it comes to public safety?"

"Since the threat came from Christians for Christmas. Some local TV evangelist is all lathered up about sharing the event with Kwanzaa and Chanukah."

"I don't see a problem. Bust his ass for inciting a riot. Make Jesus proud."

"Tell you what. You run the seminar and I'll go chase that pretty senorita around your office for a couple of hours." Jimmy slid a manila envelope across the table. "We got a few good prints off the mouse. She's in the system, Pete."

It took Ryan a second to catch up. "I was afraid of that."

"Her name is Martha Henderson, youngest daughter of John and Camille Henderson of Rising Sun, Indiana. Her mother's a teacher, father owns a car dealership there. She's Apple Pie American, by the way. Both her parents are third-generation Hoosiers so I don't know where the accent came from."

"The same place the fluent Spanish came from. If you're going to reinvent yourself and run from the law, you'd better get it right."

"Hear me out before you start going all Dog the Bounty Hunter on me. Martha, Maria, whoever was a third year law student at the University of Texas, top two percent of her class. Two years ago, she's working in the Austin D.A.'s office, clerking, writing briefs, that type of thing. That's why she's in the system. Everyone who works there gets printed. Anyway, they loved her, planned to offer her a job when she passed the Bar.

"Six months into her internship, the Austin P.D. makes a drug bust, a big one. A few weeks before the trial, the D.A. brings in the two undercover cops late one night to start prepping them. Martha's there. One of them takes a look at her and it's all over. He's gone. He asks her out a few times and she turns him down. She's the studious type and likes her men the same way. He's your typical undercover grunge narc, you know the type. Plus, he's got a wife and four kids at home. He starts stalking her, showing up at her apartment, following her when she leaves work, generally making a pest of his badass self. She ain't happy about it and tells her boss who ain't all that thrilled about it either but his hands are tied. They need this guy's testimony a lot more than they need her so they do zip. One night he's feeling a little frisky and does more than watch her from afar. He gets into her apartment, tries to crawl in bed with her for a little hump and rumble. She wakes up and grabs the closest thing at hand, a brass lamp on the nightstand. He goes night-night and she calls the cops. He winds up in the hospital, screaming his head off about how he's going to kill her. Oh yeah, the D.A. not only throws her to the wolves, he fires her. Needless to say, she's pretty disillusioned with the law and the justice system at this point so she drops out of Law School and hightails it out of Dodge. Now what?"

"Hump and rumble?"

"You want to hear this or not?"

"You got all this from one phone call?"

"You picked up enough from that little rant of hers to get the ball rolling: College, Austin and Cops. Once I put a name with the prints, I started with the University. They pulled her records and said she'd quit in the middle of her third year. They also gave me the information that she'd been clerking at the D.A.'s office. I called the D.A.'s office and got her supervisor, a woman. Turns out she's still pretty steamed about the whole thing, said she'd call me back when she could talk. She did, about five minutes later from outside the building. Once she started talking, I couldn't get her to stop. A couple of weeks after Martha leaves Austin, she gets an email from her. She's back in Rising Sun with her folks, looking to get a job in a small law office. She asks for a letter of recommendation and gives her the name of the firm. I called the law office. They loved her too for about three months, until he showed up. The trial's over and he's got some vacation time coming but instead of taking the wife and kiddies to Disney World, he opts to terrorize your girl and her family."

"How'd he find her?"

"Martha's smart. She figured out that someone hacked into her computer. Not only that, her parents called in a security firm to sweep the house. They found bugs everywhere, about a dozen altogether."

"That explains a couple of things, her expertise with a computer and why she didn't want to be linked to the Pierce case. Anyone think of bringing the Rising Sun police into it?"

Jimmy signaled the waitress for a refill. "Would you? I'm not sure at that point my confidence in law enforcement would be all that good."

"So she ends up cleaning hotel rooms and he goes on with his life, same as before."

"Not exactly. They got a conviction in the drug case and grunge-boy got a commendation and promotion. Now he's an asshole with a bigger gun. He's going to find her sooner or later, that's a given."

"You get a name on this creep?"

"It's in the envelope with the mouse. You thinking of doing something stupid?"

"Probably."

"Anything you want to share?"

"Probably not."

"You going to tell her you know about all this?"

"Hell, no. She'll run again. At least if she's here, I can keep an eye on her. I owe you another one, Jimmy, thanks."

"There's more. The gal in the D.A.'s office mentioned something else about your girl, the reason she wanted to study law in the first place. Her older sister married her high school sweetheart a few months after graduation, nice guy, came from a good Rising Sun family. About a year into the marriage, the couple stops going to family gatherings. A little while after that, they move to Cincinnati and the sister stops calling her family altogether. Martha misses her, doesn't understand what the hell's happening so she gets on a bus to find out. When she gets there, she finds her, seven months pregnant, eyes swollen shut and bruised all over. Martha's only about seventeen but she knows she's got to get her out of there so she drags her onto a bus and back to Rising Sun. I wouldn't say it's a happy ending but it could have been worse."

"What happened to the husband?"

"He picked on someone his own size and the other guy took exception, beat him to death outside a bar."

"Sounds like a happy ending to me."

"How'd you know she wasn't who she claimed to be?"

"I didn't. I'm shocked as hell if you want to know the truth. The only thing I knew for sure was she doesn't have much use for cops. Now I know why. I don't suppose you got as lucky with the name Charles Vaughn."

Jimmy shook his head. "We found two in California, a seventeen year old kid in Menlo Park and a thirty-eight year old guy in Santa Ana. I know you said the man involved with Ellie Kruger was older but I checked him out anyway. Five years ago he was doing 10 years in Florence for armed robbery."

"It's another alias. I don't know, Jimmy. Driving back, I almost convinced myself Ellie Kruger is hiding out somewhere but what are the odds that three women, all involved with the arts, approximately the same age and all living in relative seclusion aren't somehow connected?"

"After you called, I pulled up her old driver's license. He's sticking to type."

"Yeah, I noticed. It isn't so much that they look alike, although they all had long, dark hair, but all three of them were attractive women. The thing that doesn't play with Ellie Kruger is her body wasn't found. He wanted us to find Theresa."

"But it was a fluke that Susan Pierce's body was found. You talk about odds, what are the chances that a pilot would spot her body in the middle of the Arizona desert?" Jimmy emptied two packets of sugar into his coffee and half the pitcher of cream. "Maybe he's changing his M.O. We've seen that before. Murder doesn't cut it anymore. He wants to make a statement. That would explain the brutality of what he did to Susan Pierce. You don't get much more barbaric than that."

"Then why leave Theresa's body in the neighborhood where she was raised? That made it personal." The question was rhetorical, one they'd been over a hundred times.

"What else you got? Any idea how he finds them? It's a pretty specific group."

"At one time or another, they all had articles written about them. Theresa and Susan Pierce were featured in the Arts section of the **Chronicle** under two different by-lines. There was an article written about Ellie Kruger in some local publication a few months before she disappeared. Anyone could have picked them up off a newsstand."

"What about the storage facility?"

"Another bust. When I got back from Sedona, the kid and I went through every rental agreement for the last ten years but none with the first name of Charles. It's about as cold as you get."

Jimmy put his elbow on the table and leaned forward. "You want to tell me what else is going on? Something's eating at you."

Ryan tried to concentrate on the sounds around him, the low buzz of conversation, the tinkling of spoons in coffee mugs, anything that would block out Barbara Kruger's words: *They want to be taken care of…deaf, dumb and blind.*

"Pete?"

"How does he do it, get these women to change who they are?"

"Meaning?"

"I don't know that much about Susan Pierce, other than what her sister told me, but I knew Theresa, at least I thought I did. She wasn't desperate for a man and, according to her mother, neither was Ellie Kruger. How does this bastard worm his way into their lives and start manipulating them? These aren't casual flings. Theresa was crazy about him. Ellie felt the same way, made excuses for him, even stopped confiding in her best friend."

"You're asking me? I raised three daughters and I never knew what they saw in any of the guys they hooked up with. For awhile, I chalked it up to temporary insanity but they all seem to be working out. I'm not sure where you're going with this."

"I'm trying to reconcile the sister I knew with the person who let someone get close enough to murder her. You knew her, Jimmy. She was tough and smart. She could spot a phony a mile away."

"She was a pistol all right. I could see that the first time I met her. I stopped by the house to pick you up and she answered the door. I was what, twenty-four, twenty-five and she couldn't have been more than ten but she looked right through me with those big green eyes. Before I knew it, I was sitting on the couch and she was interrogating me about who I was and whether or not I was a suitable friend for her brother. She said you deserved only the best and if I didn't measure up, she'd kick my butt."

"Too bad she didn't set the same standards for herself."

"Is that what this is about, you're pissed at her?"

"I'm not pissed at her. I'm trying to make sense of it."

"You were a homicide detective for a lot of years, Pete. You ever see a murder that made sense?"

"You know what I mean."

"I don't think you know what you mean. What the hell went on in Atascadero anyway?"

"Barbara Kruger painted me a picture of contemporary women and I don't see Theresa fitting into it."

"Maybe that's your problem. You still think of her as your kid sister, the survivor, the girl who made something of herself. She was thirty, not exactly a kid. I don't know what the woman said to you, but I sure as hell wouldn't want my daughters painted with someone else's brush. You know my girls, different as night and day but they all want the same thing, to be loved. And I know something else, something I learned from you almost twenty years ago: we don't blame the victim."

"That's not what I'm doing." But it was exactly what he was doing, what he'd been doing since the morning they found her body. It was the reason that acceptance, the final stage of grief, eluded him, the reason he couldn't put the anger and depression behind him. The truth of it hit him like a punch to the gut.

"Those weren't just words I spoke at her funeral. I loved her too. If I could have picked a sister, it would have been Theresa." Jimmy slid from the booth and grabbed his overcoat. "I liked it better when you were blaming yourself. Make peace with her, Pete. Until you do, neither of you is going to rest easy."

Through the plate glass window, Ryan watched him cross the street. Jimmy was shaking his head, probably muttering to himself the way he always did when he thought no one was listening. He'd get over it.

Ryan reached for his wallet. The walls were closing in on him and he needed air, fresh air, free of the oppressive smells and depressing conversation. Now he had two voices to contend with. How did one make peace with the dead? He could barely make peace with the living.

CHAPTER 32

ANNIE

Her nerves at the breaking point, Annie wiped down the spotless countertop, and for the third time in as many minutes, peeked out the window. Unless the dog had sinus problems, what was taking so bloody long? She thought of leaving to run a few quick errands, but if they found something and she wasn't there, she'd never forgive herself. The good news was they'd checked the basement first and found no sign of Debra's remains.

When she finally walked outside, the handler and cadaver dog were leaving the marsh, heading for the line of tall pines. Saunders was watching from the terrace, his inscrutable expression hidden by the ever-present shades. Approaching him, she attempted a casual tone that belied the sexual tension that always lay just below the surface. "More caffeine?"

"I'm good, thanks."

"I meant for the dog."

His mouth twitched, the closest he ever came to a smile. "It shouldn't be too much longer, maybe another half hour. Speaking of dogs, where's your buddy?"

"I dropped him at the groomer. He's having a spa day."

"You should have joined him. You look a little ragged around the edges."

Keeping her eyes on the trees, she lowered her sunglasses from the top of her head to cover her eyes. Two could play at that game. "There's a mystery solved, why any woman would let you get away." The comment sounded more flirtatious than ironic and she added, "Ignore me, I'm cranky. I'm not sleeping well."

"You need sex, Annie, and I'm not talking about the violins and candles kind. I'm talking about the sweaty, head-banging, break the furniture kind."

She knew he was trying to get a rise out of her, but she also knew there was no way she would let that happen. "As romantic as that sounds, I'll pass."

"I wasn't volunteering. I was making an observation."

"Take a number. It seems everyone is lining up to tell me what my problems are."

"You're not my type. Sleeping with you would be like bedding Little Bo Peep."

"You're insane. I can't believe they let you walk around with a gun."

"He didn't alert on the suspicious areas. I don't think she's here."

"I almost wish she were. I got the feeling from her diary she loved it here."

"It's a nice piece of property."

"I guess it could be, but all I see is an overgrown money pit." The wind shifted and she caught a whiff of aftershave and peppermint, two scents she'd come to associate with him. Stepping forward out of range, she shook her head and focused on the dog. "We'll never know what happened to her, will we? She'll be another person fallen through the cracks. It's bizarre how I feel I know her, but I have no idea what she looked like aside from Helen's description."

"They were married in Paris, remember? I have a buddy in the RCMP who emailed me a copy of her passport. She was pretty."

Unbidden, an image flashed before her eyes. It was the same cold-case board but now Debra's photo was in the center, to her left a little boy with freckles and to her right a smiling woman with beautiful, familiar eyes. "You've been busy. I assume you learned her maiden name."

"Couillard. Your neighbor was right about that. Debra was descended from the first French family to settle Quebec, the 1600s if I remember right."

The words triggered a disturbing reprise of the previous evening, the reason she couldn't get to sleep. There was something she needed to tell him but she couldn't bring it forth.

"Bert Kennedy didn't die of a heart attack. He was killed in a hit and run three days after Debra's last entry in her diary."

That was it. God, now he was reading her mind. "I know, I learned that yesterday."

"More research?"

"I'm not researching anything. Bryce Stanley called me from London after you left yesterday and mentioned it in passing."

"I thought he didn't know anything about this."

"You weren't listening. I told you I asked him about the previous property manager. That's the reason I went to his office in the first place." She was still fuzzy from lack of sleep but the fog was gradually lifting. "Wait a minute. Helen said Bert Kennedy came to her house a few weeks after Debra's disappearance, not a few days."

"Time gets distorted after only a few months. It was twenty years ago. What else did Stanley happen to mention in passing?"

"He was calling back to acknowledge my call of the day before, the one I made to thank him for the driveway. We chatted for a few minutes, until the signal was lost."

"How's his kid?"

"He'll live. He broke some bones in his foot. How did it happen?"

"How the hell do I know? Maybe he fell or kicked the ball wrong."

Annie rubbed her eyes. She knew her train of thought was jumping the track but then so was his. He seemed distracted. His eyes never moved from the activity at the base of the trees but she sensed his mind was elsewhere. "Bert Kennedy. You obviously know more about it than I do. What happened?"

"His daughter and grandson lived a couple of miles from here. He went there every Thursday night for dinner. It was a little after ten when he left their place and walked outside to get into his car. Someone clipped him from behind. He was killed on impact. His body was thrown thirty feet, broke his neck."

"And they never found out who did it?"

"The case is still open."

"But I thought the police had ways of tracing vehicles from paint chips and tire tracks and…"

"Looks like we're done here."

She pivoted in time to see the dog jump in the van, its handler walking toward them. Saunders went to intercept him. They talked briefly and shook hands. Before getting into his vehicle, the man waved and she waved back.

Now that they were leaving, she felt surprisingly let down. At least while they were there, she had something to occupy her thoughts, something other than her unresolved future. She felt the familiar twinge of guilt. For better or worse, she had a future and Debra didn't. Perhaps it was the weather, the winter blahs, or maybe she'd picked up Larry's bug, a nasty case of self-absorption.

Saunders was heading back in her direction when his cell phone rang. He stopped, turned around and headed for his car. It was obvious from his body language, the way he ran his hand through his hair, that something or someone was pissing him off. Annie ducked back inside the house, out of the line of fire. Ten minutes later, he was at the side door and she waved him in.

"I'll take that caffeine now."

"I made a fresh pot right before I went outside. Is everything okay?"

"Peachy."

She fixed a mug of coffee for him and grabbed a bottle of water for herself. She was mid-gulp when he started lobbing questions.

"The call you made to Turk Storage. What exactly did you say to them?"

"It was a couple of weeks ago. I'm not sure…"

"It's important, Annie, think."

"I was trying to find a listing for Bert Kennedy when I came across the card for the storage company. It didn't register at the time and I threw it away. I took Einstein for a walk and while we were out, it hit me that the storage facility was in San Francisco. Helen said she thought Charles was from there and I decided it was worth a try."

"And you found the card tucked inside the page where Bert Kennedy's home address and phone number were listed, right?"

"Right."

"Tell me again. What was your cover story to the guy at Turk Storage, the one you used to get him to look through his files for the name Charles Hastings?"

"I said I was his sister, that he was out of the country and I was trying to locate the storage facility where he'd stored our parents' belongings."

"Did he buy it?"

"I don't know. He sounded young and a little frazzled. I thought I'd caught him at a bad time."

"And you gave him your phone number but he never called back."

"As far as I know."

"What callback number did you give him?"

"I gave him my cell number, I'm sure of it. I think I even spelled my name for him."

"And you found out the next day that some guy had called the hospice asking questions about the facility and mentioned he knew your brother Charles."

"That's right."

"What made your partner think the call was bogus? You must get calls all the time inquiring about the facility."

"She's been doing this a long time. I trust her judgment. If she says he wasn't on the up and up, I believe her."

"You're sure you didn't give the kid the hospice number."

"I'm sure."

"And the call came in to the hospice shortly after your call to Turk Storage."

"We keep a log of incoming calls. I looked it up and calculated it came in just about an hour later." The longer they talked, the more uneasy she became. Hearing the incident broken down gave it a much more sinister edge. "It has to be a coincidence, Mike. If I didn't give him the **Life House** number, how would someone know to call me there?"

"Can I use this?" He slid her laptop toward him. She was seated across from him and couldn't see what he was typing in. After no more than a minute, he turned the computer around so the screen was facing her.

"Is that me? Is that my name? What did you do?"

"I googled you. There are two links, one to your newspaper columns and the other to the **Life House** website. You're out there."

"I don't want to be out there. It's invasive."

"Then you shouldn't have a website." He clicked on the hospice site. "Now we know how he got your work number. He spends some time researching AIDS to give his own cover story credibility and makes the call."

"What was he doing, checking on my story to make sure I had a brother named Charles? He did say they didn't give out that kind of information. Maybe I was wrong about him. He didn't sound that resourceful."

His cell phone rang again and he got up to take it outside. Annie motioned him to stay, pointed toward herself then to the ceiling. She needed a bathroom break and some aspirin. Ten minutes later when she reappeared, he was off the phone, staring at the computer screen.

He looked up long enough to take in the transformation. "What did you do up there?"

"I washed my face and used some eye drops. Where were we?"

"The kid you talked to at Turk Storage was off yesterday so I left a message. That was him calling back. For the past few weeks, he's been hounded by a private investigator. The guy's been pushing him to come up with a rental agreement signed by anyone with the first name Charles, even promised to buy him a car if he hit pay dirt. When you called, the kid figured it was a lead. I'm willing to bet this is the guy who spoke to your partner." He turned the screen toward her again.

A California driver's license was displayed in the center of the screen and Annie leaned in to get a better look. He was a nice-looking man, a little on the serious side, but way above average. "Peter Ignatius Ryan. Is this a joke?"

"Why?"

"P. I. Ryan, P. I.? It sounds more like a TV show than a real person."

"I'll know soon enough. Lou's running a background check on him. For the record, did Stanley mention how he found out about Bert Kennedy's accident?"

"He said he was curious and made some phone calls." She barely finished the sentence when she felt a yawn coming on and covered her mouth. "Sorry."

"Why aren't you sleeping? Man trouble?"

She shook her head. "That's one of the upsides of not having a man in your life. You get to obsess on important things. I thought I had the sleep thing under control but I got some bad news last night. My partner's husband got a promotion and they're moving to Atlanta."

"That sounds like good news."

"Which is exactly what I said to them last night. They didn't believe it either."

"Can you find someone to replace her?"

"We've been friends for over ten years. She made **Life House** happen. There were times, in the beginning, when I was ready to throw in the towel. There was so much to learn and so much hostility toward what we were trying to do but she never lost her way. She kept me going. She kept everyone going. I'm closing it down right after the first of the year. There's a beautiful new facility in Pound Ridge. I spoke to them this morning and they're blocking space."

"You always make decisions on the fly?"

"I guess I do." Now that she said it aloud, she felt the full weight of her decision. "The truth is I've been thinking about it for days, even before I heard she was moving. It's time. We don't have a waiting list. That's a first."

"More good news."

"Very good news. The public is much more educated on preventing the disease and the meds are better. It would just be a matter of time before the money ran out and we'd have to start cutting back on things. Fundraising's gotten tougher. Either that or I've lost my touch."

"It didn't look that way yesterday. A half a million dollars must not go as far as it used to."

"I tore up the check. You were right."

"Can I get that in writing?"

She was growing accustomed to his expressions, but this was a new one, somewhere between respect and lust. She liked it, perhaps a little too much.

"What's next for you?"

"I haven't thought that far ahead. In the short term, I might do some traveling or spend a few months in London."

His eyebrow shot up.

"My sister lives there, remember? For a trained investigator, you have a lousy memory."

"That's my cue to leave. You're starting to pick on me."

"Hold on, did you just set me up again and change the subject?"

"It wasn't that tough."

"What's your theory about this guy?" She nodded toward the screen.

He clicked off the site and closed the computer. "This isn't a theoretical discussion anymore. It's a murder investigation."

Annie looked at the laptop, narrowed her eyes and looked into his. "You're a little late to the party but at least you showed up. In case you've forgotten, I'm the one who invited you. I handed you this case."

"You're right, you did, so let me do my job. There are already too many people out there who know you're nosing around. The less involved you are the better. It's for your own good."

"What am I, six? I'm not going to do anything stupid."

"Really? What if Ryan isn't legit? What if he's the one who killed Debra and he's paying the kid to give him a heads-up if someone starts asking questions?"

"That's lame and you know it."

"It may be lame but it's exactly what I'd do."

"But he's got dark hair and his name is Peter, not Charles."

He slapped his forehead. "I forgot, these guys never change their appearance or use aliases. He's the right age and he lives in California. You're out of the loop."

"Answer one more question, will you, Detective?"

"Shoot."

"Which one of your personalities am I dealing with today?"

"The only one you need to worry about, the one with the badge."

CHAPTER 33

RYAN

The downstairs door was unlocked, Ryan's first irritation of the day. In the stairwell, he encountered two more, the smell of fresh paint and a string of invectives that echoed through the building. The harangue was over by the time he reached the second floor, his vocabulary enriched by several colorful metaphors.

Maria was seated, her back to the door, a stack of newspapers and painting paraphernalia piled neatly in one corner. She was staring at a chalkboard perched on the windowsill. A radio tuned to a soft-rock station was loud enough to muffle his approach and Ryan knocked before entering. "Humor me and lock the downstairs door when you're working alone on the weekends."

When she turned around, he almost didn't recognize her. Her hair was braided into two silky plaits that fell along the straps of her overalls. She was spattered with paint and looked unnervingly young. "Stop worrying about me."

"It's not you I'm worried about. If your bite's as bad as your bark, someone could wander in here and get hurt. Even better, take Sundays off from now on."

"I have work to do."

"So I see." The ancient oak furniture was polished to a warm golden glow, the walls and ceiling damp with fresh paint, a soft blue-green. "Nice color."

"It's called Bora Bora Breeze. It's supposed to look like water. I thought it would be relaxing."

"Maybe you can get your money back."

"You made a joke. What's up with you?" She smiled, a lascivious little smirk. "You get lucky last night, Mr. Ryan?"

"I haven't gotten lucky since the eighties."

"I'm surprised. You've very handsome in a Dick Tracy sort of way."

"Do me a favor and drop the mister. It's either Pete or Ryan."

He walked around her desk to take a closer look at the chalkboard. At the top of the board, the years 2000-2020 formed twenty-one column headings. Beneath three of them 2010, 2015 and 2020, three names were written, Theresa Ryan, Ellie Kruger and Susan Pierce respectively. The other columns were blank, all except 2005 where she'd written two names, neither of which he recognized.

Marie moved in beside him. "You see it too, don't you?"

"Who are they?"

"I'll tell you in a minute. What else do you see?"

"Right now that's all I can see. What is this?"

"Before I went home Friday night, I went on-line to see if there were any sites devoted to missing persons or unsolved murders. I got their names from the North American Missing Persons Network. It's a sister site to the Doe Network, you know, like John and Jane Doe. Anyone can access the sites. It's a way for the public to become involved and help to solve some of the disappearances. There is also a section with composites made from unidentified remains. I thought you would know about it."

"Never heard of it. You got those names off their site?"

"Yes."

"Why 2005?"

"I went back five years from Theresa's murder, the first one we know about. There's a pattern. He kills every five years. We have three murders and they are exactly five years apart."

"We have two known murders. We don't even know if Ellie Kruger's dead and we have no idea how many others are out there. It's a good theory but I don't think we can call it a pattern. Log on, let me see their profiles."

"Do you think I would be painting walls and polishing furniture if I could log on? Two minutes after I found their names we lost our connection to the internet. I have been screaming at them for almost thirty-six hours."

"Screaming at whom?"

"At our internet provider. Who do you think I would be screaming at?"

"Right now you're screaming at me. So we wait it out. What else is going on?"

Reluctantly, she turned away from the board and grabbed a notebook from the top of the desk. "Friday after you called from the road, I sent emails to everyone I could think of connected with photography, agents, unions, professional organizations. I also went to the major on-line booksellers to see if there were any books published about California beaches. The only one I could find was published in 1989. It's out of print but I Googled the photographer. He died in 1996."

"Has anyone gotten back to you?"

"How would I know that? The internet is down, remember? It's the weekend. We may not hear anything for days."

"You're asking them to search their records for a Charles Vaughn, right?"

"I thought that's who we were looking for."

"It is, but when you're up and running send them a follow-up. He might be using the name Tyrrell, Charles Tyrrell."

"You have another lead?"

"One of the shopkeepers in Sedona traced a purchase back to a Charles Tyrrell. It was a necklace Susan Pierce was wearing in a photograph. Cody's already run the name but it wouldn't hurt to cover all the bases."

"Is there anything else I should know before I waste more time? What are you doing?"

He was standing in front of the coffeemaker, the carafe in one hand, the filter basket in the other. "Does this thing come with a manual or a tutorial?"

"It's ready to go. Put the pieces back and hit the 'on' switch."

She tried logging on again, only this time she heard the familiar sound of a connection. "Yes!"

Ryan stopped what he was doing. She took him first to the Missing Persons website and familiarized him with the quickest way to navigate it. "I went to 2015 to see if Ellie Kruger was listed. When you see the name, you click on it and…"

The photo was the same one Barbara Kruger had given him. The facts were sparse, her birth date, the date of her disappearance and the location where she was last seen. "That's not much information. Are they all like that?"

"I never had the chance to find out. I did try to match Ellie's photo with the composites of unidentified remains but she's not there, I'm sure of it. If you want to look for yourself, I can bring it up."

Standing behind her, he rested his hand on the back of her chair and bent down until their heads were almost touching. Her hair smelled like vanilla. He pulled back to a standing position. "Send the link over to my office and call it a day. Go to the park or to a movie, have some fun."

"The park? What's wrong with you?"

"There's nothing wrong with me. It isn't that I don't appreciate what you're doing. You're a natural at this but you've been at it night and day for the last four days. You've started a new life so go enjoy it. Besides, I come up here on the weekends to be alone."

She scribbled something in her notebook and tore off the page. Linking her arm in his, she led him out to the hall. "Here are the names of the two women on the blackboard. I'll send you the link." He was looking at the names when her door slammed behind him.

An hour later, he was pacing, waiting for the phone to ring. One of the names belonged to a woman in her early forties, married, a stay-at-home mom with four kids. But the other woman, Rachel Dixon, was a perfect fit. She was thirty-two in 2005 when she disappeared from her home in Boulder, Colorado, single, a cellist with the Colorado Symphony Orchestra in Denver. With the exception of Susan Pierce, the other three could have been related, cousins, even sisters.

He placed his first call to the Boulder police which was a waste of time. It was a cold case and the detective in charge was unavailable. The rest of the hour was spent trolling for family members of the missing woman, anyone with the last name of Dixon in the Boulder area. Of the four names, only one was home and claimed to know nothing of a woman named Rachel. He left messages for the other three.

He opened the window, hoping the air would revive him. Almost immediately, the aroma of fresh coffee wafted in from across the hall. Regardless of her mood, he had to risk it. The downside was he'd have to admit she was right. It was beginning to look as if her theory had merit.

"Pete?"

He almost didn't hear her over the noise from the street. Her voice sounded strained. She was standing just inside the door, the color drained from her face. "We had over fifty new emails. This was sent Friday night."

Ryan took the printout from her hand.

Subj: Are You a Victim?
Date: 11/3/00 10:12:53 PM Mountain Standard Time
From: claygirl
To: rainman06

My younger brother is in the doctoral program at the
University of Michigan/School of
Social Work and is currently working on his thesis.
While researching the long-term
effects of sexual abuse on children, he came upon a
website with a link to yours and forwarded it to me.
I believe it was meant as a joke (although not a very
funny one considering the subject matter) since he
could not have known about a man I recently (very
recently) became involved with. The lifestyles of the

two women were very close to my own. I assume they're real case histories. Although I don't consider myself reclusive, I would have to say that where I live is very remote. Also, I am an artist – sculptor – and approximately the same age as the other two women. It was the word "soulmate" that grabbed my attention as Charles has used it to describe our relationship. Your website didn't give any details about his name, physical description or profession. I know I'm just being silly but I'd like to eliminate him as soon as possible as a serial killer (ha-ha). I'll be out of town for the next few days but please call me next week so I can put my mind at ease.

Peace.

Morgan Evans
480-555-7676

"Shit." He reached for the phone.

"Are you calling the police?"

"I'm calling the number in the email. I'll put it on speakerphone but unless she answers, don't say a word."

After three rings, there was a momentary hesitation followed by the voice of a woman. "Hi, this is Morgan. I'm probably in my studio so leave a message. From November 11th through the 14th, I'll be in Sedona at the Red Rocks Gallery. If you're a dealer or collector and want information on my Birds of Prey series, please leave detailed information on how I can contact you. Have a great day."

Maria turned to leave. "Today's the 12th. I'll get the number of the gallery."

"I'll do that. You find out what town uses the 480 area code. I'm sure it's not Sedona. And see if she has a website. Maybe there's a photo of her."

Minutes later, Ryan walked into her office and tried to sound more upbeat than he felt. "She never showed up at the gallery. They think she's down with some bug that's going around. I couldn't get any other information out of them so Cody's on his way over there."

"I have her website up." Maria's color was back and she was smiling. "She's blonde, Pete. All the others were brunettes. She's probably in bed with the flu and didn't want to bother answering the phone."

"What about the area code?"

She was still staring at Morgan Evans' photograph.

"Maria, the area code."

"It's assigned to several towns in the Phoenix area, Scottsdale, Cave Creek, a few others. I don't understand why you're not relieved. Look at her. Besides, it doesn't fit the pattern. It's too soon."

All of what she said was true but Ryan didn't believe a word of it. Every instinct told him she was wrong.

"Why isn't his name on the website?"

His mind was a million miles away. "What?"

"The name Charles. Why was it left out of the profile?"

"Lita wanted it in but I made her take it out. I didn't want every woman with a husband or boyfriend named Charles getting pissed off at him and turning him in as a potential murderer."

"You don't have much faith in people, do you?"

"You spend the next twenty years of your life behind that desk and then talk to me about faith in people. There's another reason I left it out. Sometimes critical details are withheld from the public in order to qualify leads."

Her desk phone and his cell phone rang simultaneously. Ryan went for his cell phone. "It's Cody. You answer the other one. If it's a call from Boulder from someone named Dixon, keep them on the line or ask them to stay put for the next ten minutes."

He was finishing his conversation with Cody when Maria walked back into his office and folded herself into an empty chair. She looked exhausted.

"That was Rachel Dixon's uncle. He was calling back to tell you not to call him again, that the family's been through enough. A TV producer has been hounding them for months about using her case for a reality crime show."

"I'll call him back. Maybe I can get him to talk."

"He did talk. I made up a story that I was trying to locate Rachel for our high school reunion. They found her remains nine months ago at a campground near Idaho Springs. Some children were playing around with a metal detector. She wasn't buried very deep. She had a locket around her neck, engraved with her name. They confirmed her identity through dental records. I guess they haven't gotten around to updating the website."

"How far is the campground from Boulder?"

"An hour."

"What else did he say? Was she seeing someone?"

"He doesn't know. He sounded old and frail."

"What about other members of her family?"

"She has a twin sister living in Michigan but he wouldn't tell me how to get in touch with her. Their parents are both dead."

"What about the police? I assume they're in contact with him."

"They talked to him right after the remains were found but he hasn't heard from them since."

"I have to talk to him."

"Why? What good will it do? She's been dead fifteen years. He's old and tired and disillusioned with the system. Don't we owe it to the living to let them rest in peace too?"

"When we find the bastard responsible. Go home, Maria, get some rest."

"Stop patronizing me, Ryan. I'm not a child."

"Look, right now we have to play the cards we're dealt. If we can't stop this guy before he kills, then we have to dig through the victims' lives until we get some answers. We're glorified grave robbers."

"I think I'll leave that off my resume."

"I meant what I said. You're doing a good job, a great job. I don't know too many cops with your initiative and ability to think on your feet. We wouldn't even know about Rachel if it weren't for you, but I don't want to be sitting here five years from now reading emails like this one. This isn't my favorite part of the job either. When Theresa was murdered, it made me sick every time I had to talk about her. It still does. She would have hated the fact that people were dissecting the intimate details of her life even though she wrote about them, but that was her choice. The dead don't have that privilege and neither do the loved ones they leave behind."

"Maybe if you say that to him, what you just said to me. Did you tell Barbara Kruger about your sister?"

"No."

"But you're asking the victims' families to trust you and expose painful pieces of themselves. How can you expect them to be open and honest when…" She stopped and looked down at her hands. "I'm sorry. I'm sure you're doing what you think is right. What did Chief Cody find out?"

"He went by the gallery. She goes up there once a month to put on a show for the tourists. They set her up near the door and she works on a piece to draw people in. When she's there, she shares a small apartment with two local girls. They haven't heard from her either."

"When was she supposed to be there?"

"She usually goes up late Friday night or early Saturday morning. It's a two-hour drive from her home, a place called Tonto Hills, a few miles north of Scottsdale. Cody's headed there now. He'll call when he gets there." Something clicked and he rifled through his drawer until he found his notes. "Call the gallery again. Find out if she was there last December 22nd. They must keep some kind of record. Tell them you're working with Cody. Also, ask them to check their sales receipts for that date and a list of salespeople who were working that day."

"I'll do it but where are you going with this? The high school reunion thing was a fluke. I'm not always going to be able to pull stories out of my…"

He put his hand up. "I get it. The gallery is in Tlaquepaque. A man claiming to be Charles Tyrrell bought Susan Pierce's necklace in a shop in the same plaza on the 22nd of December." He loosened his tie and rolled up his sleeves. "Let me know what they say and then call the café and order some food. We're in for a long day."

"I've driven that route and there's not much out there. What if she was in an accident or her car broke down? I need to get a list of area hospitals and towing services. What do you think?"

"I think the next time I tell you to take the day off, you should do it."

"Don't hold your breath."

CHAPTER 34

ANNIE

"It's banana bread, right from the oven. I thought perhaps you could make some tea and we'd visit for awhile. Is this a bad time?"

Avoiding eye contact, Helen took the foil-wrapped bread from her hand. "I suppose I have a few minutes."

In spite of the fact that Helen kept her home at a toasty eighty degrees, the atmosphere was frosty. It was her fault for procrastinating. She should have stopped by sooner, sat her down and explained her theories about Debra's disappearance, her reasons for going to the police. The poor woman was probably confused and frightened. She'd warned Mike to tread lightly in his questioning but, knowing him, he hadn't listened. Now, almost three days had lapsed, three days for Helen to fret about it.

She heard the rattle of pans and waited for things to quiet down. "Did you go to mass this morning, Helen?"

The kettle hit the burners and Annie jumped. As she walked around the tidy living room, she carefully avoided the knick-knack strewn tables. It was a porcelain forest, the place where tchotchkes went to die. She couldn't imagine owning it all, let alone keeping it clean. She ran her finger along the top of the mantle. Not a spot of dust. Some framed photos caught her eye, the first of which was a handsome couple in full wedding regalia. The next was a charming little girl, five or six, with dark ringlets and a large pink bow to match her dress. Linda, that was her name, their only child. She was posed demurely, legs crossed at the ankles, hands held loosely in her lap. Debra's drawing was last in line and Annie picked it up. She studied it for a moment and then glanced back at Linda, dead at nine of leukemia. What an incredible waste of two beautiful lives.

Helen reappeared carrying a serving tray and tea service. Two pieces of thinly-sliced banana bread were on a matching plate along with the leftover loaf, neatly wrapped in a fresh piece of foil. "This is yours, Helen, I made it for you."

"No, thank you."

"I know I should have prepared you and told you the police were coming here, but it's been a rotten week all around. Are you all right?"

"No, I'm not all right. I think it's ridiculous accusing that nice young man of murdering his wife. You should be ashamed of yourself."

Annie's jaw dropped. "Excuse me?"

"You heard me. You young women think every man is guilty of something. In my day…"

"I don't think that at all. My father is a wonderful man and I'm sure your husband was too. I have nothing against men. In fact, most of my friends are men. I even married one."

"And divorced him. What about your sister? Is she divorced too?"

"Samantha's never been married."

"That's what I thought. You never met Charles. He was clean-cut and well-spoken, not the kind of person who does that kind of thing."

Annie counted to ten, afraid she was going to snap. That logic, skewed and irrational, was all too familiar. Her own mother was still incensed over Scott Peterson's conviction. During his trial, they argued vigorously over his guilt or innocence until Annie refused to discuss it. When he was sentenced to death, her mother cried for weeks and not once did she mention Laci or her baby by name. "Your place looks nice, Helen, are those new drapes?"

"You know they want me to go down to the police station and work with someone to come up with a picture of him."

"A sketch artist?"

"I've never been inside a police station in my life. I'm not sure I'll go. I asked someone at church today and she said she didn't think they could make me do that."

"But don't you want to help them get to the truth?"

"I know the truth. She died on the way to the hospital, just like Charles said." Her gaze roamed to the mantle. "He reminded me of my late husband. They were both gentlemen, well-bred and commanding in their demeanor. The very idea that he would bury her in the back yard."

"With all due respect, Helen, her name was Debra." Annie broke off a tiny piece of the bread. When she tried to wash it down with the tea, she almost gagged. "I'm surprised Detective Saunders told you about the cadaver dog. I didn't think they were releasing that to the public."

"He didn't say a word to me. It was that other young man, the one who stopped by yesterday."

"Someone stopped by here yesterday? Was it a policeman?"

"That nice young reporter. I can't remember his name but it's in the Sunday paper right above the article."

"What article?"

"The article in today's paper, right there by your foot."

Annie picked up the newspaper. It was all there. The Westport Police had opened an investigation into the 2000 disappearance of a Canadian woman, Debra Couillard Hastings. She was last seen in July of that year by her neighbor, Helen Allen, a long-time resident of Spinnaker Lane, Westport. According to an official source within the Westport P.D., Mrs. Allen was scheduled to aid the police in their efforts by providing a description of the woman's husband, Charles Hastings. Mr. Hastings reportedly fled the scene after an encounter with Mrs. Allen in which he claimed his wife had fallen ill and died on the way to the hospital. There was more but Annie couldn't bring herself to read it. A black and white photograph accompanied the piece, the dog and his handler emerging from the marsh, the brook and one of the birch trees in the foreground.

"This can't be good. The police didn't want this information out there."

"They can't stop me. I have a right to my opinion. Anyway, he got it all wrong. I told him the whole thing was bunk. I don't see anything in there about that."

"Because that doesn't sell papers, Helen."

"Am I going to get in trouble?"

"I don't know." She reread the first paragraph. "He cites an official source within the Westport P.D. I have a feeling they'll be more interested in plugging that leak than harassing you. I'll speak to the detectives and try to smooth things over. Just promise me you won't talk to this reporter again."

"I'm getting old, Annie. My mind is finally catching up with my body. Nothing makes sense anymore and it makes me angry."

"Like what?"

"TV commercials. I don't understand half of them."

"That's because they're stupid. They're created by sixteen-year-olds for other sixteen-year-olds."

"You know, my husband lived most of his life in another era. He hated everything new and modern. I can't remember him ever listening to music that wasn't at least fifty years old. We never went to motion pictures or plays because he said they were badly-written pieces of rubbish. I always wanted to try new things but I knew he didn't approve. When he passed away, I decided to make some changes, expand my horizons you might say, but lately I'm having difficulty coming to terms with the present. I find myself thinking the same thing over and over. In my day, that didn't happen." Her eyes wandered upward and fixed on their wedding photo. "Maybe he was right. The past was safer, easier. At least you could tell the good people from the bad."

Annie reached for Helen's hand, lowered her voice and spoke slowly, as one would to a child. "That's not necessarily true, Helen. Leopold and Loeb were intelligent, well-dressed college students. They came from wealthy families and looked like the kind of boys every mother would want, except they weren't. They murdered a fourteen-year-old boy for no other reason than they thought their intelligence exempted them from the law. They killed because they could, because they thought no one would believe that cultured, well-bred people would do something like that. That was in the 1920s. They weren't the only ones, but the difference is you weren't bombarded by it twenty-four hours a day, seven days a week."

Helen squeezed her hand. "I'm sorry I fussed at you, Annie. You're a good girl and I did care for Debra, you know I did."

"I do know that. I also think it's possible you're defending Charles because you don't want to believe that Debra was betrayed by the person she loved and trusted. I had a hard time with that myself."

"When you talk to that detective, tell him I'll do my best to help them. They said they'd send a car for me tomorrow at one o'clock."

Annie looked at her watch. "I have to get back to the house and get some things done, but I can go with you tomorrow if you'd like."

"Oh, I'd like that, dear, and I'll keep the banana bread if you still want me to have it."

Walking back to her house, Annie dodged a car backing out of the lane. When the driver saw her, he slowed the car and flipped her off. No sooner had she recovered from the shock of the gesture when she looked up and saw Mike Saunders walking toward her from the driveway. He was wearing jeans and a t-shirt under a leather bomber jacket. He looked deliciously scruffy, like he'd just gotten out of bed.

"I came as soon as I heard. Did that idiot just flip you off?"

"Who was he?"

"I didn't get his name. I've been here ten minutes and that's the third car I've turned away. I'll have to step up the patrols."

"I'm surprised to see you here. I thought you'd be back at the station water-boarding your colleagues."

"Lou wanted that privilege. He's ready to burst a blood vessel."

"How did this happen, Mike? We were standing over there when the photo was taken. I didn't see anyone."

"He must have been behind the van. We weren't looking in that direction. You were giving me a bad time, as usual, and I was pretending to ignore you."

"As usual." His visits were getting to be a habit, one she was starting to enjoy way too much. "Do you know the guy, the one who wrote the article?"

"I know him. He's a bottom-feeder. He was on his way to Starbucks when he saw the van turn into your road. He recognized the driver from another case and decided what the hell, his latte could wait. He watched for an hour or so and then wandered over to your neighbor's to see if she knew what was going on. He got the basics from her."

"And the specifics from someone in your office. I just spoke with Helen. She promised she won't talk to him again."

"He's an asshole. What's the journalistic equivalent of an ambulance chaser?"

"A good reporter."

"What, you're defending him? Let me guess, you were on your high school paper."

"College."

"The Birkenstock bunch. You were going to expose society's ills and stick it to the man."

She laughed. "These feet have never touched a Birkenstock, and I was only there for the cute boys."

"Bullshit. You're a born crusader. It's one of the things I like best about you."

His tone was different today, less aggressive, more playful. She didn't know quite what to make of it but she liked it. "And I suppose you were part of the other crowd, the ones who wanted to beat the crap out of us for being conscientious."

He raised his hands and wiggled his fingers. "Not with these hands. I was a music major at UCONN, the next Oscar Peterson."

"I love jazz piano. What happened?"

"My mother passed away right after I was accepted into Julliard's graduate program. My dad fell apart. He was a cop too.

I decided to put off grad school for a year or so. The next thing I knew I was in the police academy."

The more layers he exposed, the better she liked him. She could easily fall for him, if she wasn't already there. Despite their last exchange ending on a sour note, she dreamed of him again last night. "Do you still play?"

"Every chance I get. You still trying to stick it to the man?"

It was the perfect opening and she almost walked through it. "Not so much but I still believe in freedom of the press."

"We'll see how gung-ho you are when the local townsfolk start picnicking on your lawn."

"Sometimes we have to make sacrifices for our principles."

"I can't believe you said that with a straight face."

Typical of their bizarre ritual, they'd been talking for the better part of five minutes without looking directly at one another. It was as if they both knew eye contact would lead to something more, something inevitable. The tension, combined with the cold afternoon air, was starting to get to her and she stomped her feet to get some circulation back. "I'm freezing out here, Mike. Can we take this inside?"

He followed her in and took off his jacket. The aroma of banana bread hung in the air and the room was oppressively hot.

She opened the window over the sink. "It'll cool off in a few minutes. Can I get you something?"

"I'm leaving for Seattle in the morning, a forensics conference. I've been scheduled to go for months. I'll be back on Friday. I'm taking myself off the case, Annie."

Had he said he was going to terraform Mars or have a sex change operation, it wouldn't have surprised or disappointed her more. "Why?"

"You know why. I can't do my job if I'm personally involved. Friday morning after I talked to Flynn and he told me what your ex tried to do, I wanted to go after him and beat the shit out of him. That's not good."

"But you've always been very professional."

"Not always. That morning when I showed up here and your door was open? I'd been here awhile, at least an hour. When I saw the door open and Einstein running loose, I thought maybe your ex came back and you were in trouble so I came inside the house."

"How far inside?"

"Far enough to see you were sleeping and not dead."

"Oh."

"I covered you up."

"So I guess we can add Boy Scout to your other personalities."

"I deserve a hell of a lot more than a merit badge. You always sleep like that?"

"I've never been able to sleep with clothes on, even when I was little. My parents didn't know what to do with me."

"I know the feeling."

"That was the day the guys were finishing up the driveway, the day you found Larry's check. You gave me a pretty hard time that morning, as I recall."

"I was trying to keep my mind off the fact I'd seen you naked."

"Why are you telling me this now?"

"You asked me why I was taking myself off the case. A cop would have followed procedure and called out your name before climbing those stairs."

"I took a sleeping pill the night before, and with all the racket going on in the driveway, I doubt I would have heard you if you screamed my name."

"That's not the point. I wasn't a cop when I walked into your bedroom."

"Who are you now?"

Cupping her face in his hands, he tilted her face up so she was forced to look him in the eye. "I'm the man who's crazy about you, the one who has to remind himself every time he's around you to keep his hands to himself."

"What if I don't want you to keep your hands to yourself?"

"This isn't about an afternoon fling, Annie. If I can't have more, then I'll walk away."

"I'm not sure I have more to give, Mike. One day I think I have all the answers and the next day I'm more confused than ever. What I do know is I have to reconcile the person I was during my marriage with who I really am, and I have to do it alone. I can't handle another complication, not right now."

"Then I'll have to pass." He kissed her on the forehead. "You really don't know who you are, do you? How can you be so smart and know so little about yourself? You have these lights inside you that keep changing color. One minute you're this soft, beautiful woman and the next you're a scrappy street kid who has an answer for everything. It's a potent mix."

"Again, you weren't listening. I don't have an answer for anything, that's my problem. And I'm Irish. We're all scrappy street kids at heart."

"Is it Stanley? I sure as hell can't compete with him."

"I've told you. I don't even know the man. Don't take yourself off the case. I've gotten use to having you around."

"Good, then maybe you'll miss me enough to make it permanent. I don't want to be your buddy or your verbal sparring partner, and I'm not going to stand on the sidelines and watch some other guy extinguish those lights."

"I don't understand."

"It's what men do, Annie."

"Why?"

"I don't know. Why do we spend months looking for the perfect car and then start thinking about how to modify it? Maybe it's about possessing something. We have to break it down and put it back together again before we can consider it ours."

"Is that what you'd do?"

"No, I like the parts just the way they are."

Her kitchen phone rang and they both looked down at the display. Stanley.

Saunders shook his head.

"I won't answer it."

"Sure you will. Maybe not while I'm here but you'll answer it eventually. He's doing his due diligence, Annie. You're his next acquisition. The question is can he afford you?"

"That's a rotten thing to say. I left Larry because of the money, not in spite of it."

"We'll see."

She wanted to laugh but she couldn't find the strength. He was the second man in a week who'd ripped her to pieces. Now the kitchen, once her favorite room, was more crime scene than comfort. "You said what you came to say. Just go."

"No problem, but until this case is over, stay the hell out of my way." He grabbed his jacket and slammed the door behind him.

Sadness, fatigue, even guilt that she was having dinner with Stanley descended on her and the tears followed. She didn't want him to go, not now, not ever. She could lie to herself but her dreams told another story. Halfway up the stairwell, she heard the side door open and in the next moment, he was staring up at her from the vestibule.

"Tell me something, Mike. What is about me that brings out the worst in men?"

"That's easy. It's because deep down we know we'll never have you completely. There's something inside you just out of reach, a part you'll never give up and it drives us nuts."

"How do you know that?"

"It's in your eyes. I see it when I get too close. If I didn't know any better, I'd think it was fear."

"Maybe it is. Maybe I'm petrified of getting lost again."

Ascending the stairs until he reached her, he put his arms around her. When she hiccupped through the last of her tears, he rubbed his thumb along her lower lip. "Wouldn't you just know it, you're even beautiful when you cry."

"Does this mean we're friends?"

"Don't push your luck. I can't be your friend, Annie, not yet anyway."

"My sister's play opens on the 28th. I'll move up my plans and leave for London by the end of the week. I'll be gone when you get back." It sounded too final and her next words tumbled out before she could stop them. "Please don't give up on me."

He planted a kiss on top of her head before releasing her. "Don't give up on yourself."

CHAPTER 35
CODY

He made the final turn off Cave Creek Road and hit the brakes. Directly in front of him was the largest Kachina he'd ever seen, at least forty feet tall. It was facing south, its feet anchored in the center of a circular rock garden. A dirt road, rutted and dusty, lay just ahead and snaked its way up into the low-lying hills. To his right and left were two stone walls, the words spelled out in crooked iron letters: TONTO HILLS.

He rolled up the windows to keep out the dust and eased his boot on the gas. No wonder he couldn't find it on a map. As the crow flies, it was less than a mile beyond Desert Mountain, a gated fortress of mega-homes, six first-rate golf courses and pricey eateries. But in every other way, Tonto Hills was a world removed, remote and quirky, older than its upscale neighbor by decades. Here, individuality took precedent over conformity, eccentricity over convention.

The unpaved roads were the tip of the iceberg. Road signs, if one could call them that, were skinny wooden posts painted white with black lettering. He'd circled the community twice before finally seeing the one he wanted, Jackrabbit Road, and he'd almost missed it again. The post was leaning over, its upper half hidden by a bush.

Morgan Evans' home sat just below him, about fifty yards ahead. It was smaller than most, even older from the look of it. He pulled off and cut the engine. Her property, an acre or so of earth and scrub, was surrounded by a low stone wall. To the right of the house was a detached two-car garage. A Jeep Wrangler was parked outside, and on the ground beside it a Golden Retriever lay sleeping. When she heard Cody's pick-up, the dog came instantly alert, got to her feet and started barking.

Cody kept his distance and watched the house for signs of life. The dog jumped forward several feet then retreated, barking furiously. She repeated the action several more times and began running back and forth between the house and garage. After a few minutes, she resumed her position near the Jeep.

"Can I help you?"

He rolled down the window. The face looking back at him belonged to a man of indeterminate age, somewhere between old enough to know better and too old to care. He was decked out in cowboy gear, and judging by the height of the truck, stood about five foot six.

"I don't know, maybe." Cody extended his hand through the window. "Name's Roland Cody."

The man took his hand and gave a limp and clammy shake. "Lou Fields. That's my spread down there."

Cody pushed his sunglasses to the top of his head and opened the door of the truck. The man stepped back, the top of his Stetson even with Cody's nose. His *spread* lay just below Morgan's, a drab aluminum-sided house and a patch of dirt enclosed by chain-link fencing. "Nice looking piece of property, Lou. You know Morgan Evans?"

Lou Fields licked his lips and hitched up his levis. "I know everybody here. I sort of keep an eye on things."

The clothes were western but the accent was Boston born and bred, a recent transplant. He'd gotten lucky. Standing before him was the very person he'd hoped to meet, the one person who would spill the beans about his neighbors, the Village Idiot. "I'd say they're lucky to have you. You seen Morgan around here in the last couple of days?"

The older man took off his hat and wiped his forehead with the back of his hand. It was a gesture straight out of every John

Wayne movie ever made. "Well, I might have. You mind telling me why you're asking?"

Cody put his foot on the bumper of the truck. "Don't mind telling you at all. She was supposed to be in Sedona this weekend and a few of her friends wanted me to check on her. When was the last time you saw her?"

"Saw her Friday afternoon, playing with that goddamn dog of hers. Don't know what that girl's thinking, leaving it out all night. Tell you one thing, I hear that dog barking tonight and it's going to meet with an accident, if you get my meaning."

When he patted his holster, Cody lowered his sunglasses. If there were any truth to Lita's claim, that one could read his thoughts by looking at his eyes, he didn't want the little bandy-legged buckaroo running for cover just yet. "That's some handsome hardware you got there, Lou."

"Colt .45, the real thing, not one of those reproductions."

"Morgan doesn't usually leave her dog out all night?"

"Never has and I been here almost a year. She treats that damn dog better than most people treat their kids, takes it everywhere. She's probably shacked up in there with her new boyfriend."

"You ever see this guy, her boyfriend?"

"A time or two, even talked to him once. Had his car parked right where we're standing. He seemed all right, for a Canadian."

"How do you know he was Canadian?"

"He gave me his card. Told me he was scouting locations for a moving picture company."

"A film company?"

"Isn't that what I said?"

"Do you still have his card?"

"Nah, pretty sure I threw it away. I thought I could talk him into using my place for the outside stuff, even offered to give him a better deal but he wanted to use her house. Bet I know why."

"You remember his name?"

"Last name was Richmond. I remember that 'cause I worked with a guy named Richmond."

"What about his first name? It's kind of important."

He shook his head. "Can't seem to bring it up."

"Was it Charles?"

"That's it, Charles Richmond. How'd you know that?" He glared at Cody. "You sniffing around her too? That's it, isn't it? You're here to cause trouble." His voice was raised and it roused the dog who began barking, running back and forth between the structures. "Okay, now I'm going down there and fix that bitch."

"Whoa there, kemo sabe." Cody pulled his badge from his back pocket. "You're not going anywhere, least of all near that dog. What you are going to do is answer my questions."

Lou Fields was studying the badge. "This says Sedona and I don't see no police car or uniform. In fact, you don't look like any police officer I've ever seen. I'm not sure I have to answer your questions, Chief."

His emphasis on the last word made Cody smile. "I think you might want to reconsider that, Lou."

"What kind of questions?"

"When did you first see this Charles Richmond?"

"A week or so ago. Not sure of the exact day. He was sitting here in his car looking around."

"What kind of car was he driving?"

"I don't know but it was silver, kinda small but big enough to hold some equipment in the back seat."

"What kind of equipment?"

"Looked like cameras and stuff. Had one of those things surveyors use."

"A tripod?"

"That's it."

"Did you notice the license plate or see a rental car sticker, anything like that?"

"Never paid attention."

"Describe him."

"Hell, I don't know. I couldn't see much. He was sitting down and he was wearing one of those damn baseball caps and dark glasses, big ones, bigger than yours."

"What color was his hair?"

"Light colored, blond maybe or light brown."

"Was it long, short?"

"I just told you he was wearing a baseball cap."

Cody glanced down at Morgan's house and back at him. "If you only saw him sitting in his car, how do you know they were involved?"

Fields muttered something under his breath and started fidgeting.

"You were spying on them, weren't you? You snuck up the embankment and watched them through the window."

"You can't prove a damn thing and I'm not answering any more of your questions."

"You're right, you're not, but here's what you are going to do. You're going back to your house and do the thing you do best, spy on your neighbor. If you don't see me back at my truck in twenty minutes, you're going to call 911, give them this address and tell them an officer needs assistance. And while you're waiting, you're going through every piece of trash in your house and find that business card. If your house isn't any cleaner than your clothes, my guess is it's still in there somewhere. Do you understand?"

"And if I don't?"

"I start knocking on doors. I'm sure your neighbors will be real happy to know how you keep an eye on things."

Fields was shaking so badly his hat fell off.

Cody picked it up and handed it to him. "And one more thing. I'm going to be checking up on you, and if I ever suspect an animal around here has died of anything but old age, I'm coming back and ram that fake six-shooter so far up your ass they'll need the jaws of life to pull it out. You got me, pardner?"

The older man looked at his watch and started for his home. He was moving at a pretty good speed when Cody turned back to his truck. He reached into the glove compartment and retrieved his automatic, chambered a round and tucked it behind his back. Before closing the door, he grabbed a half-empty water bottle from the cup holder.

Walking down the hill, Cody took his time and kept his pace relaxed. As he approached the Jeep, the dog got to her feet, barked once and shook her head. Cody got down on his haunches. "Come here, girl, it's okay." He cupped his hand and poured in some water. The dog advanced slowly. The closer she got, the more he could see she was groggy and dehydrated. He stayed put and waited, arm extended. She stopped in front of him and lapped at the water. When it was gone, he added more and patted her head, moving his hand slowly to her tags. He found what he was looking for. It was heart-shaped, red with gold lettering: Maggie Evans.

When she was finished drinking, she looked back toward the house and barked twice. Cody reached for her and rubbed her ears. "I'm afraid this is a one-man job so you'll have to wait in my pick-up. If she's in there, I'll find her. If she's not, then you're coming home with me until she shows up. I'm real partial to girls. Okay, Maggie?"

At the sound of her name, she looked at him and cocked her head. Only after she was safely locked in his truck did Cody turn his full attention to Morgan Evans' home.

The front door was locked and he knocked, calling out her name. When she didn't answer, he slipped on a pair of disposable gloves, ran his finger along the top of the frame and lifted the doormat. He found the key in a plastic rock amid a pile of real ones near the door.

The front room was neat and nicely-decorated with a European feel, definitely a woman's place. It was also chilly, just a few degrees warmer than the outside air. He removed his boots and walked across the room. A wood-burning stove was cold to the touch. The kitchen was the same, immaculate, all done up in black and white tile with French posters on the walls. A small iron table and two chairs were tucked away in a little nook. Behind them was a window, and in the distance the Superstition Mountains. He checked the sink and dishwasher. Everything was washed, dried and put away. Same with the cabinet beneath the sink.

A trash can was empty with a fresh liner. He picked it up and sniffed it. Bleach.

He left the kitchen and retraced his steps across the front room toward a narrow hallway. The first door on the left was a tiny office, not much larger than a walk-in closet. Two glass blocks in the wall above his head provided the only source of natural light and he flipped the light switch. This room was not as tidy as the others. He pulled a pen from his pocket and began flipping through the papers on her desk, mostly to do with her work, a couple of inquiries and some bills for supplies. On the wall behind him was a memo board, padded with criss-crossed ribbon to hold things in place. Every inch of it was filled, a crazy jumble of greeting cards and notes.

The bathroom was next and he slowly opened the door. It was decorated much the same as the kitchen with black and white tile and walls washed in yellow. A claw foot tub occupied the far end, an oval shower rod suspended from the ceiling. The curtains and towels were dry as a bone. Everything about the room looked fresh and new, including the pedestal sink and toilet. The same with the cabinet above the sink, white MDF. He opened the mirrored door, no prescriptions, not even birth control pills. The rest of the contents could be found in the bathroom of any woman, including his own, lotions and creams and God only knew what. It was jammed full, as if nothing was removed for travelling.

There was a rustling sound coming from behind him, the only room he hadn't searched. He drew his gun and eased around the corner. The room was straight ahead, the door closed all but an inch or so. He kept his back tight to the wall until he heard the noise again then swerved and kicked his way through the door.

Her bedroom was a mess. A suitcase was upended, its contents strewn about on the unmade bed. A table lamp was on the floor and a small hook rug was bunched up in one corner. The sound was coming from an oscillating fan as the breeze hit the closed wood blinds. He left it on and turned in search of something else, something not quite right. He found it on the quilt at the foot of the bed, a large dry circle of urine.

Cody looked at his watch. He'd used ten of his twenty minutes. After giving the closet a quick once-over, he made his way to the front door, put his boots back on and locked the door behind him.

Back outside, he checked the Jeep's tires against the other visible tracks in front of the house, but whatever tracks were once there had been obliterated by the dog. Chances are, he would have carried her body to his car and driven off. As far as anyone could tell, that's the way he'd done it with Theresa Ryan, and more than likely the Pierce woman. The only difference was she'd been alive and destined for a death worse than most.

With five minutes left, he turned toward the garage. A small breezeway separated the buildings and there was a fire door on the side facing the house. He tried the handle and found it locked so he walked around to the front. The overhead doors were padlocked and he continued past them, along the far side of the structure to the back wall, the one facing south. To his surprise, instead of a solid wall there were floor to ceiling windows. He tried looking inside but the shades were down, some kind of perforated vinyl. He put his face to the glass and cupped his hands to keep out the glare. Whatever was in there was big. He could make out a shape but none of the details. It looked like a bird. He scratched his head, walked back to the house and took the key from the rock. It fit the lock and he turned the knob.

The bird was huge and menacing, a Turkey Vulture, at least twice its actual size. She'd captured it in frightening detail. The bald head and hooked beak were grotesque, nightmarish. It was landing to feed, wing dipped, one clawed appendage touching down.

Morgan Evans lay dead in a pool of blood, her eyes open and opaque. She was nude, posed, her stomach positioned just below the vultures' beak. In the dim light, everything was grey, the clay bird, her body, everything but the floor. Cody knelt down on one leg. The skin above her neck wound was bruised with dark thumb impressions just above the slash. She'd been strangled to unconsciousness, carried to her studio and revived for the final kill.

Before getting to his feet, Cody touched her hand and offered a prayer for her spirit. And then he wept.

CHAPTER 36

RYAN

Ryan rotated his neck and used his hand to work out the kinks. How could anyone spend eight hours in front of a computer? He'd been at it less than an hour and his upper body was already stiffening up. And where the hell was Cody? Even with traffic, he should have reached her home by now.

"If you want me to wave a white flag, I'll have to take off my tighty-whities."

Ryan kept his eyes fixed on the screen. "I wouldn't. I have a gun and I know how to use it."

Grinning, Jimmy took the guest chair closest to the door. "I stopped by earlier this morning and kept Maria company for awhile. She wasn't sure you'd be in today."

"I thought you had Raiders tickets for this afternoon."

"I didn't feel like driving all the way out there. Besides, we need to talk." Jimmy nodded toward Maria's office. "She gone for the day?"

"You just missed her. She ran home to change clothes and pick up some food. What's up?"

"I don't want to make a big deal out of this, but I crossed the line yesterday morning. Theresa was your sister, not mine. I don't know where my head would be if it were someone close to me."

"You gave up Raiders tickets for this? Look, Jimmy, if I got pissed at you every time you were right, I'd have ended our friendship long before now."

"Run that by me again. Did you just admit you were wrong?"

"No, I simply implied you might be right."

"What's the difference?"

"The last twenty-four hours. It was one thing when Theresa's murder was an isolated thing, a romance gone wrong, but I think we've got a serial killer on our hands." Ryan laid Morgan Evans' email in front of his ex-partner. "That was sent Friday night. Maria wasn't able to open it until a couple of hours ago." He waited for Jimmy to read it then recapped the events of the morning, including Cody's mission to Tonto Hills. He ended the summation with the discovery of Rachel Dixon's remains and their futile attempts to get more information.

Jimmy was silent through the entire recitation. When it was over, he said, "I'll lean on the Boulder police, have them send over a copy of Rachel's file. What about the uncle? You want me to hit him with a little cop talk? I'll get the sister's phone number from him."

"Let's wait. Her contact information might be in the file."

"When's Cody supposed to get back to you?"

"Could be anytime now."

"Listen, Pete, you give any more thought to Maria's problem?"

"On and off, why?"

"Because at some point someone's going to start connecting these cases and it's going to be big news. If this Morgan Evans winds up missing, they won't have a choice, they'll have to reopen the Pierce case because of the Sedona connection. Maria may not have seen the guy but she was in the house with him and she knows Susan Pierce wasn't alone. This'll be big and she'll be right in the middle of it. She can change her name all she wants but she won't be able to hide and you won't be able to protect her."

"She doesn't know anything, Jimmy. You know how much I want this bastard. If I thought for a moment she could help the investigation, I'd…"

"You'd what?"

"Can we just drop it for now?"

Jimmy got up and closed Ryan's door. "You remember about seven years back, a geeky little P.I. named Herbert Chum?"

"Sharkbait? I forgot all about him."

"Everybody forgot about him. Hell, you could forget about him when he was standing right in front of you but the guy had balls and nerves of steel. If he wanted to get the dirt on someone, there's nothing he wouldn't do, disguises, hacking into computers, whatever it took. He looked harmless, like he didn't know how to tie his own shoelaces but that's how he got away with it. I heard a story about how he followed the estranged husband of some woman who wanted to know what he was up to. Herb snuck into the guy's apartment and spent the entire day and night under his bed. When he went to work the next morning, Sharkbait took a shower in his bathroom and cooked himself breakfast in his kitchen. He also got enough on the shmuck to set his wife up for life."

"Is this a testimonial?"

"In a way. He got into a scrape about five years ago and I sort of went to bat for him. We've stayed in touch. You want to know where he's living?"

"Not particularly."

"Austin. He opened a shop selling electric scooters. The college kids and teachers are eating them up, can't keep enough of them in stock."

Ryan made a point of looking at his watch. "You know, if you leave right now, you can still make the kick-off."

"He still does a few jobs on and off, Pete, and he owes me. If that slimeball who's after Maria is dirty, and I think he may be…"

"Are you nuts? This isn't some skirt-chasing husband. He's a well-connected cop. Your friend could wind up dead and you could lose your shield. Let's just drop it, okay?" There was a shuffling from the hallway and Ryan cocked his head toward the door.

Maria gave two quick raps and opened the door. "Oh good, Jimmy, you're still here. I saw you walking up as I was rounding the corner so I got you something to eat too. Maria was working at the café today so blame her if it's wrong. Cheeseburger, no bacon, extra tomato. She also said the two of you should be watching your cholesterol and substituted coleslaw for French fries. And don't look at me like that, either of you, I'm just the delivery boy. Did Chief Cody call?"

Both men were gawking at her. The pigtails and painting garb were replaced by a tousled up-do and clean, form-fitting jeans and sweater.

Ryan rose to help her with the food. "Not yet. I don't see anything in here for you."

"I grabbed a yogurt while I was changing. I can't eat when I'm nervous." She started folding the bags. "I'll leave the two of you to eat in peace. I want to get back to the phone calls. Will you let me know when Chief Cody calls?"

"I will but you know you could still take advantage of the nice weather and do something fun, pick up on the phone calls tomorrow."

Her eyes snapped. "If you say that again, I am going to scream. If I wanted to be somewhere else, I would be there. I have a job to do and in spite of the fact that my pig-headed boss is always trying to get rid of me, I intend to do it. Enjoy your lunch."

She slammed the door and Ryan winced. "I'm going to have to install hydraulic closures on the doors, I can see that." He turned to Jimmy. "It's not funny."

"Oh yeah, it is. This is much better than a Raiders game. I'm telling you, pal, what you don't know about women is pathetic."

"I know enough not to have married one. What did I say that was so horrible?"

"To begin with, you just told her she was unnecessary, that the work she was doing was unimportant and you sounded a lot like a father talking to a sixteen year old. I'm surprised you didn't hand her twenty bucks and tell her to go to the movies."

"Shit."

"She's thirty-seven, Pete, and she's just what you need around here. She's smart enough to see that, even if you aren't. Don't run her off like you've done with every other woman who's cared about you."

"I thought you said she was in law school two years ago. That would make her twenty-five or twenty-six."

"Yes, but what I didn't mention was the ten years she spent in the Peace Corps between college and law school. She was a volunteer coordinator in Guatemala."

"And you didn't think that might explain the accent and flawless Spanish, genius?"

"I didn't know about it yesterday morning. I told the gal from the D.A.'s office to call me if she thought of anything else and she did, early this morning. She also told me there's a rumor floating around that Maria's problem may have a few problems of his own. Some drug money's come up short and two of his kids have shown up at school with bruises. She knows about that because one of her kids goes to school with them."

"Good, then maybe the Austin P.D. will fry his ass and save me the trouble."

"You're dreaming. We're talking about Texas, home of the wide blue line."

Ryan's landline buzzed. "It's Cody." He hit the speakerphone button.

Cody's voice came through clear but somber. "She's dead, Pete, somewhere between twenty-four and thirty-six hours ago. I got into her house. Looks like he asphyxiated her in the bedroom and carried her out to her studio to finish the job with a knife. This bastard's as twisted as they come. He's got her posed like roadkill below one of her pieces, some damn vulture she was working on."

Ryan closed his eyes but the image of the woman's face, her own eyes wide with terror, was still there. "She sent the email at 10:12 on Friday night. He might have walked in on her while she was writing it or found it on her computer."

"The timing's right. I found the computer but it was turned off. The house was pretty clean, everything but her bedroom."

"Roland, this is Jim Januski, Pete's ex-partner. Have you notified the local authorities?"

"The cavalry's on the way. They should be coming over the hill any minute now. Hold on." There was a moment of silence and the sound of a vehicle door being opened. "It's okay, girl, we'll be out of here soon. You just lay low for awhile longer."

Ryan sat up. "Who are you talking to?"

"I'm talking to Morgan's dog. She's going home with me and if anybody has a problem with that, they'll have to find her first. That sadistic S.O.B. left her out with no food or water. This place is lousy with coyotes. I'm surprised she made it through one night, let alone two. Someone take this down. One of Morgan's neighbors talked to this Charles guy and got his business card, slipped it through an open window in my truck while I was in her house. The information's probably bogus but take it anyway so I can give it to the locals."

"Chief Cody, it's Maria Hernandez. Read it off to me."

The two men watched as she wiped her eyes and put pen to paper. Up until the moment she spoke, neither man was aware of her presence.

"Charles Richmond. Victoria Filmworks, one word, 720 Douglas Street, Victoria, B.C. V8T 4K9. The phone number is 250-555-6000. Did you get all that?"

Maria read it back to him.

"You okay, Maria?"

"I'm fine, Chief."

"You take care. Pete, they're here. I'll give them my statement and try to stick around until the crime scene crew gets here or they kick me out. I'll get back to you when I can."

When the line was dead, Jimmy shook his head. "He's getting sloppy. She could be loaded with his DNA, and even if he cleaned the house, no one's that thorough."

"He doesn't care. This guy isn't a career criminal, Jimmy, so there's nothing in any database to compare DNA or fingerprints to. I'll bet my life on it. He kills for sport. It's a game to him. He finds beautiful, artistic women, woos them and…"

Maria reappeared in the doorway. "The phone number in Victoria is a clothing store. Information doesn't have a number for Victoria Filmworks."

Jimmy got up and grabbed his parka. "There's a lot of filming going on in Vancouver. Maybe there's some kind of governing board for the motion picture industry in Canada."

Maria turned to leave. "If there is, I'll find it."

Ryan sighed. "This time he's a location scout. He told Ellie Kruger he was a photographer. God only knows what he told the others. You're wasting your time."

She snapped back. "I'm not paid by the hour so it's my time to waste, isn't it?"

"I didn't mean that the way it sounded, Maria."

"You kids play nice." Jimmy zipped up his jacket. "I'm going to head over to my office and try to get in touch with the Boulder police."

Maria stepped forward. "Don't go just yet, Jimmy. I need a favor." When she had their attention, she looked straight ahead, lost inside her thoughts. "I want to be hypnotized by someone good, someone who knows how to ask the right questions. I said I didn't see or hear anything of consequence when I was working for Susan Pierce but I didn't know any of this at the time. Maybe there was something and it didn't register but it's locked inside my subconscious. I remembered something yesterday. She wouldn't let me go into the study but there was another part of the house that was off-limits, the master suite. I didn't think much of it at the time because a lot of customers prefer to do their own bedrooms and baths. They don't want their personal space invaded. One of the smaller bedrooms and baths was also being used. I can't recall any specifics but I know I moved some things around when I was cleaning them."

The men exchanged a look and Jimmy said, "I know someone, a psychiatrist. The D.A. uses her. I'll set it up. You sure about this, Maria?"

"I'm sure. Look, I know Pete's told you I'm running from someone. I assume Chief Cody knows too because I told his wife.

That's the reason I didn't want to be drawn into the investigation, the reason I ran. But all those women he's killed…" She leaned against the door frame and folded her arms across her chest. It was the same defiant stance Ryan observed on her porch in Sedona. "I'll take my chances."

When Jimmy was gone and Maria was back in her office, Ryan felt the white-hot rage of impotence, the cold fury of failure. As his emotions spilled over, he sent the contents of his desk hurling to the floor.

Maria walked back into his office, took the remains of a half-eaten hamburger off a chair and dumped it in the trash. After she wiped off the seat, she sat down and consulted her notes. "I just sent an email off to the MPPIA, British Columbia's Motion Picture Production Industry Association. Where do we go from here?"

"What the hell kind of stunt was that you pulled with Jimmy?"

"How can you even ask me that after this morning? If there's even a slim chance that I know something that will stop him, I don't see that I have a choice."

"Do you have any idea what the press will do when this hits the fan? As things stand now, you're no threat to him. He might not even remember you were in the house. What do you think will happen when he figures out you're a liability?"

"He'll come after me, which is why we better find him first."

CHAPTER 37

CHARLES

Creator as carrion. The press would eat it up, no pun intended. To pass the time, he replayed the scene, her struggle to fill her lungs with air, how she arched her back and offered her neck, the look of terror when she felt the blade.

Normally, he had few regrets. The game was his, the rules too. He chose the prey, the time and place for the kill. It was different with Morgan. Once again, thanks to a meddling brother, he was forced to kill out of expediency instead of purpose and he felt cheated. He would have liked more time with her, more time to get to know her, to have her know him. The rage lingered and with it his doubts, but her betrayal left him no choice, no margin for error.

He aimed the penlight at his watch. Considering the hour and density of the trees, his car was all but invisible, but one wrong move would mean the difference between success and failure. In the darkness, even the smallest illumination might alert someone to his presence. It was the waiting that infuriated him. This was unlike hunting, the payoff less rewarding, but loose ends could not be tolerated. He took pride in the fact that he rarely had to deal with them. In almost every instance, time and distance took care of them, but on the rare occasion when he was forced to act, he did so with dispatch and without remorse.

In an upstairs window, a silhouette passed behind a curtain and almost immediately the house was bathed in darkness. This was the hard part, to resist the urge to rush, to stay calm and focused. Surrendering to the gloom, his head fell back against the seat.

She was walking away from the house toward her car, a brand new 1979 Buick Riviera, his father's birthday gift to her. He watched from his window as, one by one, she piled suitcases in the trunk. When she was finished, she straightened the collar of her fur coat and swung around. Her wavy black hair caught the light of the sun but her face looked pale and sad. She bent down and reached out with her beautiful hands, smooth and warm to the touch. When she played the piano, they reminded him of velvety little animals running up and down the keyboard. She glanced up once, only once. Couldn't she see him? He ran to his door and turned the handle. Someone was playing a trick on him. It was locked. He was crying, running back to the window, calling out to her. He knocked on the glass, softly at first, then harder. His brother was outside, walking toward her. When their hands touched, she brought him close and wrapped him in her arms. Now he was screaming her name, saying he was sorry, making promises. He ran back to the door and beat on it. When his fists were raw, he used his feet until he was out of breath. By the time he got back to the window, they were gone.

His eyes flew open and he shook his head to clear it. Despite the chill inside the car, he was sweating. He'd fallen asleep and the dream had come, leaving him feeling shaken and exposed, the way it always did. The way it always would.

Tempted to call it off, he examined his options. After several minutes, he opened the glove compartment and withdrew the zippered case. Beneath it were his driving gloves that fit like a second skin, top of the line and buttery soft, black to match his clothes. He flexed his fingers and thought of his mother. The wait was over.

CHAPTER 38

ANNIE

It was overcast and drizzling, the perfect complement to her mood, the kind of day that sent the natives scurrying to their computers clutching their credit cards. The destination came in second to the predictability of the weather. Iffy, bad. Steamy, good. *Bermuda, Bahama, come on pretty mama.* So where was mama headed in five days? To one of the few spots more depressing than New England in November. Old England in November.

Annie spun away from the window and surveyed her office. In its heyday, it had been an oversized butler's pantry stocked with crystal and silver. It was also one of the first things to go when they took possession of the grand Victorian. Gutted of its leaded glass cabinets and white marble countertops, it made the perfect space for her part-time presence. It was her private cocoon, chock-a-block with memories, photographs of guests with visitors, birthday and holiday parties, even a deathbed commitment ceremony, ten years of joy and loss. Now it looked sad and out of place, a remnant of its former self, a lot like its occupant.

In spite of the weekend, she'd awakened with a spirited resolve to put it behind her and forge ahead full speed. *Things turn out the way they're supposed to.* She made a face. Pollyanna on Prozac. Wasn't that what Larry called her when she used the tired chestnut? Well, so what? The concept worked for her but, admittedly, only to a point. Mouthing the words was the easy part. Believing them was the challenge, especially since they were at odds with her personal credo, that failure was not an option, that human beings were responsible for the twists and turns of their individual journeys.

Her thoughts went full circle. All things considered, Cynthia took the decision to close **Life House** better than Annie had any right to expect. There were lots of tears, selfish tears, more for themselves than anyone else. The important thing was their guests would be properly cared for, their humanity respected. Once they got past the sentiment, their practical sides took over.

She took the seat behind her desk and stared at her notebook, three pages of things to do, each item preceded by a number. To her dismay, there was almost as much work in shutting the hospice down as in getting it up and running.

No, this was good. She had to keep busy but first she had to pick an emotion and stick with it longer than five minutes. She'd been up and down all day, vacillating between mania and melancholy, Mike never more than a heartbeat away. The only feeling she couldn't summon was the one that might have helped: anger. And it wasn't as if she hadn't tried. Even her subconscious was in on the act. Twice during the night, she was jolted awake by a nightmare that left her drenched in sweat. A man was chasing her through a dense forest. When she stopped to catch her breath, she looked behind her. She couldn't make out who he was but she knew he was laughing at her, taunting her. Out of nowhere, a form materialized to her left and then another in front of her. This time she saw a face. It was Bryce reaching out to her. She pushed past him and stumbled forward. The one chasing her was narrowing the gap. The figure to her left, a featureless mass, was running beside her now, crouching low, watching. She tripped and fell. Struggling to get to her feet, the sodden ground gave way beneath her and she tumbled into darkness. It was at this point that she woke up.

As a metaphor for her love life, it needed work. To begin with, it cast her as a victim, a role she vehemently rejected. It was just a feeling, but she was sure the one running parallel to her was Mike. Would he give up on her? Only time would tell.

A two-note bell chimed from her laptop. She rarely used the reminder feature but today she was glad she did. The last thing she wanted to do was accompany Helen to the police station but a promise was a promise. Wasn't that what started the whole mess, her pledge to find Debra's resting place? Had she not read the diary and third-degreed Helen about the previous owners, she might not be sitting there feeling sorry for herself.

She drummed her fingers on the desk and looked up as fat silver droplets raced downward against the glass. That was something she hadn't counted on, a downpour. The thruway would be a mess so she had to get a move on if she wanted to pick her up and have her at the police station by one o'clock. Hopefully, Helen had remembered to call Detective Robinson and let him know she didn't need a ride, that a friend would be taking her.

As predicted, the thruway was a disaster, as bad as she'd ever seen it, a parking lot of semis and pissed-off soccer moms in SUVs. By the time she pulled into the lane, the rain had stopped but it was past one and she was already exhausted. She pulled her truck into Helen's driveway alongside a familiar white car. Detective Lou Robinson stepped out of the car and smiled.

Caught between relief and disappointment, Annie opened her door and returned the smile. "Well, if it isn't my favorite good cop. I guess Helen forgot to call and tell you I'd be taking her today." She put her hand up. "I know, I know, we're late but the traffic was horrible and I didn't anticipate the rain and…"

The detective looked amused. "Take a breath, girl. You all right?"

"Peachy."

"I've already called and rescheduled the sketch artist for two o'clock. I don't think your friend's home anyway. I've been ringing her bell on and off for half an hour." He put a hand on her shoulder. "You sure you're all right? I haven't seen such misery on a face since Mike stopped in this morning on his way to the airport. Something going on here I don't know about?"

"I doubt there's anything going on anywhere that you don't know about. It's been a lousy few days, that's all." She patted his hand. "I don't understand why Helen isn't answering the door. We talked about this yesterday and made plans for me to pick her up."

She walked up the steps to the front door and peered through the window. Something wasn't right. Like many people her age, Helen worried about falling and kept a lamp burning day and night, the one near the bottom of the staircase. But today, in spite of the dreary weather, the house was dark. Annie rang the bell and knocked. She was about to call out to her when she turned around. The detective was right behind her, punching in some numbers on his cell phone.

Annie raised an eyebrow and the detective put a finger to his lips. After a few more seconds, he asked, "You hear the phone?"

"No, and she always keeps the ringer volume high so she can hear it over the television." Before he could comment, Annie was halfway back to her truck. "I was late getting home one day and my dog was throwing a fit. Helen suggested we exchange keys so she could let him out if it happened again. I forgot all about it."

Back on the porch, she put the key in the lock and jumped when the detective put his hand on hers. "You wait here."

Shaken, Annie watched as he removed his shoes and closed the door behind him. She heard him moving around inside the house, identifying himself and calling out Helen's name. It was probably a false alarm. It wouldn't be the first time. The Tai Chi incident sprang to mind and she jumped off the porch, ran past the garage and turned the corner toward the fence. The gate was ajar and she pulled it open. Both the backyard and patio were deserted, the shades pulled down inside the house.

She was latching the gate when she heard his voice. Thank God. As she rounded the corner, his back was to her and he was speaking into his cell phone. Expecting to see the older woman swaddled into the front seat, Annie peered inside his car then swerved toward the porch. She was almost there when the detective blocked her with his body. He shook his head and mumbled something, something that confused her. If Helen was gone, did he know where she went? Was that why he was angry? It was a sketch artist, not an audience with the Pope. They could reschedule, couldn't they?

Holding her arm with one hand, he used his other to grasp the phone and finish his call. When she tried to pull away, he tightened his grip and addressed her directly. "She's dead, Annie. I'm sorry, but you can't go inside just yet."

He was still talking when Annie threw her arm up to fend off his grasp. His phone went flying. By the time it landed, she was inside the house. She ran to the staircase and used the handrail to propel her upward. At the top of the stairs, she inched forward, hugging the wall for support.

CHAPTER 39

RYAN

"You'll have to forgive my uncle, Mr. Ryan. He's not in good health and he's the only one of us left in Boulder so he's borne the brunt of the media and TV people."

Ryan adjusted the volume control on the speakerphone. Sarah Dixon's voice was coming through as little more than a whisper. "I'm sorry, Miss Dixon, but we're having trouble hearing you. My assistant Maria is taking notes. I hope you don't mind."

There was a moment of dead air. "Is that better? I don't mind if someone's there but please call me Sarah."

"I appreciate that. I understand both your parents are deceased."

"Not exactly but I'm sure that's the impression given by my uncle. He's my mother's brother so there's some bad blood there. Right after Rachel went missing, my father started drinking again. He always had a problem but it got much worse. He was driving intoxicated one night and veered into an oncoming car. An entire family was killed, two small children and their parents. He's in prison for vehicular homicide, thirty years. Three months after the trial, my mother took her own life."

Ryan looked down at the file dropped off by Jimmy an hour earlier. There was nothing in it about any of this. For a murder case, it was ridiculously sparse. It lacked everything but the basic facts, a series of cryptic dates, a few phone numbers and abbreviated jottings. Even the coroner's report was missing. "I'm sorry, Sarah. I had no idea."

"I've made peace with it. Unless you've lost someone to a tragedy like Rachel's, you can't possibly know how it changes the lives of everyone connected to it. It's as if the act itself has tentacles that reach inside your soul. You can't lose a part of yourself and ever be the same."

He glanced at Maria but her eyes never wavered from the notes she was taking. "I know this is difficult but can you tell me about your sister?"

"It's not difficult at all. I love talking about her. She was a wonderful person and incredibly talented, funny too, a natural comedienne. It was impossible to be in a bad mood around her. She just lifted you up, you know? I think that's what I miss most."

"She was a cellist with the Colorado Symphony, as I understand it, so she must have been good."

"She was phenomenal, everyone said so. She could have been second or third chair with any major symphony in the world, but she wanted to stay close to home. She was only four when she got hooked on it. We were playing in the alley behind our house and she saw an old cello leaning against a trash can. It took both of us to drag it home. It was bigger than she was, full-size, over four feet. She could hardly get her little arms around it." Sarah's voice went soft again. "She knew how to hold it even then. I've often wondered about that. It's not like we were exposed to classical music."

"You said she wanted to stay close to home. Was that because of your father's drinking problem?"

"More or less. Our parents did the best they could, Mr. Ryan, but the fact is they never should have had children. It wasn't as if they made us feel unloved or were ever cruel but their lives changed dramatically when we were born and I'm not sure they ever got past it. It's difficult to explain but Rachel and I knew instinctively that we were superfluous. I'm not saying I handled it better than Rach but I took my own path. She needed the connection to them."

"I saw her photograph on the missing persons website. She was beautiful. Were you identical twins?"

"Yes."

"You still have the last name Dixon. Were you ever married?" There was a fine line between relevance and curiosity and he feared he'd crossed it. He had to change direction and fast. "Is everything all right? It sounds like a lot of activity in the background."

"It's always that way here. I'm sorry, where were we?"

"Tell me about Rachel's disappearance."

"It was December 18th, 2015. I had a phone call from her on Thanksgiving Day. She'd met someone, a freelance writer who was doing a story on the Symphony. He singled her out because of her age, the fact that she was so young. Rachel hadn't dated much so I was happy for her at first."

"At first?"

"It seemed to be moving very quickly, as if she were trying to make up for lost time. Her music consumed her life and she didn't have much experience with men so it worried me a bit. Also, some of the things she was telling me about him sounded a lot like our father, not the alcoholism but his need for control of everything around him. I've since come to realize that Dad needed that semblance of order because he didn't have power over his own addiction, but it concerned me that Rachel might be repeating our mother's pattern of denial."

"Did you share your concern with her?"

Sarah laughed. "As if she'd listen to me in matters of the heart. You have quite a sense of humor, Mr. Ryan."

It was an odd comment but he didn't want to take the time to pursue it. "So you were getting some disturbing vibes about the relationship."

"Yes, that's a good way to put it. It was little things really, mainly to do with her time. It seemed all her plans were suddenly contingent on his schedule. She'd been invited to join a Chamber quartet and go on tour for a couple of months but she pulled out at the last minute. She never said so but I got the feeling she didn't want to be away if he were in town."

"Did she mention if he was trying to isolate her from her friends?"

"No, not that I recall but most of Rach's friends were musicians in Denver. When she wasn't rehearsing or performing there, she led a fairly solitary life in Boulder. She loved to read and hike. I do know she was planning on moving into Denver after the first of the year. I believe she even put a deposit on an apartment. Our parents were doing better. Dad was going to AA meetings and Mom was being very strong and supportive. Rachel thought it was a good time for her to move on and give them some space."

Sarah excused herself and put her hand over the mouthpiece. The background noise was picking up again. "I apologize. Anyway, the first thing we knew about her disappearance was when mother got a call that Rachel missed a performance. That never happened, not even when she was ill. Mother called me, unsure of what to do, and I told her to call the police. I knew something was wrong. I felt it all day. That morning I awakened with a horrible sense of doom. It's quite common in twins, as I'm sure you know, but this went beyond anything I ever experienced. My mother's phone call didn't surprise me."

"I assume she contacted the police right away?"

"Yes."

"And did they pursue it immediately?"

"No."

Ryan waited, noting the change in her tone. Where she had been forthcoming, she was now wary. She was shutting down and he knew the reason. Maria knew it too and was watching him.

"Sarah, I know how hard this is, believe me, and I also know the police dropped the ball. I have Rachel's file in front of me and it's a joke, but you have to help us out here."

"You were a police officer, weren't you? Isn't that what you said?"

"Yes, I left the force in 2011."

"You don't sound old enough to have reached retirement."

"I quit the force. I quit the force to find the sonofabitch who murdered four women, five counting your sister, maybe more. One of them was my sister."

"Sarah, it's Martha Henderson, Pete's assistant. I have my own reasons for distrusting the police but that's a subject for another day. What I've learned in the last few weeks is they're just like everyone else, human, good and bad, but the men involved in this case are decent, caring people so I'm begging you to do what I've done and put aside your personal feelings. We need your help. Please."

Ryan cleared his throat. The enormity of her admission, the lilt of her natural voice, stunned him. She'd known him less than a month but was prepared to sacrifice her safety and anonymity to support him. She trusted him, a truth he found oddly discomforting, almost as unsettling as the fact he trusted her.

"All right," said Sarah. "The truth is the police treated it like a joke so I'm not surprised the file reflects that. I flew out that night, the night my mother called. I was there the next day when the police finally arrived. Once they heard she was a musician, they formed their own conclusions about her. They wanted to know what drugs she was on, what bars she went to, even who she was sleeping with. They never asked a thing about the kind of person she was, what her other interests were, nothing like that. I took them to her apartment and they were laughing and making comments about where they'd find her stash. I didn't even know what that was. There was a photograph of her in a bookcase. It was a Halloween party she'd been to the previous year. Her hair was all purple and spiked up and she had on heavy make-up. She thought it was so funny, a classical musician dressed up that way. That's the photograph they took of her. I couldn't take another moment of it so I left. When I went back later, her things were everywhere. It looked as if there'd been a home invasion. Two days later, they took our father in for questioning and kept him for almost twelve hours. When they eventually brought him home, he started drinking again and never stopped. And all the while, my beautiful sister was being murdered and buried in some…I'm sorry. I've been working on forgiveness for fifteen years but apparently I still have some work to do, don't I?"

He'd heard enough. Halfway through her re-enactment, his mind went to another case, one that pre-dated Rachel's murder by almost ten years. Six-year-old Jonbenet Ramsey was found savagely murdered in the basement of her Boulder home. Even now, the Boulder police were scrutinized and crucified for their ineptitude and failure to secure the crime scene.

"Mr. Ryan?"

"I'm here, Sarah, and thank you. I know how hard that was. The man she was seeing, did Rachel tell you anything about him other than his profession, where he came from, what he looked like?"

"No, nothing like that."

"Why do you think that is?"

"I'm not sure other than the fact that I didn't always have access to a phone, and when I did, we usually talked about the family or her music or my work."

"I'm only asking because I recently had a discussion with a woman whose daughter is still missing. She's convinced that women don't share that kind of information with other women because they don't want to be talked out of the relationship."

"I don't know why that's important but it seems rather cynical and it doesn't sound like something Rachel would ascribe to. Mind you, this is speculation on my part, but I think if it were me I'd wait to see if it developed into something real before I revealed too much. Knowing Rachel, she felt the same way. I know my parents never met him, nor anyone else as far as I know."

"Sarah, Martha here. Do you know the names of any of Rachel's friends in Denver or Boulder? I know it's been fifteen years but perhaps they might remember something she said or someone may have seen him at one of her performances."

"I can do better than that. We were finally able to have a funeral for her after her remains were found. Someone brought a guest book and gave it to me after the service. I was surprised how many people showed up after all those years. Fifty-three people signed the book. I can make a copy of the pages and fax them to you."

Ryan flipped the pages of the file again. "Did you give the police a copy of it?"

"I haven't spoken to the police since a month after her disappearance. I was calling them several times a week in the beginning but they stopped returning my calls. My uncle is the one who contacted me when her body was found. Now I have a question for you, Mr. Ryan. Is there anything in the file to indicate they ran his name through a database or put out a bulletin on him or whatever it is they do?"

Ryan and Martha sprang forward in their chairs. "What name?!"

"Charles Rivers." Her sigh was audible. "That's what I thought. His name isn't in the file, is it?"

"She told you his name?"

"Yes, and she also sent me a draft of the piece he was working on. His name was on it, Charles Rivers."

"I don't suppose you still have it."

"I kept everything. I'll fax it over with the pages from the guest book."

Ryan gave her the fax number and asked, "Do you know if the article was ever published?"

"I don't. It was shortly after that when Rachel disappeared."

"But you gave a copy of the article to the police?"

"Yes, I was convinced he was responsible and I told them that."

"This is crazy. Maybe the Boulder police are playing this close to the vest and only gave us a portion of the file. If they've got this guy in their sights, they may think we'll blow it."

"That sounds more like a defense than an explanation, Mr. Ryan."

"You're right, it does. I've seen a lot of sloppy police work but this…"

"I keep forgetting you've lost someone too. That's the worst part, isn't it, how they're victimized twice, first by the person who takes their life and then by a system that sees them only as a name and a number. You don't know where to turn. Fifteen years ago, I would have given anything to have someone ask the questions you're asking."

"If there's a Charles Rivers out there, we'll find him. You have my word." There was one more thing he had to ask her, one thing that puzzled him. It was something she'd alluded to throughout the entire conversation, her disinterest in men. It could also explain why she left home and stayed away, why the police treated her with disrespect. "Sarah, one last thing that may or may not be important and it's none of my business but you've mentioned a couple of times that you don't have much of a track record with men so I was wondering…"

Martha had been doodling on the page, circling something over and over. When she heard his build-up, she began shaking her head and waving her arms. As a last resort, she pushed the tablet in front of his face and jabbed a finger at what she'd been circling.

"You were wondering what, Mr. Ryan?"

"You're a nun?!" He hadn't intended it to come out as a question and he certainly hadn't meant to shout it but he was dumbfounded. It never occurred to him.

"You sound surprised. Yes, I'm a nun, the Franciscan Sisters of Charity. Are you familiar with the order?"

"I am." It was an order he admired, their commitment to providing education and healthcare in deprived communities impressive. They walked the walk everyday of their lives, champions of forgotten people. One of his favorite quotes from St. Francis came to mind. "If God can work through me, he can work through anyone. Did I get that right, sister?"

"You said it beautifully."

"You're in Michigan."

"Detroit. We run a wellness clinic in the projects. You should visit some time."

"I might do that, sister."

"I'd like to pray for your sister, Mr. Ryan. What was her name?"

"Theresa. Theresa Ann."

"Two of my favorite saints. I'm not likely to forget that."

Ryan promised to stay in touch, hung up and glared across the desk. "You might have told me she was a nun."

"Nice going, Sherlock. I can't believe you were going to ask her if she was gay. And for the record, I had no idea she was a nun before we spoke with her. Her uncle didn't say a word about that."

"Then how did you figure it out? Never mind. You women scare the hell out of me. You must have some kind of weird radar that we don't know about or…"

"Oh, please. We're not men which automatically gives us an advantage. We listen when people talk. What I don't understand is why it was important."

"It was important because I wanted to determine if she was predisposed to disliking all men or Rachel's boyfriend in particular, something that might have colored her assessment of him."

"I guess that makes sense." She stood and gathered up her notes. "I'll call the airlines and get you on a flight to Denver."

"I'm not going to Denver and you're not going anywhere just yet. You blew your cover and we need to talk about it."

"She's a nun, Pete, not the editor of the *Enquirer*. Besides, Jimmy slipped and called me by my real name when he dropped the file off so I assume you both know everything there is to know. I figured something was going on when you replaced your mouse with a different model."

"I'm sorry about the deception."

"Don't be. I'm relieved if you want to know the truth. Living a lie is exhausting, waking up in someone else's skin, speaking with someone else's voice. I'm taking back my life, something these murdered women can never do."

"Look, Martha…"

"It's Marti, with an i."

"Marti, I can't protect you twenty-four hours a day. The last few days have been out of the ordinary. Normally, I'm not even here half the time."

"Is that what you think, that I want you to take care of me? I didn't make this decision lightly and I certainly didn't make it because I assumed I had a full-time bodyguard. I'm a grown woman, a fact that seems to escape you periodically, and I intend to take responsibility for my own safety."

"I'm dying to know how you intend to do that. Where are you living by the way?"

"Right now, I'm sleeping on the sofa in Maria's basement. I've been looking for an apartment but it's difficult with no credit history."

"There's a vacant apartment in my building, a studio on the floor below me. It's only a few blocks from here but it's empty so you'll need some furniture. Write a check for whatever you need. It's nothing fancy but the owner takes good care of the building and the security's better than most."

"I appreciate it, but I don't even know if I can afford it or if they'll rent to me."

"You can afford it and I guarantee he'll rent to you."

"You don't know that."

"Yeah, I do. I own the building. Any more questions?"

"I'm not a charity case, Pete."

"I know you're not. This is as much for me as it is for you. The case is heating up and I have to focus my attention there. And right now I need you, preferably in one piece, so as of today you're out of here before dark unless I'm here, understand?"

"I'm swapping one kind of prison for another, is that it?"

"That's it, take it or leave it."

"I'll take it but I'll pay you back every penny."

"You can pay me back when you pass the Bar and become the kind of lawyer I hate."

"What kind is that?"

"It doesn't matter, I don't like any of them."

"I've had my identity back less than an hour and you have my future figured out. I wish I were that sure."

"I don't have anything figured out, that's the problem. We'll need a list of every musician who was with the symphony when she was there. If their website doesn't list the individual performers and the dates they joined, contact the director. We'll split the list. You take the women and I'll take the men. I'll also take care of the Boulder police and call Jimmy about running Charles Rivers through the system. Let me know when Sarah's fax gets in. Now move it and don't slam the door."

She backed out of the office and slowly closed the door. "That was Maria. Marti's got an entirely different set of peculiarities. You might even find them endearing."

Alone in his office, Ryan fell back in his chair. God, he hoped not.

CHAPTER 40

ANNIE

She was numb. One minute she was in Helen's bedroom and the next she was home, slugging back her second snifter of brandy.

Lou Robinson announced his presence by rapping on the wall just inside the living room. Several decibels above a respectable level, Queen was posing the musical question *Who Wants to Live Forever*. The detective had to shout to be heard. "I take it you're a fan."

Reluctantly, Annie adjusted the volume on the stereo. "Some people have shrinks. I have Queen. Whenever I can't get a grip, my boys are always there for me. The higher the stress, the louder the music." She raised her glass. "Join me?"

"Thanks, but I'm on duty." He took a seat in one of the armchairs near the sofa. "My boy thinks *Bohemian Rhapsody* is the greatest song ever written."

"You obviously brought him up right. How old is he?"

"Twelve. I'm just grateful he's not into Gangsta rap."

If he wanted to keep it light, she could play along. "I was ten when Freddie died. I knew nothing about AIDS back then, only that he was ill. I cried for days, knowing my world would never be the same." The small-talk wasn't working for her. Her sorrow was too pervasive. "What about you? Who's your opiate of choice when the world stops making sense?"

"When I'm on the job, the world never makes sense, but if you're asking me who I listen to when I want to get down and mellow, it's Coltrane."

Annie took a sip of the brandy and lowered her head. "I'm sorry about your phone. I don't usually lose it like that."

"I could have handled it better myself. Don't worry about it."

"I was with her yesterday morning and she was fine. I got impatient with her, though, but now it seems silly and petty. You don't think the stress of having to work with the sketch artist had something to do with it, do you? I started this whole thing and maybe I should have left it alone. I had no idea she was so fragile."

"Annie, you have somewhere you can stay for a couple of nights?"

Evidently he thought she was falling apart. "I'll be fine."

"When are you leaving for London?"

"Friday, why?"

"Because until we get the results back from the M.E., I'd feel better if you were staying somewhere else. What about your friend Cynthia?"

"What about her?" There were several things wrong with what he was saying but she was having trouble following.

"Can you stay with her until your leave?"

"You're requesting an autopsy? Helen was in her eighties. It must have been a heart attack."

"Under the circumstances, we need confirmation."

"What circumstances?"

"You went around to the back of her house. Why did you do that?"

"I stopped by there a few weeks ago on my way to work. I knocked and rang the bell. I was about to leave when she came around the side of the house. She was doing Tai Chi on her back porch and I thought she might be there today."

"Tell me what you saw. Walk me through it."

"I went past the garage and turned the corner toward the fence. The gate was open a few inches so I pulled on it and walked through to the back yard. I looked around and then I heard your voice. I assumed you were talking to her."

"The gate was open? You didn't have to put your hand over it to release the latch?"

"No."

"Go on."

"That's it."

"Did you walk on the patio?"

"No, I saw the blinds were down inside the house except…"

"Except what?"

"One of the blinds was hanging outside the window."

"You didn't remove the screen and open the window to get inside the house?"

"Why would I do that? We had the key and you were already inside."

She wanted him to stop talking and go away. The next track up was *Stone Cold Crazy* and she had to concentrate on that, not the images playing out inside her head. Her hands were trembling as she put the snifter down. The anger eluding her all day finally surfaced. "I was right. I never should have started this. Charles saw the article in the paper and couldn't risk being identified by the composite. He murdered her, didn't he?"

"We don't know that yet, Annie. She could have been washing windows, the phone rang and she forgot to put the screen back in."

"She wore one of those things around her neck, that alert button for seniors living alone. Why didn't she press the damn button?"

"She wasn't wearing it. We found it on the sink in her bathroom. She must have taken it off to bathe and forgot to put it back on."

Her voice went flat. "He killed Bert Kennedy too, didn't he? He waited for him to leave his daughter's home and he ran him down. Mike tried to dodge the question when I asked him about it but it's true, isn't it?"

"He wasn't dodging it. According to the file, we should have had metal particles and glass from a headlight. We were going to have them reanalyzed."

"What does that mean, should have had?"

"The evidence is missing."

"Of course it is. What good would it do anyway? Who holds on to a car for twenty years? You never answered my question. Did the police think it was an accident or deliberate, and please don't insult me by telling me you don't know. Even I could figure that one out. There would have been acceleration marks or skid marks or something."

"You sure Mike didn't talk to you about this?"

"He didn't talk to me about squat. I'm officially, how did he put it, out of the loop."

"He was protecting you."

"What about the patrols? They have to pass her house to get to mine. Wouldn't they have seen someone creeping around?" Her mind was racing and it was all she could do to keep up. "Unless he was watching her house and waited until he saw a patrol car go in and out of the lane and then he made his move. Feel free to jump in any time and tell me I'm crazy."

"Did you see or hear anything out of the ordinary last night?"

"No, I was beat. I woke up a couple of times because of a nightmare. Einstein never barked, not even when the patrol cars came through. I guess we're both getting accustomed to them."

"Einstein?"

"My dog. I took him with me to **Life House** this morning. Cynthia and Arthur are keeping him while I'm in London. After they move, they won't see him for awhile."

"I heard you're closing the hospice. You've had a rough couple of weeks. Maybe you should move up your trip, get a change of scenery."

"I've already moved it up and I shouldn't have done that. What I should do is cancel it. I can't afford the time right now." She finished off the brandy. It burned all the way to her empty stomach and left her with a slight buzz. What she needed was food. "I don't know how people drink this stuff. Can I fix you something, a sandwich and a cup of coffee?"

"Thanks, but I have to get back. I left the crime scene techs there. You gonna call your friend?"

"No, and I don't want her to know about this until it's absolutely necessary. She has enough on her plate right now. When do you think you'll have the coroner's report?"

"Could be tomorrow or the next day."

"Maybe I'll check into a hotel for a couple of days. Do you really think it's necessary?"

"My gut tells me he isn't going to try anything with you. He wouldn't risk it. You don't know anything anyway. I thought you might want to be around people. I'll be down the road a few more hours. Whatever you decide, stop by and let me know."

The food helped but it was the shower that did the trick, hot and sinfully long, long enough for her to cry an ocean of overdue tears. When she wiped the steam off the mirror, the face staring back was familiar but different. It was something in the eyes, a glimmer of defiance. She'd worked too hard to make a home for herself and put the past behind her. If she ran now, she might never stop. There was more than a bit of truth in what she told Mike. The change would do her good. It might even save her life or, at the very least, help her figure out what to do with the rest of it.

She brushed a hint of blush across her cheeks, ran some gloss across her lips and wiggled into a fresh pair of jeans and turtleneck. For a basket case, she didn't look half bad. It was a shallow victory but a victory nonetheless. There was one last thing she had to do before her confidence waned and she dissolved back in to a gooey mess. She had to break the news to Lou. The hotel was out.

The lane was bumper to bumper with official-looking vehicles. She was traversing her way through them, just passing her mailbox when she heard a sound that brought her to a stop. Someone was in the trees, someone with a camera. As quietly as possible, she moved into the thicket. He was young, late twenties, with long hair and a ripped t-shirt. "You have five seconds to come out of there before I start screaming."

Shocked, he dropped the camera. "Jesus, don't do that. I'm with the Advocate. I'm supposed to be getting pictures of the old lady's house."

"You're press? Let me see some I.D."

He produced a ratty press card but continued to shake. "Matthews will have my ass for this. He's already ticked off he couldn't reach me yesterday."

"Gary Matthews, the reporter who wrote the story about the Hastings case?"

"It's bad enough I have to work with the prick. I don't have to read his shit."

She looked toward the crowd assembled on Helen's front yard. "Is he here?"

"Over there by the patrol car, the asshole on the cell phone."

Based on Mike's description, she had him pictured as a small man with a bad comb-over. He was attractive, well-dressed and carried himself in a manner more cocky than self-assured. She knew the type, God's gift to the First Amendment.

Handing him back his press card, she noticed he was shivering. "Where's your jacket? It must be fifty degrees out here."

"I'm freaking freezing. He gets a tip and I get dragged out of bed. I forgot to grab a jacket."

Annie looked at her watch. "It's almost four o'clock in the afternoon."

"Yeah, well, it was good weekend, what can I tell you?"

"My side door's open and there's a pot of hot coffee in the kitchen. The mugs are in the cupboard above it. Help yourself. There's a windbreaker hanging in the garage. You can use it while you're here."

"Thanks. You're not going to mention this to him, are you?"

"Not a word."

"Watch your back. You're just his type."

"What type is that?"

"Good looking and breathing."

As the photographer walked away from her, Annie moved forward a few feet and stopped in the middle of the lane. Matthews caught her in his peripheral vision, did a double take and ended his phone call. He was several yards away when he started talking. "You're Annie Heywood, aren't you?"

The timing couldn't have been worse. The gurney carrying Helen's body was being lifted into the coroner's van. She faltered but pulled it together at the last second. "I'm Annie Heywood. Have we met? "

"Gary Matthews, the Advocate. You have time for a few questions?"

As the van pulled out of the lane, two more cars drove in. Police were everywhere, huddled together or walking alone, eyes on the ground. Two or three had broken off and were crossing Compo Road toward the park.

Matthews looked around, annoyed. "Where the hell is the photographer? I told him to keep an eye on the cops."

"Young guy, long hair with a Grateful Dead t-shirt? I saw him walking across the road." She pointed toward the park. "I think he's with that group over there."

"He better be." He softened his tone. "Too bad about your neighbor. This isn't my fault, you know that, right? I mean, it was twenty years ago. Who knew the creep was still around."

Annie shrugged her shoulders. "You were just doing your job."

"Try telling that to the cops. All of a sudden, I'm a pariah."

"But you still have your official source, unless she's not talking either." It was just a hunch, but judging from a slight shift in his expression, it was spot on. Pretending not to notice, she kept her eyes fixed on the activity behind him.

"Listen, Annie, I have an idea. How about I take you to dinner? We don't have to talk about the case if you don't want to but I'd really like to hear your take on it. You're the one who found the diary, right? I'm betting you even made a copy of it before you handed it over to the cops. What do you say?"

Her response was quick and to the point. She took a half step back and lunged forward with her knee. As it connected with his groin, his eyes widened and he went down hard, first to his knees and then his back. It was several long seconds before he could speak, the words screamed in a breathy falsetto. "You crazy bitch!"

All heads turned in their direction. When no one moved and applause broke out, she knelt down beside him. "As it turns out, we both have a job to do, Gary. Mine just happens to be ridding the neighborhood of vermin. You took advantage of an elderly woman and now she's dead. You're worse than a pariah, you're a parasite." She stood up and brushed off her jeans. "I'll take a rain check on dinner. Call me when your balls are back in working order or hell freezes over, whichever comes last."

CHAPTER 41

RYAN

Ryan checked off the final name on his list and popped an antacid. A murder investigation wasn't rocket science. It was about information, the ebb and flow, the distillation of fact from fiction.

True to her word, Sarah Dixon provided them with information, close to fifty names of her sister's friends and colleagues, all eager to help. In terms of grief, fifteen years were not enough to dispel the horror of her death, but when it came to details, those years were an eternity. Like poorly-archived photographs, images lost their clarity; and conversation, once rich in tone and texture, were words out of context. After three days, despite their best efforts to elicit a solid lead, they were back to square one. It was business as usual which, as luck would have it, turned out to be the least of his problems.

Keeping well back from the window so as not to be observed from the street, he narrowed his sight through the slats of the blinds. The guy was good, too good to be hanging out in plain view, but Ryan knew he was out there, could sense his presence. He'd seen him only once, earlier that day when he made a routine stop for his morning coffee. The encounter was brief, a few seconds at most, but something was off. It would take several more hours before the tells congealed into one discomforting fact.

The baseball cap and sunglasses, props employed by Morgan Evans' suitor, raised the first red flag. Then there was right place, right time, the precise hour, give or take a few minutes, when Ryan made his daily appearance. The place was a dump, distinguished by ratty retro linoleum and enough red neon to wake the dead. It was as far off the beaten path as one could get, known only to locals willing to sacrifice ambiance for expediency. But it was the third thing, the eye contact held a mille-second too long, that eventually tipped the scales. He had a tail. Who he was and what he wanted remained to be seen.

Two candidates made the short list. If the enigmatic Charles had gotten wind of the Maria/Martha connection, he might be doing a little housekeeping of his own. The other possibility was the dirty Austin narc. If he were under the gun in his own backyard, it wasn't a stretch to believe he would create a little mayhem on someone else's turf.

"Pete, did you hear me? I'm leaving."

He pulled his eyes from the street below. "It's only 4:30, where are you going?"

"Are you kidding me? Not only did I write it in your appointment book but there are at least two post-its on your desk reminding you. I'm getting hypnotized. She sees patients until eight tonight. I made it late in the day so I wouldn't lose the entire afternoon. We talked about this."

He'd forgotten all about it. Now he had to stall long enough to figure out his next move. "In the first place, your appointment is scheduled for Wednesday, and for future reference, I don't read post-its. They're annoying, like elevator music. You know it's there but you can't bring yourself to acknowledge it. And since when do I have an appointment book?"

She was doing it again, that thing she did when she couldn't believe what she was hearing, lowering her chin and raising her eyebrows. Next would come the deep breath and slow, measured speech as if she were addressing someone with advanced dementia.

"Today is Wednesday and if I don't leave now, I'll be late. As far as post-its are concerned, I'll make a note of that."

"How are you getting there?"

"The rain stopped so I thought I'd walk. It's only a few blocks."

"Good idea. You go on ahead and I'll meet you there." He cocked his head toward the hall and added, "Gotta hit the men's room."

He hated using her as bait but it was as good a way as any to find out which of them was the quarry. The moment he heard her footsteps in the stairwell, he was on the move. Pocketing his revolver with one hand, he hit the buttons beneath his desk with the other. A third possibility occurred to him, that the lure of an empty office might be too tempting to pass up. It was a long shot, the story of his life.

At a hair over six feet tall in four-inch stilettos, Dr. Sophia Cummings' appearance in the waiting room was something else Ryan never expected. From a sitting position, his eyes went first to her legs, loitered a moment and traveled north. The trip didn't disappoint. In a film, her entrance would be accompanied by *The Flight of the Valkyries*, Wagner's paean to Norse mythology, the bodacious band of lovelies who chose those who would die in battle. His breathing stopped when he got to her face. He was a dead man.

"Pete, it's good to see you again. I heard a rumor you were involved in this case."

Ryan got to his feet and took the offered hand. The details were sketchy but the highlights loomed large. It was six or seven months ago after a late-night jam session, lots of laughs and booze. They hit it off and followed it up with several hours of carnal contortions. Now, completely blindsided, he took the offense. "You said you were a nurse."

"I said I was in healthcare. Talking to a psychiatrist can be intimidating for some men. You know how it is."

He didn't know how it was but he didn't remember doing much talking either. Before he could frame a retort, she turned her attention to Marti.

"You must be Martha. I'm Sophia. Give me a couple of minutes and then come on in. I have a quick phone call to make. Mr. Ryan can wait for you here."

Under the circumstances, he had no choice but to accept the rebuff and sit back down. Marti was across from him, her eyes glued to the pages of *People.*

"You're a bad boy, boss."

"It's not what you think."

"It's exactly what I think."

"Have it your way but a gentleman doesn't kiss and tell."

"Evidently he doesn't phone either. That's one pissed off healthcare worker. You'll be lucky if she doesn't give me a post-hypnotic suggestion to poison your coffee."

Ryan picked up a magazine of his own. "It doesn't work that way. You can't make someone do something to which they're not predisposed."

Marti leaned in and put her magazine down on the table between them. "Don't bet the farm on that one, lover boy."

They were in to their second hour. Ryan used the time to make several more sweeps of the area. Either his imagination was in overdrive or the guy was a pro. He chose door number two and Charles dropped to the bottom of the list. A stakeout of an unsuspecting victim was one thing but executing a successful tail on a former cop was something else again. Cops were paranoid by nature. Those who weren't rarely reached retirement. Looking over their shoulder didn't stop when they gave up their badge. Another cop would know that. The list got shorter and, with it, Ryan's patience.

By the time Dr. Cummings opened her door, he was fuming. She must have sensed his mood, either that or the session had bombed. She seemed less combative, not quite as sure of herself. Ryan met her halfway across the waiting room. "She's really something, Pete. I needed some background and I don't think she held anything back. She told me all you've done for her. I may be forced to change my opinion of you."

"How do you think she'd react if she knew we were being followed?"

"Are you?"

"I'm not sure, but if I had to guess, I'd say yes."

The doctor looked back over her shoulder toward her office. "She's gutsy. She gave up law school, her family, everything that mattered and became someone else. You have to be honest with her. She can take it."

"She might run again."

"There's always that chance but I doubt it. She's invested in the work and in you. Can you handle that?"

The question was loaded, intentionally so, and Ryan didn't bite. Instead, he fired off one of his own. "Did you get anything at all? Did she see or hear anything that might help us find this guy?"

"Maybe. I film all my sessions so you can have a look. It's near the end. We'll pick it up from there."

It was obvious she wanted to help and Ryan felt guilty. "Look, Sophia, I'm sorry I never called. My life for the last few years has been complicated. You happened to catch me on the one night I was able to forget how screwed up it really is."

"Tequila shooters, God's little miracle drug. That's a personal observation, not a professional recommendation."

"I wasn't that drunk. You were great, by the way, just what the doctor ordered."

"It was my pleasure. You want to make it up to me? Find the bastard."

"I'll give it my best shot."

She crooked her finger and he brought his ear close to her lips. "I've had your best shot. Try harder."

Even though the joke was at his expense, he felt looser, less tightly wound. Now he could focus on what was in front of him, not behind him. In addition to her other obvious talents, the good doctor knew the human psyche.

The computer screen flickered and Marti's face appeared. Her eyes were closed. Off-screen, Sophia's voice was soothing, unhurried.

"Okay, Marti, you're in the kitchen and she's seen you looking at some papers on the counter. She's angry and tells you to get your things and leave."

"My supplies are down the hall. I know I should get them but there's one more room, a guest room. The bed isn't made and there are dirty towels in the bathroom. I'm not sure what to do. I don't want to leave before I finish."

"Does it look like more than one person has slept there?"

"No, the comforter is thrown to one side and only one pillowcase is wrinkled."

"What do you do?"

"I go into the bathroom and pick up the towels. They're damp so I take them to the laundry room and put them in the washing machine. I go back to the bathroom and wipe the shower down, then the sink and countertop."

"What's on the countertop, Marti? Do you have to move anything to wipe it down?"

"A black case with a zipper down the center."

"A man's toiletry case?"

"It makes me think of my dad. He has one like it."

"Is it open or closed?"

"Closed."

"Are you finished in the bathroom?"

"No, I scrub the toilet and mop the floor."

"Then what do you do?"

"I go in the bedroom to clean but it's dark, not bright like the bathroom. I have to open the drapes so I can see."

"What do you see outside when you open the drapes?"

"Wilderness. It's beautiful but…"

"But what?"

"Lonely."

"Do you see any cars outside, in the driveway, or anyone walking around?"

"No."

"What are you doing now?"

"I'm making the bed. The furniture is dark wood with carving on the front, Spanish, but I don't think anyone has cleaned it in awhile. It's dusty."

"Go on."

"I dust the dresser first."

"Tell me about the dresser. Is there anything on top of it?"

"A lamp, no, two lamps."

"What's wrong, Marti?"

"The door to the study must be open because I can hear him again."

"What is he saying?"

"He's telling her she's useless, that he can't even trust her to control the help. He's screaming at her to get me out of the house."

"Do you leave?"

"I'm almost done. I want to finish my job. Why does she let him talk to her like that?"

"I don't know but you have to get out of the house so what do you do next?"

"I dust the nightstands."

"Is there anything on the nightstands?"

"Just a lamp on one but the other…"

"What about it? What about the other nightstand, Marti?"

"Books, two books. I have to pick them up so I can dust but when I pick them up, something falls to the floor. It's a keychain. It's pretty."

"What's pretty?"

"The medallion. It's old, some of the paint is rubbed off."

"Can you describe it to me? What color is it?"

"Red and white with yellow animals on it and something in the middle. I can't make out what it is."

"Take your time. It's in your hand and you're looking at it. What kind of animals are on it?"

"Lions or griffins, four of them, very small."

"Is there any writing on it?"

"No."

"What shape is it, round, square?"

"Like a shield."

"A crest, a coat of arms?"

"Yes."

"Marti, this is important, look at the keychain. Is there anything else hanging from it, a rental car tag?"

"No, just the medallion and two keys."

"Can you…what's wrong? Do you hear something?"

"I have to go. I have to get my things and go. I don't want her screaming at me again."

"Because it makes you angry?"

"Because it makes me sad."

The screen went to black and Ryan tensed. "Did I doze off and miss something?"

Sophia took the chair behind her desk and folded her hands. "Maybe it's his family's crest."

"And maybe it's just an old fob on a key ring. I have one too, want to see it?" He pulled a set of keys from his pocket and put them on the desk.

"What is that, it's creepy."

"It's a leprechaun but that's not the point."

"Look, Pete, we went through every square inch of that house except the areas she wasn't allowed to enter. That's all we got but at least it's something."

He had to admit he was impressed with the depth of her questions, even drawing Marti back to the view from the guest room. "You're right, it is something, more than we came in here with."

Ryan looked behind him. Marti had been silent since he entered the office and still seemed out of it. "Are you all right?"

"No, I'm not all right. I should have found a way to get her away from him. Maybe if I'd confided in her about my sister or stayed in Sedona and told the police what I knew."

It was Sophia who stepped up first. "Marti, she wouldn't have listened. I see women everyday who know intellectually they're in an abusive relationship but emotionally they're unwilling or unable to leave. For whatever reason, they're stuck. I didn't know Susan Pierce so I can't comment on why she allowed him to treat her that way, but you can't blame yourself. You tried to help her. You did what you could." Her eyes made contact with Ryan's and shifted toward Marti.

He got the hint. "We've been over this. Cody knew the truth but they wouldn't listen to him either. It wasn't his ballgame. The D.A. made the decision not to pursue it as a homicide, especially after the victim's sister and brother got to him. On top of everything else, it's bad juju for the tourists. Welcome to Beautiful Sedona, land of the red rocks, cold-blooded killers and man-eating coyotes."

Marti stood up. "Okay, you two, I appreciate the pep talk but I have to get back to work."

Ryan reached inside his coat and took out his checkbook. Dr. Cummings shook her head. "Put it away, Pete. I'm happy to help in any way I can. Marti, you were great. What's wrong?"

"There were three books on the nightstand. I know I said two but there were three. One of them was a paperback by Stuart Woods. It was on top. The one beneath it was a biography of Shakespeare by A.L. Rowse. I remember that because I have the same book. The one on the bottom was very old. Dickens. I just can't…Bleak House. It was Bleak House."

Ryan frowned. "That's poetic, twisted but poetic."

"Except Bleak House wasn't bleak," said Sophia. "It was pretty cheerful."

Marti stepped forward. "Maybe he identifies with Dedlock, idle, fashionably aristocratic."

"Here we go again. Look, ladies, as much as I'm enjoying this segment of Oprah's Book Club, it could be he likes a lot of different books. Not everything has a hidden meaning."

"But most things do, otherwise I'd be out of a job." Sophia rose and walked around to the front of her desk. "Let's take your leprechaun. If that were found at a crime scene, one could speculate the perpetrator was Irish."

"Or he had incredibly bad taste," added Marti.

Ryan looked from one woman to the other. "What's with you two?"

Sophia smiled, first at him and then at Marti. "We discovered we have a lot in common. We're about the same age and

I considered Law School before I decided on medicine. We're getting together Friday night for some serious girl time…alone."

Ryan glared at her. "Not the best idea."

Sophia shrugged her shoulders. "Now's as good a time as any."

He turned to Marti. "You're not going anywhere alone. I think one of us is being followed."

"Well-built guy wearing a Dallas Cowboys cap, Ray-Bans and a black sweatshirt?"

"That's him. What the…"

"He was in the vestibule when I went downstairs to pick up the mail, a few minutes before we left to come here. I wondered about him."

"Jesus, Marti, you might have mentioned him. What was he doing?"

"Looking at the directory."

"So he's not your stalker from Austin?"

"They would have heard me back in Texas if I'd run into him."

"Not if he forced you into a waiting van with a gun at your head. Did he say anything?"

"He said hello and asked if there was an insurance office in the building."

"Did he seem nervous, surprised to see you?"

"No, not really."

"But you said you wondered about him so obviously you sensed something," said Sophia.

"I suppose it could have been the cap and sunglasses, although I never really connected him to Charles. No, it wasn't that. He seemed to be studying me, not in a lewd way, in a curious way as if he were trying to place where he'd seen me."

Ryan turned her around until she was facing him. "Did you do something different with your hair?"

"Not intentionally but it was raining when I walked to work, why?"

He took her by the arm and led her toward a mirror behind the door. "That's why." Her hair, normally thick and straight, fell in soft curls around her face. "You're the right age, right coloring and now your hair's even the same style. You've seen photos of the other women, what do you think?"

"I think you need to take your own advice and go to the park or the movies. You seem to forget I have no creative talent whatsoever. I'm a geek."

"Then maybe he found out it was you in the house and tracked you here."

"He was in his study the entire time I was there. He never saw me."

"No, you never saw *him* and you're missing the point."

Sophia stepped between them. "You're both missing the point. You're not communicating. When and where did you first spot him, Pete?"

"It was around eight this morning, a dive around the corner from my apartment. I go there everyday to pick up coffee. He came in a couple of minutes after me."

Marti wasn't happy. "And you kept this to yourself for over seven hours and didn't think to tell me about it? Damn it, Pete, you've got to stop treating me like a child."

"Up until a minute ago, I wasn't sure there was anything to tell. Anyway, you were up to your ass in phone calls this morning, we both were."

A buzzer went off in the office and Sophia checked her watch. "Sorry, but my next patient is here. You can leave by the door behind my desk. It'll lead you to the elevators. I'll call you tomorrow, Marti, and we'll decide how to spend girls' night. Maybe we'll eat in. Pete, it was good seeing you. Try to play nice."

"Why does everyone say that to me?"

When the elevator reached the ground floor, Ryan stepped off first. The lobby was empty except for a security guard. Motioning for her to hang back, Ryan approached the guard. After a minute or so, the man behind the desk shook his head.

Outside on the street, Marti walked ahead, stopped and turned around. "I'm sorry I yelled at you in there but I'm not handling this damsel-in-distress thing very well. I've been on my own since I left for college almost twenty years ago. I spent ten of those years in South America taking care of everyone else. I know it sounds like I'm not grateful to you but I am, more than you'll ever know." She shoved her hands keep in the pockets of her raincoat and looked away from him. "I'm not your kid sister, Pete. I'm not Theresa. You can't bring her back by smothering me."

"What brought this on?"

"It was something Sophia asked me before the hypnosis. When I finished telling her about the last two years, she asked me if everything were normal and I could go back to my old life in Austin, would I do it. I said no, I was exactly where I wanted to be. And then she asked me if I would take off again, run away. I said yes. The day my presence compromises the investigation, the day you put yourself or the work in jeopardy because of me is the day I leave."

"Is that an ultimatum?"

"Think of it as an informed choice. Are you laughing at me?"

"No, I'm laughing at me. That little speech you just made, the part about smothering you, I heard it from Theresa before she moved to Cambria."

"Well, there you go. What was she like?"

"A lot like you, tough, quick on her feet, a biting sense of humor."

"But not a geek."

"If you're referring to being computer-savvy then no, definitely not. I'm afraid that runs in the family. She wrote all her books in long-hand. I spent a few weekends with her in Cambria right after she moved there. I'd watch TV or read and she'd be working at her desk, writing. She used pens, not pencils. One day she ran out for something and I looked through her notebooks. Nothing was crossed out, no corrections, no false starts, just line after line of script. I don't know how she did that."

"She was writing from her heart and the heart doesn't edit or judge. That's the brain's job. I think of it as the kill-joy organ. Maybe that's why so many women ignore it."

"You didn't. He's in trouble, you know, your problem back in Austin."

"No, I didn't know. What is it this time?"

"Missing evidence, money and drugs."

"They'll cover it up and make it go away. They have to, otherwise all his collars and resulting convictions will be called into question. I know the D.A., Pete, and he's not going to tolerate do-overs."

"He may not have a choice. If something comes of it and there's a trial, you could be subpoenaed by the Prosecution."

"If they have to use me then they don't have much of a case. The D. A. fired me. The Defense will have a field day with that. Besides, I want nothing to do with something that puts drug dealers back on the streets. I'll take my chances with Tony and his goon squad before I see that happen."

Goon squad. He should have thought of that. Rats travelled in packs except when threatened, then it was every rat for himself. The chances were also pretty good they didn't have Marti's gift for legal analysis, that revenge was no longer a motivation. The way they saw it was if one fell, they all went down. Ergo, Martha Henderson was a liability.

Ryan tried to make his next question sound casual, off the cuff. "This guy you saw earlier. You said he was wearing a Dallas Cowboys cap. I don't remember seeing any writing."

They came to a stop outside their building. "It was a navy blue cap with a navy blue star outlined in white. That's their logo. I lived in Texas, they're everywhere."

"What about the sweatshirt? Are you sure it was black? I thought it was dark blue."

"It was black, a hoodie, with a zipper up the front." Her voice grew soft. "You need to work on your poker face, Pete. You think he sent someone down to clean up his mess in case things go bad in Austin. If that's true, why didn't he make a move earlier when he had the chance?"

"You said he was studying your face. Have you changed your appearance since you left Texas?"

"My hair was shorter and a bit lighter with some highlights, and I also wore glasses when I was working or studying which was most of the time." She moved her upper body so she could see behind him.

"You're squinting." Ryan turned around. "What are you looking at?"

"I took my contacts out before the hypnosis and forgot to put them back in. I can't be sure but I think he just walked out of a shop in the next block."

"Which way is he going?"

"Away from us I think."

Ryan patted his pocket, felt the gun. "Go upstairs and lock yourself in your office. Move!"

Midway up the stairwell, panic seized her. It rose like bile, bitter and foul. Inside her office, she fell back against the closed door. Her skin felt clammy to the touch, her breath labored. Her hand was shaking as she scribbled the note so she tore it off the tablet and started over. The second attempt was better and she left it on the desk. She opened the door and turned for a final look. "I'll be back," she whispered. She was looking at the chalkboard when the black-clad arm reached for her from the hall.

CHAPTER 42

ANNIE

It wasn't a date. It was two people having dinner, no big deal, but it wasn't a date. She was thirty-nine, divorced, living alone with a dog. Based on cultural predictors, she was a day away from forgetting to bathe and collecting ceramic cats.

She ripped the plastic off another dress and held it up in front of her before the mirror. It was the one Samantha insisted she buy during her last visit, the red one guaranteed to banish the divorce doldrums. She slipped it on over her bra and panties and groaned. Throw on a short black wig, a garter and she'd be Betty Boop. And with that, another dress was consigned to the reject pile.

A half hour later, she made her decision. The little black Armani was safe, more high tea than hootchie-mama. She took a final look in the mirror, went in close to check her make-up and winked at her reflection. "It's not a date."

Judging from the flowers in his hand, Bryce Stanley thought it was a date. Annie watched from her bedroom window as he parked his car, alighted and took a moment to inspect the driveway. He was even better looking than she remembered and just as self-assured. His only hesitation came when he approached the house. He seemed to be confused as to which door was the front door. She was already downstairs when he rang the bell and, for reasons known only to her evil id, Oscar Peterson's rendition of *Let There Be Love* was wafting through the living room.

Their initial greeting was less awkward than she feared, a quick peck on both cheeks, very Continental. When she came back from the kitchen, he was seated on the sofa, one arm stretched out along the back cushions. He looked comfy and relaxed.

"This is a wonderful room, Annie. You have great taste." He took the drink from her hand, Black Label on the rocks with a splash of water, no twist.

"You've really never seen this house?"

"I knew we owned it, but up until now it was just a line item on an asset sheet. Is that a CD?"

"It is, but if you'd prefer, I can put on something Classical."

"No, thanks. I'm embarrassed to admit I never developed an ear for Classical music. Violins make my teeth ache. That's Oscar Peterson, isn't it? God, can he play."

"The Maharaja of the Keyboard, at least according to Duke Ellington."

"I hadn't heard that."

"Neither had I until tonight. I read it in the liner notes."

He smiled and dropped his head. When he looked up, his face was serious. "I have another confession to make. I've been nervous as hell about tonight."

"But I'll bet you didn't stand in front of the mirror for an hour telling yourself this wasn't a date."

"Did you do that?"

"I did but please don't take it personally."

"Then I have an idea. Let's not think of it as a date. We're two old friends who haven't seen one another for a few years. We're going out to dinner to catch up. How does that sound?"

"It sounds perfect. Bryce, I haven't apologized for the way I left your office last week. You were trying to be nice and I was very rude, I'm sorry. I'm not sure why I acted that way."

"You weren't feeling well for one thing, and I shouldn't have come on so strong. I'm not nearly as pompous and arrogant as I came off that day. I hope I'll get the opportunity to prove that to you."

By the time his car left the lane, the ice was broken. There was one tense moment when they passed Helen's house and she averted her eyes, but it went unnoticed. Thankfully, the crime scene tape had been removed that afternoon. Since Helen's house was visible from a busy road, a few local realtors raised holy hell. At first the police demurred but then reluctantly agreed to take it down. She was relieved to see it go. Right up there with politics and religion, Helen's death and Debra's disappearance topped her list of unacceptable dinner chatter. In her mind, there were three good reasons for this decision. One. Bryce was out of the country until the previous day and probably knew nothing about the incident anyway. Two. While the police suspected foul play, nothing was conclusive. Several reports, including toxicology, were still pending. And three. She would have to admit their initial meeting was based on a lie.

She tensed again when he exited the thruway at Indian Field Road, one of the roads leading into Greenwich. This time, to her regret, he was paying attention.

"What's wrong?"

"Nothing, I haven't spent much time here since my divorce, that's all." The very next moment, he had his cell phone out. "What are you doing?"

"Cancelling the reservation. We'll go somewhere else."

She reached over and touched his hand. "Please don't, I'm being silly. Besides, it's Wednesday night. The place will probably be empty."

Fourth in line for the valet service, Annie kept her cool. As it turned out, the *place* was Le Coq Rouge, the new in-spot for the rich and richer. Open less than a month, everything from the furnishings to the chefs, head and sous, were imported from France or Belgium. It was almost impossible to snag a reservation, even on a week night.

Before opening his door, Bryce turned to face her. "Just say the word and we're out of here. We'll try it again in six months when they start selling off the antiques to pay the rent. This is what, the third or fourth restaurant to open here in the last ten years?"

Annie laughed. "At least." Two couples were entering the restaurant and she gave them a quick once-over. "I say we stay. May as well get back in the game."

"Do me one more favor, will you?" He flipped her visor down and clicked open the mirror. "Take a look at who I see, who everyone in this joint is going to be looking at. You're gorgeous, that dress is amazing and the rest is bullshit, pure Greenwich bullshit."

Annie leaned across and gave him a quick kiss on the cheek. "Send me in, coach, I'm starving."

The interior of the restaurant was another pleasant surprise. Where its predecessors relied on trendy wall finishes and over-the-top lighting effects, this incarnation was elegantly unpretentious. If she didn't know better, she would swear she was in a farmhouse in Provence, a four million dollar farmhouse, but a farmhouse nonetheless. The room was lit by candles, thousands of them, the tablecloths of the finest Belgian lace. Simple whitewashed walls held large, unframed oils depicting the French countryside. Even the oversized red rooster, floating over the bar and discreetly lit from above, appeared authentically aged.

The placement of the bar was another rarity. More often than not, Greenwich-ites were forced to do their pre-sup imbibing in relative seclusion, secreted off to the side or near the front where hungry diners were bustled past. Here, the four-sided bar took center stage and accounted for a large percentage of the total square footage. It was a clever concept. As well as providing a relaxed mingling of diners and drinkers, the expanded bar seating increased the bottom line. The rest of the space was devoted to banquettes and tables, relatively few in relation to its size, so diners could talk without being overheard.

When they were shown to their table against the wall, Bryce asked, "In or out?"

Annie looked toward the bar and back at him. "I'm here so I might as well enjoy the entertainment."

"Atta girl."

Their drinks were served with lightning speed and Bryce lifted his glass. "To new friends."

"And old friends," added Annie.

"Okay, old pal, it's been a few years so remind me. Exactly what have you been doing since the day you were born?"

"If you insist, but I'll make it quick. I was born in California, raised in Michigan, educated in Ohio and moved to Connecticut when I got married. My dad was an engineer with an aerospace company and my mom liked to shop. They live in Florida now. Dad's semi-retired and mom's still shopping. I have a sister, as you know, living in London and I volunteer at an AIDS hospice." At some point, she'd added **Life House** to her list of things off-limits. It was too soon to talk about it without breaking into tears. "Now you."

"That's it? Don't I get to hear how you and the Beav stole Wally's baseball cards?"

"I know, it sounds nauseatingly normal. I think Sam gravitated to acting so she could get out of her skin and into someone else's."

"And what did Annie gravitate to?"

"Archaeology. From the time I was eight, that's all I ever thought about. I had an uncle who was into Egyptology. He had all these beautiful books. One day when I was visiting, I took one off the shelf and started reading it. On my ninth birthday, he gave me my own copy of *Gods, Graves & Scholars* and I was pretty well hooked from that moment on."

"Isn't that heavy reading for a nine-year-old?"

"What can I say, I was a nerd."

"What's the rest of the story?"

"I met my future husband at Ohio State. We eloped right after graduation and the next year he was off to Law School."

"And instead of pursuing your dream, you went to work to support the two of you. I wonder how many times that's played out over the last fifty years? Any regrets?"

"None worth discussing."

"Where does he practice?"

"He doesn't. He walked away from it ten years ago. Larry's on Wall Street now."

Bryce put down his drink. "You were married to that Larry Heywood, the money machine?"

"Please don't tell me there's more than one. The money machine. As crass as that sounds, he'd love it. Do you know him?"

"No, but I know some people who made a lot of money because of him."

She was about to ask how he knew that but then she remembered. Even though the wealthy kept their bank accounts as concealed as their mistresses, the one person privy to both would be their attorney, particularly their estate planner.

The appetizers arrived and Annie's smoked salmon with crème fraiche drizzle was a sculptural masterpiece. If the food was half as good as the presentation, Le Coq Rouge just might survive and prove them both wrong.

Bryce squeezed a lemon wedge over his oysters and held it up between his fingers. "I want to meet the guy who woke up one morning and said 'I know what I want to do with my life, make lemon wedge panties, a little cheesecloth, an inch or two of elastic…'"

"I know that guy. His wife came up with the first toilet paper cozy."

Bryce laughed. "I remember those things. Did anyone actually buy them?"

"My mother. She has two, one in each bathroom. I told you she was a shopper."

"So if we're staying there and you hear me guffawing from the bathroom, you'll know what it's about."

The remark caught her off-guard but she tried not to let it show on her face. "Okay, now that you know my family's dirty little secrets, it's time for some quid pro quo, counselor. Tell me about you."

He took a sip of wine. "Born in Greenwich, raised in Greenwich, went to Yale and Harvard Law. I married a classmate of mine, Sybil, aptly named as it turned out. We divorced five years ago and tonight I'm having dinner with the intoxicating Annie Heywood."

"And you have twin boys at Oxford."

"That I do. They're great kids."

"You have a brother too. You mentioned him when I was in your office."

"I have a sibling. We've never been close, not like you and your sister. Our parents split up when I was five and he was six. It affected Scotty worse than it did me. Dad tried everything, the best schools, bringing him into the business, you name it, but all he ever wanted to do was raid his trust fund and see the world. He worked for Dad for a few years and did a decent job and then took off again. Since then, he's been pretty much blowing in the wind. One year he was in Prague brokering religious icons, the next he was in Vienna researching the Hapsburgs. When Dad died, he left him enough money so he'd never have to take responsibility for anything and he never has. Five years ago, he showed up again, said he'd had an epiphany and wanted to pull his weight in the business. Like an idiot, I jumped at the idea. I was going through my divorce and, frankly, I needed an ally and someone to help with the family holdings. He lasted six months."

"Where is he now?"

"Not a clue. We look enough alike so occasionally I'm mistaken for him when I'm in London. He went to Cambridge and he's still got some chums there but nobody's heard from him in months."

"He sounds like a character from a Hemingway novel." Annie was distracted by a woman's laughter in the general direction of the bar. When she glanced up, the woman made eye contact with her and slowly turned back to her male companion, who was standing beside her, one arm resting on the bar. Bryce was saying something but her attention was focused over his shoulder. The woman was the Countess de Longchamps, nee Miranda Prescott. She could see nothing of the man except a profile. A waiter with a dessert trolley was blocking her view.

"Annie, is everything all right?"

"Sorry, I thought I saw someone I knew. What were you saying?"

"I said I doubt Scotty ever read Hemingway or any American writer for that matter. He's obsessed with everything British. All those books in my office, they're his."

"Okay, then someone out of a Maugham novel, Larry Darrell in *A Razor's Edge*."

"I can't believe you said that."

"Why?"

"That's what Dad called him whenever Scotty would disappear. He's goddamn Larry Darrell. The thing is I think Dad also had a grudging respect for him. I'm sure there were times when dear old Dad wished he'd taken off for the Himalayas instead of getting saddled with the family business."

"What about you? Didn't you ever want to take off on a spiritual quest to find the meaning of life?"

"Once, when my mother died."

"I'm sorry, Bryce. Was that recently?"

"She was thirty-four when she died. I was seven. You sure you want to hear all this?"

"Only if you're comfortable talking about it."

"Oddly enough, I am. She and Scotty were on the Sound in a catamaran. She loved to sail and was good at it. It was rough that day and Scotty leaned over the side to lose his breakfast. He went in and she went in after him. She managed to get his arms around one of the hulls but something happened and she went down. When they found her, she had a large bruise on her temple. They think she must have hit her head when she pushed him up."

Even to Annie's nautically-challenged ear, the story had more holes than a lemon wedge panty. Where were the life vests and safety lines? Who took their eight-year-old sailing in rough weather? And how could seeing your mother drown in front of you **not** alter the course of your life? "That's horrible. You weren't there when it happened, were you?"

"I was sick in bed that weekend. I can't believe I'm talking this much. Have I scared you off?"

"Not yet." It wasn't exactly a lie but it did give her pause. She thought of Larry growing up with a drunken ne'er-do-well father and the impact it had on his life. But if Larry had baggage, Bryce had steamer trunks.

"This isn't working for me, Annie. The last old friend I had dinner with looked like Peter Ustinov. Any chance we can consider this a date, especially since you know where all the bodies are buried?"

Despite the attempt to lighten things up, his last few words had the opposite effect. There was a natural progression to her thoughts, first Helen and Debra, then Mike. It wasn't the first time that evening he'd crossed her mind and nudged her to make comparisons. Bryce was attentive and funny. Mike was sass and heat, but he'd made it clear it was all or nothing and she'd stumbled at the starting gate. She managed a small smile. "I'll have to think about it. You know how it is, tonight it's a date and tomorrow you'll give me your fraternity pin and before long…"

"You want a fraternity pin?" He jerked his thumb in the direction of the street. "I keep a supply in my car. I'll get one."

"Okay, we're actually on a date, happy?"

"It's a start."

The waiter and trolley were gone but the couple was still at the bar. Every now and then Miranda would say something and the man would laugh. It wasn't Larry. This man was taller, tall enough so his face was backlit by the pendant lighting. It could have been a coincidence but Annie suspected it was by design. Whenever he leaned down to listen or comment, he would turn his face toward the bar, away from their table.

The dinner was delicious and so, to her surprise, was the company. He had an easy-going manner and a wry, self-effacing wit. She was also impressed when he switched to club soda halfway through the first bottle of wine. During their entrees, the conversation was more chatty than profound, typical getting-to-know-you kinds of things, favorite books, favorite movies, many of which they had in common. The longer they talked, the more she relaxed and went with it.

When the table was cleared, Bryce placed his hand atop hers on the table. "I know this is a little fast but I have to go to Newport this weekend. Any chance you don't have anything better to do? Everything will be very proper, separate rooms, separate tables at dinner if you'd like."

"I'm flying to London on Friday or I'd love to. Separate rooms would have been fine."

"That's right. Your sister's opening in a play, what is it again?"

"Othello."

"This is the part where I recite a line from the play and knock your socks off. Unfortunately, my knowledge of Shakespeare is about the same as my appreciation for Classical music." He brought the club soda to his lips and put it down again. "Wait, do you hear something? It's my father turning over in his grave. He raised a lowbrow."

"I doubt that. Besides, a smart man hides his limitations. A wise man acknowledges them."

"In addition to all your other attributes, you're incredibly good for my ego. Did you just make that up?"

"It's my fallback career, writing fortunes for Chinese cookies. What do you think?"

Still touching her hand, he looked deep in her eyes. "I think I'm in a lot of trouble."

A low buzzing sound caught her ear. It was coming from his side of the table. "Your cell phone's ringing."

"I'm ignoring it."

"Answer it, I don't mind."

He pulled it from his jacket pocket, looked first at the screen and then at his watch. "One of my boys. It's the middle of the night there so it could be important. I'll take it outside."

Watching him walk away from her, she waited for the rush she always felt with Mike. When it didn't come, she lowered her head and gave it a gentle shake.

"Something wrong with the wine?"

The voice was the same but more seductive, slower, as if measuring his words for just the right impact. Bryce was right about the resemblance. They could have easily been twins. His hair was darker and a bit longer but styled similarly, brushed back off his face to accentuate his eyes and bone structure.

Scott Stanley filled his brother's glass from the half-empty wine bottle. "I figured I'd introduce myself since you've been staring at me for over an hour."

If he hadn't been smiling, Annie might have taken offense at the remark. "You just missed your brother. He's outside taking a call."

"Yes, I know, and we have nine more minutes until he comes back so we need to speed things up if I'm going to steal you away and ruin his evening."

"Nine minutes? How do you know that?"

"Because five minutes ago, I called one of my nephews in the U.K. and told him to phone his father right away. For every minute he keeps him on the phone, I send him a hundred pounds, up to a maximum of twenty minutes."

"Wouldn't it have been cheaper to walk over and join us?"

"But then I wouldn't have had you all to myself, would I?" He took another sip of wine. "This is excellent. Don't you like it?"

"It's very nice but tomorrow's a working day for me."

"Temperance and moderation, I admire that in a woman." He looked away and then back at her. "Miranda doesn't like you very much."

"I'm crushed."

"You're a very bad girl. Someone ought to take you over their knee, which is something I'll be fantasizing about all night." The grin never faltered. "Does my brother know about you, Annabelle?"

She kept her gaze steady. "We haven't discussed it but you shouldn't believe everything you hear or read, Scott. Where is Miranda, by the way?"

"She left. I doubt you have to worry about Bryce reading the book. He's not a fan." He took another sip of wine. "You haven't read it either, have you? I'm guessing you're much too smart for that. The past is the past and you have no desire to revisit it. His description of you is two pages long, did you know that? He's captured you perfectly, the trim little body that a man could lift with one hand, the heart-shaped face and large blue eyes, a lower lip that begs to be bitten. Of course you'd have to be naked and in an extremely compromising position for me to see if the rest of the description fits. You annihilated him and yet he'd give up the rest of his life for another month with you. Bryce is in way over his head. How did the two of you meet?"

"I bought the Spinnaker Lane house from your estate."

His grin was replaced with a dark look. "Why?"

"Why not? It's a very nice home with a large piece of property."

"It's a hovel and it doesn't go with the Armani which you wear beautifully by the way. Who was it, the pool boy or the tennis pro?"

"Excuse me?"

"You must have been fucking one of them. Otherwise you would have made out better in your divorce settlement."

He was doing his best to push her buttons but she wouldn't give him the satisfaction of pushing back and making a scene. "I came out of the marriage with exactly what I asked for, no more, no less."

"Really."

Bryce was making his way back through the crowd at the bar. Scott looked behind him and got to his feet. The men shook hands, stepped into one another and patted each other on the back. After exchanging a few cordial jibes, Scott scooted in next to her on the upholstered bench. His proximity unnerved her, especially when he slid his hand across the seat and under her thigh.

"I'm going to the ladies room and give you two a few minutes to catch up."

Inside the ladies room, she walked through the vanity area to the sinks and stalls. After a quick pit stop, she washed her hands and retraced her steps to the small anteroom. It was compact, just large enough to hold a chaise, a marble-topped make-up table and two or three other small pieces. A few feet away, a woman was seated on a tufted stool. She was close to fifty, stunning, with a trim, athletic body. When Annie smiled at her, the woman spoke to her in a sexy Texas drawl. "I love your hair. Not every woman can wear it. I'm afraid if I cut mine that short, I'd look like my brother."

"Let's face it, I have the body for it."

"I know someone who can fix that." The woman rose and walked toward her. "Lord, you haven't had any work done at all, have you?"

"Is it that obvious?"

"It was meant as a compliment and, believe me, I rarely give them to women."

"Thanks, I needed that."

"I doubt that. Please tell me you're not going home with both of them or I'll shoot you and then myself."

It took a moment for Annie to realize she'd been ambushed, that the woman was waiting for her.

"Sweetie, you can't expect to be monopolizing two of Fairfield County's most eligible men and not have one of us gunning for you."

"One of us? Are there more of you?"

"Right now there are at least six of us at the bar, all divorced, all looking for husband number whatever. It's like a…what do they call that thing hunters use when they're lying in wait for their prey?"

"A duck blind?"

"That's it, a duck blind, a collagen-lipped, Botox-injected, silicone-implanted duck blind. Pathetic, isn't it?"

"A girl's gotta do what a girl's gotta do. Anyway, you look great. Who cares how you got that way?"

"Who are you going home with, Bryce or Scott?"

"You know them?"

"Everyone knows them, the Stanley boys, Belle Haven, Ivy League, money up the wazoo. You're not from around here, are you?"

"No."

"Swell, now the competition's being imported."

"I'm from Westport not Shanghai."

"Same thing. Bryce may be just a tad better looking but there's something about Scott, something kinda dangerous."

Annie turned back to the mirror. The conversation was taking a direction she had no interest in following. Dangerous was an understatement. He was psychotic.

The woman regarded her own reflection in the mirror and ran her fingers through her shoulder-length hair. "I guess I'd better get back and tell the girls to holster their firearms. My name's Pam, by the way."

"I'm Annie, and if it makes you feel any better, I'm not going home with either of them, not the way you mean. But don't tell the girls. Let's make them sweat a little."

"You're a good sport. I like you." Her hand on the door handle, she turned back around. Without her smile, she looked older. "Watch yourself, Annie. You may think this is the Magic Kingdom but there are a lot more rats than mice. The management gives out passes, some for an evening, some for what you think is going to be a lifetime. Problem is they're revocable at any time. My Prince Charming revoked mine after twenty-two years and three kids."

"I'm sorry."

"The boy's got flair, I'll give him that. My mama died last year and I flew home to Bastrop to bury her. He didn't go, said funerals depressed him. When I came back, I was standing in the baggage area at JFK when I saw a man holding up a sign with my name on it. I figured my husband sent a car since I was so upset and all. Turns out he was serving me with divorce papers."

"And you never saw it coming?"

"Honey, in the Magic Kingdom you never see it coming. You're on the ride of your life."

"What did you do?"

"Right then? First, I called the meanest sonofabitch lawyer I could find and then I took a shuttle to the International terminal. I caught the first flight out to Paris, checked into a five-star hotel and spent the next two weeks shopping my ass off with his platinum card. By the time the charges showed up on his statement, we'd already reached a settlement. He never saw that coming either. You take care now."

Finally alone, Annie perched on the vacated stool. This life, these people, it was everything she ran from. She knew all about the ride. It was bright and fast and dizzying. She rode it until she couldn't stand it anymore and then jumped off. Now she was back, at least for a few hours. The woman jarred her back to reality. For all her beauty and brashness, she left in her wake the scent of hopelessness, something for which there were no cosmetic solutions.

Bryce was alone when she made her way back to their table. He looked happy to see her. "I was worried about you, especially when I saw Pam hot on your heels. What were the two of you talking about?"

"Disneyland. Did your brother leave?"

"He took off a couple of minutes after you left the table, but he did manage to spring one surprise on me. He owns a piece of this place, a third to be precise."

"And you had no idea when you made the reservation?"

"No, but that's typical. I ordered espressos. I hope that's all right."

"Of course. How's your son?"

"He needs money, what else is new? Are you okay, Annie? You seem far away."

"I'm fine. The dinner was wonderful, thank you."

The waiter appeared with the espressos, followed closely on his heels by Scott. He was holding three large snifters of cognac, moving them expertly around in his hand to release the aroma. After placing them on the table, he pulled over an empty chair from a nearby table. "Now where were we?"

With as much enthusiasm as she could muster, Annie raised her glass in Scott's direction. "To the success of Le Coq Rouge."

Scott, in turn, raised his. "And to your excellent accent. Miranda insists it's pronounced cock, not that I'm surprised."

Bryce glanced over both shoulders. "God, she's not here, is she?"

"I poured her into a cab and sent her home. She was here drowning her sorrows. She and her fiancé have hit a rough spot on the road to connubial bliss."

"Her fiancé? Isn't she married to a Duke or an Earl or something equally pretentious?"

"Count Nikolas de Longchamps. They're being annulled."

"That was quick. What happened this time?"

"The Count flushed her credit cards down the royal crapper. Mummy and Daddy had her on a plane home the next day."

"And she's already engaged?"

"Yes, and it appears she's marrying up this time, cash-wise that is."

Annie tensed. For a few minutes, she'd managed to relax, happy to have the emphasis off her. Now her antenna was fully extended. To cover it up, she brought the brandy to her lips but couldn't bring herself to drink it. The smell reminded her of the hours after finding Helen.

Bryce pushed his glass to the side. "Who the hell would be stupid enough to marry Amanda Prescott?"

Scott looked at Annie. Bryce, confused, eventually looked her way. "That would be my ex-husband, the money machine."

Before Bryce could comment, Scott said, "Oh, but it gets better. I found out why things are a bit rocky at the Heywood manse. Apparently he came home late one night in a cab, some excuse about his car breaking down. He climbs into bed randy as hell which suits Miranda just fine. Everything's taking its normal course until she smells something other than the liquor on his breath. Strawberries and soap. Early the next morning, he calls another cab to take him back to his car. Miranda's suspicious and has a lot of time on her hands so she starts snooping through his things. She finds a check stub dated that very morning. It's for half a million dollars payable to something called **Life House**. She's not sure but she thinks she's heard that name before so she calls the cab company and finds out where he was dropped off that morning."

Even by candlelight, Annie could see Bryce's face darkening, his patience wearing dangerously thin. "The cab dropped him off at my house. He showed up the night before and he'd been drinking. I didn't want him driving home in that condition. If you want any additional details, I suggest you ask Larry."

"That won't be necessary, will it Scott?" The look Bryce threw his brother's way was anything but warm but he smiled at Annie. "I assume **Life House** is where you volunteer?"

"It's an AIDS hospice." There was finality to her reply, a suggestion he may never hear the rest of the story.

Scott laughed. "Volunteer, is that what she told you? On top of everything else, our girl is also modest. She opened the hospice ten years ago and took quite a bit of heat for it. You might not know it, Bryce, but this lovely creature also has quite a reputation for being a badass, at least according to Gary Matthews."

"Who the hell is Gary Matthews?"

Finally understanding the dynamic, Annie kept silent. Scott's behavior had less to do with pushing her buttons than embarrassing his brother.

Scott leaned back in his chair. "He's a reporter for the Advocate and a frequent patron. He sits right over there at the end of the bar. He was in here Monday night an hour after Annie brought him to his knees in front of a gaggle of Westport's finest. He was still limping when he came in."

Annie glared across the table. "Actually he wound up on his back, and if you'd like a demonstration, it would be my pleasure."

Bryce rose from the table. "Now I know what it feels like to be the ugly girl at the Cotillion. Will you both excuse me for a few minutes?"

She blew it. Instead of ignoring Scott, which she had every intention of doing, she took the bait and made Bryce feel like a third wheel. But there was something else that was bothering her more. "How do you know so much about me, Scott?"

"The book, of course, but I had no idea at the time who you were other than the name. When Matthews came in the other night, I put the two together and looked you up on-line. And then I remembered hearing stories here and there about this Heywood woman, married to a highly-visible and filthy-rich asshole, who wanted absolutely nothing to do with the other children in the sandbox and never missed an opportunity to puncture their pomposity. You sounded so far removed from that bevy of Botox babes at the bar that I was trying to figure out some way to meet you. And then, to my utter shock and dismay, you waltz in here tonight with my brother."

"Say what you want about me, Scott, but don't ridicule them. They're just trying to get through the day and be what they think every man wants. Behind every Botox babe, as you put it, there's a company making billions perpetuating the lie that beauty equals happiness."

"My god, you're the real thing. Frankly, I thought you were an urban myth like the Chupacabra or Mothman. You're not in love with him, are you?"

"I don't know him. This is our first date and, thanks to you, it's not going well."

"I've decided to keep your secret, Annie. He's infatuated with you which should make your destruction of him just that much sweeter. Don't thank me now. Maybe one day I'll think of some way you can repay me."

"I doubt there's anything I can do for you that you can't get elsewhere."

"I disagree. I read the book, remember? There's nothing more challenging or exciting than a submissive with brains."

"I was nineteen and stupid, Scott."

"You started college at sixteen, maintained a 3.9 average and could argue Schopenhauer with a Rhodes Scholar. You were anything but stupid. You knew exactly what you were doing every minute." He signaled a passing waiter and raised his brandy snifter. "I was going to leave and let you two lovebirds enjoy the rest of your evening, but I've changed my mind. Perhaps it's time we learned to share our toys."

Rather than argue with him, Annie made a decision. She would make a clean breast of things and then leave, alone.

When Bryce returned to the table, he was subdued. She waited until he was looking at her and then she smiled. "Bryce, Gary Matthews wrote a story in Sunday's paper. You were out of the country so you wouldn't know about it. Shortly after I moved into the house, I found a diary belonging to a woman who lived there briefly with her husband in 2000. It's rather convoluted but the woman seems to have disappeared while she was living there."

"Is this a joke?"

"It could well turn out to be just that, or a misunderstanding."

"Do the police know about this?"

"They do but it's a very cold case, if there even is a case." She was deliberately playing it down, hoping to put it to rest.

Scott would have none of it. "I doubt Annie's neighbor would consider it a joke. She died the night before she was supposed to provide the police with a description of the husband. It's all very mysterious."

"What does that mean, mysterious?"

Scott ran his flattened hand across his throat.

Annie felt the blood rush to her head. She grabbed her coat and bag, pulling them behind her, knocking the wine bottle and its contents into Scott's lap. Cool and unfazed, he remained seated.

It was Bryce who jumped up from the table. "That's enough, Scott!"

He was saying something else but she was too far away to hear. Passing the bar, her eyes met those of the patrons, daring them to challenge her. Once outside, she approached the nearest valet and handed him a ten-dollar bill. "I need a taxi, please. I'll be waiting down there, just around the corner. If anyone asks where I've gone, play dumb." It was a cowardly thing to do, cowardly and childish, but she was determined to make her escape without another scene.

Bryce caught up with her as she was rounding the corner. "Annie, where are you going? You think I care that you didn't share your entire life history with me over a dinner? We have the rest of our lives to get to know one another. You'll have to learn to ignore Scott. I know he's annoying but…"

"Annoying? Is that what you think, that I'm annoyed? I'm not annoyed, Bryce. This is me incredibly pissed. He's rude and…" She almost said insufferable, a word she never used, a word she rarely heard uttered outside of a British drawing room. "Cruel."

He reached for her but she eased her shoulder back, away from his hand. "He's also a misogynist. You're not the only one who left some things out of our conversation. Scott hates women, particularly nice women, although I doubt he comes in contact with many of them. I told you our parents divorced. What I didn't elaborate on was how acrimonious it was. There were battles over everything and Scott and I were at the center of it. He's always been difficult. You see this scar?" He pointed to a spot just above his left eyebrow. "I woke up on my fourth birthday and he was holding a toy fire truck over my head. If I hadn't moved in time, he could have killed me. And this." He raised his sleeve above his wrist and turned it toward her, palm up. There was another scar, this one longer, running parallel with a vein. "He did this with a kitchen knife when I was five and wouldn't eat the vegetables off his plate. There were other things too but Dad refused to get him help. He was big on personal responsibility and looked upon mental illness as a weakness. Mother finally gave up. She got custody of both of us but at the last minute decided she couldn't handle him so I went with her and Scott stayed with Dad. He cleaned up his act as he got older but he never forgave her for abandoning him."

Annie pulled her eyes away from his. They were the color of the evening sky, infinite and sad. Feeling herself beginning to waver, she had to end it while she still had the strength. "Personal responsibility? He was a little boy. What's wrong with you people?"

"You people? So that's it. Funny, you're about the last person I would have suspected of being a bigot."

"A bigot?"

"You heard me. Intolerance is a slippery slope and because you think you're on the side of the angels, it doesn't make it right. Tell me to take a hike because you don't like me as a person or because I can't tell Shubert from Shostakovich but don't label me. I have no control over the circumstances of my birth or the fact that my family is fucked up."

"You're right. It was a hateful thing to say and I'm sorry."

"Don't do this, Annie. We made a connection in there. It may have only lasted thirty seconds, but I felt it and you did too. You're grounded and honest and I want someone like you in my life. I want you in my life. I'm tired of coming home to an empty house with no one to talk to but my housekeeper and dogs."

"I'm not that honest, Bryce. I lied about the reason I came to your office. I'm not writing a book. I was trying to get information on the couple that was living there in 2000. That's why I asked about Bert Kennedy. He was managing the property back then."

"I couldn't care less why you came to my office. The point is you did and I'm not letting you go."

A cab drove up to the curb and the valet signaled to her. She shook her head and another couple was motioned toward it. As it pulled away, she looked back up at him. "What kind of dogs?"

"What?"

"You said you have dogs. What kind?"

"A Bernese Mountain dog, a Portuguese Water dog and a shepherd mix." A slight smile crinkled the corners of his eyes. "Too bad you just blew any chance of meeting them. They're very picky and, besides, they'd get used to having you around and then you'd leave me for a homeless guy. We'd all end up in therapy." He took her hand. "I'm sorry about the evening, Annie. Let me make it up to you. What time does your flight leave on Friday?"

"8:30, but I've already arranged for a shuttle."

"Cancel it, I'm going with you. I'll book two seats in first class."

"You just got back from London and you're supposed to be in Newport, remember?"

"Newport can wait and as far as going back to London, I have clients there I should have seen but came back early for a very important date. I can't guarantee I'll stay for her opening, but I'd like to meet your sister, maybe take the two of you out to dinner Saturday night if you don't have other plans. What's the name of her play again?"

"Othello."

"God, why can't I remember that? On the flight over, you can give me a synopsis so I don't make a fool of myself."

"Palace intrigue, beautiful wife, jealous husband, she dies. Consider yourself synopsized."

"I think I can remember that." A look of unease crossed his face. "What Scott was saying about your neighbor. If you're in any danger, I can get our head of security at the Windsor facility to camp out until our plane leaves. He's good at what he does, a former cop."

"I appreciate that but the police are patrolling every few hours just as a precaution. I don't know anything about Debra's disappearance that would put me in jeopardy. All I did was hand over her journal. As far as that goes, the cause of Helen's death hasn't been determined. It was probably a heart attack."

"If you change your mind…is that rain? I'll grab the keys from the valet and find out where they parked the car. Wait under the awning."

Annie ran for cover, staying well away from the plate glass window. If the girls weren't buzzing about her untimely exit and Bryce's pursuit, it was only because they were too blotto to notice. For lack of something better to do, she looked at the menu posted just outside the door on the brick façade. It was behind glass, secured in an ornate brass frame. At the very bottom were the names of the three proprietors: Jonathan Hazelwood, Timothy Springer and C. Scott Stanley.

She pulled her coat tightly around her body and stepped out from beneath the awning. When a valet reappeared, she flagged him down. "Do you know the three men who own this restaurant?"

"I see them around."

"You wouldn't happen to know what Mr. Stanley's first name is, would you? The menu says C. Scott Stanley."

"No, ma'am. Everyone just calls him Scott or Scotty. I could go inside and ask someone if you want."

"No, please don't do that."

Bryce's car was just pulling up when the valet ran toward her with an umbrella. Escorting her to the car, he leaned down. "Mr. Stanley was standing just inside so I asked him what the C stood for. Told him I was curious. It stands for Cornelius, an old family name."

Annie thanked him and slipped him a five-dollar bill. The interior of the car was already toasty when she sank back into her seat. Cornelius. It was a ludicrous name, puffed up and pretentious. It fit him like a glove.

CHAPTER 43

RYAN

Needing a better vantage point, Ryan crossed the street and proceeded north. Many of the shops were closed which increased the odds in his favor. There were fewer open doors for the tail to escape detection, fewer shopkeepers to question.

Three blocks from the office, a pharmacy provided a candidate for Marti's sighting. A man in a cap and dark parka was at the rear of the store. He was arguing with the pharmacist about his prescription, demanding a refund. Hanging back, Ryan waited for him to turn around. When he did, he was at least twice the age of the man in the diner. The pharmacist was still shaking his head when the disgruntled customer left the store and he noticed Ryan. "You believe that guy? He wanted me to give him a refund for his Viagra."

Making a mental note to take his prescriptions elsewhere should the need arise, Ryan walked back out to the street and checked his watch. Twenty minutes had lapsed since he left Marti at the office. There was another explanation for her sighting, one that now seemed all too plausible. The tail doubled back or used a rear exit in one of the open shops. Even if someone were unfamiliar with the area, it would take him less than five minutes to reach their building.

He made it back in three. The ground floor offices were locked up tight as were most of the surrounding businesses. It was getting dark, that time of day when light played tricks and shadows played havoc. Locking the downstairs door behind him, he advanced up the stairs. He was several steps from the landing when he took the gun from his pocket. Something was off, a small thing he couldn't put his finger on. The light in the upstairs hall was on a timer, already lit when he reached Marti's office.

Blackness awaited him. Her door was open, not closed and locked as he instructed. Slowly, as if not wanting confirmation of what he already knew, he reached around the doorframe and flipped a switch. The overhead fluorescents buzzed and blinked before staying lit. The office was a disaster, a chair overturned, desktop items scattered on the floor. His chest tightened. He'd fallen for the oldest maneuver in the book and it hurt like hell, worse than he ever imagined. At some point, he'd have to look at that in depth but first he had to get her back. But that meant moving, and it also meant calling in help.

His cell phone was dead, and since her office was a crime scene, using her phone was out of the question. He took the hall in a single stride and opened his door.

Marti was leaning against his desk, arms folded across her chest. He took a tentative step toward her but stopped when she nodded in the direction of the opposite wall. Still holding the gun, he pushed the door fully open.

A man wearing a black sweatshirt was slumped forward in a chair, a navy blue cap on the floor beside him. In its place was a plastic baggie filled with ice. When he lifted his head, his eyes were bloodshot and unfocused. "Go ahead and shoot. Just don't let her near me."

Ryan turned to Marti. "What the hell happened?"

"I was in my office. I opened the door to go to the ladies room and…"

"I told you to close and lock your door."

"Don't start with me, Pete. He came up behind me and put his hand on my shoulder."

"And what, you picked up your desk and hit him over the head with it?"

"I'm not exactly sure what I did. One minute he was behind me and the next minute he was on the floor. I know a few self-defense moves but I had no idea I could do that."

"Who is he?"

She handed him a wallet. Ryan studied it, looking first at the photo and then at the face in front of him. "Call them. Make sure they describe him down to the last hair follicle. I.D.s can be faked. And try to find out why he's here."

Mike Saunders raised his head again. "I'm in the room. Anyone want to ask me why I'm here?"

Ryan and Marti answered in unison. "No!"

"Then you may as well know, the department thinks I'm in Seattle at a Forensics conference."

"That's convenient." Marti took a bottle of aspirin from her pocket, shook out two tablets and offered them to him in the palm of her hand. "I'll get you some water."

"Don't bother, you've done enough already. Call my partner, Lou Robinson. It's after ten there so you'll have to get him on his cell phone." He gave her the number, put the aspirin in his mouth and started chewing.

"If it's all the same to you, I'll call the Westport P.D. and have them patch me through to him."

Saunders removed the ice bag and touched the large lump on his forehead. "Who is she?"

"For the moment, she's the one you have to worry about." Ryan put the revolver in his desk drawer and took Marti's place against the desk. "Why are you here?"

"You made a couple of calls to a woman in Westport, Annie Heywood. You made the first one not long after she called Turk Storage and dropped the name Charles Hastings. When I contacted them, they said a private investigator was also looking for information on someone with a first name of Charles. I want to know why."

"And I want to know why this couldn't have been handled in a phone call, why you flew three thousand miles to tail me and stake out my office."

"Technically, I flew seven hundred miles. I was already in Seattle." He reached in his shirt pocket and pulled out a three by five inch black and white photograph and handed it to Ryan. "Her name's Debra Couillard Hastings. She married a Charles Hastings in Paris in June of 2000. At least we're going on that assumption until we get confirmation one way or another from the French authorities. That's a copy of her passport photo. In July of that year, she and her husband moved into a vacant house in Westport. She disappeared a week later. I think he killed her and disposed of her body somewhere she'd never be found. Except for your hair color, you fit the general description of the husband."

Marti walked up behind Ryan and put her hand on his back. "He's legit. He's crazy but he is who he says he is." Her eyes widened when she saw the photo in his hand. "Oh, God."

Saunders got to his feet. He was a little unsteady but at least he could stand up. "You know her?"

The phone buzzed on Ryan's desk. "I'll get that. Show him what we've got."

"Let's go, detective, back to the scene of the crime."

When they were both inside her office, Marti closed the door. Behind it, a large bulletin board was affixed to the wall. There were five photographs, blow-ups tacked across it. She took the passport photo of Debra and secured it to the left of the others.

Saunders went in for a closer look, stopping in front of each of the photos. "They all look enough alike to be related, except the last one."

"Morgan Evans. I'll get to her. Have a seat. You look a little green around the gills."

He took the chair behind her desk and Marti stood in front of the first photo, the one to the right of Debra's. "This is Rachel Dixon from Boulder, Colorado. She was thirty when she disappeared in 2005. She was involved with a man named Charles Rivers, who claimed to be a freelance writer. Her remains were found buried in a campground an hour away from her home.

"Ellie Kruger disappeared from her home in Templeton, California, in 2015. She was seeing a man named Charles Vaughn, a photographer. She was thirty-seven. No one's seen or heard from her in five years. Her mother has a brain tumor and is refusing treatment. She wants to die so she can be with her daughter.

"Theresa Ryan. Her body was found in an abandoned building site in 2010, a few blocks from here. She'd been strangled and beaten. She lived in Cambria, a beach town near San Luis Obispo. So far there's no connection to Charles but we know she was in love with someone she described as the love of her life, a phrase we've heard before."

Saunders leaned forward. "That's pretty thin. Ryan. Any relation to your boss?"

"His sister."

"Is that why he left the force?"

"You'll have to ask him. Susan Pierce, age thirty-eight. Last month she was taken from her rental home in Sedona and left to die in the middle of the desert. Her remains, what there was of them, were scattered over fifty square miles. She was living with a man who called himself Charles Tyrrell.

"And this is Morgan Evans, thirty-nine. Last week her body was found in the studio of her home near Scottsdale. She'd been strangled and her throat slashed."

"What about DNA?"

"Sheriff Cody got a copy of the autopsy report. They found evidence of a spermicide in her vaginal cavity but they also think he must have worn a condom. Her body was washed clean, no hair or fibers. One of her neighbors had a business card from a man claiming to be a location scout for a film company in Victoria, B.C. The name on the card was Charles Richmond. His business address in Canada is bogus."

"Debra was Canadian, from Montreal," said Saunders. "So he kills every five years for twenty years, all brunettes, and then breaks his pattern and kills twice in one month and the last one's a blonde. Any chance Morgan Evans' murder was a copycat?"

"No. We know that the man claiming to be Charles Tyrrell was in a plaza in Sedona on the same day that Morgan was working there. It was last December, a few days before Christmas. Pete thinks he saw her that day and filed it away for future reference. As far as we know, no one's connected these cases, least of all the press. How would a copycat know about them?"

"Maybe Sedona's the connection. The guy read about the Pierce murder and figured what the hell."

"Good theory except the authorities closed the file on Susan Pierce less than twenty-four hours after her remains were identified. Suicide."

"That doesn't make sense. They would have been all over the boyfriend."

Marti walked away from the bulletin board. "I need some coffee, and I'm sure by now Pete's going through withdrawal."

Saunders replaced her in front of the board. "There has to be some common denominator to these women besides hair color and age. Geographically, they're all over the place."

"They were all involved with the Arts in some way or other. Rachel was a cellist, Ellie an artist, Theresa was a writer and Susan Pierce composed music. Morgan was a sculptor. Did Debra have any creative bent you know of?"

"She was an artist too, a good one. Annie found some drawings of hers. She also found her journal, which is what started the investigation on our end. The irony is that it doesn't tell us a thing." Running a hand through his hair, he turned around. "Look, Marti, I know my brain's a little jumbled, but when we were talking about Susan Pierce and I mentioned the boyfriend you changed the subject. What's that about?"

Ryan tapped on the door before entering. "I thought I smelled coffee. I was starting to go into withdrawal. What did I miss?"

Marti handed him a mug of coffee and sent him a look that said she knew he'd been listening at the door. "Mike was asking why the authorities didn't pursue the Pierce case as a murder, especially since she was living with someone."

Ryan shrugged it off. "No one knew she was living with someone until it was too late. That's the way this guy operates. He's a natural born predator. He finds his prey and isolates them from their family and friends. No one ever sees him. The only thing he leaves behind is a corpse. The powers that be decided it was more politically expedient to call it a suicide and clean up the mess than have a murderer running around. Her family was also putting the pressure on. A murder investigation would have held up their inheritance. She was worth millions."

"Any chance they'll reopen it now that Morgan Evans is dead?"

"Doubtful. It was bad enough when there were two counties involved, Yavapai and Coconino. Now you've got Maricopa County in the fray. Besides, it's an election year. You tell me."

"Maybe they don't want to make an official statement but they're working it behind the scenes."

"I'm not sure who **they** are but unofficially they told the Sedona chief of police to pound salt when he took exception to their suicide call."

"I'm sorry about your sister, Ryan. You've been working on this for ten years?"

"On and off, whenever I can. Up until a few weeks ago, I thought her murder was an isolated case."

Saunders looked around the office, taking in the blackboard, bulletin board and sundry other items either tacked or taped to the walls. "A few weeks ago? How many people are working these cases?"

"You're looking at them. I have a friend on the force who's run all of Charles' aliases but so far nothing matches up. Roland Cody, the police chief in Sedona, was a big help when I was there but his hands are tied. Besides, he's got a town to worry about."

"Are you telling me the two of you put all this together?"

Ryan pointed to Marti. "She's the brains, and until an hour ago, I thought I was the brawn."

Saunders looked at her. "You use VICAP?"

"No, I don't trust it. It's only as good as the people who use it, assuming they do use it. I found Rachel Dixon on the North American Missing Persons Network or the Doe Network, one of those. We found out about Ellie Kruger because of an email her mother sent in response to our website. Our information on Morgan Evans came to us the same way but we were too late."

"I don't get it."

"Which part?"

"None of it. I'm not familiar with the two networks you mentioned and what website are you talking about?"

Marti booted up her computer. "This website. We're averaging fifty responses a day now but two weeks ago we were averaging over three hundred. I go through them and qualify them and we start making phone calls if they sound relevant. Even if they don't, I try to get back to the person who sent it and let them know there's someone who gives a crap."

Saunders joined her at the computer. "This is smart. Did you do this?"

"Design the site? No, Chief Cody's wife and daughter put it together. The two networks I mentioned were also started by women to get the public involved in trying to help law enforcement find missing persons. I had a hunch about the five-year pattern. Susan Pierce was murdered in 2000, Theresa in 2010, Ellie disappeared in 2015 so I started looking through the sites for information on women who disappeared in 2005 and Rachel's photograph was there. Now what?"

"Counting Debra, there are six murders in four states. Are you sharing any of this information with law enforcement in those other states?"

Rolling his eyes, Ryan was tempted to retreat back to his office. The chances of Saunders surviving the day were diminishing by the minute.

"Gosh, no, I never thought of that. Did you think of that, Pete? Now listen up, Detective. On any given day, twenty-one thousand women in this country are missing. If they're white, young and attractive, they may get a few weeks of news coverage and a file gets opened on some cop's desk. When they can't pin it on a family member, the file goes cold real fast or sometimes it even gets lost. You already know how the Arizona authorities handled Susan Pierce's case but ask Pete about the Boulder police or the Templeton police, how much they cared about Ellie or Rachel.

And there's another pattern here that may have escaped your rapier-like mind. It was women who started those two missing persons sites and a mother of seven and a sixteen-year-old girl who had the presence of mind to design our website."

"And a woman put it all together, not to mention another woman who brought the Debra Hastings case to my attention. You'd make a good lawyer."

"Don't even think about trying to get on my good side. I'm curious. You've known about Debra's case, what, a few weeks? How many hours have you devoted to finding her or the person who killed her?"

"Not enough. When Annie brought me Debra's diary, I didn't know what to make of it. I sat on it for a week but she wouldn't let it go."

"Why is that, Detective? Were you too busy? Is there a crime wave in Westport we don't hear about?"

"You've made your point. I need to know what you know. I'll be an extra set of eyes and ears. I have to be back on Monday but that gives us four days."

Ryan pushed off from the wall. "On one condition, reciprocity. We hear and see everything you have on Debra's case and I mean everything, the diary, evidence, all of it. You okay with this, Marti?"

"I'm okay with anything that helps us find this monster. We can use the help but if he jerks my chain again I can't guarantee I won't kill him next time. Now if you'll both excuse me, I never made it to the ladies' room." She hesitated at the door. "I have two more conditions. Our files don't leave this office. They're up to date and orderly and they better stay that way. The second condition is we start tomorrow morning, not tonight. I want to go home and nobody's touching the files when I'm not here."

When they were alone, Saunders stepped back to the bulletin board. "Marti reminds me of someone. Come to think of it, she hates me too. Is she always like that?"

"Rarely. You got lucky and caught her in a good mood."

CHAPTER 44

ANNIE

Annie picked up another photograph, wrapped it in bubble-wrap and added it to an open carton. There were half-filled boxes everywhere, on the floor, the desk, even atop the filing cabinets. She was doing it all wrong. She should concentrate on one thing, the photos for example, get them all in one box and tape it shut. Her mind was elsewhere, everywhere but on the task at hand.

"You need some help?" Cynthia was watching her from the doorway.

"No, thanks. I just need to figure out a system." Annie raked her fingers through her freshly-trimmed hair. "No, you know what I need to do? I need to cancel the damn trip. Sam will understand. When I agreed to go, I didn't know we'd be closing in less than five weeks. I don't know what I was thinking. I can't leave you alone with this mess."

"Annie, you love me, right?"

"I adore you, you know that."

"Then do us both a favor and go home, let the girls and me pack all this up while you're away. This is hard enough. I don't need you around here breaking down in tears every ten minutes. Pamper yourself a little, get a facial and have something waxed. There must be something on that skinny body of yours that needs waxing."

"I'm doing all that first thing in the morning before I stop in here to say good-bye. I'm having the works."

"I know what that means. I watch Sex and the City reruns. When you get on that plane tomorrow night, I don't want you looking back. I saw something on your face this morning I haven't seen in a long time. You looked happy, the kind of happy that usually has a man behind it."

Just not the right man. She was so sure Mike would call but it was beginning to look like he meant what he said. "I'm not ready to have a man in my life, not that way. Bryce is a nice guy, although there was a moment when I thought I was having dinner with Gomez Addams. He comes from a pretty screwed up family."

"More screwed up than a woman who lost her mama to a murderer?"

"That's different. You're different. I don't want to be that woman, the kind that always needs a man around."

"There's that n-word again. I don't recall anybody saying anything about need. Arthur and I made a decision a long time ago that we were together because we wanted to be there, not because we needed to be there. You know what I think when I hear that word used in a relationship? I think uh oh, somebody's in trouble and they're looking for someone to fix it. I know you well enough to know you don't need nothin', especially a man. I'm talking about wantin'. I'm talking about cuttin' yourself some slack and having fun. You promise me you'll try."

"I promise." Annie looked at her watch. "Right after I meet Detective Robinson at Helen's house. He called an hour ago and asked me to meet him there at three. I have no idea what that's about. He was in a hurry and said he'd talk to me about it when he saw me. I'll let you know if I need bail money."

"Don't call me. Call that fine lookin' rich man you're trying so hard to avoid."

Turning into the lane, she pulled off to the side of the road. The crime scene tape was back up and two cars, side by side, were nosing Helen's garage door. She sat for several minutes before she finally found the courage to confront whatever awaited her.

Lou Robinson met her at Helen's front door. "Thanks for coming, Annie. I'll try to have you out of here in just a few minutes."

The house was cold, colder than the outside air. Without Helen's warmth and attention, it felt as if the house died with her. The gloom was suffocating. Annie wrapped her arms around herself and remained near the door. If he asked her to go upstairs again, she wasn't sure she could do it.

The detective moved her gently away from the door and closed it behind her. "Annie, when was the last time you were in this house?"

"Sunday, no Monday, the day we found her. You were here with me, remember?"

"I remember. I meant the last time you were in here with Mrs. Allen."

"Sunday around ten a.m. I'd baked some banana bread and brought it over to her. She made tea and we talked for forty-five minutes or so. We made plans for me to pick her up on Monday and take her to the police station. She didn't want to go alone."

"Have you spent much time in this room?"

"Not really. Before last Sunday, I'd been here two or three times, why?"

"I need you to do me a favor. I want you to take your time and look around this room. It's okay, it's already been dusted for prints. Tell me what you see, if anything looks out of place. That woman sure loved her knick-knacks."

"It's where tchotchkes go to die. I can't believe that went through my head when I was here." She stepped further into the room and positioned herself behind the camelback sofa. From there, she could take in the entire space.

Helen's reading chair was in its usual place, a lamp table beside it. The Sunday paper was where she'd left it, sections of it still on the ottoman, the rest on the floor. She turned in place, avoiding the staircase. The door to the kitchen was next. "I didn't go into the kitchen on Sunday. Do you want me to go in there?"

He shook his head and Annie turned her body slightly. A sideboard was to the left of the kitchen door. The porcelain figurines were there, two to three inches apart, just as she remembered them. She faced the fireplace, scanned the mantle and turned her attention to the television in the corner. It was at least twenty years old, chunky, not sleek like the newer models. It was sitting on a cart sold specifically for that purpose, dark wood to complement the mahogany pieces in the room. A large bay window was to her immediate left. It looked out to the lane.

She jerked her head back, focused on the fireplace and closed her eyes. When she opened them, she walked around the sofa and went directly to the mantle. "This Lladro's been moved. It was here, all the way at the end on the right. Her daughter's photograph is missing."

"We didn't know she had a daughter."

"She died of leukemia when she was nine. It was an eight by ten in a silver frame, black and white or sepia. Her bow and dress were pink like they'd been hand-colored. I don't understand. Are you testing me?"

"Not at all. I thought something didn't look quite right. You were real helpful when I asked you to tell me what you saw in her backyard. Not everyone has your powers of observation."

"But I still don't understand what it means. You think someone took the photograph of her daughter?"

"I think he stood right where you're standing and took the thing most precious to her, but instead of rearranging the photographs, spacing them out better, he grabbed that statue and stuck it in the empty space."

"How could you possibly know that?"

"Because I'm a man and that's what I'd do. And because of my grandmother. She was about Mrs. Allen's age when she passed. She had a thing about symmetry." He walked up to the mantle and pointed to a statue on the far left end. It was another Lladro, the approximate height of the one now occupying the place where the photograph had been. "I figured she would have placed that other statue on the right to balance this one."

"Are you going to tell me the results of the toxicology reports or am I still out of the loop?"

"I should get back upstairs with the tech."

"Why did it take so long for the tox reports to come back?"

"There was a screw-up at the lab." He led her back outside, away from the house and lowered his voice. "She was given a lethal dose of insulin, somewhere between two hundred to three hundred units. The effects are…"

"I know what the effects are, Lou. That high of a dose in someone with normal blood sugar levels would have produced sweating, spasms and eventually a coma or death. That explains the bruising I saw on her arms. She must have been thrashing around on the floor. Why would she just lay there and let someone inject her?"

"Annie, you know I can't discuss the details of the investigation with you."

"Then I'll tell you. You can stand here and listen or you can walk back inside the house."

"If we find this bastard and he ever goes to trial, we never had this conversation."

Annie glanced up at Helen's window. "Why didn't he just smother her with a pillow? There would have been petechial hemorrhaging but that's fairly common in cardiac arrest."

"Maybe he didn't know that. Every damn one of those crime shows uses petechial hemorrhaging as evidence of asphyxiation. What else you got?"

"He had to subdue her while he injected her. That wouldn't have been difficult with her size and frailty. The bruising on her arms. Maybe that wasn't caused by rolling around on the floor. He could have had his elbow on one arm, reached across and held her other arm with his hand. That would leave him a free hand to inject her. Was there any bruising on her chest or abdomen?"

"Yes."

"But even that could have been associated with a heart attack. People often knead those areas when the pain gets too intense. What about the injection site? That's a lot of insulin. If she was moving around, how did he think someone wouldn't notice evidence of an injection?"

"It almost got past the M.E. It was only after the tox reports came back that he examined her again. She had a child by Caesarean section. The scar never healed properly. He injected her there."

"That means he pulled up her nightgown. She was such a proper, modest woman."

"This wasn't sexual, Annie. It was about as cold and calculating as they come. He had a job to do and he did it."

"And he almost got away with it. He would have gotten away with it if he hadn't left the window open. Why would he do that?"

"We think he parked over there on the Baron's property, probably in that group of trees. The pine needles were disturbed. He timed it between the patrols. Normally they're pretty consistent, every hour and a half, but that night there was a domestic disturbance call a few streets over. After the patrolman finished up there, he decided to make another swing down your lane. He was almost forty minutes early. The guy might have gotten spooked by the headlights, tore down the stairs and out the window the way he came. He could have been back in his car and out of sight by the time the patrol car turned around in your driveway and headed back out."

She looked down at the ground and moved a pebble with the toe of her shoe.

"You got something on your mind, Annie?"

"Who knows about this, that Helen's death wasn't from natural causes?"

"Probably half of Fairfield County. Your reporter friend's been nosing around the M.E. He did a follow-up story in yesterday's paper. Speaking of M.E.s, how do you come to know so much about medicine?"

"When my friend and I decided to open the hospice, I didn't want to be just a paper-pusher or the person who put the squeeze on people for money. I wanted to learn everything I could about the human body, particularly the immune system. For two years, all I did was read medical books and journals."

"Did it help?"

"Sure, at least I could pronounce all the words as I was pushing paper and pleading for money." She waited a few seconds before asking the question that was uppermost in her mind. "I don't suppose you'd tell me if you had someone in your sights."

"Right now, we're looking at everyone. There's a problem, though. The last people to rent your house for any length of time moved out in 1993 so it's been vacant for twenty-seven years. A lot of people knew about it, even knew where the key was hidden. From what I gather, your home saw more hot pillow action than the Westport Inn. I even talked to a cop who took his girlfriend there on a regular basis."

"Swell. Not only am I not in on the action but I'm going to be haunted by the ghosts of lovers past."

"I talked to Mike last night."

"Nice segue, detective. How is he?"

"He's in San Francisco. He asked about you. You still going to London tomorrow?"

"For at least two weeks. I was planning to stay longer but I have to get back and finalize things at **Life House**. Speaking of which, I better get going. I haven't done laundry in a week and I want to start packing." She looked back toward Helen's house. "What about funeral arrangements? I don't even know if Helen has family living. She never mentioned anyone."

"She has a brother in Idaho. He's in a rest home but his two sons are flying out to escort her body back for the funeral and burial. They're good men. I've talked to both of them."

"I'm glad."

"You had a flower delivery about an hour ago. It's on your side porch. I've checked them out and they're very much alive."

Annie advanced on him and gave him a hug. "Thanks, Lou. Take care of yourself and try to catch the bastard before I get back. If you talk to Mike, give him my…" Love? Did she almost use that word? Was that what it was? Was she so jaded she didn't know the meaning of the word? "Never mind. I'll tell him myself when I get back."

There were thirteen red roses, so flawless in shape and color they might have been artificial if it weren't for the scent. But even their beauty paled in contrast to the vessel, an eighteen-inch blown glass sculpture. It was bizarre and beautiful, the type of thing she loved, the type of thing she might have purchased if money were still no object. The top half was comprised of back to back male faces, highly-stylized with large blue eyes. The bottom portion was elongated and bell-shaped. The colors fused within the piece were all her favorites, jewel tones of blue, red, amber and green, the precise palette of her living room. Evidently she wasn't the only one blessed with powers of observation.

When it was safely inside the house, she extracted a small white envelope from the spray of flowers. She recognized the discreet silver logo of the florist, The Flower Shop of Greenwich. The owner was not only an artist when it came to floral design but she was also a friend, the kind of woman Annie admired, independent and energetic. They'd done business together for years.

The card inside was handwritten and Annie read it aloud. *I am a jealous lover. I deny her release for I fear the place to which she escapes. With love, the good looking brother.* What the hell?

She was carrying it to the sink to add water when her cell phone rang. Before she could say hello, the voice on the other end began speaking. "Annie, thank God you picked up. Did you get a flower delivery today? Wait, let me rephrase that. Did you get a really expensive glass jug with some roses coming out of the top?"

Annie laughed. "Yes, why? You sound upset."

"I am upset. I told the new kid not to leave it if no one was home. I don't know what I'm going to do with him, maybe send him back to Nebraska to live with his dad. That'll teach him."

"Alice, you're terrible but I miss you."

"Me too, so let's catch up. You've been holding out on me. What's with the hunky secret admirer?"

"Not so secret. I had dinner with him last night."

"So I heard. I also heard you accidently spilled wine all over him."

"I spilled wine on his brother and, just between us, it was no accident."

"Maybe I misunderstood. Anyway, he was waiting for me outside the shop when I opened up this morning. He had that piece in a supermarket bag, if you can believe it."

Annie reread the car. She still didn't get it. Who was he talking about and what was the deal about release? Even odder was the reference to his brother, particularly since he tried his damnedest to ruin their evening. Or perhaps he used humor to diffuse conflict, a tactic she often employed herself.

"Annie, did I lose you?"

"Alice, I know this is against protocol but did he pay with a credit card?"

"A Centurion black Amex no less. I see a few of them now and then, usually when the hubs has been naughty and needs a peace offering before he goes home to the lady of the house. Jesus, have I always been this cynical?"

"Aren't we all? One more favor. What was the name on the card?"

"This gets juicier by the second. Hold on."

Judging from the background noise, the tiny shop was in typical chaos mode. While she waited, Annie pulled a vase from beneath the sink, filled it with water and transferred the roses to it. After she towel-dried the sculpture, she took it into the living room and placed it on the coffee table. It looked right at home, as if the room were designed around it.

"C. Scott Stanley."

Annie grabbed the phone from between her shoulder and ear. "What?"

"The name on the card was C. Scott Stanley. I take it that isn't what you wanted to hear."

"Let's just say it's the last thing I expected to hear. Listen, Alice, I know you're busy but I have to ask. A week or so ago, you didn't by any chance make a delivery to me of some dead lilies, did you?"

"What are you talking about?"

"Someone left an unmarked floral box on my doorstep. Inside was a bunch of dead lilies. You might have thought it was a joke."

"No way. That's not even funny. I keep a few unmarked boxes but I haven't used one in months. What's going on with you, Annie? Are you in some kind of trouble?"

"I'm not sure, but I'm going to London tomorrow and I won't worry about it until I get back."

"Have a great time and try to relax. Wait, before I forget, are you still running? I miss our runs together."

"My bad, Alice. I haven't run since I moved. At first, I was too busy with the house and then my sleep cycle got messed up and I was too tired in the mornings. I miss it."

"No worries. I'll crack the whip when you get back from London. One more question and then I'll let you go. Hold on just another sec."

Sitting on the edge of the sofa, Annie turned the sculpture around. At first glance, the faces appeared alike with similar expressions, but the more she studied it, the more she detected a subtle difference. It was the shaping of the eyebrows, a small anomaly in the glass that gave one face a look vaguely sinister. Whether the artist intended it or not, it was definitely there.

"Earth to Annie."

"Sorry, I zoned for a minute. What did you say?"

"I was wondering if you knew what the C stood for. My daughter's pregnant again and this time it's a boy. Lately, I've been obsessed with names."

Annie censored her first response. She stared at the face and the face stared back. "If I had to guess, I'd say it probably stands for creep."

CHAPTER 45

RYAN

Marti lifted the last of the files from her bottom drawer and put them on the edge of the desk. "This is everything we have on the five murders, including all the emails from the website. I figured if Mike saw what we have to offer, he might be more forthcoming with his own information."

"Paranoid and manipulative, my kind of woman. What's with the donuts?"

"They're just donuts, Pete, flour, sugar and lard. There's no hidden meaning, no gratuitous statement about the eating habits of cops. I'm going to be the very model of cooperation."

"We'll see. Where is he anyway?"

"He was waiting outside when I got here at eight. We chatted for a few minutes and he got call on his cell phone. I haven't seen him since."

"Maybe he went to have a CAT scan."

Saunders leaned in from the hallway. "Sorry about that." He rubbed his hands together. "I thought California was warm all year round. We going to start this dog and pony show in here or in your office?"

Ryan walked across the hall and slid a chair from his office in Marti's. "Might as well do it in here, closer to the coffee and donuts."

When the three of them were finally seated, Saunders clicked open a battered briefcase. There was little preamble, just a slow recitation of the facts. "Annie Heywood purchased her home in September from the Stanley estate, an old Connecticut family going back to the mid-1800s. They made their money in tobacco, some type of leaf used for cigar wrappers. The plant's still in operation. Sometime in the late 1800s, they started buying up property in Westport and a couple of surrounding towns. Annie's house was one of the last pieces to be sold off. It generated rental income for the estate until 90s when the long-term tenants moved out. After that, someone got the idea it would make a nice retreat for business associates of the family so it was furnished with odds and ends. What they didn't count on was the fact that every horny guy in town would find out about it and use it. They even had a signal. If the roller blinds were pulled down in the upstairs bedroom, the place was occupied.

"So Annie buys the place and moves in. Five weeks later, she's having some floors refinished and finds a diary lodged behind the radiator. She doesn't think too much of it and almost throws it away until she learns about Debra and Charles from her neighbor." He handed Ryan and Marti photocopies of the five journal pages. "There's not much there. She must have started a new journal the day before she left for Paris to get married. The final entry, July 10th, 2000, is the last day anyone saw her alive.

"According to the neighbor, Helen Allen, she saw them eating dinner on the back terrace around dusk. Debra writes about that. Sometime around midnight, the Allen woman hears their car leaving the lane. There are only two houses on that road and Annie's house is at the end. Two hours later, she's awakened again when the car comes back but this time there are no headlights. She knows they're new to the area and thinks maybe there's some kind of trouble so she walks down to the house. Charles is there alone. He claims Debra became ill and he was driving her to the hospital when she died."

Ryan flipped over the final page of the diary. "So this woman is an actual witness, someone who can put a face to the name."

"She was supposed to work with a sketch artist on Monday. Annie went by her house to pick her up and found her dead. It looked like a heart attack but it wasn't. Sunday night someone got into her house and injected her with three hundred units of insulin. She was eighty-six years old, a shitty way to die."

"How did he know she was going to work with the police?" Ryan asked.

"A local reporter got wind of the story. It made the front page of the Sunday paper."

"And less than twenty-four hours later she's murdered? Christ, Saunders, I'm going to ask you again. What the hell are you doing here? He's living right under your nose, he has to be."

"I left for Seattle Monday morning. Her body wasn't discovered until later that afternoon. And I already told you. I need to know what you know. I'm sorry about your sister but this isn't your personal crusade. I could have come in here with a warrant and taken your files."

Marti got to her feet. "Stop it, both of you. Pete, you agreed to this. Let's hear what he has to say. And you," she turned to Saunders. "How dare you judge him. He's invested ten years in this investigation. You've been involved what, all of three weeks?"

"Yeah, I know, I'm late to the party. I've heard it all before. Whoever killed Mrs. Allen took something of hers, a photograph of her dead daughter. Any of the other women have something missing, something important to them? What about your sister?"

"Her house was burned to the ground, no way of telling."

Marti pulled a file from the pile on her desk. "Cody talked to Morgan Evans' brother. He mentioned something about some tools being missing from her studio. Here it is. It was a set of Boxwood sculpting tools in a metal case. They had a lot of sentiment attached to them because her late father gave them to her. What about Ellie Kruger's van, Pete?"

"It's possible. Her mother said she loved the damn thing. Contact Sarah, Rachel's sister, and ask her if anything was missing when they cleaned out her apartment." He turned back to Saunders. "I suppose you've already checked out the restaurant mentioned in her diary, the one he took her to on her birthday."

"There are several that fit the description, one in particular right on the Saugatuck. Lou showed her photo around but nobody remembers her. Same with the necklace. There was nothing special about it, a gold heart with an emerald in the center. We've asked local jewelers to check their old receipts but I don't think there's a chance in hell they'll come up with anything."

Ryan got up and stretched. "Let's go back to the night Debra disappeared. Is it possible he did take her to a hospital and they lost her records? I'm sure it wouldn't be the first time."

"Anything's possible but no hospital is going to release the body of a twenty-six-year-old woman without an autopsy. A postmortem was never done, no death certificate, nothing. We contacted her nearest living relative, a cousin on Vancouver Island. She confirmed they were close but she hasn't seen or heard from Debra since July of 2000.

"Look, I'll be honest. I didn't do the legwork on this. Annie and her hospice partner did most of it. All we did was confirm what they already knew. They have connections in the hospitals and were relentless. Annie's also the one who came up with the name Bert Kennedy. He had a small property management business twenty years ago. When old man Stanley found out about the activities going on at the house, he hired him to pull the plug. A few days after Debra and Charles disappeared, he started earning his keep and nosing around. Less than a week later he was killed by a hit and run driver outside his daughter's apartment. When we started backtracking, we found the evidence was missing. We know from the file we had photos and tire impressions but they're gone."

"How did the Heywood woman find out about Turk Storage?" asked Ryan.

"She didn't know Bert Kennedy was dead. She got his name from Helen Allen and tried to find him to talk to him. She found his name in an old phone book. The page was marked with what looked like a key tag from Turk Storage. She called them, you called her and here I am. What's your connection with Turk Storage?"

"You first. There's a notation here about a take-out bag from a Chinese restaurant. What's the story?"

"Not long after Annie found the diary, she was cleaning out her garage and came across a plastic bag from **Panda Palace**, a typical Chinese take-out joint that changed hands in 2003. She remembered Debra had written about Charles bringing home Chinese food. Inside were some crinkled up pages from a sketch pad, beautiful stuff Debra had drawn of the house."

"He cleaned up after himself," said Marti. "He did the same thing with Morgan's home. We know he'd been inside but there were no fingerprints anywhere."

Ryan's cell phone rang and he walked across to his office to take the call.

"Your friend Annie sounds like someone I'd like to know."

"You'd like her. I'll never forget the day she walked into the station. She had all this stuff in large baggies, the kind with the plastic zippers. She wouldn't shut up. She just kept talking, building her case."

"Does she know how you feel about her?"

"She knows. What's with the two of you?"

"It's complicated. Right now there isn't room in his life for two women, even if one is alive. For the time being, I'm content with the fact that Pete and I are friends."

Ryan was back. "What about Annie Heywood? Is she in any danger?"

"We're not taking any chances. A week or so after she first came to me, she got a delivery of some dead lilies. There was a typed message on the card. It said 'Debra is at peace. Let her go. Charles'. Right after that, we started regular night patrols down her lane. As of Monday night, she's had consistent surveillance on her home, but she doesn't know it. She leaves for London tomorrow to visit her sister."

"Talk to me about the Stanley family. What do you know about them?"

"The old man died years ago. He had two sons, Cornelius and Bryce, both in their late forties. Cornelius is older by a year, the black sheep. His middle name's Scott which he prefers for obvious reasons. He thinks of himself as a Renaissance man. This week he's a restaurateur, two years ago he was selling religious artifacts over the internet. Never married. Bryce is an attorney specializing in estate planning. He took over the family business when his father passed away. He's divorced with twin sons at Oxford."

Ryan glanced at Marti. "My money's on the lawyer."

"Mine too," said Mike.

"Way to keep an open mind, you two. Not every lawyer is pond scum."

"Bryce is clean and, trust me, I dug pretty deep. He's a model citizen, well-liked, rescues dogs, never even had a parking ticket. His brother, on the other hand, has a lot of time on his hands."

"Here's what I don't get," said Ryan. "He's been running the same routine for twenty years. This isn't a spree kill. He targets them specifically, makes his move and they fall head over heels for the guy. No one's that lucky. What's the attraction on their end?"

Marti looked at Mike. "Do you have a photograph of Cornelius?"

"No, but his brother has a website and they look a lot alike. You can google him."

After a few seconds, Marti sat back in her chair. "I think I know what the attraction is."

Mike shook his head. "I've seen it, thanks."

Ryan walked up behind her and looked at the screen. "It's probably an old photograph. Isn't there some kind of computer program that makes images look better than they are?"

"And they say women are catty. Sorry, boss, he's what we ladies call yummy, good hair, great eyes. Not my type, though. I prefer my men petulant and snarky."

"After two weeks with you, that's a given." Ryan sat back down. "I knew nothing about Susan Pierce until her sister hired me to find her. That's how I found out about Turk Storage. Susan sold her house last September and had the contents stored there. Susan and my sister had enough in common that I thought maybe the same guy was involved. That's the only reason I took the case.

We had a tip she was in Sedona, but by the time I got there, she was already dead."

"What kind of tip?"

"Before her sister hired me, she got a phone call from Sedona warning that Susan was in trouble. Since my client really didn't give a damn if her sister was in trouble or not, she sat on the information for almost two weeks."

"Who was the person who called her? There must be some way to trace the call."

"He did trace the call. He traced it to me. I'm the one who called Susan's sister."

"Then you're also the person who knew someone was living with her. What the hell's going on?"

Ryan started to say something but Marti cut him off. "It's okay, Pete. It seems like every day another body turns up and the stakes get higher. If Mike thinks I should make a full disclosure of what I know, then that's what I have to do."

"You bet I do. What I don't understand is why you don't, Ryan."

"Let her finish."

"Two years ago, I was attacked in my apartment in Austin. I defended myself and put him in the hospital. He threatened to kill me so I've been on the run ever since. I was doing house-keeping work in Sedona and one of the homes I was sent to was Susan Pierce's. I left Sedona right after they found her remains and Pete gave me a job here. I underwent hypnosis yesterday afternoon to try and uncover something, anything I might have seen or heard in the house but there was nothing. I never saw the man living with her. I only heard his voice but there's no way I'd recognize it."

"Why didn't they arrest the guy who attacked you?"

"He was working undercover and the D.A. needed him to testify in a drug bust," added Ryan. "Marti was working in the D.A.'s office when it went down. It was my decision to keep her out of the Pierce case, so if you have a problem, take it up with me."

"No problem here. I know how badly you want this guy, and if you don't think it'll help the case to get her involved, I'm not making waves. Let's go back to the storage company. Maybe we need to run the last name Stanley by them, see if we get any further with that than you did the name Charles."

"It's worth a try, especially if you flash your badge at them. They don't need to know I'm involved. I scared the shit out of the kid the last time I saw him." Ryan's cell phone rang again and he looked at the display. "I have to take this. Start looking through the files. If you have questions, Marti can answer them."

Behind his closed office door, Ryan listened while Jimmy talked. He asked few questions and took no notes. When the call was finished, he grabbed his coat and headed downstairs. He needed to cool down and think things through. What he had in mind was risky, not to mention illegal. If either party blinked, it could mean the end of everything, including the investigation.

In her second floor office, Marti said good-bye to Sarah Dixon and placed the phone back in its cradle. "They never found Rachel's cello. Her sister's pretty sure it was the only thing missing from her apartment."

Disgusted, Mike closed the file on Rachel Dixon's murder, the one sent over from the Boulder police. "I've seen thicker files on jaywalkers. There isn't even a notation about a missing cello. You were right, this is bullshit."

"You think you're depressed now? Keep reading, detective."

A little over an hour later, Saunders leaned back in the chair and rubbed his eyes. "Christ, who is this guy? He appears out of nowhere, ingratiates himself to these women through a series of false identities and then kills them. There's not a single reliable witness, no fingerprints and no DNA, and he's been doing it for twenty years without even raising a red flag."

"He's not doing it for the money, that much we know. So what's his motive, Mike?"

"He likes it."

"Which is going to make it almost impossible to prosecute him even if we catch him. Without forensic evidence, everything is circumstantial."

"You even sound like a prosecutor. What were you doing for the Austin D.A.?"

"Clerking. I was in my last year of law school at the University. Before things fell apart, they offered me a job when I passed the Bar."

"Did you always want to work for the prosecution?"

"I'm not the first woman in my family to find herself at the mercy of a man. My sister was physically abused by her husband. What I wanted to do was work within the system to see these monsters put away. Ironic, isn't it? The system I trusted was the same one that sold me out."

"What's next for you?"

"If you'd asked me that two days ago, I wouldn't have known how to answer, but last night a few things fell into place. I almost made the biggest mistake of my life yesterday and I have you to thank for not going through with it."

"I'm lost."

"When you reached in and touched my shoulder, I was saying good-bye. I panicked when I thought Tony found me, and then when I saw Pete running down the street, I just couldn't bear the idea of something happening to him because of me. It was irrational and stupid but I was going to run again. No woman should ever have to feel that helpless. It's degrading."

She searched the pile of manila files and pulled out one an inch thick. "These are the emails in response to our website, over two thousand women so desperate for someone to help them that they're reaching out to a faceless entity. For the sake of argument, let's say fifty percent of them are just angry or bored. That's still a thousand women who have no place to turn. We're implementing zero tolerance for schoolyard bullies but when it comes to domestic violence, you have to be broken and bloody before law enforcement takes it seriously."

"We're doing the best we can, Marti."

"That just it, you're not. Something's been nagging at me about those emails, something I couldn't make sense of until I took them home last night and reread them. Over three hundred are from wives or girlfriends of police officers. According to two recent studies, at least forty percent of law enforcement families experience domestic violence and that's just the ones willing to come forward. It's also four times higher than the national average. It's hard to serve and protect when four out of ten of your fellow officers are going home at night and doing the same thing."

"You sure about your numbers?"

"I'm sure. You look surprised. I was too. But what's really shocking is that the other sixty percent of you let them get away with it."

"You're going to become a vigilante for abused wives of cops?"

"I'm not doing anything until I get my life back. I have to finish Law School. Good intentions are great, but these women need an advocate with some teeth. In the meantime, I'm doing something important here and I'm happier than I've been in a long time."

Saunders reached into his back pocket and withdrew his wallet. After sorting through several business cards, he pulled one out and handed it to her. "Call this woman. She's the one who came up with the acronym S.A.B.L.E., spousal abuse by law enforcement. Her website's at the bottom of the card. When you're ready, she'll know best how to use you."

Marti took the card. "Do I want to know why you have this?"

"I'm not one of the forty percent if that's what you're thinking. We had a guy on the force my partner and I suspected was beating up on his wife and kids. We did some research and found her website. You think it's hard being a civilian and bringing it to light, try being a cop."

"What happened to him?"

"His wife left him and he moved down South. I heard he was working security at a Walmart."

"At least that's one less fox protecting the hen house."

Saunders smiled and bounded out of his chair. "You're not only beautiful, you're fucking brilliant. I have some phone calls to make and then I'm headed over to Turk Storage. I'll catch up with you later."

"Wait a minute! What do you want me to tell Pete?"

"Tell him he's a lucky guy and to take his head out of his ass."

"Mike?"

"None of these women are the key to finding this guy. He's too clever for that but there are a limited number of people who had access to the evidence on Bert Kennedy's hit and run. We find what happened to that and we find a trail back to our killer."

"That's it? That's your big ah-ha moment? Mike, you don't even know these cases are related to his hit and run. Maybe he was just in the wrong place at the wrong time. I worked for a D.A., remember? Evidence has a way of disappearing."

"Maybe in Austin but not in Westport."

"That may be so but twenty years is a long time to backtrack. You don't even know when the evidence was taken."

"Best guess? It was taken within a week of Bert Kennedy's death when the chain of custody is the weakest. A lot of people are involved in the first forty-eight hours, enough so there's always someone to blame. Besides, whoever wanted to make it go away couldn't risk an arrest."

"But I still don't…"

"Somebody got paid off, either with a wad of cash or a job offer he couldn't refuse."

"You're pretty persuasive. Is there anything I can do while you're gone?"

"Yeah, find a place where the three of us can go tonight and blow off some steam, someplace fun. With any luck, we'll have something to celebrate."

Saunders gave a final wave and Marti turned her attention back to the computer and clicked open her mailbox. After reading only a few lines, she closed her eyes. When she opened them, she took a pencil and put it to paper. Several minutes later, she had a reasonable facsimile of the crest she'd seen under hypnosis.

The animals were lions, not griffins. She still wasn't certain about the representation in the center but she drew it as a rectangle. After making a few more adjustments, she thought it might be a book on its side, binding up. Now all she had to do was figure out what, if anything, it meant. She started making a list, family crests, universities, country clubs, but stopped when Ryan walked into her office and took Saunders' vacated chair.

"Where's Mickey Spillane?"

"He's off solving the case."

"Good for him. How's he planning on doing that?"

"He thinks if he can find who lifted the evidence in the hit and run, it will lead him back to our guy. Where have you been? I thought you'd run away from home."

Ryan produced a folded sheet of yellow lined paper from his pocket and held it up. "Funny, I was about to say the same thing to you. How is your dad by the way?"

Marti recognized the note immediately. It was the one she'd written right before Saunders made his appearance outside her office. "I was hoping the cleaning people picked that up. I panicked, it's as simple as that. It won't happen again."

"You're right, it won't. You're fired, Marti. I can't have you working here if I can't trust you."

"Can't trust me? This isn't funny, Pete."

"It's not a joke. As of 11:35 last night, you got your life back. Go live it."

"What are you talking about?"

"Tony Belmont's dead. He was arrested yesterday afternoon for throwing his five-year- old boy down a flight of stairs. His wife turned him in. They had him in a holding cell with a couple of gangbangers. One of them heard the cops talking about who he was and broke his neck."

"What about his son?"

"They induced a coma to relieve the pressure on his brain. He'll be fine. I also talked to your old boss, the D.A. In exchange for you not going public with what you know about Belmont, he's willing to reimburse you for your last year of Law School and a year's salary, what you would have made working for him. I tried to get two years but he stood firm on one."

"You blackmailed the D.A.?"

"I prefer to think of it as giving him an informed choice."

"Screw you and screw the D.A. I don't want his money. Have him send it to Tony's wife and kids, they've earned it. When I go back to Law School, it will be on my terms with money I've earned, not the D.A.'s and not yours."

She walked around her desk until she was standing in front of him. "This is what you've been waiting for, isn't it? Up until now, you haven't had an excuse to get rid of me. You're just like them. You think you can snap your fingers and I'll either roll over or go away. This isn't about some stupid note I wrote in a moment of panic. It's about you. You're so entrenched in your own misery, so frightened to let someone in that you'll grab on to any excuse to keep them out. You want me to leave? Fine, I'll leave but there's something you should know. You think Lita set this whole thing up, that she encouraged me to come here and help you. She didn't. I've loved you since the moment you walked up to my porch in Sedona and you feel something for me, but that's the problem, isn't it? We have Catholic guilt in Indiana too, Pete. I'm your penance, the thing you give up for Lent." Her purse and coat in hand, she stopped briefly in the doorway. "You're worse than them. They tried to break my spirit. You're breaking my heart."

***

He'd lost track of time. It was dark when Saunders returned and flipped the light switch by the door. "I've been in morgues that were more cheerful. What's going on?"

"Not much. What happened with Turk Storage?"

"No paperwork with the last name Stanley but twenty years ago they didn't need I.D. to rent a space. He could have used any name. The kid's pulling a list of renters that go back twenty years or more. Maybe we can narrow it down that way. I had better luck on the home front. Two guys left the force within a month of Kennedy's hit and run. Either of them could have gotten rid of the evidence. Lou's tracking them down. Where's Marti? I'm starved."

"I sent her home."

"Call her, tell her to meet us at the Atlas Café. I passed it on my way here and it looks like fun. And tell her to bring an umbrella. It's starting to rain."

"I've been trying to call her all day. She's not answering her cell phone and she's not at her apartment. Best guess, she's headed back to Indiana."

"What's going on, Pete? She was fine when I left here a few hours ago."

"You've been here twenty-four hours. What's all this to you?"

"I like her. I think you're pretty much of an asshole but she's terrific."

"You're not as dumb as you look. The guy who was stalking her died in custody last night. I figured the only way I could get her to rejoin the human race was to cut her loose. I was thinking of her."

"Sounds like you were thinking **for** her. Women don't like that, especially women like Marti. I'm the last one to give advice in the romance department but even I wouldn't fuck up that badly."

Ryan turned off his desk lamp. "Come on, I need a drink."

The Atlas was packed but Maria found them seats at the bar. When their drinks were ordered, Saunders turned around on his stool. "I was right about this place. I'd like to own something like this when I retire. They have music here every night?"

"Thursdays and Saturdays."

"The keyboard player's pretty good." When Saunders turned back around, Ryan was being dragged off his stool and hustled toward the other musicians. After a brief protest, he lifted the violin to his chin. He was still playing a half hour later when Saunders saw a familiar figure huddled just outside the door under the narrow overhang. After signaling the waitress to save their seats, he left the café.

Marti had stepped away from the door and was leaning against the building when Saunders joined her. "He's a man of many talents. There isn't a dry eye in the place." He handed her a folded handkerchief. "Or out here either."

Marti took it and wiped her eyes. "I'm a sucker for Irish ballads. It's amazing how he can have that much sensitivity when it comes to music and so little when it comes to everything else."

"Come on in and join us."

"I can't. I just stopped by to pick up some food. I had no idea you'd be here. When you go back inside, tell Maria I'm out here but don't let Pete know."

"He's been trying to reach you all day."

"I've been at the library most of the afternoon. After I left the office, I went back to my apartment to finish some research but my computer's on the fritz."

"I hear congratulations are in order."

"Thanks, but I really haven't had time to think about that." She risked a glance back inside the café. "I want to find this guy as badly as he does. If he doesn't want me around, I'll find a way to work on my own."

"He said he cut you loose so you could rejoin the human race."

"I don't want to be part of the human race, I want to be with him." She smiled and shook her head. "It's too late, Mike. I said some horrible things to him and, even worse, I told him I loved him."

"Tell me again. I don't think I heard you the first time."

Marti whirled in the direction of the voice. Ryan was behind her, drenched from walking around the building. Leaving the shelter of the overhang, she went to him, reached up and raked the hair from his eyes. "I've loved you from the moment you stepped on my porch in Sedona."

He lifted her chin and brushed her lips with his. "One more time."

CHAPTER 46

ANNIE

Typical of her travel M.O., Annie was ready several hours early, bags packed and zipped, passport and money tucked inside the pocket of her bag. She'd said her good-byes at **Life House** and hugged Einstein until he whimpered. She had one more thing to do before she could go home, relax and prepare herself for the eight-hour plane trip. It was the last thing on her list, one she wasn't looking forward to.

She looked around the squad room and waited, glancing every now and then at the empty desk behind her. When Detective Robinson finally appeared in front of her, he looked harried. "Annie, I thought you'd be on a plane by now. You come to say good-bye to me?"

"I have something for your son. It's a compilation DVD of Queen music videos. Someone did it for me as a gift and I had another copy made."

"That's real nice, Annie. He'll appreciate this." He took the DVD from her. "You got something else on your mind?"

"I do. It's just going to sound a little crazy."

"Crazier than coming in here with a box of dead flowers and a telephone book in a plastic bag?"

"Good Point. I met someone the other night."

The detective offered her a large smile. "Good for you. You make sure he treats you right."

"What? Oh no, oh God no, it's not like that. I know you can't discuss the case, but you need to look closely at someone, Cornelius Scott Stanley." There, it was out. "He's the older surviving son of…"

"I know who he is."

"Of course you do. He seems to know a lot about the case, the fact that Helen was murdered."

"You talked to him about this?"

"Wednesday night."

"I told you yesterday, there was an article in the paper on Wednesday afternoon. How come you didn't say anything about this when I met you at Mrs. Allen's?"

"I needed time to sort it out because it's an awkward situation. His brother and I are friends. We were having dinner when I was introduced to Scott but the evening turned out to be a disaster. Scott was rude and obnoxious. I ended up dumping a bottle of wine in his lap and running out of the restaurant. And then yesterday, those flowers you saw on my side porch, they were from him. Here's the card. Is it my imagination or is that just a little over the top, especially from someone I obviously can't stand? And there's something else. The sculpture the roses came in is a six thousand dollar art piece."

"It was butt-ugly if you ask me. You can't blame a guy for trying to get on your good side, Annie. Maybe he felt bad about being a jerk."

"There's more. He has a history of mental illness going back to childhood. He not only tried to hurt his brother on several occasions, but he was with his mother when she died under suspicious circumstances."

"What kind of suspicious circumstances?"

"They were sailing a catamaran off Belle Haven and Scott fell in the water. She pushed him to safety but then she went under and drowned. When they found her, she had a large bruise on her head."

"When was this?"

"I'm not sure, sometime in the early seventies I guess. Scott was eight."

"Eight years old? Annie, you gotta stop this. You can't go snooping in people's lives."

"I wasn't snooping. Bryce told me about his history. He was trying to justify his brother's ridiculous behavior."

"You share any of your suspicions with your friend?"

"There was a discomforting emphasis on the word *friend,* but Annie let it go.

"Of course not. You think I'm nuts, don't you?"

"I think you're a good person who's trying to do her civic duty. I've always thought so, but it'd be best if you let us do our job. You plan on seeing your friend Bryce anytime soon?"

The question took her aback but the lie came easily. "No, why?"

I got a brother a couple a years older than me. We never did get along. He was always getting in trouble, small stuff mostly, but it was real hard on my family. One day a couple of cops came to the door to take him away, claimed he was involved in an armed robbery. I almost got myself arrested trying to keep them from taking him. I said some pretty bad things to those cops but they never even took offense. Come to find out, they both had brothers too."

"Was your brother guilty?"

"He did ten years, got out and went right back in six months later. He's been in and out of prison for thirty-some odd years but I still can't believe he did any of those things."

"I take it this is a cautionary tale about blood being thicker than water."

"I'm just saying if you want to keep your friend as your friend, I'd keep your suspicions under your hat."

"But you'll at least think about what I've told you, right?"

"I'll tell you this much. This case is fluid and we're looking at lot of people, including a Canadian man who went missing from Montreal the same day Debra left for Paris."

"But Charles wasn't Canadian. Debra told Helen he was an American." She saw the look on his face. "Okay, okay, I'm leaving."

She was in her truck when she remembered the envelope, the one she intended leaving on Mike's desk. It was a funny card about friendship, meant to poke fun at herself as much as him. It was signed *Love, Annie,* a baby step. There was no way around it, she'd fallen for him. There was rarely an hour when she didn't think of him. She still felt guilty about the way they left things, but it would mean more to apologize in person when she got back. Rejection hurt like hell and all the silly cards in the world wouldn't take away the sting.

CHAPTER 47

RYAN

The buzzer was persistent. Reluctantly, Ryan turned the shower off, grabbed a towel and stalked to the living room. After a quick exchange through the intercom, he hit a button and unlocked the front door. He had just enough time to throw on some clothes before he heard Saunders in the living room.

Holding a coffee carrier with three large paper cups, he was standing in the sparsely-furnished space. "Nice place. Who's your decorator, the Dalai Lama?" He handed a coffee to Ryan. "When you weren't at the office by nine, I figured you could use an eye-opener, unless of course you've already had one. Where is Marti, by the way?"

"None of your business. What do you want?"

"After you two lovebirds left last night, I heard from the kid at Turk Storage. He got a name, one name, someone who rented a bay in May of 2000. An envelope arrives every month with cash, two one-hundred dollar bills folded in a piece of plain white paper. Other than the number of the bay, there's nothing on it, not even a return address."

"Postmark?"

"He doesn't remember. All he does is rip open the envelope and enter the amount on a statement." Saunders cocked an ear toward the bathroom and raised his voice loud enough to be heard behind the closed door. "Morning, Marti."

Wearing an oversized robe and a towel wrapped turban-style around her head, Marti walked into the living room, took a coffee and leaned against the arm of the sofa. "What's going on?"

Saunders repeated what he told Ryan and added, "The name is C. S. Lewis. The rental agreement gives a phone number and an address in Salinas, California. The phone number's no good and information doesn't have a listing for anyone with that name. I don't have a computer with me or I would have looked up the address. It's 2301 Gresham Way. When you get to the office maybe you could…"

"C. S. Lewis on Gresham Way. Is that what was on the paperwork?"

"Yeah, why?"

"C. S. Lewis was a writer who died in 1963. Among other things, he wrote the *Chronicles of Narnia* and was married to the American writer Joy Gresham. That's not a coincidence." She saw the look on their faces and added, "My mother's an English teacher. She encouraged us to read by making a game of it around the dinner table. It was her version of *Trivial Pursuit*. Lewis died the same day JFK was assassinated. It stuck in my mind."

"Shit. I knew the name was familiar but I couldn't place it. We need to get inside that bay, Pete. You think your ex-partner can get a warrant?"

"Based on what, using a fictitious name? No judge in his right mind would sign off on a warrant with what we've got."

"So we do it the old-fashioned way. You game?"

"We don't have a choice."

"It's an outside bay in the older part of the complex. The buildings are single-story with back to back bays. If we can get through the front gate, we should be able to cut the lock."

"I'll get through the gate but I'll do it alone. You don't want any part of this."

"The hell I don't. I may be late coming on-board but there's no way I'm sitting this one out."

Marti removed the turban and shook out her hair. "Hold it, Butch. You too, Sundance. I hate to be the voice of reason, but you know as well as I that even if you find a freezer full of bodies, a defense attorney will get the case thrown out faster than you can say Fourth Amendment. You can't go in there bolt-cutters blazing. Your best bet is to pick whatever lock is on there and put it back. I assume one of you knows how to pick a simple key lock. A combination lock will be more of a challenge. You can't break it and you can't stand there all morning working combinations. I have an idea."

Disappearing into the kitchen, she was gone only a minute or two before it sounded like someone was tenderizing a Volvo with a jackhammer.

Saunders' eyes went wide. "She scares me."

"You don't know the half of it."

Marti rejoined them and held out her hand. In the center of her palm was a piece of flattened aluminum two inches long by half an inch wide. Protruding from the long side was what looked like a front tooth, roughly a quarter-inch square. The piece appeared several layers thick, thin enough to bend but rigid enough to hold its shape. "I have no idea if this will work but here's the theory." She held her other hand up, index finger and thumb pointing down to form an inverted U. "If you bend this around the shackle on the side that would pop up when the correct combination is dialed in, this tooth should go down inside the lock and trigger the release."

Ryan took it from her hand. "Learn this in Girl Scouts, did we?"

"Look, I know you want to get inside but if you do something stupid you might ruin any chance of getting a conviction if he's our guy. And if it turns out to be nothing, you could be arrested for breaking and entering." She looked from one man to the other and threw up her hands. "Fine, have it your way. If it ever goes to trial, I'll testify to the fact you're both nuts."

Inside the elevator, Saunders pressed the button for the lower-level parking garage. "You forgot your raincoat. It's pouring out."

"My raincoat met a fiery end at three o'clock this morning. Marti burned it in the fireplace. It's a long story. I have a windbreaker in the trunk of my car."

"Bolt cutters?"

"Next to the windbreaker."

"You've got your hands full, pal, but I'm happy for both of you."

When the elevator stopped, Ryan pulled out a set of keys. "It's the black Toyota in the second row. Bring it around and meet me out front in five minutes."

Back inside his apartment, he looked through to the bedroom and watched as Marti made the bed. She was still wearing his bathrobe. He took a moment to catch his breath and approached the bedroom door.

Marti looked up and smiled. "You forget something?"

"Yes." He took her in his arms. After he kissed her, he held her by the shoulders at arm's length. "What if I'm no good at this?"

"If you were any better, I'd be dead."

"You know what I mean. This. Us. I've spent my entire life avoiding entanglements. When I was a cop, I saw too many relationships disintegrate and I didn't want to start something that would end badly. When Theresa died, I had an excuse for locking people out. What if I screw this up?"

"I don't know anything that comes with guarantees, Pete, least of all relationships. Of course you'll screw up and so will I. You'll snap at me or forget my birthday and three days a month I'll make Medea look like Mother Teresa. We'll take it as it comes. I'm not looking for forever, not yet anyway. All I want is tomorrow."

"That I can guarantee. Medea, huh?"

"Go. I have to get downstairs and put on some fresh clothes." She followed him to the door. "Don't get your hopes up, Pete. You could get inside the bay and find nothing but a twenty year accumulation of girlie magazines he doesn't want his wife to know about. My dad keeps his in a footlocker at his car dealership. He think it's a secret. Mom's known about it for years, even knows where he keeps the key. Every now and then she'll mess with him and slip in a copy of the Christian Science Monitor or Good Housekeeping. It makes him crazy."

"That's where you get your evil streak. I don't have a prayer, do I?"

"Nope, I learned from the best."

Ryan pulled the car to the curb and let it idle. A block long and just as deep, Turk Storage made no pretense of being anything other than what it was, a minimum security prison for stuff, all the things people couldn't live with but couldn't live without. With the exception of the office which was loaded to the rafters with over-priced moving supplies, the entire complex was enclosed by twelve-foot high chain-link fencing topped with razor wire. Two rolling gates, one positioned near the office and another half a block down, provided vehicle access in and out. Located just outside the gates were keypads mounted on metal posts.

To limit their exposure, Ryan chose to wait near the gate farthest from the office. After almost ten minutes, the rain stopped and he cracked a window. "You still have time to change your mind. There's a diner a block down. If you're smart, you'll wait for me there."

"Smart has never been my strong suit." Saunders turned the rearview mirror so he could see the cars approaching from behind. "There's a black paneled van with its blinker on. He's turning in."

Clearing the sidewalk, the van stopped briefly beside the keypad. As the gate began to roll, the van edged forward. It was almost through the gate when Ryan put the car in gear, turned the wheel and made it through with seconds to spare. Once inside, the van turned right and Ryan whipped the wheel to the left. After a series of turns, he pulled to a stop.

Unit 305 was an end bay toward the rear of the facility. It was one of the larger units, twenty feet wide, and judging from the depth of building, at least thirty feet deep. With no other vehicles in sight, he got out and opened the trunk. He took two pairs of disposable gloves from a box, gave one to Saunders and slipped on the other pair.

Saunders was the first to reach the overhead door. "It's a cheap combination lock, ten bucks at any hardware store." He held it loosely and rattled the shackle up and down. "Where's Marti's gizmo?"

Ryan handed it off and Saunders wrapped the piece around the shackle with the tooth inside the chamber and moved it slowly clockwise. There was no discernible click, nothing to indicate the mechanism released but when he pulled down on the chamber, the shackle swung free.

The overhead door whined its ascent and stopped eighteen inches off the ground. When they both tried to lift it, it held fast. Saunders lay on the ground and scooted beneath it. "Looks like he's rigged something to keep the door from going up. It feels like picture wire, maybe a little heavier. Hand me the bolt cutters."

Ryan pushed a flashlight beneath the door. "Do us both a favor and follow the wire. If it's not attached to something that could go boom, I'll get you the cutters." He took several steps back and sat on his haunches. As he listened for movement, he saw the flashlight beam recede.

It was several minutes before Saunders' face appeared under the door. "It's no use. I tried the overhead lights but they don't work. I followed the wire as far as I could but it's too damn dark and crowded in here, a lot of stuff, probably furniture but it's hard to tell. Everything's covered with tarps. You have two choices. I either cut the goddamn wire or you mess up your clean white shirt."

Retrieving a second flashlight from the car, Ryan rolled beneath the door. Once inside, he pushed the door closed and directed his flashlight toward the ceiling. "Someone took the fluorescents out." He trained the beam around the empty canopy, the cobwebs so dense they looked fake, like the packaged product sold to decorate homes for Halloween.

The air inside the space was musty and still. With only the light from their flashlights, it was impossible to see beyond a few feet. As they worked their way through the canvas maze, the single sound was fabric against fabric.

Ryan stopped and sniffed the air. "You smell something?"

"Yeah, could be motor oil. Give me a hand with this, will you? He's got it wrapped tight."

It was a tall piece, a little over seven feet. When it was free of the canvas, Ryan took a step back and played his light against the front. "It's some kind of armoire or linen press, an old one, but it's in good condition. The inlay's still intact."

Saunders opened one of the doors. The interior was empty except for a magazine on the top shelf. He took it down and examined the cover, a Flamenco dancer in blue against a cream background. "It's a May 1940 issue of something called *The Magazine ANTIQUES.*" He flipped through it, stopping at a dog-eared page.

Ryan turned around and began pulling back the canvas on another piece, this one smaller. He stopped when he heard Saunders' intake of breath. "I'll be damned. There's an article about a 17th century cabinetmaker, Andre-Charles Boulle. He made furniture for Louis XIV. I think this is one of the pieces pictured in the article."

"You know anything about antiques?"

"Enough to know this baby didn't come from IKEA."

"Does the article mention if the piece ended up in a private collection?"

"No, just that he made pieces for the French aristocracy. Maybe we're off base here, Pete. The guy's probably an antiques dealer. That could explain the extra security."

"I don't think so." Fully revealed, the piece in front of Ryan was a dressing table, the mahogany drawer fronts expertly carved with scrollwork and fleur-de-lis. Quarter-inch thick glass was cut to fit the scalloped top and beneath it an additional bit of carving in a child's scrawl, the name Debra Couillard.

Saunders shone his light on the top of the dressing table. "We've got him." They uncovered six more pieces, all old and valuable even to an inexpert eye. "Nice retirement fund."

Maneuvering diagonally through the bay, Ryan's beam followed a wine-colored stain that snaked along the floor. When he reached the source, he knelt down and ran his fingers across the concrete. Transmission fluid. He lifted the edge of a tarp, a little at first, and then tugged until it fell free. Moving his light across the lower half of the bus, he took in the beautifully rendered birds and flowers on the turquoise background. When he could speak, his voice sounded strangely like his fathers, angry and bitter. "It's not his retirement fund, it's his trophy room."

Saunders came up behind him and used the tips of his fingers to push down on the rear door handle. With a little encouragement, the door slid open. "Holy Christ." The glow from his light caught the frenzy of Ellie Kruger's final moments, the roof liner awash with blood turned brown in the intervening years.

"He must have been sitting in the driver's seat when he reached over and cut her," said Ryan, pointing to the liner. "Arterial spatter."

The rear of the bus was empty, no paintings, no seats. A remnant of white shag carpeting held a large irregular circle of dried blood. "He put her in the back to bleed out," added Saunders. "Where are you going?"

"To get some air."

"Pete, either you call it in or I will. We need a forensics team out here."

"I'll call Jimmy when you disappear. This could cost you your badge."

"You think I give a shit about that? Screw illegal search and seizure. We'll worry about that when we get the bastard in a courtroom."

Ryan reached down and yanked on the overhead door. "You don't get it, do you? I don't want him in a courtroom."

Thirty minutes later, the first of the vans rolled in, the bomb squad followed by the Crime Scene Unit. No one inside the vehicles made a move until a car drove up and Jimmy got out. When he gave them the nod, a large man in a safety suit and headgear was the first to enter the bay.

Ryan pushed off from his standing position by the Toyota. "I assume this means you got a warrant. What'd it cost you?"

"Didn't cost me a thing," said Jimmy. "Hammond was happy to do it."

"Hammond hates my guts."

"True, but I said it didn't cost me anything. It cost you your P.I. license."

I.D. in hand, Saunders stepped between them. "Pete didn't want any part of this. It was my show."

"Yeah, and now it's my show. Relax, cowboy, it's only a ninety day suspension. After thirty years, I expect this kind of thing from him but you're still a cop. You should know better."

"I do know better. That's why I didn't destroy the lock."

"Another wiseass. You going home anytime soon?"

"Sunday unless you make it an official request."

"Sunday's good."

The three men watched as portable lights were pushed beneath the bay door. When Ryan separated himself and walked off to stand alone, Jimmy lowered his voice. "He okay?"

"You've known him thirty years, you tell me."

"You find anything of Theresa's in there?"

"We stopped looking when we found the VW bus."

"Bad?"

"Bad enough. He's driving down tomorrow to break the news to the Krugers before they hear about it on the nightly news."

"That's Pete, the world's oldest altar boy."

They heard the clatter of the overhead door as it rose unimpeded and stopped at the top of the opening. The man in the safety suit approached them, headgear tucked under his arm. "You're good to go. The wire led to a car battery. Whoever rigged it probably did it as a visual deterrent. The only way it would have exploded is if an H-bomb landed on it. Better safe than sorry. I disarmed a device last week that wasn't much more than an Altoids tin, some jewelry wire and a AA battery. Fucking internet."

Ryan rejoined them as the man walked back to his van and the crime scene team entered the unit. "I'm going back to the office." He looked at Saunders "You coming?"

"Damn right he's going," said Jimmy. "Do me a favor and stay low, both of you. If the press gets wind of your involvement, your head won't be the only one on Hammond's wall. That was one of the conditions of the warrant."

Saunders cocked his head toward the bay. "What about them?"

"You leave any fingerprints or DNA in there?"

"Of course not."

"Then leave them to me."

When they reached the office, Saunders took a cell phone call and Ryan headed for the men's room. They joined up a few minutes later in Marti's office and related the details of the morning.

Marti listened but seemed remote and distracted. Finally, she lowered her eyes and moistened her lips. "I need you both to hear me out before you say anything. I think I know who we're looking for."

Ryan rubbed his eyes. "I have to make some phone calls, Marti. Can this wait?"

"No, it can't." She grabbed a thin sheaf of papers and put them in front of her. "It was the reference to C.S. Lewis that bugged me so I went on-line and got some additional background on him. He was born in Belfast but he died in Oxford, England. There's a British connection here." She looked at Saunders. "When I went under hypnosis, I remembered three books that were in the guest room of Susan Pierce's house in Sedona. One was by a popular American fiction writer, one was Bleak House by Dickens and the third was a biography of Shakespeare. There was something on top of the books, a keychain." She took the drawing and put it in front of them. "I drew that yesterday. It's a sketch of the fob on the keychain. I wasn't sure of that thing in the middle until I looked up Oxford University. It's a book. Every university I clicked on, Princeton, Harvard, Yale, they all have books in their seals."

Saunders picked up the printout from the Wikipedia page on Oxford. "This doesn't match your drawing, not even close."

"No, but this does. It's the seal for Cambridge University."

With the exception of a few minor details, the sketch and the coat of arms were exact duplicates. Ryan was unconvinced. "You can probably pick up one of those key chains in any tourist shop in the U.K."

"And he very well may have," said Marti, "but Cornelius Scott Stanley also attended that University. I confirmed it with the Registrar's office about an hour ago. That's C. S. Stanley, in case you missed the connection."

"That phone call I just got. It was Lou, my partner. There were two guys who left the force within a month of Bert Kennedy's hit and run. One of them was a patrolman who took early retirement when his wife was diagnosed with M.S. The other was a detective before my time. For the past twenty years he's been head of security for Windsor Farms, the Stanley family's tobacco plant."

"Nice gig," said Ryan. "He lifts some evidence and doubles his salary."

"Try proving it. Annie showed up in Lou's office again, suggested he take a hard look at Scott Stanley, that he's some kind of psycho. She claims he killed his mother when he was eight. You can imagine how much weight Lou gave that tidbit of information."

Marti's tone was sarcastic. "About as much weight as you gave any of the stuff she brought you on a platter."

"Look, as distasteful as this may sound, this isn't some low-life drug dealer we're talking about here. The Stanley family goes back generations in Connecticut. The old man gave millions in endowments and scholarship funds. Bryce is no slouch in that department either."

Ryan and Marti exchanged a glance but it was Marti who challenged him. "Yesterday you were ready to feed them to the sharks and today you're nominating them for sainthood? What gives, Mike, or should I ask who got to whom?"

"No one got to anyone, Marti. Lou had lunch with a retired prosecutor, an old buddy of his. He laid out a few things friend to friend. We have to have the goods or we'll never get him into court, not with his money and connections, and we're not there yet, not by a long shot."

"What if we could link him to the other names, the aliases he used with the women he murdered?"

"How the hell are you going to do that?"

"I've already done it, just a few minutes before you got back. Every one of the names, Hastings, Rivers, Vaughan, Tyrell and Richmond, they're characters in Richard III."

"I doubt he's the first whacko to pull an alias from literature."

"No, but I'll bet he's the first one arrogant enough to pull from a source that includes his own last name. Stanley is another character in the play."

Ryan managed his second smile of the day. "That's my girl. What'd you do, call your mother?"

"I Googled them. I put the five names in and the play came up as the first link. Stanley was listed as another one of the characters."

Saunders got to his feet. "It's still not enough. Assuming we could get an indictment, no jury's going to convict on a circumstantial case involving a couple of dead writers, even if one of them is Shakespeare. They want the science, ballistics or DNA, preferably spoon-fed to them by some egghead in a lab coat. They want evidence, not theoretical bullshit."

"He's right, Marti," said Ryan. "This guy's got everything going for him and we don't even have Debra's body. Besides, when the story of what we found today gets out, he'll go underground and stay there."

Marti was angry. "Whose side are you on?"

"What kind of question is that? I'm on the side of eight dead people, including my sister. What we should do is drop it in the hands of the FBI and let them deal with it. I don't have the resources or the energy to invest another ten years of my life. I'm done."

Getting to her feet, Marti grabbed her coat. "I have to get out of here. I don't even know who you are."

When the room was quiet, Saunders said, "You better go after her. Even if we can't finish it, she broke the case."

Marti was waiting for him half a block down from the office. When Ryan reached her, she was smiling. "You're done, Pete? Only someone who's known you a couple of days would believe that."

"So that last bit in there, it was an act?"

"It was the only way I could get you alone. I had a pretty good idea of what Mike's take would be and he's right, you need a lot more than what we have." She pulled an envelope from the pocket of her coat. "This is Scott Stanley's home address in Rowayton and your flight number. You're booked on the 4:10 into JFK. It's Friday so you should leave early so you can check in by two o'clock. That leaves you a little over an hour to pack and get to the airport. I'll walk around the block and then go back and tell him you needed to cool off, that you decided to see the Krugers today. That should give you about a seven hour head start."

"You trying to get rid of me?"

"I'm trying to hold on to you but that's not possible until this is finished."

"I don't know what to say."

"Say you won't throw it all away and choose revenge over justice."

"And if I can't?"

"Then say when the moment comes to make that decision, you'll think about us."

"I doubt I'll be thinking of anything else."

She kissed him on the lips and turned away. "I love you and I'll settle for that."

With twenty minutes to spare, Ryan took a seat near the departure gate and browsed the front page of USA Today. Something drew his attention to the television on the wall to his right, a word or phrase, he wasn't sure which. An attractive woman was holding a microphone with the call letters KGO-TV. Behind her was a drab gray structure enclosed by tall gates and razor wire.

Ryan got up and moved closer. A flatbed truck was clearing the gates. Secured to the bed was Ellie Kruger's VW bus.

Mike Saunders dropped his bag at Ryan's feet. "If I were the sensitive type, I might think you were trying to run out on me. You have a chance to call the Krugers?"

"Barbara Kruger took an overdose of sleeping pills three days ago. Her husband wouldn't take my call."

"I have a daughter. I'm not sure where my head would be if it were her."

"You're here so Marti must have caved."

"Nope, she was great, played her part perfectly, right up to the moment I explained the difference between a devil's disciple and a devil's advocate."

"Maybe you'd better explain it to me."

"I said we didn't have enough evidence. I never said I wouldn't help you get it. I was born and raised in Connecticut, and I know my way around. We'll have a better chance of getting something on him if we work together."

"So there's nothing personal in this, nothing that could cloud your judgment."

"You asking me that as the brother of a victim or an ex-cop?"

"Both. I just want to know who's got my back."

"I'll have your back but I won't lie about the fact I don't like where this is headed. Annie's too close to this thing. She had dinner with Scott on Wednesday night and Thursday he sent her flowers. The card said something about being a jealous lover and denying her release."

"Where is she now?"

"On her way to London."

"Which is where we should be going."

"Lou ran his credit cards. There's been no activity since the flower purchase on Thursday morning. In fact, no one's seen or heard from him since then."

"Which could mean he's already in the U.K. If he went to school there, he knows the lay of the land."

"I'm sure he does but I'm betting he's gone to ground in Connecticut where he feels protected. He's one of them, Pete, the uber-rich. They may sell one another out for a membership to a country club, but they circle the wagons when it comes to outsiders taking down one of their own. It took twenty-seven years to get Michael Skakel behind bars for killing his fifteen-year-old neighbor. That was Belle Haven, by the way, less than a mile from the Stanley home. That kid from Darien, Alex Kelly, spent eight years cavorting in Europe on his father's dime before they got his ass into court on multiple rape charges."

A loudspeaker announced imminent boarding and they stepped in line. "Three days, Mike, and if we haven't picked up his scent by then, I leave for London and I go alone."

"Over my dead body. How do you propose we get him back?"

"In a body bag."

PART THREE

CHAPTER 48

ANNIE

Saturday passed in a blur, a dizzying kaleidoscope of color and images. By the time she fell into bed, Annie was exhausted. Sunday morning she awoke slowly and hunkered down to enjoy some alone time, a few minutes to recharge and reflect.

The night flight over was enjoyable, so very different from travelling with Larry who despised everything about air travel, a fact he shared freely and often. If it wasn't the service, it was the turbulence, both of which he saw as a personal affront to his comfort. Bryce was low maintenance, acutely aware of her presence but never intrusive. When they weren't making small talk, he was reading or dozing. She liked the way he looked in sleep, peaceful, a boyish version of himself. The scar above his eye was the only blemish on an otherwise perfect face, and more than once she caught herself staring at it, resisting the urge to touch it and heal the childhood memory. Ninety minutes after landing, his driver dropped her at Samantha's Notting Hill flat.

Their reunion was boisterous as always, but to Annie's consternation, sleep would have to wait. Samantha wasn't having it. Was she daft? It was Saturday. Who could sleep with the Portobello Market a block away? It was only after several hours of serious shopping that she was allowed to fall into a delicious, dreamless nap. When Samantha finally coaxed her to consciousness, she had less than an hour to bathe and dress for dinner, an invitation she wished she'd declined.

An evening on the town with her sister was rarely relaxing. As her popularity increased, the ruthlessness of the paparazzi grew exponentially. She'd grown comfortable with her role as an appendage to her famous sister but she feared how Bryce would respond. She needn't have worried. Thanks to the arrival of an A-list Hollywood couple in town to promote their latest film, the paparazzi were otherwise engaged. Nonetheless, they were into their first course before she allowed herself to loosen up.

With little effort, Bryce had steered the conversation to topics near and dear to the hearts of both women. He was particularly interested in Samantha's work with PETA UK and her very public abhorrence and contractual refusal to wearing anything made from the skin or fur of animals. It was a side of him Annie hadn't seen and she liked it. When he reached for her hand over coffee, she offered no resistance.

Slipping from beneath the quilt, she stepped into a pair of sweatpants and grabbed a t-shirt from her open suitcase. With Sam in rehearsal for the better part of the afternoon, the day was hers to do with as she liked. She could dress or not dress, go out or stay in, read a book or go back to bed. But at the moment, she was starving.

Samantha was in the kitchen, unruly hair piled atop her head and secured with a bright purple clip, reading glasses on the tip of her nose. Laid out on the table were yogurt, fruit and two cranberry scones, Annie's contribution from the farmer's market.

She poured a glass of juice and leaned against the tiled countertop. "You might have waited for the car to stop before jumping out last night. What did you think was going to happen when we were alone?"

"I was hoping he'd whisk you back to his place."

"I'm not ready to be whisked anywhere."

"Oh, you're ready, Annabelle. You just don't know it." Pushing the glasses to the top of her head, Samantha cocked her head. "Well?"

"Well what?"

"Aren't you going to ask me what I think of him or are you going to make the same mistake you did with Larry the loser?"

"It was dinner, Sam. Don't make it into something more."

"He's perfect for you."

"No one's perfect."

"He's the anti-Larry and that's good enough for me. They couldn't possibly have less in common except, well, you know?"

"A penis?"

Samantha made a face. "Yuk, no, I wasn't thinking of that, but now that you mention it, I'll bet he's dynamite in the sack."

"And you surmise this because you've had so much experience with men?"

"Asks the woman who's been with two men in thirty-nine years."

"Touché."

"I'm talking about quality. Bryce is everything Larry aspires to be without the irritating baggage."

Bryce's family history was the last thing she wanted to discuss, the last thing she wanted to think about. "There's always baggage, Sam. How did Larry get into this conversation?"

"Who should we be discussing, the cop?"

There it was again, the gnawing in the pit of her stomach whenever she thought of him. "Can we leave Mike out of this?"

"I don't know, can we? I know the way your brain works, sis. The problem you have with Bryce is he and Larry look the same on paper, handsome, rich and successful. The cop is the wild card, the bad boy you never got to experience when you were a teenager."

"That's ridiculous."

"Is it? The last time you saw him, when you were ready to jump him, describe him to me."

"I don't remember."

"I do. You called me after he left. He was wearing jeans, a white t-shirt and a leather bomber jacket. His face was scruffy and he smelled like peppermint." She tore off a piece of scone and popped it in her mouth. "Bad boy."

"He's a detective, a father, and a jazz pianist, not exactly one of the Sons of Anarchy. Give it a rest." She picked up an oversized envelope from the edge of the table addressed to Bryce's London home. "What's this?"

"Bryce mentioned his boys were fans of the show and asked if I had any photographs lying around. I was going to drop it in the mailbox on my way to rehearsal but then I thought you might be seeing him today so…"

"Oh, you thought that, did you?" The truth was she and Bryce had no plans beyond last night's dinner, which suited her fine. The trip was about supporting her sister. Jumpstarting a romance was the furthest thing from her mind. If he could rearrange his schedule and stay for opening night, that was okay too, but she had no intention of chasing him around London.

"Talk to me, kiddo. It's the evil brother, isn't it? He's the reason you're holding back, which is silly. You have no proof his brother is anything more than an insensitive twit. There's one in every family."

"Not in ours."

"Good grief, Annie. You're not seriously comparing our family to other families. We were the Ingalls with better plumbing."

Annie laughed. "Do I detect some latent hostility about our childhood?"

"Mom and Dad did the best they could. It's not their fault they loved one another unconditionally and brought us up in a safe, nurturing environment."

"Please tell me you're still in therapy."

"For the sake of argument, let's assume the guilt over thinking his brother is a murderer is part of it. If it's not the cop, what's the other reason you're holding back?"

"That's the second time you've used that expression. He hasn't asked anything of me so I can't be holding back."

"He hasn't tried to get you in bed?"

"Nope, he's been the perfect gentleman. Last night before I got out of the car, he kissed me for the first time."

"And?"

"And it was nice. The first time I met him, he touched me on the back of my neck and it freaked me out. It's like he's known me for years and he's inside my head. Anyway, that's as far as it's going."

"You could do worse, you know."

"What's with you, Sam? Are you on his payroll?"

"I'm just saying…"

Annie nodded at the clock behind Sam's head. "Don't you have to be somewhere at noon?"

Samantha threw a look over her shoulder. "We'll pick this up later."

Smiling, Annie held up two fingers giving her the peace sign. "Groovy."

Alone in the flat, Annie drew a bath and grabbed a book from her carry-on. An hour later, pampered and shriveled, she was bored out of her mind. Her attempt at a nap was also a bust. Who could sleep with Samantha's voice in her head? She tossed and turned and finally gave up. Introspection was something she could do anytime, anywhere. What she needed was fresh air and exercise.

At a little past two, she was dressed and ready to go. On her way out, she made a detour through the kitchen and penned a note to Samantha. The envelope for Bryce was right where they'd left it, stamped and ready to go, and she slid it into her bag.

She started walking south. Absent the crowds and kiosks of yesterday's market, Portobello Road was just another street in another big city. It had rhythm and energy. Westport was a compromise, she knew that now, close enough to maintain her ties but far enough to give the illusion of freedom. It was familiar and safe, but being safe was not the same as being alive. Safe was an escape, the place you ran to when your life was in shambles. Safe was a spirit killer.

The farther she walked, the more the lark became obsession, a game of pros and cons, what-ifs and if-onlys. What if she had gone with her original plan and moved to Manhattan? What if she could do it now, sell the house and buy an apartment in

Greenwich Village? What if, by moving again, she could truly start over and find the missing piece of herself, the part that knew how to be happy? Seclusion wasn't working for her. Left to her own devices, she created drama from solitude, murder from the mundane.

She ducked into a pub and took a seat by the window. After ordering an Irish coffee, she waited for the other side to weigh in, the intellectual party-pooper. When it came, it came with a vengeance. Was she out of her mind? Now was not the time to be making big decisions. Her life was a question mark, a series of unanswered queries and incomplete tasks. She was responsible Annie, practical Annie, list-maker and rule-follower, the one who stuck by her choices and sucked them up when they turned to crap.

Even as she tried to tamp it down, her excitement built. With the closing of **Life House**, there was nothing holding her in Connecticut. Maybe she was one of those people for whom emotion was a better compass. It was beginning to look that way. The hospice was a good example. It felt right and it was right. She'd jumped right in and made it happen, no second thoughts or hesitation. Her marriage was a different story. It took months to accept his proposal and years to admit her mistake.

With a single phone call she could put the wheels in motion. Kay still had a key to the house which meant an appraisal could be done and the paperwork started. It was one less thing to worry about when she returned from London. She reached for her tote bag and fished around inside for her phone. What she pulled out was the envelope for Bryce. Why the hell not? It was another baby step, a way to confirm she could change who she was. After paying the bill, she walked outside and hailed a cab.

It was a mistake. She knew it the moment she entered the cab. Polite Annie didn't drop in unannounced. It was rude, not to mention risky. There were a dozen good reasons why he might not want to see her. He could be entertaining friends or brunching with his sons. And of course he lived in Chelsea, where else? Home to rock stars, film stars and a former Prime

Minister, it was the wealthiest borough in one of the most expensive cities in the world. For all she knew, he kept a mistress in town, maybe two. That would explain his frequent trips to London, why he never pressed her for more. Why rent the cow when he could afford to own the dairy? By the time they reached Cheyne Walk, Bryce Stanley ceased to exist. She was cold-calling on Caligula.

She leaned forward to get the cabbie's attention. "I've changed my mind, I'm not staying. I have to drop something at the door and then you can take me back to Notting Hill."

As her foot touched the pavement, her eye caught movement in a ground-floor window. Bryce was there, not twenty feet away, his back toward the street. He was talking on the phone, shaking his head. She was almost to the door when he glanced in her direction. She raised her hand to wave but he turned around and continued the call. What did she expect? Confused and embarrassed, she continued forward envelope in hand, the longest few feet of her life.

The door opened but it took a moment to register. She'd never seen him without a jacket, not even on the plane. Today he was dressed in casual clothes, chinos and a clingy turtleneck. He was muscular and fit, a body to go with the face. When her eyes reached his, she had to look away. He was staring at her with such intensity that the things she wanted to say, the explanations and protestations were completely forgotten.

From a place outside herself, she watched him brush past her and walk to the curb. She looked back through the window. It was his study, walls paneled in cherry and highly-polished to reflect the light from a fire. In the center of a mahogany desk, a laptop sat open. That was all she saw before his hand found the small of her back and propelled her through the open door. When it was closed, he pushed her back against it. She felt the warmth of his hands on her face, the heat of his breath on her neck, the smooth firmness of his lips as his mouth ravaged hers. Lost in a floodgate of sensations, she barely noticed when he picked her up and carried her to the stairwell.

The bedroom was cool and dark. With the drapes drawn, she could make out shapes but little else. He sat her on the bed, pushed her gently back and pulled the turtleneck over his head. When he got to his knees in front of her, she closed her eyes as he unzipped her jeans and slid them down over her hips, kissing a spot just below her navel. His skin was hot but she didn't trust her senses. She was caught in a slow, silent erotic dream. Sitting next to her, he pulled her into his lap facing away from him, her back against his chest. She felt him swell beneath her as he unbuttoned her shirt, unhooked her bra and cupped her breasts. The dream continued and she went with it, brain and body no longer hers. She thought of nothing but his hands, their slow and practiced descent down her body. Her breath came in short, urgent gasps as she tried to move, but he held her to him, so tightly she could feel his heart. His fingers strayed and lingered, teasing and exciting her. When she tried again to wriggle from his touch, his hand found the strip of silk between her legs and ripped it away.

CHAPTER 49

RYAN

Surveillance was a pain in the ass. The wear and tear on the back and bladder were the least of it. Staying focused was the challenge, forcing the eyes to distinguish details and training the brain to recall them.

Sunday stakeouts were problematic. Any other day of the week, a lone car and occupant might be ignored for several hours. It would be one among many, but with so many shops and businesses closed, that same car and driver could attract unwanted attention. He'd moved the car three times in the last six hours, far enough to avoid curious eyes while maintaining visual contact with their missing quarry, a disappointing no-show.

Saturday, their first full day, came and went. They used the time confirming what they already knew: Scott Stanley had disappeared and no one had seen or spoken to him since Thursday morning at 9:07 a.m. when he purchased flowers for delivery to Annie Heywood.

His business partners accepted his absence with a measure of frat boy humor and envy. That was Scotty. Rumor had it he was holed up somewhere banging his brother's hot girlfriend. Annie Heywood was her name. There was even reference to a book Ryan never heard of in which Scotty's fuck du jour was exposed as quite the piece of ass, a detail he omitted from the notes he was sharing with Saunders.

In the guise of a concerned friend, he placed a call to Bryce Stanley but even that failed to elicit anything beyond an exasperated response. *No, he had neither seen nor communicated with his brother since 10 p.m. on Wednesday night. And yes, he remembered exactly what his brother was wearing — half a bottle of Chateau Margaux 1966.*

With each round of questions, one thing was clear, all roads led to Annie Heywood. By Saturday night, he was intrigued and Saunders was sullen.

Ryan crushed a paper cup, tossed it in the backseat and lifted the binoculars. They caught a break with the location of Scott Stanley's home. Situated on a promontory, it overlooked Five Mile River and was visible from several spots in the village. An older home, it had a Spanish vibe, whitewashed exterior walls with some wrought iron here and there and a tile roof, very different from the other homes in the area, mostly clapboard Colonials. It was also private, a good fifty yards or so from its nearest neighbor and cocooned among dense trees.

Saunders opened the passenger door and slid in. "His partner was right about one thing. The house he's renting has been on the market for six months. Scott leased it with an option to buy. I pulled the listing off the internet and called the broker. Scott and the seller came to an agreement on the price and the closing is next month. What we're seeing from this angle is the main part of the house but there's also a studio and detached garage."

"Did you call the airline?"

"I called them. Their flight landed at Heathrow yesterday morning."

"Their flight?"

"I had a hunch, so I asked Lou to pull Bryce's credit cards. Sometime Wednesday night, he booked two seats to London in first class, one for himself and one for Annie."

"That doesn't mean they're together. We know Scott caused a big enough scene in the restaurant that she ran outside in the rain to get away from him and Bryce was hot on her heels. Maybe he did it to make amends for his brother spoiling the evening or he knows his brother is a psychopath and wanted to protect her. For all we know, Scott chartered a private jet, paid cash and is living it up with his Cambridge buddies in London. I talked to Marti an hour ago and she wasn't halfway through the list of charter airlines."

"Then that's where we need to be. Maybe I called this wrong, Pete."

"If he left in a hurry, he'll leave signs of a hasty departure, missing toiletries, drawers rifled, a note to his cleaning lady. It'll be dark in an hour. If he's home, there should be signs of life, an inside lamp, outside lights, something. There's a bar and grill in the village. We'll grab some food and come back. I need to use the head anyway."

"And if the house is dark when we come back?"

"You know anything about security systems?"

"I know enough not to trigger them. You get some food and I'll meet you back here in an hour. If we're going in there, we need something other than flashlights. Otherwise, we'll have every Neighborhood Watch type breathing down our necks."

"Night goggles?"

"Yeah, my daughter has a thing for caves, the deeper and darker the better. I bought two pair last Christmas, one for her and one for me."

"How old is she?"

"Seventeen. She starts college next year, wants to be a geologist." He was out of the car when he ducked his head back in. "Christ, what is that? You smell it?"

"Smell what?"

"It hit me when I parked my car but I thought it was coming off Five Mile River. The wind must have shifted. Now it's stronger and it smells like decomp."

"Could be anything, a raccoon, even a deer. I saw two in Stanley's yard today."

"Maybe."

It was pitch black when they made their way through the trees, with each step keenly aware of a dead animal in the vicinity.

Despite the darkness, the house was quiet as a tomb, no lamps, no flickering TV, not a single discernible sound from within. If Stanley were inside, he was hunkered down in the dark.

Bypassing the main structure, they headed for the garage and to its left a smaller building, presumably the studio. By pre-agreement, Ryan swerved left. The knob turned easily and he walked inside. A few scuff marks here and there but otherwise the hardwood floor was in good shape. An entire wall was mirrored with a ballet barre secured in place at both ends. The other walls held prints of ballet dancers, a few by Degas but most he didn't recognize.

Saunders joined him as he was closing the door. "An empty ballet studio. What's in the garage?"

"Enough horsepower and chrome to fund my kid's education through grad school, a brand new Maserati Quattroporte and a Harley-Davidson Low Rider S, top of the line. The rest is stuff you'd find in any single guy's garage including mine, some tools, skis and poles, a life vest or two. Wherever he is, he didn't drive there."

Ryan inclined his head toward the house. "You ready?"

"Let's do it." Producing a pair of wire cutters and a lock-pick set from the pocket of his leather jacket, Saunders added, "If there's an alarm system, I'll find it."

Backtracking across the front of the house, Ryan walked the perimeter until he came to a window facing his car. It was partially open, the screen in place, the unmistakable odor of decomp strongest here.

Saunders caught up with him at the front door. "You smelled it too. I cut the wires to the system."

Like the doors to the studio and garage, the lever handle gave easily under his hand. Immaculately clean, the Saltillo flooring and oversized furniture looked new in the large front room, the lampshades still wrapped in plastic. It was the same in the kitchen and what they assumed were guest rooms and baths. The Master Bedroom told a different story.

Slumped against a massive headboard, C. Scott Stanley's blood and brain matter coated the wall behind him, a 9mm Glock on the floor just inches from his right hand.

Ryan couldn't take his eyes from the creature before him, his body grey and bloated beyond recognition. He'd waited ten years to send this bastard to hell, ten long years spent in his own private purgatory and for what, so the coward could take the easy way out.

Behind him, Saunders' voice cut the eerie silence. "With that much decomp, he's been dead two to three days. He left a note, Pete."

"What does it say?"

"He admits to killing Theresa and the other five women, as well as Helen Allen and Bert Kennedy. It's rambling but it's all here. He must have been drunk or high when he wrote it. He closes by saying he's shuffling off this mortal coil on his own terms and signed it with an S."

"Hamlet, a poseur to the end."

"Theresa's at peace. They all are. Call Marti and…"

The unfinished sentence dragged on and Ryan finally pulled his eyes away from the body and turned. "Call Marti and what? What's the problem?"

"I don't know. Maybe it's what you said about him being a poseur but something feels off, the timing, the venue, the weapon, maybe all three. He creates elaborate personas based on a play by Shakespeare and then offs himself by putting a gun in his mouth and messing up his pretty house. It's anticlimactic."

"Anticlimactic or not, it's over. Do I wish I were the one to pull the trigger? You bet your ass I do, but at least no other woman will suffer like my sister."

"I have to call Lou. He'll get the crime scene unit in here and he'll want your statement, Pete."

"He'll get it in the morning. Right now, I'm going for a walk to blow the stink off. If I'm lucky, I'll find a bar along the way."

CHAPTER 50
ANNIE

Annie opened one eye and groaned. "This is London. Why is there sun?"

"I opened the blinds. It's one o'clock and I've wasted half my day off watching you sleep." Sitting cross-legged at the foot of the guest room bed, Samantha pushed a breakfast tray forward.

Annie scooted to a sitting position and tucked the extra pillow behind her. "Wow, this is nice, thanks."

"Save your thanks. I want details and they better be good. You were MIA for ten hours yesterday, no phone call and no text."

"I know I should have called and I'm sorry. How was rehearsal?"

"I worked my ass off. What were you working off?"

Samantha was glaring at her, never a good thing, especially before coffee. She took a sip and moistened her lips. "I cabbed it to Harrods and had a late lunch. Then I walked around for a while and stumbled on an art house. I watched The Godfather again, all three films. I had a good time."

"I'll bet you did." She pulled a box from behind her, the approximate size and shape of a man's shoe box. "Who sent you these, Al Pacino?"

"What is that?"

"It's a dozen pair of La Perla Black Label bikini briefs, two hundred and forty dollars a pop. You must have really enjoyed those films."

"You opened a box addressed to me?"

"You snooze, you lose, Sleeping Beauty. It came a few minutes ago by special messenger and I was bored. There's a note in the box but I thought I'd let you open that."

"I appreciate that." An envelope was on top of the panties and she slit it open with a knife from the tray. After reading it, she put it aside and dumped the contents of the box on the bed. On top of the pile was another envelope, thicker than the first and beneath it something wrapped in gold foil. She ripped the foil off and stared.

"It's a shovel. I hope that's not a metaphor for how much he digs you. If it is, he lost some points."

"It's a trowel. Archaeologists use it for cutting compacted sediment and compressed soils. I can't believe he remembered."

"And I can't believe there isn't a diamond bracelet hidden in there somewhere. What's in the other envelope?"

"It says he knows I'm sad about closing **Life House** and wanted to give me something to look forward to. He's arranged for me to spend six weeks on a dig in Greece starting in February. All expenses are paid including first-class air travel back and forth. I can't accept this, Sam."

"The hell you can't. It may not be my cup of tea but it's an amazing gift. Besides, he can afford it."

"That's just it. I made a big deal out of the fact that he has money. If I take this, I'll be a hypocrite and bigot."

If it were a diamond bracelet, maybe you'd have a case but a lot of thought and time went into this. He's giving you your dream, Annie. You can't throw that back in his face." Sam retrieved a box of tissues from the dresser. "Blow your nose. I saw him drop you off last night, and judging from the good-night kiss and replacement underwear, I'd say things are progressing. How did that happen?"

"After you left yesterday, I took a long walk and somewhere along the way I lost my mind and decided to drop the envelope of photographs off at his home. I told the cabbie to wait so he could bring me back after I left it at his door."

"And?"

"It didn't work out the way I planned."

"Do you want to talk about it?"

"There's nothing to talk about. We had a lovely day."

"I'm happy for you, but from where I sit you look like someone ran over your puppy."

"Okay, sure, why not? During one of the most important weeks in your life, let's make this about me."

"You're right, it's much too pretty a day to sit inside and talk. I'll call Wimbledon Stables and book us in. Nothing clears the head like bouncing around on the back of spirited horse. What do you think?"

Annie fell back on the pillows. "I think you're vicious and cruel. Be honest, Sam. Haven't there been moments over the past few months when you've wanted to scream at me to get it together and keep it together longer than an hour at a time?"

Reaching for her sister's hand, Samantha entwined their fingers like they did when they were kids. "I've never told you this, Annie, but I have almost no recollection of my freshman year, not a class, not a professor, not even a girl. What I do remember is sitting on your dorm room floor night after night talking to you about how confused and miserable I was. Was I gay, was it real or experimentation, how could I possibly tell Mom and Dad? You were really busy with your studies and activities but you never, not even once, cut those talks short or made me feel I was taking you away from something more important. I was important and you let me know it in a million ways you're not aware of. And you did it with such grace. I've thought about it over the years and wondered where a nineteen-year-old girl found the courage and confidence to help her sister through the most difficult time in her life. People in my position commit suicide everyday because they can't reach out to their families, but you reached out to me and saved me. With any luck, I'll have a lot more opening nights but I'll never have another sister."

"You were seventeen. I'm thirty-nine. I shouldn't be this nuts."

"You're not nuts, you're human. In the last three months you've gone through a divorce, made the decision to close **Life House**, your partner and friend of eleven years is moving to another state and your neighbor was murdered. Most people don't go through that much turmoil in a lifetime and almost none of them go through it without the help of good pharmaceuticals. You did get laid last night, right?"

Annie laughed. "Yes, Samantha, I guess that's what you'd call it."

"What I'd call it? What would you call it? Have you silly heteros changed the definition and forgotten to tell us?"

"It was intense."

"Good intense or bad intense?"

"Intense, and that's all I'm saying."

"Come on, Annie, throw me a bone. I've been working so much I haven't had a date in two months."

"It was dark in the room, so dark I never saw his face. We rarely talked, not much more than a few words in almost eight hours."

"Like a deprivation chamber with benefits."

"If you say so."

"He's a sexual superman who doesn't talk which means he doesn't have to be reassured every five minutes. He's gorgeous and gives perfect gifts. Tell me he cooks and I'll pay for his sex-change operation."

"He cooks. He made dinner before he brought me home. It was good."

"I can see why you're so unhappy. You're a brave girl hanging in there for almost ten hours."

Annie plucked a strawberry from the tray, nibbled at it and put it down. "What would you say if I told you I'm moving to Manhattan?"

"I'd say I told you to do that three months ago when you opted for little house in the boondocks. I'd say it's a great idea if you're doing it for the right reasons."

"And I'm sure you're going to remind me what the right reasons are."

"You already know the right reasons. The wrong reason is running away. You'll never find what you want by looking behind you. When I moved to London, it was because I always wanted to live here, not because I was escaping the states. When did you make this decision?"

"Yesterday before I went to his place."

"Where does Bryce fit into this?"

"He doesn't."

"That's not what it looked like from my window."

Annie's cell phone chimed and she jumped. Before she could grab it off the nightstand, Samantha snagged it and put it in her pocket. "It's no one you want to talk to, believe me. What's going on, Annie?"

"Nothing's going on and nothing has changed since we spoke yesterday morning. I don't want a relationship." She almost added *with him* but thought better of it. For whatever reason, Sam was promoting Bryce like he was a candidate for office and she was his campaign manager. The question was why.

"Maybe you're in love with him and you're scared. Moving to Manhattan is a pre-emptive strike. You want to dump him before he disappoints you. You know what frosts my ass, Annie? You're letting Larry win. He let you down so now every man is presumed to be a shmuck. Bryce is in love with you, I know that for a fact. He told me at dinner the other night when you went to the ladies' room."

"And you didn't think to share that with me over breakfast yesterday?"

"It wasn't my place. Had I known you were sleeping with Marcel Marceau, I might have mentioned it. You know now so what difference does it make?"

"It makes all the difference in the world. I wouldn't have gone over there."

"You're right, you're nuts."

"Can we drop this so I can take a bath?"

"Is it Markham? It is, isn't it? Annie, it's been twenty years and you're the one who made the decision never to see him again.

Please don't tell me you're going to spend the rest of your life alone when there's even a remote chance you'll find happiness, real happiness, with a man who loves you."

"They're too much alike, Sam. Touching him yesterday was like touching Lucas. Their body types are similar, even the feel of their skin. There were moments in his bedroom when I thought… never mind what I thought. Maybe it's the timing. I don't know."

Samantha held up the second envelope. "That's what this gift was supposed to say to you. It's about giving you the space and time to figure all that out. Bryce knows you're not ready for a long-term commitment but he's willing to wait it out."

"I knew it." Annie jumped from the bed and struggled into her robe. "That was quite the little chat you had the other night. Too bad I didn't go out for a cigarette or you would have had the wedding planned. The good news is I don't have to worry about my life with the two of you manipulating it."

"Believe what you will but neither of us was in that cab when you went to his home yesterday. You did that all on your own. He talked to me, told me how he felt about you. What was I supposed to do, get up from the table?"

"Whose idea was the six weeks in Greece?"

"Hello, have we met? The closest I ever want to come to dirt is when it's mixed with water and slathered over my body. It was his idea, all his. He started working on it the morning after your first date."

"It wasn't a date. Is that my cell phone again? Give it to me."

Samantha read the display again and put it back in her pocket. "Not a chance, it's Larry again. I'm telling you, he's the Devil, all-seeing, all-knowing."

"Why is he calling me? What time is it in Connecticut?"

"It's a little after 9 a.m. If he calls again, I'll take care of him. One last question. When we were talking about the benefits thing, that was code for something else, right?"

"Yes, Samantha, it was code for something else. Do I have to draw you a picture?"

"You're right, he's a loser, dump him. The thing is you still haven't said how you feel about him."

"I don't know what to call how I feel about him. I'm overwhelmed by him. When I close my eyes, I see his face. It's as if he's inhabiting me and it creeps me out."

"Fear is a habit and whether we choose to break it or embrace it defines our destiny."

"That's awful, who said that?"

"You did. We were having one of our marathon talks. I thought it was crap too but I never forgot it. It's my mantra before every audition. You've always been smarter than everyone else, Annie. Maybe that's your problem, you think too much."

The water was hot, just the way she liked it. Parting the bubbles, she looked down the length of her body, shocked at the bruising on her thighs and breasts. Despite her best efforts to wash him from her mind and body, she could still feel him inside her and taste him on her lips.

Although at times irritating, Sam's inquisition crystallized a few things. What happened between them was an anomaly, a one-off, and she had to end it before either of them got in any deeper. Before the day was out, she'd call him and return the gifts — by messenger this time. Once that was done, she'd call Mike and say all the things she should have said before he left.

Relieved, she turned the dial on the battered portable radio, a relic from her sister's college days, rested her head on the back of the tub and closed her eyes. With the volume up, she could concentrate on Edith Piaf, not the incessant ringing of phones. She loved Sam's world but only as a guest and only in small doses. It was noisy, full of gossip and angst, drama begetting drama.

Sensing a presence, she opened her eyes. Samantha stood in the doorway, her eyes bright green against her pale skin. "You need to get downstairs now, Annie. Right now."

"What's wrong?" She sprang to her feet and grabbed a towel. "Is it Mom and Dad? Samantha, what the hell? Talk to me."

"Downstairs now."

With the towel wrapped around her, Annie raced down the stairs and stumbled into the darkened lounge. The blinds were closed, the only light in the room from a TV in the corner. A montage of six women filled the screen and below them a chyron streaming news about the suicide of a serial killer. "Who are these women? What is this?"

"Scott Stanley committed suicide. You were right about him, Annie. He left a letter confessing to the murders of eight people. Debra is the woman on the upper left. He murdered Mrs. Allen too, the son of a bitch."

A million things were going through her head, how the bastard invaded Helen's house and pumped her full of insulin, Debra's joy at her new life and death at the hands of a madman, the scene in the restaurant. "When did this happen?"

"They discovered his body last night after they found his trophies or whatever they call them. They kept it quiet until they could notify the victims' families. I wouldn't have known about it if I hadn't answered Larry's last call. He was frantic, ready to board a plane if he didn't get in touch with you. He knew you had dinner with Scott Wednesday night."

"That's BBC. Why are they covering it?"

"Scott went to Cambridge and has ties here. This is a big story and Bryce is their focus now. They showed the outside of his Cheyne Walk house and the press is all over it."

Annie grabbed her cell phone off the coffee table. "Has he called?"

"I don't know. All the phones were going off at once so I turned the ringers off. They're here too, Annie. That's why the blinds are closed."

"Who's here, the press? Why would they be here?"

"Some little rat-bastard photographer caught the three of us walking into the restaurant Saturday night. It's a clear photo too. There's no way we can deny it's us."

"Oh my God, the play. What are you going to do?"

"What can I do? My publicist is working on a statement."

"I'm so sorry, Sam. I brought this mess into your life at the worst possible time."

"You didn't do this, sweetie." Samantha's phone vibrated on the coffee table. "Shit, it's my director."

"Do you have to answer it?"

"May as well get it over with. I'll take it in the kitchen."

Scrolling through her recent calls, Annie counted twelve, none of them from Bryce. Like her, he probably had no idea what to say, but unlike her he was also grieving. Her hand was shaking as she punched in his numbers but stopped before the final number. Dead or not, Scott was having the last laugh. If she needed further proof that a relationship with Bryce was doomed, his brother provided it.

The coverage was extensive. Each segment brought forth more disturbing images, a VW bus aboard a flatbed truck in San Francisco, crime scene technicians carrying boxes from a storage facility and Stanley's home, mementos of his kills. The photos of the murdered women reappeared on the screen and she turned up the volume. Details of their lives were coming in, information that propelled them from victims to human beings. They were all involved in the arts, a writer, musicians, artists. It was as if, by killing them, he wanted to destroy not just their beauty but their passions.

Samantha joined her on the sofa. "Look at them. Look at the lives he's taken. Every one of them got up one morning believing she was loved. She took a shower, had her coffee or tea and planned her day. She had no idea it would be her last."

"You don't know they believed they were loved."

"I had CNN on in the kitchen. That's how he got close to them, by convincing them he was in love with them. Some of the family members are coming forward with their stories. They're angry. They're saying law enforcement dropped the ball, that twenty years is too long to have a monster on the loose and no one looking for him."

The photograph of the three of them outside the restaurant flashed on the screen. It was remarkably good, almost as if they were posing. Bryce was in the middle, his arm around her waist. The voiceover was delivered in a British accent, clipped and credible.

Annie leaned forward. "What did he say?"

"He mentioned our names, identified you as my sister and Bryce as Scott's brother."

"I heard that part. Did he also say Bryce and I are romantically involved?"

"Rumored to be romantically involved. It didn't take Sherlock Holmes to figure that one out. Everyone in the U.K. knows I'm gay, and you can tell by the way Bryce is looking at you, like he's on a diet and you're a bacon cheeseburger."

"I can't watch this anymore. I'm turning on CNN. Maybe they'll have more information about the women."

"I wouldn't, sweetie. CNN is trying to make the most of the backstory and you're part of it. I saw the tail-end of an interview with Miranda Prescott. She claims you were sleeping with both brothers, playing them against one another and that's the real reason Scott committed suicide. Some reporter even found out that Scott sent you flowers the same day he killed himself. He claims you're unhinged, by the way, that you attacked him."

"How do you do this, let them invade your life?"

"This isn't the pretty part of what I do, but I chose this life and you didn't. What if we have my publicist put out a statement from you?"

"And say what? At least fifty people saw me at dinner with them and Scott did send me flowers. For all we know, someone was watching when Bryce brought me home last night. What about the play? Is your director replacing you?"

"The world's more fucked up than you think. Within an hour of the story breaking, it was sold out for the entire run. They're thinking of extending it another four weeks."

"I have to get out of here. I have to run."

"Run? You can't run from this."

"I'm not running away, I'm running. It's what I do when I'm about to lose it. Isn't there a way out through the garden?"

"There's a padlocked gate but I lost the key. The wall is almost eight feet. You'll break your bloody neck. Besides, the weather is turning bad."

"It's either that or I'm going to throw up all over your expensive new furniture."

"The painters left a ladder here last week. You can use it to get over the wall but how are you going to get back in?"

"Through the front door. I'm unhinged, remember?"

"Annie, you may as well know the two men who broke the case, the ones who found his body, are going to be interviewed."

"So?"

"I wrote their names down. Peter Ryan is one of them and he's also the brother of one of the victims. He'll be speaking on behalf of the families. The other one is Mike Saunders. Isn't he your cop?"

Was my cop. The tears she'd been holding back threatened to spill over and she laughed. "That's perfect. It's not enough that all the crazies are crucifying me. Let's give the police a venue to whack me around. I'm going."

Minutes later, wearing black tights, a sweatshirt several sizes too large, running shoes and a baseball cap, her own mother wouldn't recognize her. She climbed the ladder, poked her head over the wall and looked both ways down the narrow street. The coast was clear. Some kids playing nearby watched open-mouthed as she made the jump. Landing easily, she smiled and waved.

After a few warm-up stretches, she started running. She was almost to the end of the street, about to make a turn, when an SUV came from behind and pulled in front of her, blocking her in mid-stride. She had only enough time to notice the tinted windows before two men jumped from the vehicle. One of them picked her up while the other held open the rear passenger door. Within seconds, it was done and the SUV was in motion.

She was in the second row of seats alone. In front of her, two men were in the front and a third was behind her in a spare seat. "Who are you? Are you police? Where are you taking me?"

The driver eyed her through the rearview mirror, his thick Irish accent tinged with humor. "We've got a bit of a drive, miss, so you might want to settle back and relax."

"What do you mean a bit of a drive? I'm not going anywhere with you. Let me out of here." She tried opening the door closest to her but it held fast. "Look, maybe you have me confused with someone else. There are a lot of people who live on that street. Why are you doing this?"

She tried the handle again, her initial panic giving way to anger. She needed something to use as a weapon and felt around on the floor and seats, running her hand between the cushions. She didn't have her cell phone but who took their cellphone on a run? She had to think, to make the most of what she had, which was nothing. There were only a few reasons why someone was abducted and none of them good.

"If it's money you want, I don't have any money. No one in my family has the kind of money that would justify…" Samantha. Were they using her to extort ransom money from Samantha? If that were the case, she'd die before she let that happen.

Fat droplets of rain hit the window and she touched them with her fingers. It would be dark soon and that's when the real terror would set in. She checked her pulse and tried to control her breathing. Her head was throbbing from the tension. Her stomach lurched and she fought the nausea. She had to close her eyes until the feeling passed. When she opened them, the vehicle was pulling to a stop.

They were in front of a large stone house, three floors high. Flanking it on one side was a six-car garage with what looked like living quarters above it, and on the other side a row of stables. The driveway was circular, at its center a limestone fountain with jumping dolphins. It was dusk, enough daylight to see they were in the middle of nowhere.

When the locks released, she threw open a door and leapt from the SUV, running back toward the road. The rain was pounding the grass and she lost traction, fell and twisted her wrist. Before she could get back on her feet, one of the men picked her up and threw her over his shoulder. She beat on his back with her fists and tried to kick him but he held her legs in a vice-like grip.

At the front door, her captor opened it and put her on her feet. When she looked behind her, he was gone. She was shaking, partly from the rain but mostly from her nerves that were shot.

She heard footsteps approaching and held her breath.

"Bryce?" Instead of relief, her rage erupted and she ran toward him.

He deflected the blow just inches from his face and held her by the wrist. When she stopped struggling, he released her. "Calm down. I didn't know any other way to get you here."

"Don't tell me to calm down. Where are we and why wouldn't they tell me where they were taking me?"

"I hired them for their muscle, not their social skills. We're a half hour out of London at the estate of a family friend. They're in Vail for the winter. What's wrong with your wrist? Did I hurt you?"

"I fell trying to run away. Are we alone here?"

"Except for ten very large, very capable men camping out over the garage when they're not on duty."

"Bodyguards? Why?"

"I'll explain later. I had to get out of London. On top of everything else, I have clients and a family business to hold together, and I can't do anything with the press all over me. They beat you up pretty good too."

"I've had worse things said about me. Someone once called me a Republican. I want to know why I'm here and why you didn't call to ask me if I wanted to come."

"I couldn't risk our conversation being overheard. Someone sitting in a car across from Samantha's flat would hear everything with a long-range microphone. No one would have noticed them with all the press milling about."

He took a step forward and she backed up. She had to think and she couldn't do it with his scent invading her space. If she didn't look directly in his eyes, she might be able to make sense of it all, including his hold on her.

"Annie, look at me. I understand you're upset and I'm sorry. You're cold and wet. Our room is up the stairs at the end of the hall. Get out of those clothes and take a hot bath. We'll talk later."

"I'm not a child, Bryce. You can't send me to my room. Tell me what's happening."

"Or what, Annie, you'll throw another temper tantrum? Go ahead, be my guest. It will do you good. Hell, I wish I could throw one too. My serial killer brother committed suicide, I've got the foreign and American press breathing down my neck and I have a death threat to deal with. And what's going through my head right now? That you look about sixteen and I could be arrested just for thinking what I'd like to do to you." He walked a few paces and took a vase from the foyer table. "Here, have a ball. I can afford to replace it."

She took the vase from his hand. "Not this you couldn't, it's priceless. Tang Dynasty, Changsha Kiln, over a thousand years old." After setting it carefully back on the table, she shook her head. "You said you had a death threat. I don't understand. Why would someone want to hurt you? You had nothing to do with any of this."

"I got the call an hour after the BBC started broadcasting the story, a half hour after they aired the photograph of the three of us outside the restaurant. The threat was made against you, sweetheart."

Had she heard right? She knew what she wanted to ask but couldn't form the words.

"They want money, three million dollars and we'll never hear from them again. Apparently, this isn't unusual. Whenever there's a sensational story, all kinds of nefarious types come out of the woodwork. It may be a hoax but I'm not taking any chances. I have the money with me if it comes to that, but in the meantime I've hired the best investigators in the U.K. to track them down, all ex-Interpol. We need to lay low for another twenty-four hours or so."

She pointed toward the door, her voice unrecognizable as her own. "Can you please ask them to take me back?"

"Back where, to London? You're not going anywhere. I can't protect you in London."

"The police."

"They said they'd know if we brought the police in and the deal would be off. Besides, they wouldn't do a thing more than we're doing and my guys don't have to follow any rules. I know what I'm doing."

"What about Samantha?"

"In addition to the team of investigators, there are twenty men, two shifts of ten watching her flat and this house round the clock."

"She'll hate that."

"She can't know about it. She might panic and call the police. If she goes out, they'll be with her but she won't see them. You have to call her, Annie. Tell her we're together and you'll keep her posted. Ask her to pack a bag with whatever you'll need for a few days including your passport and someone will pick it up in an hour. But you can't say anything else, understand? This will all be over soon, I promise."

"You've thought of everything. Then what?"

"That's up to you. What I'd like to do is take you away somewhere until this mess dies down but that has to be your decision."

"What about your boys?"

"I got them out on a private charter earlier today. Sybil's meeting them in Spain. Her family owns a villa in Tarifa."

"I don't know what to say to you. I want to say I'm sorry your brother is dead but…"

"I'm not sorry. I only wish he'd died before he took the lives of eight innocent people. As soon as his estate is settled, I've instructed my attorney to divide it up among the victims' families. I don't know what to do about Mrs. Allen. I know her husband and daughter are deceased. Do you know if she has other family?"

"She has a brother in a rest home in Idaho."

"I'll let my attorney know and he'll track him down."

"Bryce, I have to talk to you about Scott. There are some things you need to know."

His cellphone rang. Before he answered it, he nodded in the direction of the library. "There's a phone in there. Call your sister."

The call was short. She followed his instructions to the letter and the timing couldn't have been better. Samantha was preoccupied returning phone calls and fending off the press. She suspected nothing. When it was finished, she walked back to the foyer. Bryce was on the terrace talking to two of the men from the SUV. He looked relaxed and confident, another side she hadn't seen, the take-no-prisoners professional.

While she still had the strength, she mounted the staircase. *Their room* was at the end of an expansive hallway, an open suitcase on the bed. She entered the first guest room she came to, the one farthest from his. It was beautifully-appointed, the bathroom large and inviting. Exhausted and emotionally spent with neither the will nor patience to wait for the tub to fill, she stripped and turned on the shower. With the water as hot as she could stand it, she let the spray soothe her tension and warm her skin.

Closing her eyes, she turned toward the wall and hit it with her fists. She wanted him out of her head and out of her life, but now even fate was conspiring to push them together. The trick was keeping her distance. If he got too close, she might never be able to pull away. The tears started and she let them flow. Holding them back was the worst thing she could do. This was not the time nor place for a breakdown.

Out of the corner of her eye she detected movement and wiped a circle of condensation from the thick glass shower door. The room was empty. She was toweling off when she saw the cup of tea. It was hot and sweet and made her sleepy. She took a robe from a hook behind the door and tried to put it on but her arms were like lead. On shaky legs, she made her way to the bed, the sheets cool and smooth.

As she drifted off, the day replayed itself inside her brain, every word, every image, a continuous toxic loop. Faces emerged from the mist, beautiful faces, daughters and sisters just like her. He cut them, watched them die and took what they treasured most. Their sin was love and the punishment was death.

Another face invaded her dreams. Bryce. She recognized his touch, the way he'd made love to her, the unhurried feel of his hands as he found her most intimate spots and took her over the edge again and again.

CHAPTER 51

RYAN

"Where are you?"

"I'm still in Westport, police headquarters. We're tying up a few loose ends and then I'm off to the hotel to pack."

"What time does your flight get in?"

"Seven something in the morning. I'll call you from the airport before I take off. Plan on playing hooky tomorrow, boss's orders. I have plans for you that don't include a computer."

"Mm, can't wait. Pete, I know this didn't end the way you wanted it to, but are you okay? I mean really okay."

"I am now. It ended the way it was supposed to. Looks like you're stuck with me."

"Then I'll keep you. Did I forget to mention how handsome you looked on CNN? It was a great interview. You spoke from your heart. How's Mike doing? He did a good job too, but I got the feeling he's not totally on-board with everything."

"He thinks we've jumped the gun going all in on the suicide. He has another theory."

"He thinks Bryce is our serial killer and framed his brother to take the fall after he murdered him. Am I close?"

"Creepy close. Did he call you?"

"No, but I figured he'd be a wreck if he saw the photograph of Annie Heywood with Bryce Stanley. He's in love with her, Pete."

"Yeah, I got that."

"I miss you. Hurry home."

"Tell me again. I don't think I heard you the last fifty times."

"I've loved you since the moment you stepped on my porch in Sedona."

"I know the feeling. I'll call you later."

Ryan was disconnecting from the call when two short raps on the closed door preceded Saunders' entrance into the smallest of the interrogation rooms, the one farthest from the chaos of the squad room, the place he hoped to hide from Saunders' incessant naysaying.

"We have a problem."

"No, you have a problem and I have four hours till my plane leaves. I don't want to hear it."

"Well, you're going to hear it. We found Dickson and he caved. Bryce Stanley hired him to head up security at the tobacco plant. It wasn't Scott."

"Unless he admitted to destroying the evidence, that's not caving. It's responding to a question."

"He claims he approached Bryce for a job, but I don't believe it."

"You don't want to believe it because it shoots the shit out of your theory that Scott's not our boy and his brother staged the whole thing. My problem with your theory is you want it too badly."

"It would have been easy for him to get into his brother's house, set it up and write the confession. He did it on a computer and signed it with an S, not even his full name."

Watching from the door, Lou Robinson nodded at Ryan before joining the fray. "Two analysts looked at that confession and said the way it was typed was consistent with someone drunk or on drugs, in his case both. They also said the quirky syntax was typical of other documents and emails on his computer. His fingerprints were all over the damn thing, Mike."

"Okay, let's talk about the fingerprints. The only piece of evidence linking Scott to any of the murders is the partial print they found on one of your sister's journals, right?"

"You mean other than the confession and a storage unit full of the victims' property?"

"All I'm saying is it could be Bryce's print. You know as well as I that family members often share the same fingerprint patterns. We've seen it before."

"That's weak, Mike."

"Then how about this. I found the story on their mother's drowning. It wasn't Scott in the boat with her the day she died, it was Bryce."

"Wouldn't be the first time a reporter got it wrong and mixed up the names."

Ryan rifled through the growing pile in the middle of the table. "Is there a photo of the mother?"

"Yeah, and you're not going to believe this." Saunders dropped a blow-up of a newspaper article in front of him.

Anita Stanley was in her thirties, beautiful with long black curly hair, a classical pianist.

Ryan read the article and added it to the pile. "The bastard was killing his own mother over and over again and Freud's in hell doing the happy dance. What else?"

"Why now? He just bought a third of an interest in a successful restaurant and put a down payment on a house. That doesn't sound like someone who wakes up one morning and decides to eat his gun and admit to eight murders. And what about the flowers he sent to Annie? The florist said he was upbeat and completely rational."

"We know he was capable of appearing rational, otherwise he wouldn't have been able to pull off the subterfuge he used with the six women, including my sister. I can't speak for the rest of them but I know Theresa. She was wary of crazies. She was raised by one."

"You said I wanted this too badly, Pete. Maybe you don't want it enough. Maybe you're glad it's over and you can go back and start living your life."

There was more than a grain of truth in his argument and Ryan sat back down. "Make your case, but we'll start with your question first. Why now? Why after twenty years did Bryce Stanley wake up one morning and decide to kill his brother and pin the murders on him?"

Saunders pulled another photograph from the file and put it down in the middle of the table, a photograph of three smiling people entering a restaurant. "Because of her, his next victim. Bryce didn't like that his brother was getting close to her and he had to end it. Maybe he found out about the flowers and decided to eliminate the competition."

"Scott wasn't competition. You're off base there, Mike. I talked to Annie the day after the ruckus at the restaurant. She couldn't stand him, said he was rude and obnoxious."

"That Prescott woman, what's her name. She claimed Annie was sleeping with both brothers. Maybe Bryce believed that too."

"That woman's a nutcase. She was Larry Heywood's fiancée until an hour after she gave that interview when he broke off their engagement and put out a statement saying what she claimed was bullshit. Unfortunately, it never made the major news outlets. Face it, Mike, you got nothing, less than nothing."

"You believe that too, Pete? You willing to walk away from this and take the chance we'll have another dead woman on our hands or are you going to have my back like I had yours? What if it were Marti?"

Low blow but it worked. Ryan picked up the photograph taken outside the restaurant. If they missed something and got it wrong, they owed it to the victims to get it right. "I'll cancel my flight for twenty-four hours on two conditions: one, there's someone I want to consult, the psychiatrist who hypnotized Marti. She profiled a rapist a few months ago and nailed him. If she thinks your case is valid, we take it from there; two, I run the show unofficially, at least until we find out if there's a case against this guy. This has to be handled discreetly and strictly under the radar, nothing official."

Running his hand through his hair, Saunders nodded. "You know my answer. Lou, you in?"

"We're partners, remember? I'm in. When and where do we start?"

"We've been at this all day and it's almost 3 a.m. in the U.K., too late to contact anyone. We start first thing tomorrow morning. I want to know where all the players are. Lou, try to find out if Bryce is still in London or if he's on his way back to the States. Then get in touch with Annie Heywood. You have contact numbers for her, right?"

"She gave me her cell number and her sister's home and cell numbers in London."

"Call her but make it casual. You're checking in, friend to friend. Tell her you're sorry about all the bad press she's getting. See if she mentions Bryce. If she doesn't answer her cell, don't leave a message then try the sister but don't panic her. Give her the same story about checking in. This is about getting information, not ruffling feathers, got it?"

"Got it. I thought of something else. My wife and I were in London a couple years back. We were in a restaurant and started talking with another couple at the table next to us and ended up spending the evening together. We've stayed in touch by email. He rides a desk at Scotland Yard. I'll call him in the morning, shoot the shit about all the excitement, maybe suggest he do some unofficial digging to find out where Bryce is and what he's up to."

"Do it."

With Lou gone, the atmosphere turned grim. Ryan liked Saunders and felt for the guy. The last time he saw a man this miserable over a woman, he was looking in the mirror. "We don't know they're together, Mike."

"He has her. I know it in my gut. He's been after her for weeks. I dropped by her place the Sunday before I left for Seattle and told her I was taking myself off the case, that I couldn't be objective with her in the picture. He called while I was there but she didn't take the call."

"Were you sleeping with her?"

"No, but it was inevitable and we both knew it. She's not that woman, Pete, the one those vultures and the press are making her out to be. She's funny and smart and she worked her butt off to keep the hospice afloat. She's feisty. After the incident with the dead lilies, we had patrols going up and down her lane every hour. One of our patrolmen caught the tail-end of a stand-off between her and her drunken ex. He came by for a little late night nookie and she damn near killed him. The next morning a worker found a check he left for her, a half million dollars. She tore it up. She knows who these guys are, the super-rich. If she's with Bryce, she's not there by choice. I'd bet my life on it."

"You should have made this case two hours ago. Go home and get some sleep. Tomorrow's going to be a long one and it's late."

"That's what's killing me, that maybe it's too late."

CHAPTER 52

ANNIE

Gasping for air, she sat up in bed and fumbled for the bedside light. That couldn't be right. The clock read 3:06 a.m., almost eight hours since she fell asleep. She was groggy and dehydrated and couldn't remember the last time she ate. Not good.

Her valise was on a bench at the foot of the bed. There was almost zero chance Sam remembered her glucose pills but there had to be something edible in the kitchen. When she managed to stand without falling over, she looked around for the robe she pilfered from the bathroom but it was gone. Rummaging through the valise, she found a robe if one could call it that, a Fredericks of Hollywood number with half a yard of silk and lace where modesty should be. It would have to do. She needed a shower and food and then she needed to plan her escape route back to London.

The house was quiet as she made her way toward the staircase. Behind her, Bryce's door was closed and she breathed a sigh of relief. The last thing she wanted was another encounter like yesterday's. He was angry with her, angry and frustrated, and she didn't blame him, but the high-handed way he got her there still ticked her off.

Downstairs, she saw the flicker of a television and followed the light. It was coming from the library, the very same library where she used a phone to call Samantha. At the far end of the room, a flat screen TV was mounted on the wall. A Chesterfield sofa was positioned in front of it, its back to the door. Bryce was sitting at one end, leaning forward, elbows on his knees. She stood just outside, out of sight.

On the screen, Mike Saunders was responding to a question posed by the host of the program.

Yes, I know Miss Heywood and I'm glad you asked me about her because there are a number of allegations concerning her that need to be addressed. To begin with, she was never involved with Scott Stanley. In fact, it was Annie who first brought him to our attention in connection with the disappearance of Debra Couillard and the murder of Helen Allen. She's been tireless in her efforts to get the authorities involved in this case. Furthermore...

The screen went to black.

"Let me ask you something, Annie. Aside from my brother, is there anyone in Connecticut you haven't fucked? I know you're there, I can smell you. Strawberries and soap. Isn't that what Miranda smelled on your ex? And the detective. He's in love with you too, isn't he? I don't blame them, by the way, you're addictive. You're beautiful and clever, very clever, and you have the little girl lost routine down to a science. I was a sitting duck. You figured the best way to nail Scott was through me and you were right. What was it he just said, tireless in her efforts? He has no idea or does he? Are you still working with him, Annie? Are you still playing me?"

She backed up, wanting to explain but knowing if she tried, he wouldn't listen. Her legs turned to water as she climbed the staircase. Hearing him behind her, she started running. He caught the hem of the robe and she lost her footing on the carpet runner. Falling forward, she used her hands to cushion the fall, her wrist throbbing as she continued upward. And then he was on top of her, grabbing her around the waist, lifting her up. She kicked, her feet finding nothing but air. He opened the door to his room, dropped her on the bed and walked back to lock the door.

"Don't do this, Bryce, please." Her throat closed up with a new surge of tears. "I know you're angry but I can explain."

"Undercover work has its hazards, sweetheart. It won't be as much fun for you this time but I'm going to enjoy the hell out of it."

She got to her hands and knees. "Is this your idea of protecting me? Ask me anything and I'll tell you but don't do this."

Still fully-clothed, he started toward her. She was scrambling off the bed when he grabbed her ankle, flipped her over and pulled her back. The robe fell open and his eyes ran the length of her body. She pulled the robe closed and wiped at her tears. When she saw his hand moving toward her face, she flinched and turned her head.

Her reaction startled him. "You think I'm going to hit you? Jesus, Annie, I'm not my brother."

"And I'm not that person, the one you accused me of being."

"I don't know who the hell you are. Just when I think I have you figured out, I get another curveball thrown at me. You're like poison. Every minute I'm with you, you get deeper into my system."

"Then take me back to London. You said yourself the death threat was probably a hoax. Have them drop me at a hotel and I'll stay there until they find whoever's behind it. I'll pay you back the money you're spending on my behalf, I swear I will."

"Is that what you want? Look at me, is that what you want?"

"Yes, but first I want you to stop yelling at me and let me explain. I've never played you. I went to the police and told them about Scott after the incident at the restaurant. And then when I received his flowers…"

"What flowers? Scott sent you flowers?"

"He sent me roses in a Miyagi sculpture."

"Les Visages? That was his favorite piece. Was there a card?"

"Yes, but I can't remember what it said, something about a jealous lover. It was signed the good-looking brother."

"And you thought he was coming after you? Why didn't you tell me any of this?"

"You're his brother. I didn't know you, not like I know you now. I tried to tell you earlier before you took that call. What else do you want to know? I haven't been with Larry in over a year. The night he came to my house things got physical but I fought him off. I was taking a bath when he came to the door so I'm sure Miranda did smell me on him."

She didn't know how to describe Mike. A lifetime ago, she thought there might be hope for them but Scott destroyed that dream too. Despite what he said in the interview, he would never trust her and she couldn't fault him for that. "Mike Saunders and I are friends, nothing more. You're the only man I've been with since my divorce."

"I heard you in the shower when I brought the tea. You were hysterical. I wanted to pull you out and comfort you, but I decided to let you cry it out. Was that a delayed reaction from being brought here or something else?"

"That's one question you can't ask."

"Then I'll ask another one. Do you love me?"

"I don't know."

"Are you afraid of me, is that why you want to go?"

"It's what I do, I run away. I've put my feelings on hold for so long, I don't trust them. They're like demons I keep at bay. What you witnessed in the shower was my pathetic attempt at an exorcism. There's a piece missing inside me, the piece that knows how to be happy. Sometimes I feel if I could just explode maybe the pieces would come back together the way they're supposed to."

"And Sunday, what was that?"

"It was sex. You have to let me go, Bryce. I can't breathe."

His hand found its way inside her robe and cupped her breast. "You're breathing pretty well now."

She pushed his hand away. "I can't do this."

"You can and you will, right now, you and me in this room. You've been fighting me since the day you walked into my office, so go ahead and give it your best shot. I can take it. You can scream and cry as much as you need to but whatever's bottled up inside and making you afraid needs to come out so we can move forward. I love you, you know that, but there's only room in our relationship for two people. Your demons have to go."

She slapped him hard across the face. "And you have the nerve to call me clever, you manipulative bastard. You've found a way to turn rape into therapy. That's sick."

"Good, now we're getting somewhere. This isn't about sex, Annie. This is about something much more intimate. It's about honesty. Demons hate that. They thrive off the lies we tell ourselves."

"What are you, some kind of genetic freak, a man who wants to talk about feelings or is psychotherapy a hobby?"

He moved across the bed and fluffed the pillows, locked his arms behind his head and closed his eyes. "That's an old-fashioned lock on the door. You use a key to get in and out and I have it. Wake me when you're ready to start talking."

Unless he'd grabbed a nap while she was sleeping, he had to be exhausted. Within minutes, his face relaxed and his breathing deepened. With as much stealth as possible, she slid off the bed and padded to the door, the thick carpeting beneath her feet absorbing all sound. The knob turned but the door held. The only other possibility was the window across the room and she made a bee-line for it. Pulling back the edge of the drape, she saw that the window was open but not enough to wiggle through. There was a small balcony outside and she pushed the window open to take a better look.

"We're two floors up so don't even think about it."

She let the drape fall back in place and turned to face him. "This isn't going to work no matter how long you keep me locked up. I don't want a relationship."

"I don't want a relationship either. I want a life, preferably with you. You're a complicated woman, Annie, and you'll probably be the death of me but I'm willing to risk it."

"Trust me, you don't want me. I'm poison, remember?"

"Then what do you want, sex? At least there's one room in the house where I know I can satisfy you."

"You're pretty sure of yourself. How do you know I wasn't faking it?"

He laughed. "Sweetheart, any man who claims he can't tell the real thing from a fake shouldn't be allowed to procreate."

Twenty years ago, she heard the same thing from Lucas. On the one occasion when she tried to trick him and make him eat his words, he knew and he wasn't amused.

"You can start by telling me who hurt you. Was it the same person who gave you those scars?"

"No one gave them to me. Before my senior year in college, I was backpacking through Italy and I slipped down a craggy hill."

"That must have been some sight, you backpacking through Italy naked. I'm guessing someone used a belt on you. What I want to know is why."

"I'm tired, Bryce. I want to go back to my room."

"You slept for almost eight hours."

"I know and I don't understand it. I always have trouble falling asleep. Did you put something in the tea?"

"A mild tranquilizer. I had work to do and I can't concentrate when you're around."

"You had me abducted and you drugged me? I could have you arrested."

"You do that, just as soon as we get out of here. Perhaps I didn't make myself clear. We're not leaving this room until we figure a few things out." He patted the space next to him. "You're shivering and white as a sheet. I won't lay a hand on you unless you want me to. Pinky promise."

It was an offer she couldn't refuse. The bed was inviting and she was freezing. When she tried to keep some distance between them, he put his arm around her and pulled her close. "Body heat. Now start talking."

"You said some horrible things to me downstairs. Maybe we should talk about that."

"Maybe we should. I'm more sorry than you'll ever know and I'll spend the rest of my life making it up to you, but that's what happens when you shut people out and don't trust them enough to be honest with them."

"You can't make me talk, Bryce, so we might as well have sex."

"I'm beginning to understand why someone would use a belt on your ass." She tensed but he held her and kissed the top of her head. "Tell me some things I don't know about you."

Safe ground. "I read Nietzsche and Schopenhauer for kicks. My favorite rock group is Queen and I know the lyrics to all their songs. I believe in God but I think organized religion will destroy us all. I drink my coffee black, wine gives me a headache and I smoke a joint several times a year. Now you know more about me than my mother."

"Who taught you about sex?"

"Is that a critique?"

"It's a compliment. I've been around, Annie, and I've never been with any woman more comfortable with her body or more accomplished at giving and receiving pleasure. You look innocent, like you walked off the page of a children's book but that little body of yours tells a different story."

"I was married for seventeen years, remember?"

"You were married to someone whose priorities were making money and abusing alcohol. Were you faithful to him?"

Yes, I was faithful to him. I was tempted a couple of times but I could never go through with it. Were you faithful to Sybil?"

"God, no. When the boys left for boarding school, our favorite pastime was hurling our infidelities at each other. The only difference is I preferred away games and she liked playing the home field. I'm surprised you never heard the rumors. I thought everyone in Greenwich was in on the joke."

"I was never part of the in-crowd. That was Larry's domain."

Suddenly very tired, she turned toward him and put her hand on his chest. If she closed her eyes, she could almost believe she was lying next to Lucas. They were similar in many ways, their bodies, the way they looked at her, even the way they tried to plumb her emotions and get inside her head.

He took her hand off his chest and kissed her palm. "You weren't going to see me again, were you?"

"No, I was going to run again. There was someone I cared about a long time ago and you remind me of him. It ended badly. Trust is a funny thing. When it's destroyed, it takes a lot of people down with it."

Instead of responding, he rolled toward her and took both her hands in one of his and stretched them over her head. He secured her legs with his knee and held her face with his free hand. It happened so fast, her eyes went wide. When his mouth came down on hers, she closed her eyes.

He pulled back. "Open your eyes, Annie. When you're in my bed, you're with me, not Markham."

She turned her face away and chose her words carefully, hoping to inflict the most amount of pain possible. "At least your brother was honest with me. You're nothing but a fraud and a liar."

He let her go but when she tried to sit up, the room was spinning, colors blending into one another. In slow motion, she managed to get her feet to the carpet, her legs like rubber when she tried to stand. She was burning up one minute, freezing cold the next. She needed water. The bathroom was to the right and the door was open. She looked behind her, certain he was following her but he was standing at the window, staring into the night. Sinking to her knees, she crawled inside the bathroom and used the sink to help her stand. The woman in the mirror frightened her and she looked away. The water was cold, but when she tried to bring the glass to her lips her hand couldn't hold it and it slid to the marble floor.

Someone was holding her head, talking to her, angry that she wouldn't look at him. "Open your eyes and try to focus. You're cold as ice. Your glucose pills, baby, where are they? Annie!"

CHAPTER 53

RYAN

Saunders set the carrier of coffees on the conference room table and raised an eyebrow. "Remind me again why we're meeting here and not the police station?"

Thumbing through the files in his attaché case, Ryan threw him a look. "Two reasons, three if you include the fact it's not the police station. We're working under the radar, remember? How long do you think it would be before someone started nosing around and questioning why I'm still here and you're still obsessing over the Stanley case instead of dogging your active cases? It's a five-minute drive if you need something and the hotel gave me a good rate for the use of a conference room for the day."

"I'm sure they did. The last time this conference room was used, Benedict Arnold was planning his attack on New London." He took a seat at one end of the table and powered up his laptop. "They have Wi-Fi, I'm shocked."

"And a speakerphone. Did you remember to call Lou?"

"He's here. I passed him in the parking lot. Dickson left town. I called his home early this morning and got their pet-sitter. He and the missus took a last-minute trip to Puerto Vallarta."

"Which means they wanted to ditch the crummy weather here and work on their tans. It doesn't prove he destroyed evidence."

"Let's get the shrink on the phone. We can bring Lou up to speed when he gets here. I know it's early there but maybe we'll get lucky."

"She's an early riser and usually in the office by seven."

"Do I want to know how you know that?"

"You definitely don't."

The phone rang several times before Dr. Sophia Cummings finally answered. "Sophia, it's Pete Ryan. We have a situation here and we could use your expertise. Are you with a patient?"

"Today's paperwork day so no patients. Congratulations, by the way. I saw you on CNN. I'm glad it's over, Pete, for your sake and for the sake of the families. Where are you?"

"I'm still in Connecticut. You're on speakerphone with Mike Saunders, the detective I've been working with. He did the interview with me. His partner Lou Robinson will be joining us shortly."

"How can I help?"

"How much do you know about Scott Stanley? Have you been keeping up with the case?"

"I've read everything I can get my hands on, particularly since I've been on the fringe of the case."

"In your professional opinion, does he fit the profile of our serial killer?"

"He's textbook, a loner, never married, estranged from his family, arrogant, narcissistic, erratic when it comes to his professional life and with enough time and money at his disposal to find, seduce and murder his victims."

"Any hypothesis on what might have pushed him over the edge to take his own life and confess to the murders?"

"Weren't there some recent articles about the Canadian woman's disappearance that precipitated the murder of the older woman? Prior to that, he'd been operating in total obscurity for twenty years. If he believed the noose was tightening, that would be motivation enough."

"What about the confession?"

"People leave confessions for any number of reasons. As their final act, some like reliving the details of their crimes, some do it as a way of giving resolution and seeking forgiveness and some do it to embarrass the ones they leave behind. Each case is different."

"There was an altercation in a restaurant the night before involving Scott, his brother Bryce and Bryce's date. Evidently Scott said something and the woman spilled wine on him and ran from the restaurant. Bryce went after her."

"Do you know what he said that made her react that way?"

"According to Annie Heywood, Scott knew a lot about Mrs. Allen's death but she didn't elaborate."

"Annie Heywood, why do I know that name?"

"She's had a lot of bad press, particularly here on the east coast because of her involvement with Bryce and because Scott sent her flowers the day of his suicide."

"I know who she is. Didn't one of her friends claim she was sleeping with both brothers and pitting them against one another?"

"The woman who said that is no friend. She was the fiancée of Annie's ex-husband. He's since dumped her and repudiated her comments."

"I heard about the flowers. Do we know if there was a card and what it said?"

"It's here somewhere. *I am a jealous lover. I deny her release for I fear the place to which she escapes.* It's signed the good-looking brother. That sounds like a confession to me, maybe a threat?"

"There's something familiar about that. Read it again, Pete."

He reread it and waited.

"I found it. *I am a jealous lover. I deny her release for I fear the place to which she escapes. She knows this and taunts me. Quivering beneath me, she arches her back and offers her throat, lips parted, pink and swollen from my kiss, eyes flutter, pleading, and in that time and place the delusion is mine — that I am in control.*"

"What the hell is that? It sounds like fifty shades of bullshit."

"It's a quote from Lucas Markham's latest book. Annie Heywood's full name is Annabelle Hogan Heywood, isn't it?"

"Yeah, why, and what does any of this have to do with the flowers Scott sent her?"

"Scott used only the first two sentences of a longer quote. It may have been his way of letting her know he knew who she was."

"Who she was? What does that mean?"

"Markham dedicated his book to her. He was one of her professors at Kent State. They lived together for a month when he was thirty-eight and she was nineteen. It was tempestuous, to say the least."

"It sounds like he held her against his will. What's all the stuff about pleading and release, being in control?"

"You need to get out more, Pete."

"Very funny."

"Maybe Marti and I can arrange a movie night for you."

"Stop corrupting my woman. I like her the way she is."

"Smart man. Markham's a sexual dominant. He's referring to her climax. She's his submissive, at least he thinks she is. The reality is she has him wrapped around her little finger. She goes along with the game because she loves him and she knows he loves her but the ball is always in her court."

"Are you talking about S&M?"

"S&M is about pain. Dominance and submission is about pleasure, about trust and pushing limits. He never hurt her until their last night together when she refused his marriage proposal and he beat her badly."

"All this is in a book?"

"*Breaking Annabelle.* It's been number one on the New York Times Bestseller list for weeks. Annie sounds interesting, a woman I'd like to know better."

"Join the club."

"What was that, I didn't catch it?"

"That was Mike editorializing."

"That's right, you know her, Detective. You were very gracious about her in that interview. I'm sure she appreciated it."

"If she's still alive."

Silent until now, Saunders appeared to Ryan like a man going down for the count. That he believed her to be in danger was bad enough but the revelation about her past clearly sucker-punched him. "You need a break, Mike?"

"I'm good. Let's finish this."

"Any chance it was the book that pushed Scott over the edge, Sophia?"

"I don't see how. Other than its titillation factor, I think it's irrelevant. I'm more interested in Scott's relationship with his brother. I haven't seen him interviewed. Were they close?"

"According to the people we've talked to, they were anything but close. Their parents divorced when they were young and the boys were split up, one to each parent. They had almost nothing in common but the name. Bryce is the youngest but turned out to be the responsible one, forty-eight, divorced with twin sons at Oxford. He's a lawyer but he also runs the family businesses since his father's death. He's Ivy League, rich as Croesus. Scott was the black sheep, the one who could never get it together. He lived off his trust fund."

"Then I think you've answered your own questions about the timing of his suicide and why he left the confession. It's possible the incident in the restaurant was the coup de grace. His brother is everything he isn't and this time he also gets the girl.

"Scott's life was motivated by seducing women and making himself irresistible to them. Annie rejected him in a public display, and to top it off, she went home with his brother. If he were already predisposed to taking his own life because he knew the authorities were closing in, the confession was his way of exacting revenge on his brother by sullying the family name."

"I don't believe a word of it."

"Excuse me?"

"You heard me. I think it's all bullshit and exactly what Bryce wants everyone to believe."

"I thought the case was closed, Pete."

"It is but Mike has a different take on things. Do you have time to hear him out?"

"I'll be happy to hear him out. What's your theory, Detective?"

"I think Bryce Stanley set the whole thing up, the suicide, the confession, all of it. I think he fixated on Annie as his next victim and wanted his brother out of the picture. Either that or he found out she knows a lot about the case and got close to her to see how much she knows. He's been after her for weeks, ever since she went to his office to inquire about Bert Kennedy, the dead property manager."

"So there are really two issues here. Is Bryce Stanley the serial killer and is Annie in danger either as a serial victim or potential threat."

"Bingo."

"Before I can make any sense out of any of this, I need to learn as much about her as I can. You seem to know her well, Detective. Tell me about her."

Ryan spoke up. "I'm sure you've seen her photograph. It was all over the networks, the one of her, her sister and Bryce outside a restaurant in London Saturday night."

"I may have seen it, Pete, but I don't recall it specifically."

"I have it on my computer, doctor. Give me your email address and I'll send it over."

She gave it to him and excused herself to take a call.

She was still on the call when Lou walked in the conference room. "Sorry about that. It's colder than a witch's tit out there. I've been trying Annie since early this morning but no dice. All the calls went to voicemail. I finally connected with her sister, Samantha. She knew who I was so I made small talk before asking how her sister was holding up. She's with Bryce. She went out for a run yesterday and he surprised her by picking her up. She called Samantha an hour later and asked her to pack a bag for her for a few days, that someone would be round to fetch it for her. Annie said she'd be in touch but Samantha hasn't heard from her."

Saunders slammed his laptop closed. "The sonofabitch has her. I knew it."

"It's Lou, correct, the detective who spoke to Annie's sister?"

The three men turned back toward the speaker phone. "Yes, ma'am, this is Lou Robinson."

"Hi, Lou, I'm Sophia. Did Annie's sister say how she sounded when she called her and asked her to pack a bag?"

"She said she sounded tired but happy."

"Thanks, Lou. Sorry for the interruption. You're up, Detective. You were telling me about Annie. The email still hasn't come through but tell me about her, who is she? I assume she's unmarried."

"She's divorced, lives alone with her dog."

"Is she involved in the Arts like the other victims?"

"Not that I know of. She had an interior design business for awhile but I never got the feeling it was her choice. She founded an AIDS hospice with another woman in 2010, Life House. There's a website. She's a pain in the ass, quick on her feet. Nothing gets by her. That's why I don't understand this. She's smart, at least I thought she was."

"I don't like your tone, Detective."

"What does my tone have to do with anything?"

"You're implying female victims are somehow mentally deficient, that they lack some psychological prescience. Whoever Charles turns out to be, he's good-looking, educated, with enough time and money available to him that he can do whatever it takes to get them under his control. Are you married, Detective?"

"Divorced. Why?"

"I'm sorry about your divorce but obviously something went wrong in your relationship and one of you was not the person the other thought they were. Whether one is a PhD or a drag queen in the Castro, no one asks for it."

"You're right, I was off base. I have a daughter and I'd kill the person who second-guessed her."

"And I'd help you. I'm looking at the photograph now. Annie's on the left, the one with the short hair, correct?"

"Yes."

"She's lovely but…"

"But what?"

"She looked familiar for a moment. It's nothing, really. He's in love with her."

"And you know that how?"

"His body language for one thing, the way he has his arm around her. He's announcing to the world that she's his and he'll protect her at all costs. It's also written all over his face. The last time a man looked at me like that was the night my ex-husband proposed."

"Is that a professional opinion?"

"It's my opinion as a professional and a woman. Physically, she doesn't fit the archetype of his other victims either. Her hair is very short and blonde, although I think one of his victims was blonde, am I right, Pete?"

"Morgan Evans, the sculptor. What else?"

"She's compassionate, a trait he would find simpatico with his own philanthropy. She's beautiful, smart and feisty, all the things that complement him, things he would find appealing in a mate, not a victim. This isn't an exact science, gentlemen, but I'll stake my professional reputation on the fact he's madly in love with her."

"I think you're right and the tip-off is the sister. Charles isolated his victims from their friends and family. Here he's on the town with Annie and her sister. I've talked to most of the family members of the other victims, and I'm including myself in this. We all shared one thing, bad vibes about him based on what we were told."

"Lou, when you were talking to her sister, did you get any sense of how she feels about Bryce?"

"I didn't ask specifically, but I didn't get the feeling there was any animosity toward him."

Ryan felt the vibration of his cellphone and checked his watch. There were two calls and two new voicemails, both from Marti. "What about your friend at Scotland Yard. Did you reach him?"

"Bright and early this morning. He'll do some digging and call me back."

"Okay, let's regroup here for a minute. If I'm hearing you right, Sophia, you're ruling out serial victim."

"Actually, I'm ruling out serial victim and potential threat. If he thought she were a threat, why not kill her like he did the Allen woman? He's shown no compunction about getting rid of potential witnesses. If he were going to eliminate her, he would have done it before the entire world knew they were involved and when he could have included her death in the written confession. In my opinion, that makes an even stronger case for Annie being the real deal for him. Detective, are you still with us?"

"I'm still here. For the sake of argument, let's say he is in love with her. He could still be Charles and that's the reason he had to murder his brother and set him up to take the fall for the murders. He's closing the door on one life and opening the door on another. What would you say?"

Lou's cell phone rang. "That's my buddy calling back. I'll take it outside."

"Well, doctor?"

"What would I say? I'd say you should be writing screenplays."

"Then explain this. He has offices in Greenwich, Palo Alto and Santa Fe. The house in Westport is a twenty minute from his Greenwich office. Rachel's home in Boulder and Morgan's home in Tonto Hills is a two-hour flight by plane. Ellie's home in Templeton and Theresa's home in Cambria? Three hours by car from his Palo Alto office. Susan Pierce's home is forty-five minutes from Palo Alto."

"Now you're reaching, Detective."

"Cops reach, Doc. It's what we do. It was a reach to stake out Scott's house and yet, here we are."

"Point taken."

Looking like he went three rounds with a Mack truck, Lou walked back in the room. "You're not going to like this. Bryce is thirty minutes outside of London on an estate owned by the Spaulding family. The family's wintering in Vail. There was a report on file. Some country doctor called them to report he'd been hauled out of bed a little after two by someone claiming to work for Bryce Stanley. He found Annie passed out on the bathroom floor. One of his sons is hypoglycemic and he recognized the signs. Turns out her blood sugar levels were low, she was dehydrated and suffering from anemia. The doctor put her on an I.V., got some glucose into her and shot her full of B12."

"Screw this, we're wasting time." Mike was on his feet.

"Lou, Sophia here. I assume she was conscious or he would have hospitalized her. Did the report mention why the doctor called it in to Scotland Yard?"

"He recognized Bryce Stanley but couldn't remember from where. The guy's a hundred years old. He thinks every rich American is mafia. He knew the Spauldings were out of the country and here's this strange guy living in their house with a gang of bodyguards. Bryce didn't try to conceal his identity and gave the doctor a thousand pounds for his trouble. The inspector who took the call thanked the doctor and filed it away."

"Do we have the name of the doctor?"

"I just got off the phone with him. He said she reminded him of his grand-daughter. She was nude, lying in this big bed. When he turned back the sheets to examine her, she was bruised up and down her body. Bryce told him she took a fall down the stairs earlier in the day. She had some cuts on her from where she fell on a broken glass."

"Did the doctor talk to Annie?"

"He said she was pretty out of it, but she told him she hadn't been taking care of herself and it was all her fault."

"Jesus, what is it going to take with you people? For all we know, he threatened her and told her what to say or maybe he slipped her something to make her compliant."

"Mike, you know as well as I do, that girl's a hellion. I told you what she did to Gary Matthews. He outweighed her by a hundred pounds and she brought him to his knees and didn't even break a sweat. When that girl gets her Irish up, you don't want to be anywhere near her."

"Then maybe she fought back. You should have asked him if the bruising was consistent with a fall or…"

"Or what, Detective?"

"You know what I'm talking about, rape or rough sex."

"Pete, I have another call coming in and I have to take it. Can I call you back in five minutes? I have your number on my caller I.D."

"Sure." Almost immediately his cell phone vibrated. He checked the display. "I'll take this outside. I need some air." When he was outside the building, he hit the talk button. "I'm outside where they can't hear me."

"You know exactly what I'm going to say."

"He's a good cop, Sophia."

"He's a man first, a man with an agenda. That makes him a dangerous cop."

"I need an answer, Sophia. From what you know of Bryce Stanley, is there any possibility Mike's theory holds water and he's our serial killer?"

"Pete, all I can tell you is he isn't even close to fitting the profile. Based on what you told me, there's nothing in his personal or professional life that would raise any red flags. Charles lacked empathy. I doubt he was capable of love. Women were a means to an end, a way to satisfy some betrayal or resentment he's been harboring most of his life."

"It's his mother. I saw a photograph of her. The resemblance to five of the six women is uncanny. She was a classical pianist. Speaking of photographs, let's talk about the one of them outside the restaurant. You saw something and when Mike called you on it, you covered it by saying you thought you recognized her. What was that about?"

"You don't miss much, do you?"

"What did you see?"

"It's just a gut feeling but I don't think she wanted to be there. Her sister and Bryce were smiling like they were enjoying themselves but Annie's smile seemed almost obligatory, for lack of a better word."

"Her sister is a celebrity. Maybe she felt awkward with the paparazzi hovering around."

"I'm sure that's it. What are you going to do, Pete?"

"I'm going back inside and tell them I'm done, and then I'm going to the hotel and turn off the phones until the airport shuttle picks me up in time to make the red-eye."

"I mean about Mike. He's not going to let this go. He's obsessed with her. Someone better keep him hosed down and on a very short leash."

He was almost home free, ten feet from the conference room door when his cell phone vibrated. He was tempted to let it go to voicemail but at the last minute checked the display. "You must be reading my mind. I was just thinking of you. We're about to wrap this up. I'll call you back when...."

"Pete, Jimmy's here. He needs to talk to you."

The panic in Marti's voice stopped him in his tracks. The next voice he heard was Jimmy's.

"I'm sending you a photo via text. A crime scene tech found it this morning tucked into one of Theresa's notebooks from the box taken at Turk's. There were over a hundred and this was in the second to last."

It was a black and white photograph, a Polaroid judging from the white border, a close-up of a man dozing. It was Scott Stanley, except it wasn't. There were subtle differences but the one that made him break out in a cold sweat was the scar above the left eyebrow he remembered from his website.

"Who knows about this, Jimmy?"

"No one yet."

"Make sure it stays that way. You have to trust me on this and keep it under wraps. If the press finds out, we'll have another dead woman on our hands. He has Annie Heywood isolated on an estate outside of London with a small army of bodyguards."

"Jesus Christ. I'll give you forty-eight hours and then I have to take it to the Chief. In the meantime, I never saw it. What can I do from my end?"

"I'll let you know. Put Marti on."

"Pete, did I hear right, Annie's with him? You're going after him, aren't you?"

"I don't have a choice. Book me on the first available flight from New York to London."

"What about Mike?"

Sophia's words echoed in his ears but were drowned out by a louder voice. *What if it were Marti?*

"Book one for him too. Call me when you have the flight details."

"I'm on it. What else do you want me to do?"

"Start researching honeymoon destinations, preferably those that guarantee sun but without internet or television."

CHAPTER 54

ANNIE

Still damp from a bath, Annie turned off the tap at the sink and cocked her head. When she heard the knock again, she grabbed a towel and knotted it between her breasts. "It's all right, I'm decent."

"What are you doing out of bed?"

"I feel much better. I've been up for hours and even scrambled some eggs. I'm a little stiff, but oddly enough the only thing that hurts is my tush. Are you sure that doctor wasn't a large animal vet? It was a very big needle."

"He gave you two shots of B12."

An awkward silence followed and she lowered her eyes. "I'm sorry about last night. I overreacted." When she looked up at him, his eyes were fixed on her. There was a sadness there she hadn't seen before, a vulnerability. "Thank you for sitting with me until I fell asleep. Your door was closed when I went downstairs to the kitchen. I hope you got a few hours sleep."

"Several hours actually. I'm flying to Bellingham this afternoon. A chopper will pick me up in an hour and take me to the airport. I've left instructions that you be taken back to Samantha's tomorrow morning. Two of the men behind the death threat are in custody and they have a lead on the third. You'll have round the clock protection until he's apprehended."

"You're not coming back?"

"I'm flying directly to Connecticut from there. You're free. I thought that's what you wanted."

Twenty-four hours ago, she wanted nothing more than to repeat her pattern and run back to London, but the thought of returning to a throng of press scrutinizing every corner of her life wasn't as appealing today. For whatever reason, it was clear he didn't want her there alone. A hotel was still an option, but if the press got wind of it, she was no better off than at Samantha's. Also clear was the fact he was dismissing her, damn cheeky considering he'd dragged her there against her will. "Toys aren't much fun when they're broken, are they?"

"You can't possibly believe I'm doing this because you're sick or I've thought of you as a plaything."

"I don't know what to think. I'm not sick. I have two common, very controllable issues I've been neglecting."

He unfastened the towel and turned her around in front of a full-length mirror. "Look at yourself. Look at what I did to you."

She was bruised from head to toe, her wrist wrapped in a skin-colored bandage with faded orange antiseptic splotches on her arms and legs.

"I know the exact moment when I gave you every one of those bruises. The ones on your legs are from when you fell on the stairs trying to get away from me, and the ones around your waist from when I yanked you off the stairs."

"Bruising is common in people with anemia. I fell on the glass. It's not like you pushed me."

"Didn't I? I knew you were hypoglycemic. You told me the day you came to my office. Instead of playing mind games, I should have been taking care of you."

"I don't want you taking care of me. I'm not your bloody ward."

"Maybe I should send you back to Markham for more training. You're as submissive as a pit bull."

She threw up her hands. "Markham again. Why can't you let it go?"

"Why can't you? Watching you sleep, I had a lot of time to think and even identified one of your demons. He must be sitting in Ireland laughing his ass off. Even after twenty years, he's still dominating you."

"What are you talking about?"

"You're still in contact with him, aren't you? He knew you were filing for divorce."

"Yes, but…"

"When was the book released, Annie? How long after your divorce was final?"

"Less than a month, why?"

"That was no coincidence. As long as you were with Larry, Markham knew he had no competition, but he couldn't stand the idea of you finding happiness with someone else. He was counting on the fact that once you knew about the book, you'd be paranoid about letting another man in your life. We'd all be suspect. You knew it would bring out all kinds of men, the assholes like my brother who embrace the lifestyle and the ones who just want to bed the hottest little piece of ass this side of the Pecos. Why do you think you reacted like you did when I mentioned Markham's name?"

"Because I thought you lied to me. This has nothing to do with a few bruises. You can't get past the book. How long have you known about it?"

"Since yesterday afternoon. It was on Spaulding's desk. I must have moved the fucking thing six times before I finally picked it up and looked at it. I had no idea, Annie, and that's the truth. I don't like Markham's stuff. I read *Sojourner* and thought it was a pile of shit."

"I know, I typed it from his handwritten notes. Why didn't you just tell me you knew about it? Why were you baiting me with all those questions?"

"Because I wanted you to tell me about it, to let me in. I needed to know if there was something you needed, something I wasn't giving you, that you'd trust me enough to ask for it. After I read the book, I went on-line and did some research. Some of the most powerful and talented women in the world are submissive in the bedroom, the one place they don't have to worry about being in control."

"I've had the tutorial but thanks for the refresher course. That was his thing, not mine. We were together eight hours on Sunday. Since you've done your homework, was there ever a moment when I behaved like a…"

"Submissive? Frankly, I was more concerned with not having a heart attack, but in retrospect, no. The truth is, I don't give a damn what you are. We're good together."

"What do you want from me, Bryce?"

"Everything, and in return I'll give you the world. Come with me. Let's blow this mausoleum. I'm chartering a private jet and it will take us anywhere we want to go."

"What's in Bellingham?"

"There's a boat company there I've been trying to buy for five years. The owner emailed me and said he was ready to sell. I have to go before he changes his mind."

"I didn't know you were into boats."

"I'm not into boats. I'm into selling boats. I own a boat company in Newport which was where I was supposed to be last weekend, remember? Right now, all we manufacture is a line of wooden sloops. The company in Washington makes catboats, beautiful catboats. I want his company. Samantha's opening isn't for another week and I promise to have you back for it. I'll wrap the business part up in a couple of hours and then we'll go somewhere for a few days, somewhere off the beaten path."

"Bellingham is near the Canadian border, isn't it?"

"About as close as you can get, why?"

"I read about a place called Shawnigan Lake on Vancouver Island and looked it up on-line. It's remote and very pretty, about forty-five minutes from Victoria by car. There are several B&Bs on the lake and I doubt we'll be recognized."

"Make sure they have big beds and room service."

Her expression must have betrayed her because he placed his hands on her shoulders. "Separate rooms?"

"Separate beds will be fine."

"Whatever you want, you call the shots. Whoever that asshole was who made an appearance last night, he's gone. Besides, if my master plan works, I'll have a lifetime to make love to you."

"You may as well know I have an ulterior motive for wanting to go to Vancouver Island."

"As long as it's not an old lover, I'm good with it."

"No old lovers." When he dropped his hands, she turned toward the sink. If she was going to lie, she didn't want to look him in the eye when she did it. He deserved better than that. He also deserved a break from any reminder of his brother's victims. "It's a girlfriend, actually more like a pen pal. We met on-line and found we had a lot in common. I promised if I were ever in her neck of the woods, I'd drop by to meet her in person. An hour should do it."

***

Annie opened her eyes to find the sun streaming through their windows and a smiling Bryce sitting on the edge of her bed. That he was staring at her was disconcerting enough but the extreme change in weather was weird to say the least, happily so. Not twelve hours ago, they arrived at the B&B amid a downpour of Biblical proportions, her worst fear realized, that despite the separate beds they'd be cooped up together with nowhere to escape.

The chartered plane was barely off the ground when she had second thoughts about her decision to dodge the press by accompanying him. It was a reprise of the cab ride except this time they were thirty thousand feet above the ground and a course correction wasn't in the cards. Why she refused his offer to return her to Samantha's flat was another mistake she could add to the ever-growing list. Another decision 'made on the fly' as Mike would say, this one not as successful as the others. *Mike.*

"Penny for your thoughts."

Ignoring the bait, she sat up, pulled the blankets over her breasts and followed her nose to the nightstand separating their beds and the two large Styrofoam containers. "Is that coffee? How long have you been up?"

"Long enough to shower, answer a dozen emails, finalize the boat deal and forage coffee for my caffeine-addicted woman. I even managed to bring the sunshine."

"So what you're saying is I'm a slacker."

"A total slacker, and I love it. I also solved a mystery, one that's been bugging me for weeks. Remember when you were in my office and I said you looked familiar?"

"I thought we decided it was because of my resemblance to Samantha."

"It was a party at the Bishops, seven or eight years ago. It was the hair that threw me. It was long and pulled back off your face in a ponytail at the nape of your neck. You wore no jewelry except a watch, very little make-up and you looked like you wanted to be anywhere but there. I thought you were someone's daughter who wandered in from a sorority meeting."

"I remember that party. It was around Thanksgiving and bitterly cold. I walked outside to get some air and saw an elderly man in a wheelchair looking up at the sky. He was all bundled up. It turned out he was the father of our host and he liked to sit outside at night. I went over to introduce myself and we started talking. He was so sweet. I don't know how long I was out there, but I got chilled and all of a sudden this man walked up behind me and threw his jacket over my shoulders. I turned around to thank him but the light from the terrace was in my eyes and I couldn't see him. When I finally went back inside, I tried to find someone without a jacket but no one knew who it was so I left it with the hosts. That was you?"

"By the time I rejoined the party Sybil was already getting drunk and hitting on the bartender, so we left. I never did get the chance to ask who you were."

"I wanted to get up and thank you but he was holding my hand so tightly, I couldn't leave him like that."

"I wonder what would have happened if we'd met that night."

"Nothing would have happened. We were both married." She hugged her knees to her chest beneath the blankets. "Bryce, about the sleeping arrangements…"

"You're calling the shots, remember? This might surprise you, but I love you just as much out of bed as I do when I'm inside you. But if you don't stop biting your lip and looking at me with those sleepy, bedroom eyes, we could both be in trouble. It's a good thing I have a conference call in thirty minutes."

"And I have a friend to visit. I'll jump in the shower and be out of your hair while you make your call."

"Do you know where she lives?"

"I do and she's only a mile or so from here. I asked at the General Store across the way while you were registering yesterday. I figured there couldn't be that many Jacqueline Gauthiers and I was right."

Twenty minutes later, dressed in a new pair of tights and hoodie purchased at a mall in Bellingham, she was ready. "Have you seen my running shoes?

"By the nightstand."

The first one went on fine, but when she tried to slip her foot into the other one, something was stuffed into the toe. Reaching inside, she pulled out a small black velvet box. The ring was set in platinum, the center stone a large pink diamond in the shape of a tear and on either side two perfectly-matched solitaires, slightly smaller but exactly the same shade.

"Bryce, what is this?"

"I know how you feel about the African diamond trade so I went the Australian route. It's the color of your cheeks when you're angry or flushed. I had to guess at the size."

"It's beautiful but…"

"I researched it on-line Saturday when we landed and had it flown to London. I knew I'd wear you down eventually, at least I hoped so. I told Samantha at dinner I'd wait as long as I had to but I can't keep that promise, not now."

"We've only known one another a little over a week."

"How long did you know Larry before you agreed to marry him?"

"Four years."

"I knew Sybil over five so I don't think time is really an issue, do you? As far as being sure, I knew I wanted you from the beginning. Dinner sealed the deal. You're not only beautiful and smart but you make me laugh. I haven't had a lot of laughter in my life, Annie."

"I'm not ready for this, Bryce. I'll think about it and let you know when I get back from Greece."

"I've thought about that too. I'll set up camp in London and fly over for conjugal visits, help you wash the dirt out of wherever you crazy people get dirt. Besides, that's all part of my master plan."

"What master plan?"

"We're getting out of Connecticut. I'm closing the offices in the U.S. and relocating them to the U.K. We'll either keep my flat in London or buy something larger and we'll get an apartment in Manhattan. You're going to do what you should have done twenty years ago, finish your education and get your doctorate. What you do with it is strictly up to you. You can put it in a drawer, teach, write a book or travel the world in search of the Holy Grail. The point is you deserve it and it's something I can give you."

"You've thought of everything."

"I always do." He took her hand and slipped on the ring, a perfect fit. "Try not to get mugged."

Every muscle in her body poised for flight, she walked until she knew he couldn't see her from the window and then she ran. It wasn't like the normal run she enjoyed while testing her endurance or capturing an endorphin high. This one was prompted by panic, the realization she was being swallowed whole by another wealthy man she didn't love who would strip her bare and reinvent her in the image of her worst nightmare, a society wife.

If the directions were correct, Jacqueline Gauthier's house was just around the bend, but she wasn't ready for that yet. She needed somewhere quiet to pull her thoughts together and make sense of the carnage of the last week, both externally and internally.

A narrow dirt road leading to the lake was on her left and she veered off the pavement. Minutes later, an abandoned picnic table offered the ideal spot. Her first thought was of Mike. It was now or never. If the Fates were conspiring against them, they'd have a fight on their hands. She wanted to hear his voice, and if there were even a slim chance to repair the damage, she had to try. She could lie to herself for eternity but he was the reason she never contacted Kay to list the house. As much as she liked the allure of a big city, Manhattan was too far away. If he didn't want to be her friend, she'd offer him more. She'd offer him everything he wanted. She loved him. It was just that simple — and that complicated.

Reaching for her phone in the pocket of her hoodie, she took the ring off when it snagged on the fabric and dropped it in the other pocket. It was past time to end the charade and take her life back. She wanted to tell him earlier when she mentioned the sleeping arrangements but he changed the subject, his ploy of choice when he suspected she was ready to walk away. It happened far too often to be coincidence, another thing she'd overlooked, his uncanny ability to manipulate every situation to his advantage.

When Mike's phone went to voicemail, she thought of leaving him a message but clicked off at the last minute, relieved she remembered to block her number. She didn't need another scene if he called her back and Bryce intercepted the call or saw his name pop up on her phone.

Her next call was to Samantha. Like Mike's, it went to voicemail but this time she left a message. She was on Vancouver Island and would be returning to London alone on the first flight she could get. She was fine and would explain everything when she got back.

More cottage than house, Jacqueline Gauthier's was on a slightly larger lot than most of the others surrounding hers, but they all had one thing in common, authentic old-world charm.

Despite the chilly November air, the door was open, a screen door obscuring a view of the interior. She knocked once, then twice, and was ready to give up when a woman appeared through the screen. "May I help you?"

Annie tried to hide her surprise. She assumed Jacqueline was around the same age as Debra which would put her at forty-six or forty-seven, but this woman was years older than that, her hair pure white.

"Is this the Gauthier residence? I'm looking for Jacqueline or Lisa if she's home."

"Who are you?"

"My name is Annie Heywood. Jacqueline doesn't know me but I spoke to her daughter a few weeks ago about Debra Hastings. I don't know if you watch BBC or news from the U.S. but something has happened involving Debra. It's a very big story in the states and the U.K. and…"

"I know who you are, Miss Heywood. I am Jacqueline Gauthier. We don't own a television and we have nothing to discuss. Debra's untimely death was twenty years ago. Debra is at peace."

"I suppose untimely is one way of putting it. Debra was the victim of a serial killer, the first of six as far as the authorities know. He also murdered her neighbor on Spinnaker Lane, Helen Allen, a woman Debra cared about according to her diary. I'm sorry to have bothered you. Thank you for your time."

She was turning to retrace her steps back to the road when the woman's voice reached her. "This man is dead, this serial killer?"

"He took his own life last week after leaving a confession regarding Debra and the other seven victims. The man your cousin knew as Charles Hastings was Scott Stanley. His family owned the property on Spinnaker Lane. When I spoke to Lisa, I mentioned finding Debra's drawings. I would have brought them with me but the police took them as evidence. I'll send them off when the police return them."

"I apologize for my rudeness, Miss Heywood. You're shivering. May I offer you a cup of tea or coffee?"

"I am a bit chilled. If it's no trouble, I would love a cup of coffee."

The interior of the house was another surprise, this one far more pleasant. It wasn't large by any means, but what it lacked in size, it made up for in ambience. With its working wood-burning stove, Matelassé cushions and well-worn Aubusson rugs, it was like stepping back into another century. Even the coffee press was vintage.

But it was the walls that held her in thrall, hundreds of breathtaking sketches tacked up everywhere, most in pen and ink but others in watercolors, even an occasional oil, but not a single one of them was signed. "These are beautiful. Your daughter mentioned she was studying art. They should be in a gallery."

"My daughter has no interest in commerce. She wants to teach."

"I'm sure she'll be a wonderful teacher. What you said to me earlier, that Debra was at peace. You sent me the dead lilies with the warning, didn't you? I don't understand."

"There is much you do not understand, but now is not the time nor place. My daughter will be home soon, and the less she knows about this whole ugly affair, the better. There is a reason why we do not own a television. The outside world is a brutal place."

"So you've created your own world inside these walls." As the words left her lips, a watercolor on the opposite wall jumped out at her, a baby crawling across a boulder among tall grass. There were others too, the birch tree and the brook, the tall line of pines that formed the boundary of her property. "These are drawings of my house. There's no way unless…" Annie's breath left her body in a rush. "You're Debra. I see it now, the resemblance to the photograph in the montage, but how? Everyone assumed…"

"That I was dead? Their assumption was correct. Debra Couillard Hastings died an hour after making the final entry in her journal."

"None of this makes sense."

"Betrayal seldom does. Have you ever been so frightened, so mortified at your own naiveté that inside you wished to die but a force outside yourself took control? You needn't answer. I pray you have not.

"My life as I knew it ended shortly after supper. We were in the kitchen and I was tidying up. He wanted to be intimate. My monthly was late and I was very tired, but when I tried to explain, he got angry. I had never seen him like that and then his hands were at my throat. I don't know how long I was unconscious. When I woke up I was in the dark and felt motion beneath me. It took me several minutes to understand I was in the back of his automobile."

"You were in the trunk."

"I could not believe he would do that to me, but it was when he stopped the car that the real terror set in. When he opened the trunk, I struck him with something heavy. I believe I even drew blood and it enraged him even more. It was then I saw the knife and felt the blade at my neck, which is when I lost consciousness again. The next time I awoke, I was in a filthy and foul-smelling metal container and I heard large vehicles in the distance. I was so weak from loss of blood that I knew I was going to die there."

"He left you to bleed out in a dumpster at a truck stop?"

"Yes, a truck stop. That's what the woman called it."

"What woman?"

"The woman God sent to save me. She was a teacher returning home from a meeting of some sort when she pulled off to use the restroom. She also had a bag of trash in her car and when she opened the receptacle to dispose of it, she heard me crying. It was when she was helping me out of that wretched place that I was the most frightened. She kept insisting that she take me to the hospital and alert the police, but I begged her not to. I was afraid Charles would find out and come for me.

"She took me to her home. The wound wasn't very deep and she dressed it as best she could. She let me use her phone and I called Jacqueline. I had no idea if the woman would keep my secret from her friends and colleagues, but she did. Two days later, Jacqueline arrived and together we made the long drive here. I was home and safe."

"You felt threatened by my call and conversation with Lisa. Under the circumstances, I don't blame you. Where is Jacqueline? Does she live here with you?"

"My cousin died in a boating accident seven months after she brought me here and one month before my daughter was born."

"You took her name. Didn't the locals think that odd?"

"This isn't America where everyone's personal life is exploited in the media for profit. Do you know much about Vancouver Island, Miss Heywood?"

"Nothing beyond what I've read on-line."

"It's a mish-mash of humanity, a liberal enclave where people mind their own business. I'm sure there were those who wondered about it, but I'm equally sure there are those who believe I took her name in deference to her memory."

Footsteps on the stoop preceded the opening of the screen door and a whirling dervish of sandy blonde hair and blue jeans rushed in. "Mama, I'm sorry I'm late but class ran over and now I must hurry to the kiosk. Did you remember to wash my uniform?" She did a double take at Annie's presence and blushed. "I apologize. I didn't know you had a guest."

"Your uniform is hanging in your closet. This is Miss Heywood from Connecticut. She was kind enough to drop in and introduce herself."

"I'm so happy to meet you, Miss Heywood, and again I apologize. It seems I'm always rushing off somewhere."

While still a lovely young woman, Lisa Gauthier looked less like her mother than her father and another piece of the puzzle fell in place. "I completely understand, Lisa. I had several jobs when I was in college too so I know how it is. I'm just happy we finally met."

Smiling broadly, Lisa turned and started to leave the room when she stopped and readdressed her mother. "Mama, are you expecting another guest this afternoon? One of the tires on my bicycle is low, and while I was walking it, a man pulled up beside me and asked if I knew where the Gauthiers lived. I know how you feel about strangers so I told him I never heard of them. I hope I did the right thing. You know what was odd? He looked familiar."

The hairs on Annie's neck stood up and she checked her watch. Three hours had passed since she left the B&B but the missing time was only part of it. There was something she had to reconcile from Debra's earlier recounting of the night she almost died, something minor that should have been a footnote but refused to go away.

Annie waited until she heard the door close to what she assumed was Lisa's room and ran to the window overlooking the road. She didn't see the rental car but she knew it was Bryce. It had to be.

Debra was on her feet. "What is it?"

"Debra, think back to that night. I know it's unpleasant but you said you hit Charles with something. Was it heavy enough to hurt him? You said it might have drawn blood. Where did you hit him?"

"I was lying on my back and my right hand touched something cold and metal. It felt like a heavy steel bar. When he lifted the door, he leaned in to pick me up and I struck him as hard as I could." Her fingertips touched the spot above her left eyebrow. "I struck him here."

Mind-numbing panic threatened to suffocate her but she had to think it through. In and of itself, that wasn't proof of anything. Helen never mentioned a bandage on his forehead when she saw Charles that night. *All the lights were off.* "Do you remember if he had a scar there before that night? It's important, Debra."

"No, he didn't have a scar there but he had one on his arm, a long scar. He told me he took a fall skiing and cut it on his pole. What is it? I see your distress. What are you not telling me? Who is the man looking for me?"

"It's Charles. He's looking for me but he won't hesitate to hurt you and your daughter. He's with me here in Shawnigan but I thought, everyone thought it was his brother. I brought this nightmare back into your life and I'll end it here. Is there a back door?"

"Yes."

Annie fumbled for the cellphone in her pocket and pressed it into Debra's hand. "Take this. Get Lisa and go out the back door. Get as far away from here as you can and call the police. Tell them it's Bryce Stanley and not Scott who's the real murderer." Her face a mask of stunned disbelief, Debra stood immobile. Fearing she was losing the battle to make her understand the urgency and may in fact be in shock, Annie took her by the shoulders. "You have to move and get Lisa to safety, can you do that?"

"Mama, that's the man."

Looking first into the ashen face of Lisa staring at the screen door, Annie's head pivoted long enough to know they were out of time. "Run!" She pushed Debra toward her daughter before lunging for the solid front door in hope of locking him out, but it was too late.

The first blow caught her on the side of the head and she went down hard, her bandaged wrist taking the brunt of it. With her vision blurred, she saw Lisa pulling her mother down the hall. When she heard a door slam at the rear of the house, she tried to stand but the second blow, a backhand to her face, sent her reeling.

By the time her head cleared, Bryce was standing over her. "I was wrong about you, Annie. You're not just complicated, you're very clever but you made one fatal mistake. I do my homework, remember? It took five minutes to research the fact that Jacqueline Gauthier died in a boating accident in 2001. I have no idea who these people are but I hope this little misadventure of yours was worth it. You'll soon learn I won't be lied to. Now get up. We're going back to the B&B and from there we're driving to the airport where another charter plane is waiting to take us back to New York. You'll be confined in my home in Greenwich until after the wedding."

He was mad, stark-raving mad, but how had she not seen it? "I'm not going anywhere with you."

"Don't be ridiculous. We're getting married." He grabbed her wrist. "Where's your ring?"

"I threw it in the lake."

"Then I'll order you another and another after that if it comes to that. There are protocols, my dear. You're about to become the wife of a very important man."

"You're insane. I'll die before I marry you."

It started in his eyes, black and fathomless, the man she knew replaced by a stone cold killer. His rage was a living thing, time measured not in minutes but in pain. His hand went around her throat, lifting her off the floor. Lodged between his body and the kitchen island, she watched his face soften back to something approximating a human being. "Say the words, Annie. Tell me you love me and this will all be over."

"I detest you. You're a monster."

She saw the bloody knife and knew it found its mark while somewhere in the distance sirens wailed. He slowly raised the knife again and she slipped into the void, a world of darkness and despair.

CHAPTER 55

LIFE HOUSE

"He's back. It must be thirty degrees out there. Maybe if we ignore him, he'll freeze to death and we can have the city dispose of him. He's persistent, I'll say that for him. This is the third time this week."

Cynthia took another dinner plate from the cupboard, wrapped it and placed it in a cardboard box. "I still think we should hear him out."

"Why do you keep saying that?"

"It's been six weeks since they carried her out of that house, five weeks since we brought her home. In all that time, she hasn't talked about it once, hasn't cried a single tear. That ain't normal. You have to get on that plane tomorrow, Samantha, or you can kiss your career good-bye. You want to go back, knowing maybe he's got some answers we don't?"

"I don't want to go back at all, not yet."

"You're going back if I have to kick your ass every mile from here to there. Whatever else is going on in that head of hers, she doesn't need guilt over screwing up her baby sister's career. She's proud of you. We're all proud of you. You must be damn good at what you do for them to put off the opening for two months."

"I keep telling you it has nothing to do with how good I am. It's all about revenue. Ticket sales shot through the roof when they thought it was Scott, when I was just the sister of the woman dating the brother of a serial killer. They went to the moon when it turned out to be Bryce. It was easier to delay the opening than refund the money. You really think we should talk to him?"

"I do and I think we should get him in here now while she's still outside with the dogs. I'm not sayin' we're gonna let him see her. Let's see what he has to say first."

At the front door, Samantha wrapped the sweater tighter around her body and motioned him forward.

Pushing off from the oak tree in the front yard, Mike Saunders stopped at the bottom of the front steps. "Are you going to let me see her or not?"

"If it were up to me, you'd be in a paddy wagon on your way to Bellevue but Cynthia seems to think we should talk to you. We'll make a decision on whether you can see her after that."

"Why didn't you let me see her in the hospital?"

"She didn't want anyone to see her, not even our parents. If you're coming in, you'd better do it now while she's still out back."

Following Samantha into the kitchen, he went directly to the window overlooking the large fenced yard. There was a temporary reprieve in the snowfall but Annie was knee-deep in a week's accumulation. She was standing up, arms outstretched, face upturned toward the sky. Taking a tentative step forward, she fell face down. When she rolled over, four dogs raced to her and licked her face, vying for their place in her universe.

"I recognize Einstein but where did the other three come from?"

"They were Bryce's. She never saw them but he mentioned them once. It was one of the first things she asked about when she could finally communicate. 'Make sure they don't take his dogs to the pound. Get his dogs, Samantha, I mean it.' She kept repeating it over and over. Cynthia called Arthur and he went to the shelter and got them all out. He kept them until we got back from Canada. They won't leave her side. It's like they know she saved them. Crap, she's coming back in."

Annie was on her feet and the two larger dogs, the Bernese and the Portuguese Water dog were positioning themselves on either side of her. She put her hands through their collars and began slogging through the snow. Directly in front of her, Einstein took up his position as lead dog and the Shepherd brought up the rear. It was a perfect formation of love and trust.

"Who taught them to do that?"

Cynthia joined them at the window. "No one. Started a few days ago. She was out there alone with them and she stood up and they moved in on her like they did there. They brought her right to the steps of the porch. She'll come in first to give them treats. You stay back out of the way and don't say a word."

He stepped back as Annie stomped the snow off her boots and opened the back door. When the five of them were inside, she knelt down and whispered words of love and appreciation to each of them. Standing up, she used her hands to feel her way around the room and eventually to the treat jar. Once the dogs received their treats and left the kitchen, she removed her boots, cap and jacket. The scarf came off last revealing a two-inch slash that missed her carotid artery by a fraction of inch. "Why is everyone so quiet? Is someone else here?"

Ever the thespian, Samantha's tone was breezy. "I wish. We could use the help. I'd like to get this packing done before I'm old enough to play Angela Lansbury parts."

"I thought I caught a whiff of something…peppermint."

Cynthia harrumphed. "Wish I caught a whiff of somethin' besides wet dog. Peppermint tea with a little honey and lemon sounds good right now. I'll make some. It'll be good for your throat."

"Save it for me. I'm going upstairs to take a hot shower. When I come back down, I'll finish taking the ornaments off the tree."

"Baby, you just had a bath three hours ago."

"I know, Cyn, but I got chilled outside."

When he heard the sound of running water above their heads, Saunders put one hand on the side of the refrigerator and scrubbed his face with the other. "Christ."

Samantha rolled her eyes. "Yeah, this was a good idea. He'll be a great help."

"It's not supposed to last this long." He turned to Cynthia. "You're a nurse. Why hasn't she come out of it?"

"How much do you know about hysterical blindness?"

"Only what I've read, which is everything I could find on the subject."

"Temporary means nobody knows. It's different for everybody. It should have been gone by now but for whatever reason she's not coming out of it. They think it has something to do with the last image she saw before she lost consciousness. There's some kind of logjam in her head preventing her from processing the information."

"What was the last thing she saw? Has she told you?"

Samantha shook her head, her face a tapestry of sadness and regret. "Debra told us. Once she got her daughter to safety, she went back to help Annie. She was at the door when she saw him take the knife away from Annie's throat and run it through his eye into his sick brain. He couldn't kill her so he turned the knife on himself. Her eyes were open and she saw the whole thing. That's when she passed out."

"Does she talk about him, about any of it?"

"She's been home five weeks and she hasn't mentioned a word about anything. We don't ask but we let her know we're here for her. She flatly refuses to see a psychiatrist."

"Let me try."

"Are you out of your mind? We're the two people closest to her in the world and she won't talk to us. Our parents were here for a week and they finally went home in tears because she wouldn't talk to them."

"She loves the four of you. Maybe she doesn't want to transfer that pain to the people she loves the most."

Cynthia gave him a sideways glance. "You love her too."

"That's beside the point. She was almost loved to death. The last thing she needs is another man in her life right now. And no offense, but all the loving and coddling she's getting from the two of you hasn't helped a goddamn bit."

"That's not true. You saw her. She's back to her beautiful self. You didn't see her in the hospital. She was bruised and bleeding from head to toe. Her face was swollen and she had three cracked ribs, not to mention a broken wrist. Another fall and one of the ribs could have punctured a lung. It's a miracle she's alive, and she's healthy. She has her anemia under control and her hypoglycemia. I know my sister. She'll be fine. Tell him, Cynthia."

"I'm not so sure, Sam. She may be healed on the outside but she's not all right on the inside. One of us has been with her twenty-four hours a day and she hasn't cried, not a tear. She never even cried in the hospital when she was in pain. Doesn't that worry you?"

Mike lowered his voice. "Has she gotten angry? She was in love with a man who turned out to be a serial killer, who beat her and almost cut her throat. Has she gotten angry?"

"No, but that's not necessarily a sign that anything's wrong. We talked about it when I was here in September, about Larry and the divorce. She said after awhile it was easier to walk away than get angry with him."

"That's bullshit. I've been on the receiving end of her anger and I can tell you she knows how to dish it out."

"What makes you think you can get through to her and get her to open up?"

"Because I know her secret. There's a piece of her she refuses to give up, a part of herself she withholds. That's the part I need to reach."

"Did she tell you that?"

"Not in so many words but when I accused her of it, she didn't deny it."

"When was this?"

"The last day we were together, the Sunday before I left for Seattle. I had to see her again, to tell her how I felt about her. She turned me down and we had some heated words. I stomped out of the house like a rejected teenager and went right back in to apologize. She said she brought out the worst in men and I said it was because she withheld parts of herself and it made us nuts. I wasn't trying to get her into bed, by the way. I told her a man would be a fool to want her only for an afternoon. You have something to share, Samantha?"

"I don't know. It's very personal and I hate betraying her confidence but maybe that's what she was trying to tell me the day after she and Bryce got together, you know, sexually. Sorry, but you started this."

"They were together a little over a week. I've come to terms with the fact they weren't playing chess all that time. What day was that?"

"Monday, the day the story broke about Scott."

"Sunday was the first time? They'd been seeing one another for several days before that."

"This is Annie we're talking about. She made Larry wait almost six months before she slept with him. Her nickname in college was Annie Blueballs."

"I don't know where you're going with this."

"I don't know where I'm going with it either except she was miserable that Monday. I told her she looked like someone ran over her puppy. She said she was going to sell her house and move to Manhattan. I asked her where Bryce fit into it and she said he didn't. I tried to get her to say she was in love him and was scared he'd let her down like Larry but she would never admit to that. The next thing I knew, she was in the bathtub and the press was beating down my door."

"What happened next? When did he pick her up and take her to the house in the country?"

"We watched the coverage on CNN and BBC for a few hours and she was very upset. She became even more agitated when they showed the photograph of the three of us outside the restaurant. She said she had to get out of the flat and go for a run."

"You told Lou she called you a little later and said Bryce picked her up during her run, that she'd be staying with him for a few days and wanted you to pack her a bag. You said she sounded tired but happy."

"Did I say happy? I don't remember saying that but maybe I did. I was trying to juggle several things when he called."

"Try to think, Samantha. How did she sound? Was she happy to be there or not?"

"No, I don't think she was particularly happy. Her voice was flat, like the phone call was something she had to get out of the way. I was confused because what she was saying wasn't making any sense."

"How so?"

"I couldn't understand how he could have picked her up during the run when she went out the back way over an eight-foot wall. How did he know she was going to do that? Anyway, all that went through my mind and then I was on to other things."

"Maybe she called him before she left your apartment or during her run and told him where she'd be."

"She didn't take her cell phone with her and they never spoke that morning. I know that for a fact."

"But his brother's been found dead and confessed to killing eight people. Didn't you think it was odd she wasn't calling to comfort or support him?"

"It was a strange day, Mike. After awhile, she seemed detached."

"When did you hear from her again?"

"Wednesday. I was in rehearsal all day. She left me a voicemail. I should have known something was wrong. She didn't sound like herself. She said she'd be coming back to London as soon as she could arrange a flight. I tried to phone her back but she didn't pick up. Two hours later I got the call they were airlifting her to a hospital in Vancouver."

"How did they know to contact you?"

"We have each other's numbers in our phones as ICE, you know, in case of emergency. Cynthia is in her phone too. She got there eight hours ahead of me. They had the inquest three days later but they never spoke to any of us. Debra told them everything."

"Do you want your sister back or not? And you, do you want your best friend to be a walking imitation of the woman you've known for eleven years? She needs to get angry and I can make her good and angry. I'm not saying it'll cure her blindness. That'll happen when she's ready but maybe this logjam bullshit is because she's holding everything in, the pain, the anger, all of it."

"How do we know you're not just saying this so you can get in there and make her pay for choosing him over you?"

"You don't."

"And how do we know you're not going to break her?"

"She's already broken. There's something else I want. I want both of you to leave for the afternoon and take the dogs. I want her to know she's here alone with me and no one's coming to her rescue."

"No way. Cynthia, say something. She trusts us. We can't do this to her."

"Mike's right, Sam. Loving her and protecting her isn't enough to bring her back."

"And if she ends up hating us for this?"

"She won't hate you. She'll hate me."

"But you care about her. How can you be willing to give up the possibility…"

"I owe her. That Sunday she asked me to be her friend and I said I couldn't, not yet anyway. Maybe if I'd left that door open, she would have confided in me. Or maybe if I'd been a better cop, I would have focused on Bryce earlier and spared her all this."

"This is my fault. I should have been paying attention."

"How the hell is any of this your fault, Samantha?"

"I kept pushing her toward him. I thought he was the real deal. That night at dinner, he brought up things about me, my career and activism he couldn't have known off the top of his head unless he researched them. I fell for it. I fell for all of it. The next morning, I told her he was perfect for her but she fought me at every turn. I didn't know you, Mike, and when she wouldn't talk about you, I assumed it was a one-time fling, but looking back, every time I brought up your name, she'd get this haunted look like she was in real pain. It was always you and I missed it completely."

"There's more than enough blame to go around but let's put the bulk of it where it belongs. Stanley fooled eight people into trusting him enough to get close to them and then murdered them in cold blood. Let's be grateful he didn't make it nine."

"I've heard enough. Sam, you go up and tell her we're leavin' for awhile. I'll put the dogs in the van. We'll go to her house and work on gettin' you packed. You'll call us when you're done, Mike?"

"I'll call you from my car and wait until you get here before leaving."

"We don't have to tell you what she means to us, do we?"

"She's lucky to have you."

"Somethin' tells me her luck just ran out."

Back downstairs, Annie started taking the ornaments from the tree. She removed only two before she stopped and lowered herself to the piano bench. "How did you get in here, Mike?"

"Through the back door. I waited until they left and then I found a door unlocked."

"That's a lie. Why are you here?"

He pulled a chair over and sat directly in front of her, far enough away so she wouldn't feel threatened. "The day the cadaver dog was at your house and we were watching from your terrace, I made a joke about your problems. You told me to take a number, that everyone was lining up to tell you what your problems were. It's my turn, Annie. My number came up."

"Are you here officially or did you draw the short straw as my surrogate shrink?"

"This isn't an official visit. I'm at the midway point of a sixty-day suspension."

"Why did they suspend you?"

"Good cops don't lie to their superiors and they don't let their personal feelings get in the way of a murder investigation. I did both."

"Then I guess you're here to straighten me out. You're wasting your time. I don't want to talk to you."

"Talking's one thing but you haven't shown any emotion at all."

"In other words, I'm not acting in a way that everyone thinks I should. What is the accepted behavior for someone in my position? Am I supposed to fall apart? That sounds a lot like what a victim might do and I'm not a victim."

"No, you're the smartest kid in class and you're embarrassed you're human like the rest of us. You fell for the wrong guy. That's the reason you haven't cried or gotten mad. As long as you keep it all inside, you're above the fray. Hell, you might even regain your sight and that's the last thing you want. Then you'd have to deal with the look on everyone's face. You know the look, Annie, the one that says what the hell was she thinking? I always thought she was so smart. I said it about you myself."

"Is that the best you've got because you'll have to up your game if you want to play around inside my head."

"Is that what Bryce did, played around inside your head?"

"I've had multiple offers to write a book about it and I've turned them all down. I'm not giving it away for free, least of all to you."

"But you didn't have a problem giving it away to Bryce for free, did you? Oh, that's right, when they undressed you at the hospital, they found a five carat diamond. That's a pretty good pay-off for what, a few days in the sack."

"I see we're trying the tough-love gambit. Break her down and put her back together again. Isn't that what you said men do?"

"I said men do that when they want to make something theirs. I don't want you anymore, Annie, you're damaged goods."

It was the closest she'd come to tears and she closed her eyes and turned away from him. "You're all alike. Only the packaging and weapons are different."

"That would have made a great exit line. Too bad you can't find the door without tripping over the furniture."

"When did you become so cruel?"

"When you decided to give up."

"I haven't given up. I'm just dealing with things in my own way in my own time. I have to do this myself or I'll be lost and that frightens me more than anything."

"Your way isn't working. You're still blind."

"I know and I also know the doctors think it's because I blew a fuse when I saw him turn the knife on himself but I don't think that's it. If I hadn't lost my sight, I wouldn't have allowed myself the time to figure out how I let him into my life. I would have been on to a hundred other things that didn't matter. It's surprising how much one can see when there are no distractions. And I don't believe for a moment your cruelty comes from thinking I've given up on myself. You think I lied to you about Bryce. I didn't."

"I know you didn't. You'd be amazed at the things I know, like the fact that you left both Scott and Bryce in that Greenwich restaurant when you paid the valet not to tell anyone where you were, that the day after you slept with him for the first time you told your sister he didn't fit into your plans. I also know he ordered your engagement ring from a diamond merchant in Sydney less than twenty-four hours after your first date. You didn't let him in, Annie. He'd already made up his mind about you. There was no way you could keep him out."

"I know what you're trying to do. You're saying I had no control over what happened but that isn't true. I got into that cab and went to his house."

"Why did you go there?"

"I was going to drop off some autographed photos of Sam he requested for his sons."

"That's it?"

"I don't know, maybe I wanted something to happen. I was feeling good that day. There had been so much turmoil back home and I realized I made a mistake moving to Westport. My original plan was to move to Manhattan, so I decided to make a fresh start and put everything behind me."

"Including me."

"As I recall, you rejected me."

"You recall it wrong. I rejected an afternoon fuck. I wanted it all. Let's get back to Bryce. Were you still planning on moving to Manhattan, even after the day you spent with him?"

"I was more determined than ever."

"Then why did you go with him when he picked you up during your run?"

"He didn't pick me up. I had just started my run down the street behind Samantha's flat when an SUV cut me off. There were three men inside. They put me in the vehicle and locked the doors so I couldn't get out. They wouldn't tell me where they taking me. I was terrified and when we got to the house and I saw Bryce, I was furious."

"Did he explain why he had you picked up?"

"Because of the death threat. He never told me if they found the third man."

"Exactly what did he tell you?"

"He told me that after the photograph outside the restaurant aired, he got a call from someone threatening to kill me if he didn't come up with three million dollars. He said he'd hired a team of bodyguards to watch that house and Samantha's flat and he'd also hired some investigators to catch the men who made the threat. At some point, he said they apprehended two of the men but there was still a man out there somewhere and we had to lay low for another couple of days."

"There was no death threat, Annie. Scotland Yard interrogated the bodyguards. Bryce told them you were his sister, a drug addict, and he was sequestering you in that house to try and get you clean. The bodyguards were there as much to keep you in as to keep out the press."

"I need some water."

When she started to rise, he took her hand, surprised when she didn't pull it back. "I'll get it. Cynthia made you some tea. I'll bring that too. I don't suppose you have anything stronger hidden away somewhere."

"Unless they already packed it, there's a bottle of whisky in the cabinet over the refrigerator."

When he came back, he handed her the bottle of water and she drank half of it and set it down. He wrapped her hands around the mug of tea and she brought it to her lips.

He was walking away when he heard the mug drop to the floor. Turning back, he saw the first tears running down her face. Getting to one knee in front of her, he used the pad of his thumb to wipe away a tear. "It's all right, I'll clean it up and make you another cup."

"No tea. He made me tea."

"When did he make you tea?"

"Right after they took me to that house. It was raining and I was wet and cold from falling when I tried to run away. I went up to take a shower and when I came out there was a cup of tea on the countertop. It made me sleepy and I went to my room and got in bed. I slept eight hours and I kept having these dreams. When I woke up, the robe I was wearing was gone."

"Tell me about the dreams."

She shook her head.

"The dreams were about him, except they weren't dreams, were they? He drugged you."

"He said he gave me a mild tranquilizer because he needed to get some work done. What did he put in the tea?"

"It could have been a number of things, maybe GHB, but it sounds more like Rohypnol. It's illegal in the U.S. but you can still get it in the U.K. with a prescription. The effects last longer and it induces a form of amnesia."

"Why would he do that?"

"Does it matter?"

"It matters to me."

"You said you went to your room. You weren't sharing a room?"

"I didn't want to. It was a large home with several guest suites and I took one down the hall from the master suite where he had his things."

"Maybe he was pissed you weren't going to sleep with him and stacked the deck."

"I should have known the death threat was a lie. When I first got to the house, he said he didn't know any other way to get me there, and then later he said he knew I wasn't going to see him again. Why didn't I put the pieces together, Mike?"

"Because he didn't want you to. Pete Ryan brought in a hot-shot psychiatrist from San Francisco to consult with us on the case. The D.A. uses her for profiling. She banked her professional reputation on the fact that Bryce wasn't our guy. I have to make a quick phone call and then I'll clean up the tea. Stay put, okay?"

"I don't need you to clean up my mess. I can do it."

"Look, just this once, don't give me a hard time and do as you're told."

She needed air and felt her way to the front door, opened it wide and took several deep breaths. The wind was kicking up. When her cheeks began to sting, she closed the door, made her way back to the tree and removed another ornament. She could picture it in her mind, blown glass in the shape of a pine cone and inside a sprig of holly. Taking her body against her will was the least of it. He took something much more precious, her last Christmas at **Life House**, her last chance to look at their faces and tell them what they meant to her and how much she loved them.

As her rage built, she slammed her fist on the piano but it took several seconds for the pain to register. Using the fingertips of one hand, she felt the chards of glass imbedded in the other.

"What the hell was that? Jesus, woman, what have you done? Open your hand." He led her to the kitchen and turned on the cold water, forcing her hand beneath the faucet. "Where's the first aid kit and some tweezers? I have to get the glass out."

"The infirmary is around the corner near the stairs. The tweezers are in one of the drawers."

"Keep your hand under the cold water." He came back and sat her in a chair at the table. "How did this happen?"

"You got what you came for. I'm angry and I'm crying. I hope you're happy."

"I'd be happier if you'd done it without props. You have to keep still. There's a lot of glass."

She wiped her eyes with her free hand. "I suppose I'll have to cancel my handball game tomorrow."

"Did you just make a joke?"

"It's better than being a joke."

"You're not a joke, Annie. We can't help who we fall in love with. I'm living proof of that."

"I wasn't in love with him, Mike. I was overwhelmed by him, by his ability to do everything right except when he was doing everything wrong, which was most of the time. The truth is, I didn't like him very much. He was too mercurial and manipulative."

"But you agreed to marry him."

"No, I didn't but then he never actually proposed. He slipped the ring on my finger and told me where we were going to live and what I was doing with the rest of my life. That's why the ring was in my pocket. I was giving it back to him when I returned from Debra's."

"That's when you called Samantha."

"I'd left the room in the B&B. He told me to walk not run because I was still weak. I walked until I knew he couldn't see me from the window and then I started running as fast as I could. I felt buoyant, like at any moment I was going to fly through the trees. I didn't understand it at first until I realized I was breathing, really breathing for the first time in a week. I found a quiet spot on the lake and called Sam."

"He loved you. You were probably the only thing in his entire miserable life he did love."

"And it was the death of him. I'm a lousy risk."

"What if I were willing to take the risk?"

"I'm not. I have a demon to purge and some serious trust issues to deal with, and until I do, I'm no good to anyone."

"I have to leave in a few minutes, but this time I'm not coming back. It's too painful. I have a daughter to think of and she needs me too right now. I'm sorry."

"Don't ever apologize for being a good father. It's one of the things I like best about you."

"That's a start." He finished bandaging her hand and held it loosely in his own. "This might smart for a day or two, but it wasn't as bad as it looked. You can take the bandage off tomorrow before your handball game. Annie, that call you made to Samantha from Shawnigan. What time was it?"

"Around 10 a.m."

"I had a call about that time but I picked it up too late. I was going to call the number back but it was blocked. Was that you?"

She dropped her head. "I called you before I tried Sam, but I didn't want you calling me back in case Bryce picked up my phone so I blocked my number."

"And if I'd picked it up?"

"You would have heard all the things I wish I'd said that Sunday before you left for Seattle."

"Why am I not hearing them now?"

"Look at me, Mike. I'm a mess, not just on the outside but inside too. You deserve a woman who has her act together, not a caricature of herself. You were right about me. There is a part of me I hold back but I don't even know what it is. I can't fix it until I identify it and I can't ask you to wait."

"You're not asking. I'll wait for you, Annie, but know this. The next time you and I cross paths, you're not running me off."

CHAPTER 56
SAN FRANCISCO

"Please tell me you're Annie."

Laughing, Annie slid out of the booth and hugged her first real pen pal. "We meet at last. How's baby Ryan? More importantly, how's Daddy Ryan, still being overly-protective?"

Marti smoothed her hand over her belly before sliding in across from her. "He's a pain in the ass and now I have both of them on my case. They had a meeting yesterday and decided I should cut my hours back. I don't know which is worse, when they're going head to head over a case or when they're in one of their boy-bonding periods. That's when I usually mention my female plumbing and they scatter."

"They really did it, huh? Ryan and Saunders Investigations. I never thought Mike would leave the force."

"You know why, don't you?"

"No, not really."

"Mike left the force for the same reason Pete did, because the system failed the women they loved. They think they can do a better job without those pesky parameters, and you know what? They're right, they can."

"Do you have many cases?"

"Are you kidding? We have more than we can handle. They're considering bringing on another investigator." Marti reached across the table for Annie's hand. "Enough about us. How are you?"

"Nervous at the moment. Marti, I've never really thanked you for your letters these last few months. They were my lifeline to Mike."

"Six months is a long time. I'm not sure I could have gone that long without breaking down and communicating with Pete."

"I thought about it every day, but I made a promise to both of us that the only way it would work is if I got my act together, not just my sight, but whatever was inside me that held me back from embracing what everyone deserves, the right to happiness."

"You're here so you must have figured it out."

"I did and, ironically, it was something Bryce said the day we left for Vancouver Island. We were arguing and he brought up Markham again. He said even after twenty years, Lucas was still dominating me. I thought about that a lot while I was in Greece, so when I left there, I flew to Dublin. It was the best detour I could have made. He's still a force of nature, but I realized I was never really in love with him. I was caught up in the whirlwind he created around himself. I said good-bye and meant it this time. No more letters, no more contact. If Mike still wants me…"

"If he still wants you? The guy's a walking Nicholas Sparks novel, one of the sad ones."

"So what's the plan, Fearless Leader? I'm getting anxious. You mentioned something about a grand opening, but I didn't catch what was opening."

"Yeah, about that. Pete and Mike didn't simply join forces in the P.I. biz. They sort of bought a bar."

"A bar as in tequila shooters and sexy barmaids? Sounds like I got here just in time."

"More like a bar with fancy martinis, the best burgers in town, a jazz pianist and a fiddler."

"Mike's playing again? That's wonderful but how did that happen? Why didn't you tell me about it?"

"I didn't know how you'd feel about it, and when you wrote that you were ready, I didn't want to jinx things. It's been one of Pete's favorite haunts for years and Mike loved the joint, so when the owner wanted to sell and retire to Florida, Jake and Elwood pooled their resources and bought it. It was Mike's idea to name it **Theresa's Tavern**. Five days a week, it will be your garden variety bar and lounge, but Thursday and Saturday nights, your guy will tickle the ivories and mine will do whatever one does with violin strings."

"And today's the grand opening?"

"That was a week ago but we're still mobbed. I'm sorry, Annie. I'm afraid this won't be the quiet, romantic reunion you were hoping for."

"Maybe not but it sounds like fun, and if it makes Mike happy, that's good enough for me. So why are we sitting here?"

"Because you're right, we need a plan." Marti smiled and snapped her fingers. "And I think I might just have one."

Even from half a block away, Annie felt the change in energy, partly from the people mingling outside the bar and partly from the Mission District itself. It was so different, so much more colorful and alive than the San Francisco she knew from previous trips. Could this be her life now?

Despite Marti's assurance that Mike's feelings hadn't changed, she wouldn't be convinced until she saw his face. He'd relocated to the other side of the country to start a new life and she was part of the old one, the one he left behind.

Still several yards from the entrance, Marti put her arm through hers and pulled her down an alley. "We're going in through the back door. Stay close to me, and if you see Mike, duck and run to the ladies' room."

Mobbed was putting it mildly. The bar was at least four people deep, every table filled, all eyes riveted on the grand piano and the guy giving the late Oscar Peterson a run for his money. It was the best rendition of 'I love Paris' she ever heard.

From her spot down the narrow hallway, she watched Marti approach a man seated at the bar and whisper something to him. He turned around and smiled, cocked his head and motioned her forward.

After she thanked him and took his seat, she felt Marti thrust something in her hand. "You'll know when the time is right. Just press the button. I'm off to find my man. You found yours."

One song rolled into another and Annie was reluctant to break the spell but when he finished 'Love For Sale' and asked for requests, she knew the time was right.

From her perch at the bar hidden by those standing in back of her, she hit the button on the microphone. "I have a request. Let's Fall in Love."

He was well into the first bar of the song when he stopped, stood up and looked toward the bar. Squeezing her way through the throng, she stood motionless at the perimeter and knew she was home when he grinned and took her in his arms. "Sorry, lady, you're too late. I'm already in love."

"It better be with me."

"Who else? Let's get out of here."

Ignoring the cheers and catcalls, he led her out the back door. Their first kiss was everything she imagined it would be and so much more. Every part of her ached for him.

When they finally came up for air, he took her face between his hands. "I love you, Annie, but nothing's changed since the last time I saw you. You're not getting rid of me again."

"That's the last thing I want. In the past six months, I learned a lot about myself and even purged a demon or two, but the thing that shocked me most was the realization that you're the first man I've ever really loved."

"And the last. How long are you staying?"

"Forever if you'll have me. I got rid of all my baggage, including the house and everything in it. I'm homeless."

"The hell you are. Where's Einstein?"

"He's in a doggy day care a few miles from here."

He kissed her again. "Let's get our dog and go home."

"And then what?"

"And then we break some furniture, every last piece of it if I have my way. You were a decorator. You can replace it."

"Hallelujah! I thought you'd never ask." She was still laughing when he dragged her down the alley toward the street.

THE END

BOOKS BY SHELBY KENT-STEWART

Surviving Sydney
Wicked Tails Series – Book 1

Runaway Brat

Blessing
Wicked Tails Series – Book 2

Once Upon a Faerie

Serenity's Child

Storming Jericho

***

Coming Soon

A Journey in Seventeen Syllables

For Love of Honor
Wicked Tails Series – Book 3

Healing Hannah
The Mulcare Legacy – Book 1

The Siren Wore Scarlet

ABOUT THE AUTHOR

A native of Southern California, Shelby is no stranger to the wonderful world of words. With the publication of her first story at the ripe old age of ten, she was hooked. In one capacity or another, she's been writing all her life, advertising copy, political speeches, screenplays and books. Depending on her mood, it can be a mainstream thriller one day, a sexy adult fiction the next, whatever floats her literary boat.

You can visit her website at www.shelbykentstewart.com

AUTHOR'S NOTE

According to the Centers for Disease Control and Prevention and The National Institute of Justice, **domestic violence** in the U.S. has reached epidemic proportions with close to one-quarter of Americans reporting physical or sexual abuse by a husband or partner at some point in their lives. In households with children where domestic violence occurs, the children are abused 60 percent of the time.

There are ways we can help. If you know someone at risk, find a way to let them know help is out there or report the abuse. Since most victims suffering at the hands of a violent spouse or partner arrive at shelters and safe houses with little more than their children in tow and the clothes on their backs, donations of money and clothing are gratefully accepted.

We're in this together.

U.S. Hotline: 800.799.SAFE (7233)
Teen Dating Abuse Hotline: 866.331.9474

Peace, Shelby

9 781641 842617